DANCING in the DARK

OTHER TITLES BY HELÉNE HOLMSTRÖM

TV24

Time to Rise

DANCING *in the* DARK

HELÉNE HOLMSTRÖM

TRANSLATED BY MARLAINE DELARGY

AMAZON CROSSING

This is a work of fiction. Names, characters, organizations, places, events, and incidents are either products of the author's imagination or are used fictitiously. Any resemblance to actual persons, living or dead, or actual events is purely coincidental.

Previously published as *Dansar i mörkret* by HarperLove in Sweden in 2023. Translated from Swedish by Marlaine Delargy. First published in English by Amazon Crossing in 2025.

Published by Amazon Crossing, Seattle
www.apub.com

EU product safety contact:
Amazon Media EU S. à r.l.
38, avenue John F. Kennedy, L-1855 Luxembourg
amazonpublishing-gpsr@amazon.com

ISBN-13: 9781662534416 (paperback)
ISBN-13: 9781662511523 (digital)

Cover design and illustration by Elizabeth Turner Stokes

Printed in the United States of America

DANCING *in the* DARK

1

Every wine bottle has its own history. Some begin at vineyards that have been passed down through generations, with wine from vines that might be a hundred years old, or older. Or vines that have survived fires, droughts, and floods. Or that have traveled to the other side of the world to be planted in places where no one believed that wine-worthy grapes would ever grow successfully.

Whenever Bente Hammar recommended a wine to her customers, she always told its story. Tonight, her account of the grower who cultivated seventy-year-old vines in volcanic earth on the steep hillsides of Sicily, a stone's throw from Mount Etna, captured the full attention of the wine bar's first clients. The three young women watched expectantly as Bente walked from their table to the bar to fetch the bottle of red. *Its fiery taste and slightly earthy tone will perfectly complement their seasonal vegetables with whipped herb butter,* Bente thought with satisfaction. In moments like these—introducing people to new wines that elevated their dining experience, telling an interesting story—Bente loved her job.

She was just about to head back to the women's table when she felt a hand on her arm. She turned to meet her friend Ellie's clear blue gaze.

"Guess what?" Ellie said. "The new wines have arrived, and I've persuaded Tomas to let us do a first tasting after we close."

Bente grinned. "How did you manage that?" The idea that Tomas would let them taste the wines before he did sounded too good to be true.

"By pointing out it will help us match the wines with tomorrow's menus. Increased sales!" Ellie tapped her temple with her index finger.

The place where they worked, Rendezvous, was a mediocre local bar and restaurant, but it had an excellent wine list. Bente had been the sommelier there for almost two years: creating the bar's wine lists, advising customers about which wines went best with their meals, and ensuring that the wines were served properly. Tomas, the owner, insisted on stocking good wines, believing this would impress the choosy clientele around Mariatorget. He wasn't entirely wrong; customers were impressed with Bente's selections. But it would take more than a good wine list to improve the wine bar's reputation.

Bente went over to the table and held up the bottle to the light flooding in through the tall windows. The sun was low in the sky, and it cast a golden shimmer over the room, making the deep-red wine glow through the bottle's green glass.

The women nodded their approval. Bente then took the corkscrew from her apron pocket and opened the bottle, uncorking it with a satisfying plop. She waited for the first woman to taste it before she served the others.

She returned to the bar and, as the roofs of the buildings across the street swallowed up the last rays of the sun, sorted the previous day's opened bottles on the solid wooden bar top framed by ribbed birch paneling. There was nothing wrong with the venue—dove-gray walls, pale wooden furniture, and low-hanging lamps with wide shades that spread a soft glow over the rectangular tables. The slightly darker wooden floor contrasted well with the cool color palette. Tomas hadn't skimped on the decor or the building materials, but somehow the place lacked a feeling of warmth, despite the staff's efforts to fill it with positive energy.

Some first-time guests did return, but by then it usually felt like a different place because Tomas had made changes and was trying something new. He was incapable of deciding what kind of business he wanted Rendezvous to be. When he took on Bente, it had been a simple wine bar; it later became a restaurant and bar. Now it was something in between. The one constant through all the changes was Tomas's lack of engagement—he showed his face, counted the night's receipts, and issued orders, and that was about it. He was never fully involved, yet he expected the business to run seamlessly, a disconnect that resulted in poor management on his part, insufficient staffing, and poor customer service.

And there was another problem. Tomas had recently informed the staff that he'd put the place up for sale, and now their hearts were no longer in their work because no one knew what was going to happen next. Their shared creativity was what had always made Rendezvous special. One example was this evening's charred seasonal vegetables, which had been added to the menu by the impressive chef.

In a reversal of their usual problem, they actually had too many serving staff on tonight, so Bente and Ellie let the other waiter, a young student, finish early so he could get back to studying for his exams. After the kitchen closed, the chef went home too. A few guests lingered while, behind the bar, Bente and Ellie began to prepare their after-hours tasting. They unpacked the bottles and read the accompanying information, writing down the wines' names and years and their expectations from the wines.

As soon as they were alone, they switched the music to soft Swedish pop and turned it up, setting out their glasses to the sound of Veronica Maggio's singing. They took off their aprons and left the tall candles burning on the tables all around them.

Once everything was ready, six identical glasses sat in front of each of them. They lined up the wines and poured them—four reds and two whites. Tomas always left the writing of the wine descriptions to Bente; he felt that her skill lay in explaining wine in a way that people understood, and she didn't disagree. This ability had once led her to a career as a TV sommelier. Tomas loved to mention this fact to customers, which made Bente feel like a performing monkey.

She and Ellie sat down opposite each other and swirled the first glass in order to release the wine's aroma. Two of the red wines were from

Burgundy, one was from Portugal, and one was from Liguria in Italy. The oak-aged Chardonnay came from California, and the Sauvignon Blanc from Australia.

The soft glow from the overhead lights made the wine in the first glass look almost golden as Bente held it up to inspect the color and clarity.

"By the way, you haven't replied to my invitation yet," Ellie said.

Ellie had recently bought a house in Huddinge. The photos revealed an idyllic residential area, the sort of place that sent chills down Bente's spine. Bente could already picture the May evening of the housewarming: late spring, with the smell of barbecues and the scent of hawthorn blossom in the air, and the sound of children's laughter echoing among the houses. Ellie had been longing to buy, and was looking forward to moving in. Who wouldn't, at this time of year? Piles of leaves and cut-back plants in the gardens after the spring clean-up, chatting over the fence or drinking flasks of coffee at rickety wooden tables that had been left outside all winter. Some kids might even be out grilling sausages. Bente hadn't set foot in an area like that since she'd left home at the age of thirteen. In all the years since, she hadn't known anyone who lived like that, at least no one she felt obliged to visit. It wasn't that she couldn't handle attending; for goodness' sake it was only a housewarming. She just didn't want to.

She smiled. "Of course I'm coming."

Ellie gave her a searching look. "It'll be cool."

They'd met when Bente started working at Rendezvous, and had quickly become friends. Bente didn't ever talk of her childhood, and Ellie respected her friend's boundaries, which Bente appreciated.

They were well into the oak-aged Chardonnay, noting down words like *cardamom*, *burnt butter*, and *toffee apples* when Bente's phone vibrated with a message. It was from her friend Camille in France.

> Mon chérie! You remember I was invited to join a diving expedition to a shipwreck off the coast of Brittany last month? It was crazy.

Another message immediately followed:

Look what we found down there—a genuine treasure. Some pretty average wines, but also some of real quality, plus this: a small box containing a single bottle, with something that looks like a Swedish inscription. Can you help with the translation?

Camille loved diving, and she was one of the best sommeliers Bente knew. She had a highly trained nose, and could distinguish between different wines from neighboring vineyards in Burgundy. She and Bente had met back when they were both pitching wine in a messy wine bar in Montparnasse, in Paris, fifteen years ago. Being well-qualified sommeliers wasn't the only thing they had in common; both women had also long dreamed of joining an expedition to search for wines in a shipwreck. To Camille's great delight, the French government had finally granted permission to investigate a wreck that had been located a few years earlier. The ship had struck a mine in 1945, just before the end of the Second World War; wine had made up a considerable share of its cargo. Bente guessed that her friend had been first into the water when the expedition got underway.

An image of a wine bottle appeared on her phone screen. The bottle had been cleaned, and the dark-green glass looked almost cloudy. In the middle was a small, round metal plaque, embedded in the glass, with a large tree—an oak—etched onto it. Among the oak's branches, so small that they were barely visible, were four words.

Bente quickly replied:

No problem. I'm still at work with Ellie, will take a look as soon as I get home.

Camille responded immediately:

Say hi to Ellie—tell her she has to come back here and dance on the tables with me.

Bente smiled. She was so grateful for her little gang. She and Camille had remained friends even after Bente left Paris for Stockholm, TV appearances, and a job at one of the city's Michelin-starred restaurants. Camille had also been one of her staunchest supporters after Bente's TV career came crashing down and she was swept up in a storm of negative attention and publicly humiliated. Her two friends had gotten to know each other when Bente took Ellie on a weekend trip to Paris a year or so ago.

She and Ellie finished the tasting, then cleaned up and changed out of their work clothes before setting the alarm and locking up. The March evening was chilly, and Bente was glad she had chosen her warm coat and pushed her wool hat into her pocket at the last minute. She pulled on the hat and tied her belt.

Ellie set off toward the subway while Bente cut across Mariatorget and climbed the stairs to her sister Hanna's enormous apartment, which was blissfully empty tonight. Her sister was working late, and her mother, Agneta, was visiting a girlfriend. Bente was looking forward to a couple of hours of much-needed peace and quiet.

She missed her own apartment so much—her little Parisian-style flat in Stockholm's Söder district. She was currently renting it out; she had brought her most precious possessions here, and put the rest in storage. It was a temporary solution until she had saved sufficient capital to be able to move back. Right now Bente and her mother were both parasites, living off Hanna's enormous success in the tech world. Fortunately she had plenty of space.

Bente's mouth felt dry from the wine, and tea would probably only make it worse, but she was craving a strong Earl Grey. She boiled the water, dropped in an overfilled infuser, and spooned in plenty of honey. She blew on it and took a cautious sip; the heat hurt her tongue, but the honey soothed her mouth.

She grabbed her thick woolen sweater from the hook by the double doors and stepped out onto the crescent-shaped balcony with attractive wrought iron railing, which overlooked the square. The murmur of conversation from Hotel Rival drifted through the air; people crossed the square, entering and exiting it from the surrounding streets. In the distance was the constant hum of the traffic on Hornsgatan.

She sat down on the garden furniture that was left out all year round, took out her phone, and looked closely at the photo Camille had sent. There was nothing on the bottle apart from the brass plaque; obviously the label had perished on the seabed.

At the bottom of the plaque was a date—*1944*. Bente tried to zoom in on the branches of the oak tree so she could read the inscription, but the image was too blurred.

Can you send me a sharper image?

A second later the screen flashed, and a clearer photo appeared. She took a sip of her hot tea and zoomed in again.

The words *Saknar dig* appeared between two of the branches. Then: *Din*, and down the trunk: *Dejje*.

MISS YOU
YOUR DEJJE

She sent the translation to Camille and got an immediate response.

How strange. Could it be a message to someone?

Bente nodded to herself. It could be. Her screen flashed again:

The bottle is going to be sold at auction along with the other wines. It would have been great if we could have told its story.

Bente understood that sentiment more than anyone. She replied:

What do you know?

Camille repeated what Bente already knew about the ship being sunk just before the end of the Second World War. Then she added:

According to the ship's log, the origin of the cargo was Bordeaux.

Bordeaux. The west coast of France. Bente took another sip of tea while she waited. The three dots were pulsating.

Hard to set a price when we know only the year and geographical location. Thanks for the translation anyway!

No problem, Bente answered, ending with a kiss emoji.

She put down her phone and gazed out over the treetops in the square; tiny drops of moisture had formed on the branches. After several minutes, she went indoors and, feeling inspired, headed for the well-stocked wine refrigerator and picked out a Bordeaux. From a simple château, not very expensive; she just wanted to savor the moment.

She opened the bottle and poured herself a glass. She figured she could use the rest for her next YouTube episode, which she was going to record the following day. The topic of Bordeaux could be good; she hadn't talked about classic wines in a while. Recently she had focused on smaller producers with a more modern style.

She took her father's old waterproof jacket from the hallstand and put it on before going back out onto the balcony. It was pretty cold out there now.

Once again she gazed at the photograph of the bottle and wondered how it had ended up on board that particular ship. The idea struck her—this could be a fantastic subject for a TV show! Looking at wine in a historical context, a shipwreck wine from the Second World War . . . But a second later she squashed the thought, remembering: Her TV career no longer existed.

She was a has-been.

2

The glare of the spotlights was merciless, and Didrik Holgersson had to make a real effort not to squint at the cameras and the audience. He couldn't see the people in the studio because of the bright lights. Still, the thought of all those faces turned toward him made his skin crawl.

"Welcome back to *The Experts*." The show's host, Madeleine Hägg, was one of Sweden's finest, in Didrik's opinion, and her tone was warm. "For new viewers, let me introduce our program's historian, Didrik Holgersson." Madeleine then introduced the other members of the panel and the week's special guest, a former minister of education. The day's topic was education. Madeleine turned to the minister. Didrik exhaled, then drew in as much oxygen as he possibly could. Why was his bow tie so tight? It was almost choking him, and he thought he could feel his tweed jacket chafing him through his shirt.

The Experts aired on TV24 on Thursday evenings, and Didrik was a permanent member of the panel, which also included a sociologist and an economist. An appropriate guest joined them each week to discuss a new topic. The show was one of TV24's most popular offerings, and Didrik usually loved the live tapings. There had been some lively exchanges tonight, and everyone knew their subject, but right now Didrik just wanted the recording to end so that he could get away.

The minister had finished talking, and Madeleine turned to Didrik. He bought himself a few seconds by taking a sip of water, tried to focus his senses—make eye contact with Madeleine, listen to the question, push aside all thoughts of Lovisa. He concentrated on his breathing. He couldn't have a panic attack in front of the audience.

"So what's your view, Didrik? To what extent do schools play a greater role in society today than in the past?"

Didrik formulated the response in his head, thinking about history and all the parallels he could draw to make the studio audience and the viewers think the matter through. Then he said something off the cuff that generated laughter in the studio—delivering clever answers that made history easy to understand was his forte. Slowly he let out a long breath. He loved his job, and recording shows like this was part of that enjoyment.

His mind wandered to what had happened. Lovisa, his wife, had said that she was leaving him. Was it his work that had led to this decision on her part? Surely he hadn't been away that much—no more than Lovisa. *She* was the one who'd had her hands full recently, with that prestigious international study.

Applause rang out, and Didrik was brought back to the moment. Madeleine wrapped up the show and thanked the participants. Didrik stood up and quickly wiped his palm on his pants before shaking hands with the other panelists.

Lovisa's words echoed inside his head. He broke out into a cold sweat. He had to get out of here. His shirt was beginning to feel damp beneath the thick tweed jacket.

He gave the production team a quick wave and prepared to sneak out—he didn't need to stay around for polite chitchat. He was turning to leave when he heard Madeleine's voice behind him. "Didrik, do you have a moment?"

He stopped, turned back.

"I wanted to talk to you about the new idea we ran by you—I believe you received the outline? I thought it sounded really exciting. You were going to get back to us?"

"Oh yes, I was . . . Yes . . . absolutely." He looked around. He had no memory of what he had promised to do.

Madeleine was still looking inquiringly at him.

"Like I said, I'll get back to you. Thanks for a great show." Once again he turned away.

His bow tie felt like a snare, was it tighter than usual? Or had his neck swollen? He thought he was going to be strangled at any second. He hurried out into the corridor, finally escaping from the stuffy studio, and tried to get some oxygen into his lungs, but it was hot here too. Jesus, had they cranked up the heating in the entire TV24 building? Didn't they know that the price of electricity had gone through the roof?

This isn't working anymore. That was what Lovisa had said, and she had meant it.

Those words had come as a shock to him on Sunday evening. Sure, in the days leading up to it—weeks, now that he thought about it—she had been evasive, but he knew she had a lot to do at work, and had assumed that was all it was. There were periods when they were both incredibly busy, and they sometimes fell into bad habits, not paying each other enough attention.

Lovisa had been sitting on the sofa with a cup of tea. He'd registered the absent look on her face, and she hadn't even glanced up when he came in. As usual, he'd suggested one of those crime shows they both liked.

"I'm going to get ready for bed." She had stood up.

"Is something wrong?" he'd asked.

She'd taken a deep breath. "This isn't working anymore."

"Have you been talking to my mom again?" Didrik had sighed. "I know you both think I'm doing too many recordings, but I've got a break coming up in a few weeks."

Didrik's mother and Lovisa were touchingly in agreement on many things, most of all the fact that his TV work was a terrible idea. It took up a lot of time, and as a result his academic career suffered. Nothing was really happening on that front at the moment, which annoyed them both.

When Lovisa didn't say anything, Didrik went on: "I know I've been out for a lot of evenings, but things are calming down now; we'll finish recording *The Experts* in a couple of weeks. And I've arranged a meeting with one of the professors at the university to discuss jumping in as a guest lecturer. You remember we talked about that, he's the one who wrote . . ."

"I don't mean that. I mean this." She'd waved her hand in the air between them.

"What? You mean . . . ?" He still didn't understand.

"Us. I mean us." She raised her voice, which she never did, as if there were a problem with his hearing, when in fact the problem lay with her lack of clarity. Because he still didn't get it. What was she trying to say?

"I don't think it's working. I don't feel as if . . . I don't want this."

"What don't you want? We're married!"

"I don't want to be married to you anymore." Her shoulders appeared slumped, as if she had been carrying a heavy burden.

"But . . . I love you," he said feebly, hearing how pathetic he sounded. "Where has this come from?" He still couldn't take in what she had just said. "Don't you love me anymore? Or . . . I don't understand."

Lovisa said nothing. She simply shook her head. It was impossible for Didrik to work out whether she was confirming that she no longer loved him, or if it was a sign of resignation. But he could see it in her eyes.

"Can't we talk about this? What is it you think isn't working?"

Lovisa sank back down onto the sofa. "You and me. We . . . I don't know. We don't have anything in common anymore."

"But we're . . ." Didrik sat down beside her. "Children. We're trying for a baby."

Lovisa gazed at him in silence.

"For God's sake, I love you! How can you throw this in my face?" He was the one who raised his voice now. Lovisa looked shocked; they didn't behave like this. Until now, their marriage had always maintained a calm, low-key equilibrium that was based on mutual respect.

"I'm moving out tomorrow." She stood up again and headed for the bedroom.

Moving out? Where to? How long for? For good?

"I need to think," she added.

No problem, he could give her time to think. Give her a few days to sort out her thoughts. Of course he could.

"I'll sleep on the sofa," she called from the bedroom.

"No, I'll sleep on the sofa," Didrik said wearily.

◆ ◆ ◆

The following morning had been dreadful. Lovisa didn't want to talk; she was distant and silent as she picked up her suitcase and slammed the door when she set off for work. Didrik had somehow made his way to his office at Gärdet to prepare for the TV show. Lovisa hadn't been in touch all day, and by Tuesday morning he couldn't bear it any longer. He had to know.

When are you coming back?

He closed his eyes. A message with absolutely no dignity. The reply had pinged back almost immediately:

I need time.

Didrik hurried along the corridor, greeting those he passed but avoiding meeting anyone's eye. He needed to get to the changing room, and fast.

"Didrik. Hi."

Shit. It was one of the directors from the morning show, a guy Didrik had lunch with occasionally. Under normal circumstances, he didn't mind chatting to him at all.

"I've been trying to get ahold of you—I wanted to get your input about . . ."

"Yes, absolutely, give me a call tomorrow when I'm in the office." Didrik forced a smile and kept walking. His phone vibrated—was it Lovisa? Was she ready to see him? Perhaps she would tell him that it had all been a mistake, she'd changed her mind, she didn't know what had come over her, these things happen. Their relationship was definitely working. They were fine. They loved each other, after all.

How could she think anything else?

Thirteen years. They had been a couple for thirteen years, married for eight. They had been trying to have a baby for six years. He had believed their efforts and failures had brought them closer together. What had he missed?

He practically ran along the corridor to the dressing room, then opened the door, sank down on the bench, loosened his bow tie, and took it off. Undid a few shirt buttons. Shrugged off his jacket and took a deep breath. With shaking hands, he grabbed a bottle of sparkling water from the table, unscrewed the cap, and knocked it back so fast that the bubbles went up his nose, making him snort and cough. He put it down and took another deep breath.

When he checked his phone, his shoulders slumped. It was only a message from Elnaz, the features editor from the production company that was working on new program ideas. She wanted to confirm that they were meeting for drinks this evening.

In a way he was relieved not to have news to face, but then his phone vibrated again.

Lovisa. The name flashed on the screen.

He didn't dare open the message.

What if she really had changed her mind about being married? Or maybe the message was about something practical, a reminder to take out the trash. He exhaled and clicked.

And there it was. No room for doubt.

Four words that smashed everything within him to pieces.

I want a divorce.

3

The acclaim had come so quickly ten years ago. One day she was periodically giving tips about wine on the morning show, and the next, she had a show of her own. Bente had been unprepared for what came next.

The attention had been unexpected; she was even more surprised by the hatred that came her way as her fame grew. It started with the odd dig here and there, nasty comments on her YouTube videos, which gained an avalanche of new subscribers after she began to appear on TV. These were followed by a few unpleasant headlines in magazines and gossip columns concerning how she came across on-screen, and some poisonous remarks on the TV station's Facebook page. *I think the other wine expert is better* was a common thread. Needless to say, any expert these people preferred was always a man. However, Bente took this all in stride; the world of wine was a male-dominated industry, and she had grown a thick skin over the years.

Once she and the celebrity baker Henrik Eklund became a couple, the tone of the comments and articles softened, as if having a boyfriend made her more or less okay. But the relationship ended, Bente was blamed for allegedly cheating on Henrik, and everything came crashing down following the "dine and dash" incident—a misunderstanding that ultimately ended Bente's TV career.

She had visited a restaurant with some friends—influencers and TV personalities who occasionally got together. Fame had brought her these new acquaintances—a group of women who met up for dinner or lunch, hung out in bars. After their outings, everyone always posted fantastic pictures on social media, accompanied by breathlessly enthusiastic captions. *Dinner with Bente Hammar, such an energy boost!*

It had been a long evening. They ate and drank, ordered more food, more bottles of wine. High-quality wines, and the final check had added up to considerably more than the monthly food budget for a family with three children. (A sensationalist gossip site had later drawn the comparison.)

They had been celebrating the premiere of a new television show on which one of the other girls cooked and Bente offered advice about wine to accompany the dishes. After the restaurant, they moved on to a bar, then to a club where someone in the group was on the VIP list.

It wasn't until the following morning, when they were chatting in their WhatsApp group and trying to work out who had paid for what and who owed money to someone else, that they realized they had left the restaurant without paying. It had been a chaotic departure, with a couple of the girls chatting to a news anchor, Bente visiting the bathroom, and the other girl trying to find a cab.

Bente had immediately tried to call the restaurant, but they didn't open until the afternoon. She went to their Facebook page to try to resolve the matter straightaway, knowing from her own experience within the industry that an unpaid check that big could easily lead to the involvement of the police. Above all, she was ashamed and embarrassed. This situation was absolutely not okay, and she clicked on the page, feeling sure that the matter could be quickly resolved. Unfortunately, the restaurant had already posted about the incident.

> Thanks to the four girls who did a runner without paying the check yesterday evening. Our staff worked hard serving you three courses, wine, and Champagne, and you didn't even leave a tip for the waitress. Unfortunately the table wasn't booked in

> advance, so we don't have your names—but if this is you, please get in touch.

Shit. With a lump in her stomach, Bente clicked on the post with the intention of commenting, but then realized that it would be better to send a DM rather than expose her name and picture. That was when she noticed the number of reactions below the post.

A thousand. *Jesus.* And then the comments. Hundreds. And just as many shares.

She knew that certain posts could go viral on social media, like those of cute kittens or babies laughing, but she had never heard of a "dine and dash" going viral before. As she tried to take it all in, the numbers kept on going up, with the original post getting shared over and over again.

She broke out in a sweat.

She quickly typed a message to the restaurant, saying that it was her party that had forgotten to pay. She couldn't help going back to the comments to see what people were saying. It wasn't long before she saw that someone had identified her.

> I was sitting at the next table! They were so noisy, ordering lots of food and giving the staff a hard time. I recognized one of them, it was Bente Hammar, that woman who talks about wine on TV.

Bente thought back to their behavior. She always made a point of being pleasant to the staff, and she had taken up the battle over tips in the past. She thought the Swedes were very poor in that department, and she had said so publicly on more than one occasion. Admittedly her party had done the wrong thing in forgetting to pay, but surely they hadn't also been rude to the waiters and waitresses? Bente had always caught their eye and thanked them properly, wanting them to know that they were seen and appreciated. She knew that her companions could be a little casual toward the staff, but she didn't think anyone had been impolite.

Someone named Lizette Jansson had replied to the comment that identified Bente. What a leech, when restaurant owners are already barely scraping by. She probably thought she could eat there for free! Stuck-up bitch! And she cheated on Henrik Eklund. He deserves someone better.

The first stone had been cast.

Next was someone by the name of Peter: Can't stand her on TV, smug bitch, not surprised that she ran out without paying.

Bente watched in real time as a tsunami of hatred poured down on her. All she could do was sit there, utterly powerless.

The thread was completely out of control now, the number of comments spiraling. If this were medieval times, there wouldn't have been much left of her stoned body. As Bente was scrolling, the comments were switched off. Presumably someone at the restaurant didn't like their Facebook page being used as a platform for a lynch mob.

They hadn't replied to her message, so as soon as the restaurant opened she called and explained as apologetically as she could that they had simply forgotten about the bill. The person on the other end of the line said curtly that it would be fine for her to come in and pay.

Looking like the main character in an espionage novel, she went down there dressed in a baseball cap and sunglasses, and with the collar of her coat turned up to hide her face. She paid and apologized once more. Fifteen minutes later the restaurant deleted the post, and Bente let out a sigh of relief. The whole thing had blown over.

However, later that evening when she was recovering on the sofa with the new novel by her favorite writer, Valérie Perrin—Bente liked to read French authors in order to keep up her language skills after having lived there—she received a message from one of her friends.

Have you seen this?

There was a link to a blind item on the entertainment page of one of the tabloid papers.

> Female presenter leaves luxury restaurant without paying check
>
> At a Stockholm restaurant, a TV star and her friends consumed food and drink to the value of thousands of kronor. Then they left—without paying.
>
> "This could definitely constitute fraud," says a lawyer with expertise in this kind of crime.
>
> It all began like a normal restaurant visit. The TV star and her friends arrived at the classic Stockholm venue at about 7:00 p.m.
>
> "I recognized her right away," says a diner who was there when the group arrived.
>
> According to a guest who sat at an adjoining table, the four women were quiet at first. They started with a bottle of Dom Pérignon 2009 and enjoyed two dozen oysters with the vintage Champagne before ordering the rest of their meal.
>
> "We are of course proud of our entire menu, but this party ordered our most spectacular dishes. French toast with truffle and a 63-degree egg to start, followed by beef tartare on lobster for the main course. They chose to have the beef topped with Kalix caviar, and after studying the dessert menu went for a sorbet made from Italian lemons and specially aged vodka," says Fredrik Larsson, the restaurant owner.
>
> The check came to 12,326 kronor, excluding tips. At this point in the evening, the party disappeared without anyone paying.

A picture of the check was included, with the caption A vulgar order.

The fact that Bente had since paid was irrelevant; the budding disaster was now a reality.

On top of everything else, the rumors about her alleged infidelity had resurfaced. And in the eyes of the public, the fact that she had previously stood up for restaurant workers, their pay and conditions, and said that everyone should leave a tip of at least 15 percent didn't help; it simply made her a hypocrite.

The following day an "expert"—it wasn't clear in what field this person's expertise actually lay—publicly stated that behaviors such as *kleptomania* and *infidelity* were often linked, and that these problems frequently revealed narcissistic tendencies, as in this particular case. Before long the writers were naming Bente in the articles, since everyone knew she was the one being talked about anyway.

Her misstep hadn't led to any major headlines—she wasn't that famous. However, the attention was enough to cause the hatred that previously had only seeped out to come gushing forth. Lies now mixed with wild speculation in the comment boxes, and Bente realized that the truth didn't actually matter to these people. They *wanted* her to be a horrible person. In that context, the facts were irrelevant.

She couldn't stop reading.

Her mother and sister noticed the effect it was having on her, and eventually persuaded her to take a break from the spotlight. TV24 didn't object.

Even though her mother and sister were standing by, ready to support her, Bente had rented out her apartment, packed two suitcases, and taken the ferry to the island of Gotland and Aunt Lydia—the only member of the family who placed no value whatsoever on Bente's activities, and who never questioned her ambitions in the world of TV.

Lydia's husband had left when their son, Uno, was a baby, and mother and child had spent a great deal of time with Bente's family since then. Bente's father had later died and her mother had spent some time in jail; during that time, Lydia had been the natural support to

Bente and Hanna, and over the years, Bente, her mother, Hanna, Lydia, and her cousin Uno had become a close family unit.

By the time of Bente's crisis, Lydia and Uno lived on Gotland, and moving into her aunt's house just outside the Visby town wall, being spoiled with Indian teas and home-baked cakes and cookies, and being called *sweetheart* had helped enormously.

Bente had stayed with Lydia for almost six months. During that time she had carried on posting her wine tips on YouTube on a weekly basis, even though she was no longer especially popular. A few mean comments slipped through, but eventually people grew tired of the scandal and only a few loyal followers remained.

When Bente returned to Stockholm, she moved in with her sister, Hanna, in the enormous apartment on Maria's Square. Her sister's fortune could be compared to a digital version of Scrooge McDuck's bank vault. Hanna was then already supporting their mother, who had served her jail time and taken early retirement from her accounting work, and was happy to provide Bente with food and somewhere to live while she looked for work as a sommelier.

Eventually, Bente got the job at Rendezvous and, in spite of Hanna's protests, started to pay rent. Bente gratefully accepted the emotional support, however. Living with her mother and sister, spending time with them every day, reminded her that she was not alone. The break in her TV career had already lasted three years. By now, Bente had accepted the truth.

The world of TV had forgotten all about her.

4

The message from Camille had prompted Bente to read up about Bordeaux, the Second World War, and shipwreck wines. Then she moved on to finding information about wine production in that area during the war years—a topic she was familiar with from her sommelier training, though she needed a refresher and wanted more detail.

She spent half the night and the morning on her research, and before she left for work she recorded a short film about Bordeaux wines, recommending the red she had opened the previous evening and adding to that a bottle of white. Her YouTube videos didn't get huge traffic, but she loved making them.

After posting the video, she got in the shower, keeping the bottle from the bottom of the sea in her mind the whole time. There was something about it that was impossible to let go. She felt as if she was on the trail of something specific that was fascinating, and the wider theme was interesting on its own.

She began to form a pitch in her head. *The link between wine and people through the ages. How war and bad harvests affected the wine and those involved in its production.* Lighthearted but informative entertainment, the kind of thing that made viewers feel smart because they were learning something. It felt wonderful to be completely absorbed, totally swept away: the same way she had had felt while learning about wine in the early days of her training. That had been a transformative experience. All the aromas and tastes she already knew had become more real once she understood the flavors: where they came from, how they had developed; which aspects had to do with the variety of grape, the climate, the soil, and which could be attributed to the manner in which the wine had been fermented and stored.

She had sent lots of questions about the bottle to Camille, who'd promised to get back to her. Maybe Bente was wasting her time, but if it turned out that the bottle actually did have an interesting history, she'd be prepared to move forward and pitch the idea to a production company.

When she emerged from the shower, she had several new messages from Camille, including lists of the addresses where the French ship's cargo had been scheduled to be sent. There was an address in Vetlanda, in Sweden, which Bente was determined to follow up on.

The walk to the restaurant was short. It was a beautiful afternoon, and she could almost feel spring in the air, which was slightly damp, a shift from the bone-dryness of winter. There was the faintest hint of budding new life.

The restaurant dining room was empty when she arrived, but she could hear clattering from the kitchen. She poked her head in and said hi to Emil, the chef, before getting changed into her work clothes.

Ellie showed up a couple of minutes later, and when they returned to the dining room, Tomas was there.

"Hi, girls. Good description of the wines yesterday, Bente. I've already updated the wine list."

Bente nodded. When Tomas was in a good mood, he wasn't slow to give praise. Maybe she was being a little too negative about the job? When she first got the post as sommelier, everything had felt so right. She would be responsible for the wines, have her own budget, and be tasked with making sure the restaurant's wine cellar was something special, as she was *such a good sommelier*. That was how Tomas had described her. He had promised that, because of her expertise, she would be able to travel to France and visit vineyards in order to source unique wines for the bar. However, those trips had never materialized. Bente made recommendations about which wines to buy, but the final decisions were always

Tomas's, because he wanted to keep an eye on expenses, and there was no further mention of a budget of her own. Apart from Tomas, though, her colleagues were fantastic, which counted for a great deal. Besides which, she *needed* this job.

Tomas had written up the evening's dishes on the chalkboard in the middle of the restaurant. If Bente had been running the place, she would have made radical alterations to the menu, including dishes with a little more finesse, that matched the wine list. She would have invested in some of those new corkscrews that allowed you to draw off the wine without opening the bottle; they made a small hole in the cork, which meant that the wine lasted as long as if the bottle had never been opened. In the wider context, it was such a small investment, but Tomas was too mean to agree to it, and as a result they always served the same old wines by the glass.

Several more colleagues arrived, some of them talking about the previous night at the restaurant. Bente always appreciated these moments when everyone was together, preparing for the evening to come. Even Tomas seemed to see the value in these discussions, and was often capable of boosting everyone's mood.

"Well done yesterday, those of you who were on duty," he began with a smile. "And our YouTuber." He looked at Bente; the nickname was loaded with contempt even though he always smiled as if it were meant kindly. "And no one ran away without paying their check." He laughed loudly and winked. No one else laughed. The joke wasn't particularly clever, and Bente was heartily sick of being the target of his humor. The fact that his jokes weren't even funny made the whole thing even more humiliating.

She stared back at him, her face expressionless. Unmoved. She had no intention of letting him see how his words affected her. To be fair, it wasn't actually the words that bothered her, but rather the sense of being exposed in front of her coworkers, who always looked uncomfortable in these situations. Ellie used to speak up on her friend's behalf, but Bente had asked her to stop—it just gave Tomas more fuel for his fire.

Tomas continued to run through the evening before them, explaining who was doing what and noting any special bookings.

They ate a quick dinner, a croque madame rustled up by the chef. *This would make a fantastic addition to the menu,* Bente thought as she bit into the crunchy bread. As usual, everyone chatted and laughed during the meal, but staff dinners weren't as relaxed when Tomas was there. He had decided to stay on for a while tonight to "help out."

Soon the first guests arrived. As the evening went on, several diners ordered wine by the glass, so Bente's job mostly involved making simple recommendations and serving the wines.

She was opening the fourth bottle of house red when she heard a voice beside the bar. "Bente?"

She turned around and saw Elnaz, the features editor with the production company Bente had worked with in the past. Seeing Elnaz here was like an echo from the past. She was perched on a barstool and was dressed all in black, her signature look, including a pair of Doc Martens. Even when they had been recording the cookery show in France during a hot week in summer, Elnaz had never taken off her beloved boots; she had, however, swapped her customary sweater for a thinner T-shirt and her jeans for a skirt. In black.

"Hi." Bente put down the bottle. She had always liked Elnaz. They hadn't exactly been friends, but they had gotten along well, and had made several shows together. Bente hadn't kept in touch with anyone from TV, and was genuinely pleased to see Elnaz, who had her laptop and a large glass of red on the bar in front of her.

Elnaz beamed, stood up, and gave Bente a hug.

"Are you working?" Bente nodded at the laptop.

"Yes—I'm waiting for someone to join me, and thought I'd deal with a few emails."

"Are you still with Palento?"

"I am, but as a producer now." Elnaz smiled, her eyes glowing with pride. She had always worked hard—her promotion was well deserved.

"Wow, congratulations! I couldn't be more pleased."

"Thanks. So I'm flat out looking for interesting ideas—we need something new. I'm actually about to discuss an exciting concept, if my date bothers to show up." She glanced at her watch.

"Sounds good." Bente was aware of Tomas's curious scrutiny from behind the bar. She suddenly thought about the bottle from the bottom of the sea, but immediately dismissed the idea.

"And are you still in TV?" Elnaz asked.

"No, not at all."

Should she say something anyway, mention the fact that she had plans for a concept for a TV show?

"Here he is." Elnaz's face lit up and she waved to someone behind Bente, who turned to see a man with curly dark hair and round glasses wearing an olive-green coat over a smart tweed jacket. She realized she was staring. The man was Didrik Holgersson, the TV historian. The hum of conversation in the restaurant stopped for a few seconds. Everyone's attention was focused on Didrik, who seemed completely unaware of the effect he was having. He raised a hand to greet Elnaz.

There was color in his cheeks as if it were cold outside, and he looked stressed—different from the way he came across on TV anyway. Nowhere near as proper and correct—his cheeks were unshaven, his hair was tousled, and there was something about his expression that Bente couldn't place. She concluded that he was much better looking in reality.

Didrik was known all over the country, and his fame had come pretty quickly. He had started appearing on TV at about the same time as Bente. The difference was that Didrik Holgersson had immediately become everyone's favorite, and these days his popularity was well established. His pitch-perfect accounts of historical events, his skill in linking them to current affairs, and his ability to communicate with everyone—even those who weren't particularly interested in history—had made viewers embrace him without hesitation.

Bente watched him as he ran his fingers through his hair, completely unaffected by the curious glances of everyone in the restaurant. He came over to Elnaz, gave her a quick hug, and sat down on the barstool beside her.

Bente slid back behind the bar and took an order from an elderly couple who wanted her to recommend a red to go with their burgers. She then fetched a bottle of Cabernet Sauvignon from the Napa Valley, opened it, and served them. When she was done, she looked over at Didrik and Elnaz, met his dark gaze, and asked if he would like something to drink.

"Have you two met before?" Elnaz asked. "Bente Hammar—Didrik Holgersson."

Bente held out her hand across the bar.

Didrik's grip was firm, his hand warm.

"Bente worked with TV24 for several years recommending wines, and we worked together on a food show," Elnaz added.

"I loved your tips on wine," Didrik said with a smile.

"Thanks. Nice to hear."

So he knew who she was. She wondered how much he knew. At least he was polite enough not to say anything; he merely asked for a glass of wine. Bente served him the same red that Elnaz was drinking, and took the opportunity to top off Elnaz's glass just as Tomas walked by.

"Maybe you should do less chatting and see if those two would like more wine," he snapped, nodding in the direction of the couple with the burgers whose glasses were still almost half full.

"This is a former colleague of mine." Bente smiled, doing her best to ignore the sharpness of Tomas's tone.

He glanced at Didrik, whom he obviously recognized, then fixed his gaze on Elnaz. "Really? Maybe you were one of the gang that ran off without paying the check!" He laughed loudly, then headed for the till.

Bente flushed bright red. She wanted the floor to open up and swallow her. How could he do that in front of Elnaz, someone she respected and admired? She gave the two of them a quick smile. "I'd better get back to work. Great to see you again, Elnaz. Good to meet you, Didrik."

She hardly dared look at him.

"Same." Elnaz was clearly embarrassed.

Bente went over to the couple with the burgers and asked if everything was to their satisfaction, then opened a bottle of fruity Pinot Noir for one of their rare regular customers.

◆ ◆ ◆

A while later Elnaz caught Bente's eyes. "We're leaving now—it really was nice to see you."

Bente came around the bar. "Thanks, good to see you too. I hope everything continues to go well." She couldn't stop thinking about the bottle—what if this was fate? Elnaz had turned up just when Bente had gotten an idea for a TV show—maybe she could mention it, see what Elnaz thought? She and TV24 had agreed on a *pause*—perhaps this might be a way back?

"Take care of yourself," she heard herself say. Apparently the little pitch she had prepared was staying in her head. She gave Elnaz a quick hug and nodded to Didrik before they disappeared out into the spring twilight.

◆ ◆ ◆

A couple of hours before closing, Tomas picked up a bottle from under the bar. "What's this? It's open." He shook the bottle, held it up to the light. "Who opened it?"

"I did. A customer wanted a glass of Pinot Noir," Bente replied.

"We have lots of wines by the glass."

"This was one of our regulars."

Tomas was clearly irritated. "This will just be wasted now. Brilliant idea, Bente. A straight loss."

"I know it's expensive, but I can sell the rest of the bottle before the end of the evening." Bente tried to remain calm and composed. Not to let herself be affected by Tomas's bad mood.

"It doesn't go with any of the dishes."

"No, because the menu is completely unimaginative," she mumbled.

"What did you say?"

She looked him in the eye. "It would have been fantastic with the steak tartare that Emil suggested." Bente wasn't the only one with aspirations in this place; the chef often came up with ideas that Tomas dismissed as being too costly. "We have good wines, but the menu isn't adapted to go with them, so nobody orders by the bottle."

"So you think the menu is poor. Why don't you go and tell Emil? What a supportive colleague you are." The guests closest to the bar had picked up on the argument and fallen silent.

"It's not Emil who's responsible for the menu—you have the last word," Bente said quietly.

"Well, I am the owner." Tomas sighed loudly. "It's obvious that you don't have a clue how to run a restaurant."

"Maybe not, but I know how to sell good wines."

"You wouldn't know it from the turnover. Things haven't exactly improved since I took you on."

Bente had no intention of letting him walk all over her. "Because you won't let me do what I'm capable of. Shape the menus, match food and wine, have a dialogue with the chef, look at the big picture."

Tomas stared at her. "You know what—if this place doesn't suit you, the door is over there."

Enough. She took off her apron, placed it on the bar. "Fine."

She headed for the changing room, with Ellie running after her.

"What's going on? You're not quitting, are you? Please tell me you're not quitting!"

Bente retrieved her things from her locker. Put on her shoes, slipped her work shoes into a cloth bag hanging from a hook. Grabbed her coat.

"I don't know, but right now I need to get out of here." On her way through the restaurant, she pulled on her coat, then walked outside.

She stopped, took out her phone, googled, and found an email address for Elnaz. Then she jotted down her idea and pressed "Send."

Before she could change her mind.

5

1944

The stench from his fellow travelers—unwashed bodies and clothes, dirt and sweat—lay heavy in the air inside the packed train carriage. Maybe the worst of the smell was coming from Sven himself. The stress and fear that someone would discover the real purpose of his journey seemed to be seeping out of his pores along with the perspiration.

Sven hadn't been in France since he'd completed his training with the Foreign Legion, before France surrendered and was occupied. The people he had encountered on the train today were completely changed from the ones he'd seen then. They sat in silence with their heads bowed, trying to make themselves as small as possible. The only people making a noise, chatting and laughing, were the two German soldiers who had embarked just after Sven. They had checked everyone's papers and then stayed on board the train, which was heading all the way to Bordeaux.

At long last the train slowed down, but when the doors opened, more hot air came pouring in. Sven got off and was overwhelmed by the swirling dust on the platform. It was still only spring, but the past week had brought an unusual heat wave.

He had almost reached his final destination. He took his documents out of his inside pocket and tried to look as relaxed as possible. He had done this several times now, and this time he nearly felt as if he really was Per Jonsson, a carpenter from the Swedish city of Gothenburg, on his way to visit French relatives in Bordeaux.

Three German soldiers were stationed at the exit, checking documentation. Two of them looked tired and, apparently exhausted by the heat and the burning sun, barely glanced at the proffered papers. The third was a young man, bright and full of energy, who examined each person's documents in detail, then smiled at them as he waved them through.

Sven hoped he wouldn't get the conscientious soldier. However, a second later the eager young man beckoned him forward. Sven took a deep breath. His papers were credible; the resistance movement had done an excellent job. At the same time, the Germans had been more on their guard ever since the Allies had grown stronger. They seemed to see members of the resistance everywhere.

The thought of those courageous individuals, with whom Sven had been working ever since General Charles de Gaulle established the Free French, France's resistance government-in-exile, made him feel immensely proud. When the occupation of France began four years earlier and the then-government signed an armistice with Germany, part of the Foreign Legion had thrown their support to the Vichy government, collaborators with Nazi Germany. But Sven's brigade in the Foreign Legion had gone over to fighting for de Gaulle's forces. Just like the brave Frenchmen who now fought from inside France, risking their lives.

The soldier looked at Sven. "What is your business in Bordeaux?" His French was perfect, but spoken with a German accent.

Sven explained, also in French. The German examined the documents, waited a few seconds, turned the papers over, looked at Sven again, then gave them back. Sven had passed through many checkpoints, but he was equally nervous each time. Afraid of being exposed. Arrested. Maybe sent to a prison camp.

Disappearing into a prison camp.

Everything he did involved risk, but that had been the case ever since he had decided to join the French Foreign Legion and fight in the war.

The soldier gave a brief nod, then smiled and waved him through. Sven was about to move on when the German looked down at his suitcase.

"I need to check that."

"Of course," Sven replied, as if it were no problem at all. He opened the case and the soldier picked up the wooden boxes.

"Nice." He nodded admiringly. "For wine?"

"That's right. My relatives own a small vineyard in Médoc."

The German turned the boxes this way and that, apparently inspecting the carpentry as Sven held his breath. The man couldn't possibly see the tiny space. The minute gap above a loose piece of wood that had been pushed to one side from the base of the box, where the document had been placed. If you didn't know it was there, it was impossible to see it. Someone might hear the loose piece of wood rattle if they shook the box, but the German simply looked at it. Gave it back to Sven without further investigation.

"So you're heading for the Médoc peninsula?"

"That's right." Sven kept his voice steady, as he had been trained to do. "Château de Chênes."

"You can travel with me." The German nodded in the direction of a car. "I'm going that way."

"There's no need, I can get there under my own steam. There's a bus due shortly." Sven looked at the silver watch his parents had given him for his twentieth birthday.

"I'm heading there anyway—that's where I'm stationed, in the village where you're going. I was planning to leave in a little while—I'm sure I can get permission to go earlier." The soldier took a step closer to Sven. "It would be nice to talk to someone with the same interests—I'm a carpenter too. Back home in Germany." He held out his hand. "My name is Max." He turned to his colleagues and said a few words in

German. The other soldiers nodded, and Max looked at Sven again. "Let's go."

Sven realized that he couldn't say no. The offer of a ride was a friendly gesture, and you didn't say no to a member of the occupying forces. Maybe the soldier was just being kind, or maybe he had a hidden agenda—it was impossible to tell. You couldn't trust the Nazis.

Max led the way to his car and Sven jumped in.

"Most of my company are from Bavaria, from urban families. They're not the children of carpenters, so there's no one to talk to about craft. And I have to say, those boxes are a fine example of your skills."

"Thanks," Sven mumbled.

"Are they made of oak or . . . is it . . ." Max frowned. "I can't think of the name for that type of wood in French." He thought hard. "Big cones." He made a large, elongated oval shape with his hands.

"You mean pine? Yes, you're right."

"That's it, pine." Max nodded.

Had it been a trick question? Max might suspect something, but Sven had given the perfect answer, as he had rehearsed before he left. He glanced at Max as he started the car; he certainly didn't look suspicious.

Max set off through the town and out onto the main highway. The car was open-topped, and the country air swirled around them, bringing with it the smell of hay and a hint of the sea breeze from the Atlantic coast. Sven could almost taste the damp saltiness of the ocean.

He sat bolt upright all the way, ready for anything. He could only hope that Max would take him to the vineyard as promised, and that he hadn't been caught out. If that were the case, Sven knew exactly how this would end.

He knew exactly what the Germans did to members of the resistance.

6

In hindsight it was almost laughable to think that they had been in such a hurry to buy a house. They had moved in on a glorious autumn day, and both Didrik and Lovisa had waxed lyrical over the beautiful maple with its leaves in shades of golden yellow and copper red, and at the back, the stately mountain ash with glowing orange berries. It was as if every corner of the garden offered up unexpected treasures.

They'd lit a fire and enjoyed their new home, dreaming of the children who would run around there one day, and they immediately started discussing what kind of protection they would need for the stove, to make sure tiny hands didn't get burned. But the months passed by without Lovisa getting pregnant, and eventually the months became a year. A year became two, then three and four. Then they both turned forty, and just the two of them living in a relatively large house made the lack of children even more tangible.

Right now, though, walking up the familiar steps to his own childhood home, whose every variation Didrik knew well, and stepping over the threshold with the chip from when his little brother Victor dropped his skateboard there, felt reassuring. Like a warm, soft blanket. And Didrik needed that today.

His mother met him in the hallway, and he handed over the plant he had bought on the way.

"Lovely," she said, but judging by the look on her face, he had made the wrong choice. "Hydrangeas are beautiful, as long as you give them plenty of water." And there it was, the little dig. As always. His mother spent a ridiculous amount of time on her plants every week, and yet the potted plant Didrik had given her was deemed way too taxing to look after.

She looked inquiringly over his shoulder.

"I'm afraid Lovisa had to work late."

His mother frowned. Shit, he should have prepared a better excuse. Lovisa never missed dinner with Didrik's parents. He had to think fast.

"There was a tight deadline for a piece of the project she's working on."

A safe bet, because Lovisa was pursuing a stellar career within philosophy research. She was a lecturer at Södertörn University, and was participating in a major international study on the distribution of society's resources, which his mother loved to discuss with her.

"I think it's fantastic that Lovisa is taking her research so seriously. She'll be a professor before we know it!" Pride shone in his mother's eyes, and the underlying message was clear: Didrik was wasting his career prospects and his academic knowledge on something as trivial as TV entertainment.

The sense of reassurance he'd felt earlier had been misplaced. He cursed his naive hope that his mother would provide consolation; in fact, she wouldn't be able to cope if he broke down here. A person had to hold their emotions in check; she had learned that lesson as the child of an Estonian father who had left everything behind and fled to Sweden during the Second World War. Didrik loved his grandfather, but any talk of feelings was out of the question, in the older man's opinion, and Didrik's mother had inherited that point of view.

"In you come," she said. "Victor and Sofia are already here—they've got some news." She was beaming, and Didrik immediately knew what they were going to say.

His younger brother had married only six months ago. In a way Didrik was grateful for his mother's not-so-subtle warning, because it gave him the chance to prepare himself mentally and force a smile when the moment came.

His father emerged from the kitchen and gave him a warm hug before leading the way into the dining room, where they sat down at the table. Didrik greeted his brother and sister-in-law. Did Sofia look different? He didn't want to stare, but it was clear that something had changed; she was glowing.

His mother had cooked her popular halibut, which she served with potatoes tossed in dill and whitefish roe. The crystal glasses were out, and a freshly ironed linen cloth covered the table, topped by matching, neatly pressed napkins. Always neatly pressed napkins in the professor's house.

His father poured the wine—Sofia declined.

Didrik had planned to drive home, but now he wondered whether he should leave the car here. Maybe a glass of wine or two was exactly what he needed to get through this? On the other hand, it was probably stupid to drink when he was in this state. He refused the wine too.

"So, are you going to tell us?" His mother could hardly sit still as she smiled at Victor, then Sofia.

Victor placed his hand over Sofia's and gave it a squeeze. "We're having a baby." He smiled, looked at Didrik, and swallowed. The smile didn't quite reach his eyes, and he was clearly a little wary.

Didrik put down his glass of water and grinned. "Seriously?" He stood up. "I'm going to be an uncle?" He walked around the table and hugged Sofia. "You look wonderful—congratulations!" Then he hugged his brother, holding on for a few seconds longer than usual. "Congratulations!" His voice was trembling slightly, but when he met Victor's gaze he felt nothing but genuine joy. His childlessness was a bitter burden, but short of having his own child, a niece or nephew was what he wished for the most.

"Fantastic!" his mother said. "I'm so happy. A grandchild *at last*, and not *a day* too soon."

When she carried on like this, reminding him of a steamroller, Didrik wondered if she'd ever heard of involuntary childlessness. He hadn't discussed the topic with her; he'd merely mentioned that he and Lovisa were trying, and had assumed his parents understood that it wasn't going terribly well, since there were still no grandchildren.

"Victor, tell us more about that study in conflict resolution—you must be nearly finished?"

Victor put down his knife and fork, wiped his mouth, and took a sip of water. "Yes, we're in the homestretch now—there's been a lot to do." He looked at Didrik, then his parents. "I'll be spending some time at the University of Bordeaux in the next few months, so you'll have to take care of Sofia." He patted his wife's arm, and she smiled.

"Of course we will," his mother replied, gazing warmly at her daughter-in-law.

Both Didrik and Victor had followed in their mother's footsteps in the academic world, and Victor was a doctor in the faculty of social sciences here in Uppsala.

As usual their father remained silent, listening to the conversation and periodically nodding in agreement. Occasionally he rubbed his bald head. He was an engineer, a civil servant; he knew a great deal about the world of academia, but never spoke up.

"How exciting." His mother turned her attention to Didrik. "And how about you? Any plans to go back to the university?"

"I have a meeting with a colleague at the university next week," he said quietly. "And I've been approached about a new TV show, one that will look into different antique artifacts and their history."

His mother's face was expressionless. "One of those quiz shows?" Ill-concealed distaste took over as she spoke.

"You could say that." Didrik avoided her gaze, glancing around the table, then out the windows at the apple tree in bud.

"Why don't you carry on with your research into the history of Estonian Swedes? I liked that idea, it sounded so interesting, researching the history of your maternal grandparents. They've got lots of material up in the attic out in the country; it just needs someone to go through it."

Didrik nodded. Maybe he'd go back to the topic one day.

"By the way, I saw Krissie at a lunch the other day," he said. "I'm going to be a guest on her show later in the spring." He speared a piece of potato drenched in roe, and looked at his mother.

"Well, there you go." She turned to Sofia. "Pass me your plate—you're eating for two now!" She happily spooned more food onto her daughter-in-law's dish. "Couldn't Krissie find anyone else, besides her nephew?" She smirked at her own joke.

"I love Krissie's show, she's so good at talking to people," Sofia said diplomatically.

Didrik's Aunt Krissie was something of a TV legend. She had started out as a journalist, moved into television, and become one of the country's most respected TV personalities. She had her own show, on which she interviewed everyone from Hollywood stars to presidents to top names in the world of sport. Didrik's mother didn't like talking about her sister's successes.

"I would have loved to conduct research into Estonian Swedes," she continued instead, handing around the potatoes. "If I'd had the opportunity to look into our family origins, I would have jumped at the chance. Obviously." She topped off Sofia's glass of water, then her own.

"You're not dead yet, Mom," Victor said, which made her laugh. Didrik would never have gotten away with a comment like that. "Don't you think it's great that Didrik is educating the viewers about history? He makes it so easily accessible." Victor spoke encouragingly, and Didrik shot his brother a grateful look.

"But does everything have to be easily accessible? Everything has become so superficial these days. If you want people to understand history, surely the least you can ask is for them to make an effort."

Didrik suppressed a deep sigh.

They moved on to dessert—Italian gelato served with strong coffee.

They chatted about their mother's job and Victor's research project, about the new library where Sofia worked as a librarian, and a little bit about the baby. Nothing about Didrik's job, until his father asked him something, a little shyly, as the two of them were clearing the table.

"What was that former education minister really like? I saw the show—it was good. You were good, as usual."

Didrik smiled. His father often tried to smooth over his wife's criticism, and Didrik knew that his father, at least, was proud of him.

"She was nice—kind of reserved, of course."

"I can believe that. I've always liked her, even if she was a member of the wrong party." His father laughed. "I thought it was an interesting discussion. Your mom thought so too."

"Mom?"

"She watches every week, although she'll never admit it."

No doubt this information was meant to cheer Didrik up, but he just felt sad that she couldn't share this with him. That she couldn't tell him that she followed his career and apparently found his show interesting.

"You're welcome to come and sit in the audience one day if you like."

"I'd love that. Why not? If Mom wants to, of course."

Didrik resisted the temptation to roll his eyes—why couldn't his father think for himself? He was a highly competent individual with a long career in engineering and management behind him, yet he still had to ask his wife's permission to do things.

"No problem." Didrik patted him on the shoulder.

Dusk was falling by the time the party broke up. Didrik hugged his brother and sister-in-law again before they both climbed onto their bikes and Didrik got in his car.

It was a long drive from Uppsala back to the northern suburbs of Stockholm, but there was hardly any traffic today. He soon reached his own little suburb and drove into the safe housing estate where all the homes looked the same—modest dwellings that, these days, sold for sums that were anything but modest.

When he and Lovisa had started dating, they'd commuted between Uppsala and Stockholm. A couple of years later, Didrik secured a post lecturing at the University of Stockholm, while Lovisa took up a research job at Södertörn University. They bought an apartment together in the Gärdet district. However, city life hadn't suited either of them.

He loved the house they had now. It was painted white and lay in a quiet cul-de-sac that was perfect for children, where they could play or learn to ride a bike without any dangerous traffic.

He got out of the car. Could he bring himself to go inside?

A movement by the front door stopped him in his tracks.

It was her.

Lovisa was there. She was home. To stay?

He quickly walked toward the door, but she was already on her way out. She closed the door behind her and put the key in the lock. She glanced up when she heard his footsteps. Looked at him wearily, as if he were an irritant.

Strands of hair had escaped from her blond ponytail. She was wearing her long gray coat over a navy-blue turtleneck sweater. Navy blue suited her. She was irresistibly beautiful. He admitted this to himself reluctantly—because she was no longer his.

"Can't you come in so we can talk?" He didn't want her to go. He wanted to make her the very best cup of tea, serve it with a slice of the walnut bread she loved. They would chat. About their work days, their dream of a family, their careers, plans for the future. The kind of thing they always used to talk about, though if he was brutally honest, they hadn't done much talking recently.

"I have to go," she said firmly, removing her key from the lock and dropping it in her purse.

"Please, Lovisa. Can't you stay? Please, I . . ." He broke off. He didn't know what to say, but he couldn't let her leave. "Don't go."

She paused as if she was wondering what to say, almost as if there was something on the tip of her tongue. But then she shook her head and looked at him with sadness in her eyes. "I'm sorry Didrik, but it's best this way. Best for us."

"Best for us? We're a family, you and I."

"We're not a family."

"But we're going to have children. Please, please stay." Suddenly something struck him. "Is that the problem?"

"What?"

"The fact that we haven't had children? But it'll sort itself out, we're going to start the process of figuring out . . ."

"It's not that."

"I mean, we've discussed adoption and . . ."

"It's not that."

He took a few steps toward her, felt desperation clawing at him. "What can I do? Do you want me to change? I'll give up the television, go back to the university." He took her hand. She didn't pull away, and he smiled at her. "Then everything will be like it was before. The way our life used to be."

"It's not that," she said yet again, her voice harder now. She shook her head, withdrew her hand. Stepped back and looked him in the eye. "I've met someone else." Even though she was speaking quietly, her words sliced through the silence of the street. A man passing by with his dog glanced at them, then looked straight ahead and walked a little faster.

Didrik remained motionless for a few seconds, trying to take in what she had said. "Are you serious?"

She didn't say anything. Of course she was serious. She turned and walked away, heading for the bus stop.

Didrik felt his world collapsing around him. The love of his life was leaving him for another man, and he couldn't change that, couldn't change the situation, couldn't change *himself*.

All he could do was stand in front of their house, where the outdoor lighting cast a warm, deceptive glow in the cold blue light of the gloomy spring evening, and watch as Lovisa left him.

7

Bente had received a reply from Elnaz the very next day. She'd thought the idea sounded interesting, and had asked Bente for more information. The problem was that Bente didn't really have any more information. For that, she'd need to conduct research at the National Archives.

Bente had decided that she would devote her time today to panic-researching the wine bottle so that she would be prepared for her meeting with Elnaz at the production company the following week. She was now sitting with her notebook open in front of her in the silence of the National Archives' reading room. She had told her mother and sister that she was going to find somewhere quiet to look for a job, because she knew they wouldn't like the real reason why she had disappeared with the laptop—to conduct research for a TV show.

She went through photocopies of old handwritten documents, hoping to learn more about the people the bottle had been sent to. She looked up the address in Vetlanda and learned that in 1945, when the ship sank, the residents had been a couple with the family name of Steen.

She was able to determine that their grown-up children had moved out—a daughter in 1941 and a son in 1939. He had joined the French Foreign Legion. Bente's heart began to beat a little faster. Could this be something? Had he sent the bottle home? If he was in the Foreign Legion, it wasn't impossible. On the other hand, she knew very little about the organization or the role it played in France during the Second World War.

Once more she looked at the photograph of the bottle.

Your Dejje

Could the mother have had a secret lover who sent a message from Bordeaux? No—too romantic and not especially realistic. The most likely scenario was that the son was involved somehow. There was no information to suggest that he had moved back home again. She consulted the list once more: His name was Sven Steen. She wrote it down in her notebook.

She opened up her laptop and searched online for *Sven Steen foreign legionnaire.* She found a blog where an ambitious amateur historian had listed every Swede who had been a member of the Legion.

And there it was.

Sven Steen b. 1916
Foreign Legion 1939
Prisoner of war 1944, d. 1944

So he had died in 1944. But surely the bottle had been shipped in 1945? Sven Steen couldn't have done it. Had someone else sent it after his death?

She made a note of all her thoughts—at least this was better than nothing. A bottle from a shipwreck, with links to a Swede who served in the French Foreign Legion during the Second World War. Who was taken prisoner, then died.

She pulled on her coat and walked out of the building. As she left, twilight was falling, but the evenings were gradually getting longer. She loved this time of year, when it remained light out at the time when she had always gone to work at Rendezvous.

She jumped on her bike and cycled home through the city, over Skeppsbron and up toward Slussen. The area around Hornspuckeln was busy with traffic and people on the move, on the way home or out for the evening. At the moment, not having a job to go to felt like something of a relief. Going back to Rendezvous wasn't an option—it would be too humiliating. She was looking forward to simply cooking for Mom and Hanna, enjoying a glass of wine, and then working on her pitch for the meeting.

As she stepped into the hallway, she could hear her mother laughing. She and Hanna were sitting at the enormous kitchen island, whose top was one huge slab of stone. Agneta threw back her head, her red curls bobbing. She was holding a cocktail—a Manhattan.

Hanna poured bourbon into her own glass, followed by vermouth. She could mix that drink in her sleep. They both looked over when Bente walked in, and Hanna held up her glass. "Want one?"

"A cocktail for the cook—thanks." Hanna took out a glass for her sister.

"Hi, Bente," said a third voice. Bente spun around and saw her Aunt Lydia waving from the screen of her mom's cell phone, which she had propped up against the vermouth bottle. In the background were Lydia's built-in oak bookshelves in her house in Visby.

"Any luck with the job search?" Hanna asked.

Bente was tipping rice into the hot oil in the frying pan, but stopped mid-movement. Was there any point in telling the truth? On the other hand, she was too excited about the project to keep quiet.

Hanna handed her the shimmering red cocktail.

"I was actually working on something else."

"Oh?" her mother said.

"A wine bottle from Bordeaux with an inscription in Swedish has been found in a shipwreck from the Second World War, and I think the story would make a good TV show."

Her mother's shoulders slumped. "TV?"

Bente nodded. "I've got a meeting with a production company next week. This story is totally unique—I think it could be great."

"Sounds exciting," Lydia said encouragingly.

Agneta managed a thin smile. "I'm sure it will be."

Hanna didn't appear convinced.

"I'm going to look for a job in the meantime, of course," Bente added quickly. She didn't want to appear ungrateful. She really appreciated her sister's hospitality, but it wasn't a given that Bente could live here indefinitely, and she absolutely didn't want to do that. She had no intention of letting her sister support her financially.

"It's not that," Hanna assured her. "You can stay here as long as you like, it's just . . ." She trailed off. "This TV business . . ." She didn't need to say any more. Bente knew exactly what her mother and sister thought.

"I don't even know if it will come to anything," she said in an attempt to smooth things over. Although if it didn't, she would be terribly disappointed.

"What about running your own business?" Agneta asked. "You've always dreamed of doing that, ever since you and Dad . . ."

"I can't just start up my own business."

"That's what your dad always said when I tried to encourage him." Agneta took a sip of her Manhattan.

Bente didn't answer. Instead she concentrated on adding white wine to the rice, which hissed and crackled. She didn't like talking about her father. It wasn't as if her family never talked about him; they had talked a great deal about him and everything that had happened. But certain memories were too difficult to revisit.

Saturday afternoons—a lasagna in the oven, red wine in a large glass on the kitchen counter. Dad sniffing the wine's bouquet, allowing Bente to do the same before he started coming out with terms for it like *sweaty horse*—a phrase he'd picked up from Swedish wine connoisseur Carl Jan Granqvist's TV show *Living Life* in the mid-1980s. He would add in words like *violets*, *aniseed*, and *cherries*—tastes and aromas that were easier for Bente to understand. And the whole time, he'd be listening to Bruce Springsteen, the smell of the lasagna spreading as Dad explained about French and American oak barrels. On those afternoons, he would sometimes talk about his dream of taking over a building in the area—an abandoned block of apartments or the run-down pizzeria—to open his own bar and restaurant.

Bente recalled feeling a sense of security during those days, but in hindsight, it also seemed that her father had kept up a kind of facade, for reasons she couldn't understand. He must have hidden so many problems.

And yet his dreams had felt so real that he had often talked about them.

If he'd been able to do what he wanted, would he maybe still be alive? Would that have made him happy?

Bente turned her attention to chopping shallots. She had hoped for a little more enthusiasm from her mother and Hanna, although she did understand their unease. Bente had experienced the very worst side of celebrity, yet still she longed for it. She probably ought to ask herself why, but she didn't want to reflect on it too much. She also sensed a niggling feeling of shame. The desire to be famous was ugly. What was wrong with her?

This situation might be different, though—she was meeting with the production company as the creator of a show, a producer. Of course she wanted to be in front of the camera, too, discussing wine—she had missed that. The chance to take the viewers on a dizzying journey through Bordeaux in each episode, revealing its wines and its history, was a dream. At the same time she would be searching for the origins of the bottle and the story behind it. This was a concept that could take her further, a 2.0 version of TV-Bente, more advanced than anything she had done before.

Throughout dinner, Bente's project wasn't referenced again. They shared a bottle of Chianti, although Bente suspected that her mother would probably have preferred to carry on drinking Manhattans. Lydia joined in, too, eating a bulgur wheat and chickpea burger.

After dinner Bente and her mother went out onto the balcony. Agneta pulled on her Tretorn boots and Dad's old oilskin coat, which she always wore when she went out for a smoke back in the day; Dad used to complain that it stank of smoke when he put it on to go hunting. Mom had stopped smoking when she was released from jail, but she'd kept up the habit of going outside for a breath of fresh air—a distinct improvement over a hit of nicotine.

They gazed down at the square and the hazy glow from the streetlamps through rain-filled air.

"Things will work out," Agneta said.

"I think so too." Bente meant it; she wasn't the kind of person to give up.

Agneta didn't say any more, they simply stood there in silence. Eventually she went indoors, but Bente stayed where she was. The wrought iron railing was cold against her fingers, and a chilly breeze pinched her cheeks. She was about to go in, too, when she heard footsteps, and Hanna appeared with two steaming cups of tea. She passed one to Bente, who blew on the hot liquid.

"We care about you, Bente—we know how bad you felt because of everything that was written about you, we know the toll it took." Hanna sipped her tea.

Bente blew on her drink again but didn't answer.

"Why do you even want to go back into TV?"

"I've got an idea for a show that would be excellent entertainment, and I've always loved working in TV. I . . . miss it."

"What exactly is it that you miss?"

"Piquing people's interest in wine and history, sparking their enthusiasm."

Hanna still didn't look convinced.

"I want to tell people that wine is about so much more than just the drink itself—it's about culture, history, several hundred years of accumulated knowledge and refinement. I want to touch on all of that. To talk about how the wine trade during the world wars was a part of the resistance movement, but was also something that the collaborators were involved in. In many countries, viticulture and even individual vineyards have survived the plague, revolutions, war—and what if this particular bottle has a fantastic story to tell?" Bente lifted her chin and looked her sister in the eye. "And besides all of that, I love teaching people about wine. This is an amazing opportunity."

"Do you want to teach people about wine, or appear on TV? Those are two completely different things," Hanna pointed out.

Bente didn't say anything, she just drank her tea.

"I don't understand why you want to go back, why you want to be famous."

"It's not about being famous."

Hanna's expression betrayed her skepticism.

"It's my life and my career and I'm thirty-five years old, so I can make my own decisions about what's good for me."

"That's exactly what I'm worried about. The fact that you're so desperately keen to get back to the world that fascinates you so much—at the expense of your well-being."

With those words, Hanna went back inside.

Bente sank down on a chair on the balcony and finished her tea, considering everything her sister had said.

◆ ◆ ◆

A week later, on the morning of the meeting, Bente's phone buzzed with a message.

It was from Elnaz—was she going to postpone? Bente had sent her the sparse information she had managed to find about the bottle. Maybe Elnaz thought it wasn't enough?

She opened the message with her heart pounding, but there'd been no need to feel anxious. Elnaz was simply wondering if they could hold the meeting at TV24. She had spoken to an executive producer there, and he was really interested.

Little flutters of joy replaced the sinking feeling in Bente's stomach. A meeting with TV24? It was usually necessary to get the production company on board first; the point of her meeting with Elnaz had been to pitch to the production company, who would then approach the TV stations. Clearly Elnaz had already done half the job, which meant that Bente's idea had taken a huge step forward.

On the way she cycled past Rendezvous. She had handed in her resignation the previous week, to which Tomas had replied that she had beaten him to the punch, implying that he had intended to sack her. She felt nothing but a huge sense of relief.

The low-lying sun was creating sparkling stripes across the roofs of Östermalm as she pedaled up the last hill before Karlaplan. She seemed to have endless energy this morning, and didn't even need to stand up to manage the incline. She continued along Karlavägen, the only place in Stockholm that felt like a boulevard—this was where she got that Paris-feeling. On to the TV24 building in Gärdet. As usual the wind was whipping across the large open space where residents gathered for recreational purposes. In the distance the Kaknäs communications tower rose up into the clear blue sky.

Bente walked into reception, which had gotten a major facelift since she was last here. The walls that had been painted in a shade of purplish blue were now covered in birch paneling. The room seemed to be enveloped in light, and she was surrounded by shaggy rugs made of thick fabric and long linen curtains.

She sat down on the lead-gray sofa.

Before long Elnaz appeared in a doorway, wearing a visitor's lanyard. She left the door ajar and beckoned Bente to her.

"So good to see you again," she said, giving Bente a hug. "And I'm so pleased you got in touch with your idea."

Bente smiled. "I'm glad you're interested." She slipped in through the door, which closed behind them.

Elnaz returned her smile as they continued along the corridor. "I love your YouTube clips on wine—you're a natural in front of the camera, and it's great that TV24 seems keen on your idea. Just a quick update: I met one of the producers for lunch the other week, and he loved the concept, so I thought we might as well bring TV24 on board right away. He and I had a meeting about something else this morning, but we chatted briefly about you, and they're definitely interested."

"Fantastic." Bente did her best to suppress the excitement that was racing through her body; she wanted to be as professional as possible.

As they walked, they met several people who knew Bente; each one greeted her as if nothing had happened, as if she was here every week, and she felt herself grow taller with each encounter.

"How are things with you?" she asked Elnaz. "How's life at Palento?"

"I think things are beginning to move—it was kind of slow at first. Your ex Henrik and his girlfriend are making a show about the newly renovated patisserie—you might remember there was a fire."

"Yes, I heard about that. Such a shame—it was a really old business, wasn't it?"

Elnaz nodded. "The oldest patisserie in Västervik."

"The new show sounds great."

"Are you still in touch, you and Henrik?"

"Not anymore. But I'm glad his Christmas special went so well, and that he fell in love at the same time."

The Christmas episode of Henrik's regular show last year had been a great success. It had aired in a prime-time slot, and the viewers had loved watching him fall in love with Nora, the pâtissier he was working with, in real time. The whole thing had made Bente happy too. He deserved every success. He was a good man, even if the love between them had perhaps never been strong enough to last.

"What did you think of his apology?" Elnaz asked.

Bente understood immediately what Elnaz was referring to. "It was . . ." She tried to choose her words carefully.

Years before, in the moment when everything collapsed around her, she had been completely alone in France. A meeting with her French ex-boyfriend in connection with the recording of a show there had triggered rumors that she was cheating on Henrik. She had protested her innocence, had assured Henrik over and over again that nothing had happened, but he had believed every word that was written.

After that, when the scandal over the unpaid restaurant bill broke, Henrik had remained silent. He didn't contact her or offer any support. True, he had been absolutely certain that she had cheated, but she had been left totally isolated. No one in the world of entertainment had been prepared to stand up for her.

Henrik had eventually posted an apology on Instagram, which was picked up by gossip magazines and online publications. In it, he'd admitted that he should have defended Bente when things spiraled out of control. He had also apologized personally in a long message to her, but it was the public apology that had been an attempt to make things right, even if it hadn't actually changed her situation.

"It was what I needed," she said eventually.

"Even if it was a bit late," Elnaz commented.

"I expect he had his reasons." Truthfully, Bente agreed with Elnaz, but now was not the moment to come across as someone who held a grudge.

Elnaz opened the door of the meeting room, where a man with a shaved head, and dressed in a white shirt with the sleeves rolled up and blue jeans, was waiting. He stood up and gave a small smile, as if he was too stressed to smile properly, and held out his hand. "Don." Short and to the point.

Bente had heard of him even though she'd never met him before. She knew that the man's name was actually Robert, but for some unknown reason he was called Don. He had been working at another channel when Bente was with TV24, and had built his reputation producing scandalous docusoaps. These days he made other kinds of shows, and had produced Henrik's Christmas special together with Elnaz.

"Okay, let's get started." Bente sat down next to Don, and Bente took a seat opposite them. She opened up her notebook to where she had written down the most important details; she hadn't wanted to stare at a computer screen throughout the meeting. She began by talking about the message she had received from her friend Camille, the bottle's mysterious background, and everything she had found out about it. She showed them pictures of the bottle on her phone.

They listened attentively.

"This is really exciting," Don said, once Bente had finished and sat back. She let out a long breath. She had nailed it.

Elnaz looked at Don, nodded, and smiled. "This would suit Didrik, don't you think?"

"Absolutely. It would be fantastic."

"Didrik?" Bente didn't understand.

"Yes, I mentioned the possibility to Don when we had lunch. We've both been in touch with Didrik Holgersson about working in a new format, and your idea is a perfect fit."

Didrik Holgersson? Hang on, had Elnaz misunderstood? This was Bente's show, a show about wine. She had come up with the concept—were they really planning to bring in someone else?

"I mean, of course you'd be involved," Elnaz added quickly, as if she'd read Bente's mind. "But we need someone else too."

Someone else too.

"It would be interesting to have a stronger history angle, and someone for you to team up with," Elnaz went on.

"Didrik Holgersson," Don clarified, as if Bente hadn't already gotten it.

They had clearly worked through their vision for the show. Bente couldn't help feeling blindsided, but then again, that was how things were in the television industry. She knew that perfectly well. Sometimes a show was based on an idea by someone who was credited only in that capacity. Bente had been naive to think she would just get her own show.

And Didrik Holgersson was famous. Really famous.

"You're both around the same age, and he's incredibly popular," Elnaz said. "I think the two of you would be a great match, with his knowledge of history and your unique vision for the story."

Bente tugged at her sweater. She had gone for a wool turtleneck with dark-blue stripes, worn with black slacks—formal, but relaxed enough for the meeting. No one wore suits at the production company. However, the top part of the sweater was beginning to feel like a brace, making it impossible for her to move her head. She felt as if it was squeezing her throat, like she couldn't breathe.

"So this is what I'm thinking." Elnaz gazed up at the shiny brass-colored sphere of the ceiling lamp as she spoke. "A format where the two of you discuss and kind of educate each other about your specialties while researching the history of the wine bottle at the same time." She glanced at Don, seeking his approval. "This would be something completely different for Didrik. He can still talk about history, but also ask questions and engage in a discussion. It's a fresh concept for him—he'll love it."

"Exactly." Don nodded enthusiastically. "It's a cool concept, and Didrik is super-popular. He's personable, people love him, he's good on TV, and he's a hot property right now. If we can get him on board, then TV24 is in."

Elnaz looked delighted. "He works hard, and he's so nice. Very professional."

Had Bente landed in the middle of some kind of in-person fangirl forum for Didrik Holgersson? No one seemed remotely interested in her opinion on the matter. She didn't doubt for a second that Didrik was hardworking and nice, and no doubt fantastic in every possible way. The many people who loved him couldn't be wrong. However, this push meant that Don and Elnaz thought the show needed someone as popular as Didrik in order for it to happen. What were the implications of his involvement as it related to her role—both behind and in front of the camera? Would she be totally overshadowed? She had already been sidelined in their discussions about the concept, and about how the show could be shaped to suit Didrik Holgersson, TV24's star.

"And he speaks French!" Elnaz's eyes were sparkling.

"So do I," Bente pointed out. "My idea was to do this on my own, with a strong wine angle. I think it would be really good," she added, managing to get a word in edgewise at last.

"If TV24 is going to run with this, we need someone like Didrik," Don insisted. "Someone the viewers like."

At least he was honest. Bente wasn't enough. They needed a star to carry the show, otherwise Bente would not be appearing on it.

"But naturally you'd be credited as the creator and a producer." Appeasing words from Elnaz. "It's your concept, after all."

Bente nodded, keeping her expression pensive.

Elnaz leaned forward. "And you will be in front of the camera, too, along with Didrik—it will be your *joint* show."

Bente forced a smile. What could she say? Besides, wasn't it amazing that they wanted a star like Didrik on her program? The fact that they wanted to buy it was incredible, but she still felt stupid and naive. What had she imagined? That her own contribution would be sufficient? She was a has-been, a nobody. Of course they needed someone that the public loved. She had to face facts—she wasn't going to pull in the viewers.

"We'll send you a contract in a few days, and you send us everything you've got. Then we'll get some of our researchers on the case to confirm whether we've got a real story. So we know if we've actually got a show."

Elnaz's tone was jocular, but Bente knew she was deadly serious.

No story?

No show.

8

1944

Mathieu gazed at his father as he walked into the kitchen. The sunbeams followed him in from outside like glowing shadows. The rows of vines beyond him swayed beneath the burning sun.

"Looks pretty good." His father wiped the sweat from his brow with the back of his hand. Parts of the vineyard had been turned over to growing vegetables, something to eat. "But the cabbage isn't going to come to anything." Unfortunately, the stony ground of the Médoc wasn't suitable as a growing medium for anything but vines.

He placed the freshly picked produce on the counter. Tomatoes, carrots, shallots.

Mathieu's mother smiled, and the frown lines in her forehead that had deepened since the occupation seemed to disappear for a few seconds. Sometimes it seemed like her constant anxiety might destroy her. Anxiety over her family, over France, over Mathieu.

"That's not bad!" she said.

The sight of the sun-ripened tomatoes made Mathieu's mouth water.

"I managed to get some eggs this morning, but we can save them until tomorrow," Mom added.

Mathieu turned his attention to the map on the kitchen table once more. Lunch could wait; he had to finish what he was doing. A Jewish family was in hiding in the neighboring village, and the map detailed their escape route. The wine bottle with the map hidden in it would be collected this evening. He carried on with his work, drawing with meticulous care and swearing out loud whenever he made a mistake. He wasn't a skilled draftsman, but he was the best out of the three of them, so the task fell to him.

He leaned back and contemplated the map. It seemed to him that it left something to be desired. He tried to rescue it by correcting the meandering main road, but ended up having to throw it away; the whole thing was illegible.

He made a fresh start, and his mother tried to persuade him to eat while he drew.

"You have to have something, you worked hard this morning." They were behind with the tasks needing to be completed in the vineyard. Mathieu was able to help out only very early in the day, when there was no risk of any of the Nazis coming by and seeing him.

He gave in and munched a juicy tomato, a slice of the dark bread, and a little salad. Then he picked up his pen once more.

"I was thinking about labeling the 1934 blend," his father said.

"Is it ready?" Mathieu asked.

"Yes, I tried it yesterday. It was excellent." His father smiled.

It was one of their finest blends, and probably the best year in the whole of the thirties.

Not that they would label it that way.

These small, silent acts of rebellion enabled them to keep going. Wrongly labeled bottles. Or, as in this case, giving their friends in the resistance movement a bottle of their finest vintage. The Germans insisted that the best must be reserved for them, and the winemakers allowed the Germans to believe that they were cooperating. At least in this village the occupying Nazis paid for their wine, albeit at a ridiculously low price. Many other wine producers in Bordeaux had simply had their cellars plundered, or even worse—had had their entire vineyards taken over.

The *Weinführer*—as the German soldier who led the occupation of Bordeaux was called—had decreed that the finer wines must be reserved for the Germans. The vineyards were permitted to sell only the more basic table wines to other Frenchmen, who could barely afford to buy wine at all these days.

Mathieu's family had worked in the resistance movement ever since the occupation began, but over time, their role in it had changed. At first the goal had been resistance itself: helping the British to infiltrate occupied territory, carry out ambushes, and sabotage the German efforts on the ground. But ever since the Nazis had begun transporting prisoners by bus and train, and going from one vineyard to the next with their lists of names, the family had focused on supporting escape missions instead. They received information about upcoming operations and passed it on by delivering wine bottles with maps and messages concealed behind the labels, and sometimes, in addition to the maps that made their way past the Nazis, incorrectly labeled bottles of finer wines also slipped through.

In the time since the Allies had achieved several successes using this method, the resistance movement had become even more active, and the family's responsibilities had changed yet again. They still worked on escape routes, but they also passed on information and maps that were directly linked to the Allies' campaign.

Mathieu was just about to return to the map when he heard the sound of an engine, and tires crunching across the gravel in front of the house. He inhaled sharply.

They weren't expecting anyone.

His mother was washing up; she stopped in mid-movement, then flew into action.

"Quick, quick Mathieu!"

He gathered up his papers and hurried out of the kitchen, then realized he had forgotten his pens and rushed back.

"Come on!" his mother hissed, peering out of the kitchen window. "It's a German soldier and someone . . . someone I don't recognize.

Hurry up, Mathieu!" His father ran into the bedroom next door, followed by Mathieu, then his mother, pushing him along.

He turned around. "Calm down."

Panic shone in her eyes.

His father yanked open the hatch, and his mother urged him down into the dark hole.

9

Didrik was sitting at his desk with his laptop in front of him, preparing for tonight's discussion topic on *The Experts*. His blue-and-white-checked pillow was poking out from behind the cupboard where he had shoved it when he put away his bedding, just in case he got a visitor. He rented the office with a few other freelancers at TV24. It was in Gärdet, not far from the studios, and sometimes friends would stop by, or his cousin Vendela, who was a reporter at the station.

He got up and pushed the pillow farther behind the cupboard. No one knew that he was staying here. He had been sleeping on the sofa for two weeks, ever since Lovisa told him she'd met someone else. The house had felt too big and lonely, like a mockery of all his shattered dreams.

He had finally called his brother the night before. Talking to him had been a huge relief, but Didrik had asked him to keep quiet for the time being. He couldn't face a conversation with his mother, who would simply add it to the list of Didrik's failures, of which she no doubt kept a meticulous record.

Victor had encouraged him to try to *feel* for a while, to be present in his emotions rather than suppressing them. Doing this had helped, and Didrik had begun to summon up the strength to deal with the situation. The first step was to see if he could find a rental apartment. They'd gotten an appraisal done on the house; neither of them wanted to live there, so it was time to sell.

He sat down and took a sip of his coffee, which was going cold. The breakfast roll he had bought from the 7-Eleven lay untouched beside it.

He stood up again. He needed to focus. Every thought stung his brain like a swarm of mosquitoes, and when an idea landed, all it did was hurt. Everything hurt right now. Maybe he could drink something strong in order to dull his feelings? Like they did in the movies when something was too difficult—knock back a glass of whiskey. He had a bottle leftover from when he and a university colleague had had a research study published in a well-established and respected journal. Actually, when he thought about it, a huge tub of cookie dough ice cream was much more appealing. But would it have the same numbing effect?

He sat down again. Went through his messages, found a reminder about an unanswered email—asking about that wine and history show. It had simply disappeared in the fog of messages and work-related tasks he had been incapable of facing up to. Elnaz from the production company had tried to get ahold of him a couple of times. She was wondering about the new antiques show they had discussed in the bar, but there was also the wine show, which was still at the idea stage. Didrik didn't know much more than that, he hadn't bothered to read the whole message. That wasn't like him at all—he always read and replied to emails right away. He was reliable, someone who set great store by turning up to meetings on time and dealing with tasks immediately. This meant that people liked working with him, or so he'd heard. Didrik didn't know if that was true. And in any case, these days, he no longer knew who he was.

Wine and history . . . It definitely sounded interesting, but would he be up for the kind of commitment an entirely new production and filming schedule would entail? Just the thought of it made him slump in his chair. On the other hand, maybe that was exactly what he needed?

He was incapable of making a decision, so he didn't answer the email now either. He had no idea whether he wanted to do the show. At this point, he could only think a day or two in the future.

Should he open the whiskey? If it dulled the pain for just a second, then . . . why not? He took the bottle out of its box, drew out the cork with a satisfying pop. Took a picture and sent it to Victor:

Do you think this is a good time to open this?

The answer came straight back:

Absolutely!

Didrik smiled, picked up the glass on his desk, and filled it half full. He had expected Victor to be upset when he told him about the breakup, but his brother had remained surprisingly calm. Now that he thought about it, Victor and Lovisa had never been especially close, even though they had a great deal in common, just like Didrik and Lovisa.

University had brought them together. They had met at a friend's thesis defense dinner in Uppsala. The minute Didrik had been asked to act as historian on a Christmas show, Lovisa had opposed the idea, but Didrik had loved it from the get-go. Making history accessible, trying to reach people, was his passion. Teaching while working on his doctorate had been his most enjoyable period at the university. Understanding history meant understanding the contemporary world, and to a certain extent the future and its challenges. The TV show had focused on historical Christmas traditions, and he had gladly accepted the challenge of making history easier to understand. The viewers had loved his contribution, and more TV work came his way. After he was given a history show of his own, success was assured. He took a break from the university, and he'd spent the last four years solely working as a TV historian.

Lovisa hadn't said much in the beginning, but once he agreed to a permanent role on a show, she made her opinions clear. Things only got worse when he became one of the stars on *The Experts*. He had thought she would come around to his point of view eventually; it was just his career, after all, not something that would impact their marriage.

Maybe he'd been wrong about that.

He took two big gulps of the whiskey. And another. It burned his mouth, and he let out a snort, spraying the liquid everywhere. Jesus. Knocking back whiskey was really quite unpleasant.

He was interrupted by a knock on the door.

He coughed. That stabbing pain in his head, the machine-gun salvo of thoughts, was still there; it hadn't disappeared. In fact, it was more painful, as if the fiery whiskey had gone straight up into his skull. His nose was hurting too.

Another knock on the door.

"Just a minute!"

He shoved the glass, the bottle, and its box in the cupboard. Glanced behind him to make sure the pillow hadn't slipped out, then opened the door.

He saw a pair of startling green eyes. He blinked and looked the woman up and down. Then up again. It was that TV sommelier, Bente Hammar, whom he'd met in the bar with Elnaz.

"Hi." She nodded a greeting, and her wavy auburn hair fell over one shoulder. She looked kind of . . . self-assured, in wide-legged pants and a white cotton shirt beneath a trench coat. Or was it the whiskey that made him think that way?

In the bar he had thought she looked vaguely familiar, but hadn't managed to place her until Elnaz introduced her. She'd been a big name on TV a few years ago, but then everything had gone wrong. He had appreciated her contributions to TV24's morning show, and had learned quite a bit about wine. He had impressed Lovisa with this knowledge over several dinners, and had even managed to impress his mother when they invited his parents for a meal.

"Hi?"

"I hope I'm not disturbing you." Bente gave him a searching look. "Can you spare a few minutes?"

"Of course, of course. Come in." He felt stupid, leaving her standing there, and stepped aside.

She still seemed unsure. He probably looked like a complete wreck.

She held out her hand. "Bente Hammar."

"Yes, I . . . I know." He shook her hand.

"We met at Rendezvous with Elnaz—I used to work there."

"I remember." What was she doing here?

"I believe Elnaz emailed you with an idea for a show last week?"

He made an effort to think back. Last week? Then he remembered that Bente's name had been mentioned in connection with the history show linked to wine—in the email he hadn't read all the way through. "Right, yes . . . I haven't had time to reply." Had she been sent here to pressure him?

"I understand, I just wanted to ask . . ." She was glancing around as she spoke.

He followed her gaze; the room was tidy, and there was no sign of the pillow. Should he invite her to sit down?

"Take a seat." He nodded in the direction of the sofa, hoping she couldn't tell that it was also being used as a bed.

She marched over and sat down, while he remained standing. "I just wanted to know what you think. If you're interested. We really want you on board."

"Interested in what?"

"The idea Elnaz sent you," Bente said slowly. Did she sound annoyed?

"The idea, right, yes, let me see . . ." Didrik went over to the desk and opened up his laptop with clumsy hands. "I'll just find the email . . ."

"Or I can give you the pitch, if you like."

"Okay, fine, yes." He closed the laptop, sat down, and rested his chin on one hand, but his elbow slid along the surface of the desk. What the hell was wrong with him? Fucking whiskey. What a stupid idea! He hadn't been expecting a visit, plus there was the matter of his lack of sleep. He didn't even want to think about how he must be coming across.

◆ ◆ ◆

Bente adjusted her position; the sofa sagged in the middle, as if he had a lot of visitors. Which wasn't surprising—everyone seemed to love Didrik Holgersson. And she had to agree—the way he appeared on TV, he really was lovable. A person you couldn't dislike. However, he looked quite different now. His hair was much messier than when she'd met him at Rendezvous, and he'd developed dark circles under his eyes. The respectable history nerd from the television looked almost crazy. He seemed clumsy, generally confused, making her think of the archetypal absent-minded professor. She gave a little smile, because the effect was unexpected and almost attractive. Beneath the smooth surface, she was catching a glimpse of a different man, one much more serious and subdued.

A week had passed without the production company hearing anything from Didrik. Elnaz had also explained that their research had come to a standstill. *Our team is having difficulty finding any more information about the bottle and the man who was in the Foreign Legion. Meanwhile, we're looking into a few different angles—will be in touch!*

Bente had therefore come here on a charm offensive. She needed Didrik, so she started talking.

He nodded as she plowed on. He was almost too attentive, as if he was making a huge effort. She noticed that he couldn't sit still and kept changing position; plus his gaze wasn't entirely focused. Jeez, had he been drinking? Wasn't there a smell of booze in here? Yes, come to think of it, she'd picked up something of the scent when she walked in. Then again, it could just as easily be hand sanitizer—people who had just sprayed their hands smelled worse than Hanna's cocktails.

Oh well. Whatever possible issues Didrik had with alcohol, she would just have to put up with them.

After receiving Elnaz's email, Bente had realized that she was going to have to do this herself if she wanted the show to match her vision. She had decided to take her camera and travel to Paris to carry out her own research. Meet up with contacts, try to find out more about the bottle, the shipwreck, and Bordeaux. But she couldn't do any of that unless she was sure that Didrik was on board with the show, so she had to choose her words carefully, sell him the whole concept. He had to say yes! Maybe she should stress the historical aspect?

"I want to follow the wine bottle, its origin and the *history* surrounding the wine. Travel around France, speak to *historians* in Paris. And possibly go on to Bordeaux to research the area during the *occupation*, how the winemakers coped, how the people lived *in the past*."

Didrik kept nodding, as if he were taking in what she was saying and considering it.

"I think it sounds very exciting," he began. Bente felt a surge of hope through her whole body. "I'd love to do it, but . . ." he added quickly.

The hope died away. "But . . . ?"

"But the situation at home is . . ." He sighed deeply. "There's a lot happening on the home front. I can't give you a definite answer today."

Bente simply nodded. An unequivocal yes from Didrik was exactly what the production company and TV24 were demanding.

"We really do need you," she pleaded. "The production company has asked some junior researchers to carry out the research, and they haven't found anything. I need someone with your expertise to tell us what to look for, to help me understand the history and find the truth." He was a researcher, after all—surely the truth and a story, together, must mean something to him.

"Okay . . . How far have you got? What have you learned?"

"Only that the bottle was sent to an address in Vetlanda in 1945. There was an inscription on a plaque attached to it, a picture of a big oak tree and then some words in Swedish. I don't know where it was sent from, or why, but the people who lived at the address in Vetlanda were the parents of a man who left home to join the French Foreign

Legion just before the start of the Second World War. He was arrested by the Germans in France toward the end of the occupation and died in prison—before the bottle was sent. I have no idea whether he sent it somehow, but there's definitely a connection. I want to look into the origins of the bottle." She took a deep breath. "Like I said, we need your expertise."

Something about him seemed to change, maybe because now he felt needed. She got the sense that this kind of thing was important to Didrik.

"Your cooperation would mean a great deal," she added.

"Okay." He slammed both hands down on the desk with an unexpectedly loud bang. "I'm in!"

She couldn't help leaping to her feet, beaming at him. She tried to dampen her enthusiasm; she didn't want to show how much she *really* needed him. "Fantastic!" she said with a laugh.

"I'll contact Elnaz about the logistics."

"Excellent—I'll book my trip as soon as everything is sorted."

"Where will you go?"

Bente realized she'd been thinking aloud, but she was ecstatic. The show was going to happen! She smiled at Didrik. "Paris. The research won't do itself, and I have some contacts there, so I'm hoping I can get some help with information about the bottle and its origin. A little bit of groundwork before we go over there to start filming."

"Paris?" He looked thoughtful.

"Yes."

"Do you mind if I tag along?" He seemed much more alert and brighter than before.

She hesitated. She had planned to do this on her own. On the other hand . . . his knowledge was invaluable. She was no history expert.

"Okay, why not?"

"When are you going?"

"As soon as I get the green light from the production company confirming that there's actually going to be a show. As soon as you agree on the practicalities."

He remained silent for a moment, then nodded decisively.

"Cool. I'll speak to Elnaz right away and ask her to book tickets for us." He smiled at her, and her stomach flipped.

Perhaps it was because she would soon be in Paris.

Or maybe it was because Didrik Holgersson had just fired off the most charming smile.

10

Bente woke on the morning of her departure with a tingling, throbbing sensation in her body. She floated into the kitchen and made herself a cup of coffee while humming along to Bruce Springsteen, the way Dad used to do on the weekends: as a kind of warm-up for an afternoon of cooking, while playing Bruce at full volume.

The sun was shining from a cloudless sky. She wrapped herself in a thick cardigan and took her cup out onto the balcony and into the damp freshness of spring. If she closed her eyes, she could imagine that she was in Paris. The smell of asphalt warming up in the sun, the green shimmer of leaves in bud, about to burst forth yet still a little subdued, the way spring always was in a big city. Like the blurred contours of a painting.

It was happening; she was about to start work on her show. Her own TV show. After the meeting with Didrik, they had kept in touch and made a plan for their research in Paris—who they would contact ahead of time, which museums they would visit. She had done her part, and she hoped that Didrik had done his. He had been difficult to get ahold of, slow to answer emails, and even worse when it came to confirming that tasks had been done. All she could do was keep her fingers crossed.

She had arranged to see Camille, who she hoped could tell them more about the bottle, and some colleagues from her time as a sommelier in Paris: people who were experts on older wines. She had also tried to get in touch with Frederic. Her ex-boyfriend's family owned a vineyard in Bordeaux, and he knew the area well. She hoped he would be able to answer several of her questions. She had to admit that she was also looking forward to seeing him. In typical fashion, he hadn't yet replied. She was pretty sure they would see each other, though; he never missed her when she was in Paris.

She finished her coffee. Time for a shower. On her way to the bathroom, she bumped into her sister.

"You're going today?"

"I am." She nodded toward the kitchen. "There's coffee if you want it."

"You could still drop out of the trip," Hanna said.

"Why would I do that? I want to go. Plus this is for work; I'm taking my camera so I can get some authentic material we might be able to use for the show."

"But will doing the show make you feel good?"

"It's going to be different this time. People have forgotten all about what happened." At least that was what she told herself.

"You love working with wine, that's your passion. You like making your YouTube videos—so why do you have to be on TV? People don't have to see that you're successful in order for you to be successful."

"Thank you for your advice, but if I want to enjoy words of wisdom with my morning coffee, I can order an embroidered wall hanging online." Bente went into the bathroom and tried to shake off the aftertaste of the conversation. Why couldn't Hanna simply be happy for her? She knew that her sister's misgivings came from a place of love, but this was something Bente *wanted*, and she was going to be fine. She had spent three years recovering, and she was mentally ready to work in TV again.

She chose her softest jeans and T-shirt, with a lovely thin cashmere sweater. She had a long train journey ahead, with transfers in Copenhagen and Hamburg.

She grabbed her wheeled suitcase and looped her big leather bag over her shoulder. Pushed her sunglasses up onto the top of her head, pulled on her leather jacket, trench coat, sneakers. She took a scarf from the hallstand at the last minute and left the apartment without speaking to Hanna again.

She ran downstairs to the waiting cab. Hanna's words still lingered, but Bente was convinced that she was wrong. It really would be different this time. Besides, Bente wasn't looking for recognition.

She just wanted to work with someone she thought was fun.

◆ ◆ ◆

Springtime in Paris could be treacherous, but in Stockholm that treachery was guaranteed. A strong wind was blowing down the street outside the station, and she hurried inside, where she was met by the aromas of coffee, freshly baked bread, and fried food, as all the restaurants that had opened over the past few years prepared for lunch. She made her way through the crowds of travelers to the platform where she and the others had arranged to meet. The place was unusually busy for an ordinary Wednesday morning.

Elnaz, who was coming along to project-manage their research, was already there, tapping away on her phone. Once it was clear that Didrik was on board with the project, the production company had decided to pay for the trip.

Elnaz looked up. "This is going to be so much fun!" She placed a hand on Bente's shoulder. "I have to say that this show—the whole concept, in fact—is incredibly exciting. There's no mistaking your enthusiasm and commitment. And the idea of filming with your camera during the research phase is genius."

Bente smiled. "Good to hear."

The burning smell of the trains' brakes mingled with the unpleasant odor of a nearby trash can, but there was also a fresh breeze blowing in off Riddarfjärden, the easternmost bay of Stockholm's Lake Mälaren, just visible from the platform (if you peered into the distance).

Tomorrow she would be in France. There was something surreal about the whole thing. As soon as they were settled on the train, she would leave Hanna's tedious words and the fiasco at the wine bar behind her. She would be on her way. She was going to work. Soon, soon she would be in Paris.

Elnaz glanced down at her large wristwatch. "Where's Didrik?"

The train would be arriving at the platform in a few minutes.

"Did he say he might be late?" Bente asked.

Elnaz shook her head. "I haven't heard anything."

They both checked their emails and text messages, but there was nothing.

The minutes passed with no sign of Didrik. Surely he ought to contact them if he was running late?

The train pulled in and stopped with a screech and a hiss.

"He'll be here, don't worry. He's punctuality personified," Elnaz said calmly.

If he was going to make it, he had to come now.

The doors opened and they found their carriage, stowed their suitcases in the luggage rack, and sat down.

Bente settled down and peered out of the window as Elnaz focused on her phone. Wasn't she nervous? The train was due to depart in mere minutes.

Soon Elnaz was also peering out of the window, as if she had just realized that maybe she ought to be worried. "Where the hell is he? This isn't like him at all, he's usually so . . ."

"Reliable and easy to work with, I know," Bente said wearily. In spite of Didrik's much-lauded qualities as a colleague, Bente was sitting here with a laptop stuffed with information, a file of printed-out documents, and a list of things they needed to go through during the train journey, and the fantastic Didrik Holgersson couldn't even be bothered to show up. Did he have any idea what a difficult position he was putting her in?

She clamped her jaws together. Hard. "I'll call him," she said. The signal rang out, but then his voicemail kicked in. She sighed, stood up, and angled her head so that she could see along the platform. *Please, Didrik, don't drop out now.*

"This train is ready to depart," a voice informed them over the loudspeakers.

Shit shit shit.

She had been so close, so close to producing and filming her own show. Was Didrik Holgersson about to wreck the whole thing?

She looked at Elnaz.

Elnaz tried to reassure her. "Maybe he got the time wrong, in which case we'll wait for him in Hamburg."

Before starting this project, Bente should have made absolutely certain that it wasn't a mistake. Didrik seemed to be the kind of person who was completely on top of departure times, who had all the details of the trip printed out and safely tucked into one of those plastic folders that looked like an envelope, but had a little button so that there was no danger of anything falling out. The folder would be carried in a practical rucksack or a briefcase with a shoulder strap. Now she wasn't so certain about any of that.

She was about to sink back into her seat when she saw him, running along wearing a woolen coat and carrying a leather duffel bag over his shoulder.

"There he is!" she exclaimed.

He jumped on the train a second before the doors closed.

Elnaz sighed and rolled her eyes. After a few minutes, as the train left the central station, he arrived in their carriage, making his way along the aisle, every head turning toward him as the passengers realized who he was. Before he reached Bente and Elnaz, he was intercepted by a woman requesting a selfie; needless to say, he obliged with a smile.

"Sorry I'm so late, but I . . . I had to post a letter. It was impossible to find a mailbox."

"There's one at the entrance to the City terminal, and Vasagatan," Bente informed him tersely.

"What?"

"In fact, there are lots of mailboxes at the central station—surely you must know that?"

Didrik appeared taken aback. "Well yes, now you come to mention it . . ."

She had seen right through him. Why lie about something like that? Maybe he was simply unreliable, an airhead who was too fond of his drink, in spite of everything—and who always got away with it?

◆ ◆ ◆

Once they had passed the city of Mjölby, Bente and Didrik went to buy lunch while Elnaz took a phone call. The dining car was relatively quiet, so Bente seized the opportunity to speak to Didrik privately. She took a deep breath.

"I can't work like this. I just want to make that clear from the start."

Didrik looked inquiringly at her as he chose a Caesar salad from the shelf in front of them.

"You hesitated before you said yes to the show, and ever since then you've been bad at answering emails and . . . and it feels as if you're not completely on board." He was the star—was it dumb of her to speak to him like this? But she had to clear the air. "And you almost missed the train. I have to know if you're committed to this project. If you're not, you need to say so right now. You didn't have to come on this trip, you could just appear in front of the camera later."

"I was late, that's all. Like I said, I had to post a letter."

"I know a white lie when I hear one."

He remained silent for a moment, and then he looked at her, his expression serious. "I really do apologize for being late and worrying you and Elnaz, but I'm here now, aren't I? And I *do* want to be on this trip."

Bente nodded. He was already a bigger part of the project than she was, despite the fact that she had spent several days preparing the trip and planning the show. She had to give him a chance. She had no choice. She was going to have to let go of her resentment.

They changed trains in Copenhagen. When Bente and Elnaz ordered wine with their meal, Didrik went for mineral water. Bente relaxed a little; it seemed that alcohol wasn't his problem. It must be something else.

Next they caught the sleeper train in Hamburg. She and Didrik worked until late, and got along very well now that they'd said what had to be said. Listening to him talking about history was captivating—he came alive as he related anecdotes and described exciting events that they could incorporate into the production. It was obvious that he was capable of raising the show to another level with his knowledge of history. The passion he felt for his subject was clear.

Bente could see now what others saw in him.

11

The production company had booked a small boutique hotel in the heart of Saint-Germain-des-Prés, a stone's throw from Notre-Dame. Didrik's room wasn't especially large, but it had an enormous bed, and the first thing he did was sprawl across it. The decor was sober, with gray-beige walls—or greige, wasn't that what they called it? There was a high headboard in dark wood, a small desk in the same kind of wood, and a chair upholstered in black-and-white-striped fabric. The only pop of color was the soft bedspread made of emerald-green velvet, which lay folded at the foot of the bed.

Getting away from home and establishing a physical distance from Lovisa and the house they had shared was a relief; he felt as if he could think again. He'd enjoyed working on the train, as he and Bente had shared their knowledge of history and wine, and he had managed to suppress his thoughts about everything else.

Only a couple of days earlier he had signed the divorce papers and mailed them. Then, on the morning that Didrik was getting ready to set off for the station, Lovisa had contacted him, wondering if he was at home. He was, he replied. However, he was determined not to let her message distract him.

He had checked the plastic folder containing all the printed-out travel documents—the folder that had always irritated Lovisa, even though she claimed to love his meticulous approach. Not that he gave much credence to such assertions now. She had cheated on him, and—what was worse—it had been going on while they were still living together. He felt so betrayed. To think that he had imagined she loved him, when in fact she'd been sneaking around behind his back. Worse, she had destroyed their life together, all his dreams; she had simply trampled on everything as if it were worth nothing.

Another text message had arrived.

On the way to you now. Need to talk. About something important.

Typical—now that he was in a hurry, it suited her to talk.

Catching a train, no time to talk now. Have sent in the divorce papers, if that's what you're stressing about.

Three dots pulsated on the screen. Then:

It's not that. Please wait. I have to tell you something important. In person.

Something important? He had a feeling it wasn't something that was going to make him happy. Was she planning to remarry?

At that moment the prospect left him strangely indifferent. It was already clear that the two of them were finished—there was no going back. She had hurt him too much, and everything they'd had—their relationship, all the things they'd shared—had been ruined.

The cab he'd called to take him to the City terminal had pulled into the driveway. He waited for a couple of minutes in case Lovisa showed up, then realized that if he didn't go now, he would miss the train, messing things up for Bente and himself. Was it really worth waiting for Lovisa?

His lack of interest in what she had to say really made him think. It had crept up on him during the weeks since she had left—the realization that the situation between him and Lovisa had been far from perfect. Something had clearly been wrong. At the same time, Didrik had believed that they could get over it, that it was nothing more than a bump in the long road that was their marriage. But when he *really* thought back, he realized that he hadn't felt loved or appreciated by his wife, and in all honesty, he wasn't sure he had been a loving and appreciative husband to her either.

Then and there, in the hallway of what had been their shared home, he made a decision: He had to let this go. Lovisa had moved on; he didn't know if he was ready to do the same, but he accepted that they would never be a couple again. So he opened the door, locked it behind him, and got into the cab. He sent a message to Lovisa, saying that he didn't have time to wait for her.

◆ ◆ ◆

He met up with Bente and Elnaz outside the hotel, and they crossed the street to a small café that was so Parisian it seemed to Didrik almost to be too much, but he quickly changed his mind about that when they walked in and he saw the beautifully made pastries. They ordered coffee, a baguette each, and a basket of croissants, and he suddenly felt hungry. He realized he hadn't eaten much lately; he'd had no appetite. But maybe this trip was the beginning of a new chapter in his life?

The clouds in the sky above Paris had begun to disperse, and the sun peeped through as he sipped his coffee and gazed at the pale sunbeams with narrowed eyes. The coffee tasted different here—the way it always did overseas. Each country had its own coffee flavor.

As they were going through the day's meetings, Bente's phone buzzed. She picked it up and a foolish smile played over her lips. A French lover? She had mentioned during the train journey that she used to live in Paris.

Once they had cleared the air, they'd had a very pleasant time together. Something told him that she wasn't the kind of person who usually confronted others; he had noticed that she looked uncomfortable as she raised her concerns, and he had detected a hint of uncertainty. But that had made it clear to him just how important the show was to her, and he'd felt ashamed of the way he had behaved. This only served to strengthen his feeling of freedom as he slowly began to release himself from thoughts of Lovisa.

Who was messaging Bente, making her laugh quietly to herself? He couldn't help being curious. Eventually she put down the phone and took off her leather jacket. It was warmer now as the sun gained strength, so he followed her example and hung his jacket on the back of his chair. The waitress served them more coffee, and Bente smiled at her. She was different now from when she had come to his office—more relaxed, content, and at ease with herself. This city clearly was her true habitat.

As they enjoyed their breakfast, Elnaz took notes, and they fine-tuned their plans for the next few days.

Bente cleared her throat. "So a friend of mine just got in touch."

A friend. Didrik smiled to himself. Maybe that was what he needed down here himself, a "friend." Someone to help him get over Lovisa and their marriage once and for all.

"His family owns a vineyard in Bordeaux, and he knows a lot about the area—can we squeeze him in?"

"I'm sure we can." Elnaz checked her notes and jotted something down.

"Hopefully Frederic—that's his name—will be able to help us find out information about the bottle. But I thought we could also talk with him about Bordeaux during the 1940s, how the winemakers lived during the occupation. Frederic has told me about his family, and about how the very best wine was hidden in those days. The Germans requisitioned the wine, and the producers put dust on the cheaper wine bottles to make them look as if they were older vintages."

"That's so interesting!" Elnaz said. "I'm sure that information would work really well. Do you think he'd be willing to appear on camera?"

Bente put down her cup. “Frederic loves any kind of attention.” She gave a knowing smile.

Didrik’s phone buzzed next, notifying him of an email from a man he had met up with the previous week, who ran a blog about Swedes in the Foreign Legion, and had promised to provide photos of the subject in question.

“Look—this is Sven.” Didrik turned his phone toward Bente and Elnaz. The photos showed a broad-shouldered man with hair so blond it was almost white. He was wearing the classic white hat of the Foreign Legion. It was hard to tell what color his eyes were, as the photo was black-and-white, but Didrik guessed they were blue.

“The photos come from that guy who runs the blog about Swedish members of the Foreign Legion,” Didrik explained. “I emailed you about him—he found the photos in one of his many books.”

“Oh, so you’ve been in touch with him?” Bente didn’t look pleased. “I thought he didn’t have time to see us until after the trip?”

“He had a window, and I rearranged a couple of things, met up with him a week ago. Unfortunately, all he knew about Sven was that he’d been taken prisoner in France and died in the prison camp—information that was already in the blog. He had no details about *how* he ended up in France.”

Bente scrutinized the photos. Nodded with a distinct lack of enthusiasm.

Did she think he should have checked with her first? That struck Didrik as illogical—after all, it was his TV show, too, wasn’t it? Surely anything that moved the show forward had to be good?

◆ ◆ ◆

The first meeting after breakfast was with Bente’s friend Camille, in a different café with a red awning that shaded the windows. A woman with her dark hair cut in a bob and wearing bright-red lipstick got up from one of the sidewalk tables and came to meet them. She and Bente exchanged hugs and air-kisses, chatting rapidly in French.

Didrik went inside to order café au lait for everyone. He returned with a tray of china cups and placed them on the mottled green-marble tabletop.

Elnaz took over Bente's camera and filmed them as they talked. Camille began by showing them photos on her phone from the diving expedition. Herself in a black diving suit, other participants; a couple of pictures of the outside of the hull, then ones taken inside it. Didrik could barely make out the outlines of boxes, covered in seaweed and algae.

"Wine exports were just getting underway again after the liberation of France, so when the ship struck a mine with all that expensive wine on board, it was a significant loss for the wine producers."

Camille took a substantial cardboard box out of her rucksack, which was on the ground beside her. She fished out a wooden box that appeared well preserved. It contained the bottle in question, and she removed it and placed it on the table.

Though the label had perished in the water, the brass plaque was still intact. They all sat in silence for a moment. There it was, the reason why they were sitting here.

"It's beautifully made," Bente said.

The etching of the oak was extremely detailed, with gnarled branches, a generous covering of leaves, and a powerful, twisted trunk.

Miss you
Your Dejje

"So what have you found out?" Camille asked.

"Not much." Bente took her through the little they knew about the Swedish address from the lists Camille had sent. And about Sven and the Foreign Legion. Didrik had done some research of his own in the days leading up to the trip, and had learned that Sven had been arrested in France. He had been helping the country's resistance movement through his links to the Legion, and had been sent to a prison camp, where he later died. Didrik hadn't been able to find out where the prison camp was.

"Now we want to know where the bottle came from," Bente explained. "To be honest, we're not totally sure that Sven Steen sent it—he died in 1944."

"But *if* it was him, then we think the bottle has a fantastic story to tell," Didrik said. "The brigade Sven belonged to fought for de Gaulle's Free French forces, and we want to find out what he was doing in occupied France. Was he there on a secret mission? How did he even get there? All these questions lead us back to the origin of the bottle—if we can track it down, we might learn more about Sven."

Camille nodded. "I'm afraid none of us on the dive team know any more about the wine. Like I said, there's nothing about the vineyard on the bottle or the wooden box. We've checked the ship's log, but there were no lists of exporters or anything like that." She shook her head slowly. "However, the rest of the boxes came from Bordeaux, so we're pretty sure that's where this wine originates too."

"You can't see anything on the cork?" Bente asked.

Camille shook her head, her dark bob swinging. "I'm afraid not. We've tried to look through the neck, but as you can see, the glass is very dark, and we can't make out any words there."

Bente turned the bottle around and held it up to the light. "No, there doesn't seem to be anything on it. Did the rest of the wine come from the left or right bank in Bordeaux?"

While Bente and Camille discussed the location of various vineyards, Didrik took a sip of his coffee. It was at least as delicious as the cup he had drunk earlier. Rounded and smooth, creamy. It reminded him of a weekend in Milan with Lovisa; they had spent the days drinking first-class coffee, visiting museums, seeking out good wines, and eating excellent food. They had only recently fallen in love then, and on the second day they had simply stayed in bed in their hotel room. They had emptied the minibar of drinks and snacks, and the following day they had rushed to a small café on the street corner and ordered virtually everything on the menu for breakfast.

"Sorry, did you hear what I said?" Camille was looking at him. She laughed to take the sting out of the situation; she had obviously asked him a question while he was lost in his memories.

"She was wondering if you knew anything about the Foreign Legion's work with the resistance movement," Bente clarified, clearly annoyed.

"My apologies." Didrik cleared his throat. He could see why Bente was finding him difficult, and he really wasn't like that—unreliable and a poor timekeeper.

Then again, according to his mother it was a wonder that he could even manage to avoid putting his sweater on inside out every day. The fact that he'd secured a job at the university had been a miracle greater than the first moon landing.

Sometimes Lovisa had been drawn into his mother's little digs. In the beginning he had found it quite sweet, but the longer they lived together, the more vicious the digs became. The more distance he got from their relationship, the easier it became to see both her and the marriage in a different light. She had never been satisfied with him, his job, what he did. For his part, Didrik had found it difficult to immerse himself fully in their relationship without constantly thinking about children. They had never raised their voices at one another, but they had bickered nonstop over the past year, maybe the past two years. She no longer listened when he talked about work; she wasn't interested in hearing about his colleagues at the TV station, or about his new show, which had made him bitter. He would find himself paying her back in the same way—changing the subject when she tried to tell him about her job. Lovisa had worked overtime more and more often, and they hadn't shared the household tasks anymore. Instead when the snow melted, he had asked Victor to help him out with clearing and burning the garden rubbish.

He and Lovisa *hadn't wanted* to spend time together—but he had hoped it would be possible to change that.

"I'm not an expert on military history, but I can certainly look into that," he answered Camille now. "As I said, Sven's brigade liaised with the Free French, the forces built up by de Gaulle when General Pétain agreed to an armistice with Germany and allowed France to be occupied. And the Free French worked with the resistance movement."

Bente nodded, her green eyes fixed on him and her auburn hair shimmering like copper in the sunlight. There was a sternness in her expression, but then she turned to Camille.

"I love the stories about how the winemakers hid the best wines from the Nazis as a way of supporting the resistance."

Camille smiled. "Me too. I heard about someone who found an entire cellar that had been hidden from the Nazis."

"Amazing! Imagine if our research takes us to undiscovered vintages from Château Margaux or Mouton Rothschild," Bente mused.

Didrik had been captivated by her during the train journey; she had been completely absorbed by the stories she told him, her sparkling green eyes reflecting the same passion he recognized within himself. There was the anecdote about a colleague who had picked up the wrong bottle—a cheap *crémant* instead of vintage Champagne—and no one in the party they were serving had noticed the difference. The memory had made her laugh out loud, and in that moment he saw the real Bente. He could tell that she was generally trying to keep her distance, holding back, almost as if she were apologizing for talking too much. This behavior was very familiar to him—people often acted that way in his company. Didrik assumed he was the problem; maybe he wasn't the kind of person you could confide in. He had experienced this dynamic on numerous occasions, most often with Lovisa's coworkers.

But right now, here in the café, he saw the passionate Bente, eagerly and comfortably chatting with her friend.

That kind of passion was what he had loved about Lovisa. The way she could spend an entire weekend reading some scientific article, studying it in detail, or meticulously scrutinizing a publication she had discovered in an antiquarian bookstore, written by one of the philosophers she admired.

Once again Camille was looking at him inquiringly.

"Maybe you know more about that?"

Didrik dragged his attention away from Bente. He was confused—Camille was clearly waiting for an answer.

"Sorry, I didn't quite understand the question," he said hesitantly, feeling Bente's disapproval.

"Mines from the Second World War—can they still turn up today?"

Didrik cleared his throat. "They can, yes. Mines from that period have been safely detonated in recent years. Do you mind if I take a closer look at the box?"

"No problem," Camille replied.

Didrik picked up the box, turning it this way and that as Bente and Camille continued to discuss the transportation of wine after the war. It was beautifully made. He noticed a tiny gap, no more than a millimeter wide, in one of the panels on the back of the box.

"Look." He showed them. "I wouldn't have seen it if the dampness hadn't made the wood a little darker just here." He used his finger to trace the area where the wood bellied out a fraction. "It's odd—could it be some kind of compartment?"

Camille leaned forward. "How exciting! There wouldn't be room for anything more than documents—could that be it? People were very inventive when it came to smuggling things under the noses of the Nazis."

Didrik nodded.

"Maybe the bottle was sent with a secret message in the box?" Bente suggested.

Didrik nodded again. "In which case the paper would have perished long ago."

"Is it okay if we borrow the bottle?" Bente asked.

"Of course. Keep it as long as you need it—it won't be going to auction until later. It would be great to see it on TV!" Camille said with a smile.

"It would be brilliant to have Camille on the show, talking about the diving expedition," Didrik said as they walked back to the hotel. A thin layer of gray clouds had moved in over the city, and the sunbeams that managed to break through spread an apricot-colored glow over the streets.

"I agree. I hope we can find out more. The fact that the bottle was shipped after Sven's death doesn't make sense—what if it wasn't him?" Bente said.

Elnaz nodded pensively. "It does seem illogical. We need to know where the bottle was sent from."

Didrik considered all the information they had gathered so far. Tried to connect all the loose ends. This was what he loved—making connections. He felt as if he were walking on air.

Working on the bottle and being in Paris made the divorce and all his problems associated with it seem very far away.

12

1944

Sven let out a long breath when the German soldier drove into the courtyard of what looked like a vineyard. So this was Château de Chênes. Behind the main building he could just see row upon row of vines, swaying in the gentle breeze. The house was covered in gray plaster, adorned by a double door whose red paint had flaked off badly thanks to wind and weather. The red tiled roof had faded in the sun, and the window shutters were the same dull shade. The plaster had fallen off one gable end, exposing a brick wall.

Next to the house stood an enormous oak. The sight of the huge tree, its crown rustling in the breeze, made Sven's heart leap.

It reminded him of home.

His long distance from home felt suddenly very real—not only in terms of miles, but in time. He had been in the Foreign Legion for five years, training and fighting, and he had just renewed his contract for another five. With the war in Europe, quitting was not an option for him, although he understood why many chose to leave the Legion when their five years were up. He would never forget the devastation and his encounters with injured civilians after the Battles of Narvik in early 1940. Nor would he forget the dead bodies—those could be too much even for the most hardened soldiers. Together with Norwegian and allied British-French troops, the Foreign Legion had helped defend

Narvik against the Germans, forcing the Germans to retreat, though the Allies had eventually lost Norway to Germany. The battles had continued for the Legion and for Sven in North Africa and Italy.

Everything he had been through since leaving home suddenly felt tangible the moment he saw the oak, making him think about the person he had been before he left Småland. He thought about his mother, and how worried she must be right now. He wrote to her every week, and she would be waiting for his next letter. He hoped he would get the chance to write her again soon.

And Father . . . Did he ever wonder about Sven? Did he worry? Maybe he didn't even want to see his son. But if Sven managed to go home on leave, then he would be able to show his parents his medals, tell them what he'd achieved. Surely Father would forgive him then? He would see that Sven had changed.

The stately tree's branches spread over the roof of the house, casting long shadows across the gravel as the German slowly drove forward. The stones crunched beneath the wheels of the car, and the soldier swung the vehicle in a wide arc before pulling to a stop.

"I think we've bought wine from here a few times," Max said. At first Sven thought he was going to get out and come inside with him, but to his relief, Max simply gave a brief nod. "Good to meet you."

"Thanks for the ride," Sven managed before the German drove away.

Slowly Sven exhaled, then he headed for the red-painted double door. He knocked and waited. The right-hand door opened a fraction, then the gap widened with a long, drawn-out creak.

A wary face appeared—a woman in her late forties, possibly younger. The war had aged people. A man came to join her. The woman was wearing an apron over her skirt and a pair of sturdy boots. The man was dressed in work clothes.

"Good afternoon," Sven began. "I've brought the wooden boxes for the special harvest of 1935. Where would you like me to put them?" He held up his bag. This was a coded message that he was supposed to deliver when he arrived. If he received the correct answer, then he would know he was in the right place.

The woman looked inquiringly at him, which immediately put Sven on his guard. Had he got it wrong? He was a couple of days early; whenever the resistance movement saw an opportunity, you had to take it. Maybe the couple hadn't been informed?

The man cleared his throat. "Next to the workshop, on the right-hand side."

Thank goodness—the correct answer.

Sven held out his hand. "Sven Steen." He spoke quietly—you never knew who might be listening.

"I wasn't expecting you for a day or two."

"We had to move the trip up. We heard reports that the Nazis were taking action in several places, but I guess no one got around to telling you—my apologies."

"Welcome," the woman said, stepping aside to let him in. They shook hands. "So you got a ride?" she said, raising her eyebrows.

"Yes, from a German soldier. He checked my papers and was heading in this direction—apparently he's stationed in the village."

The couple introduced themselves as Juliette and Hugo, Madame and Monsieur Latorre, before showing him into the kitchen. It was a simple country one, with a large table and a wooden counter. Pans hung from hooks above, and light flooded in through a narrow window that faced the front of the house and the giant oak.

"Here we are." He placed his bag on the table and unpacked the boxes.

Juliette nodded. Picked up one box and slid open the loose piece of wood. She took out the documents and read each one before passing it to her husband.

"We'll fix it—it's good that we found out now," she said.

Sven had no idea what she was talking about. He never knew what was in the papers—he was just a messenger. It was best that way, because if he was captured, he wouldn't be able to reveal anything.

"Would you like something to eat? We've just finished our lunch, but there's some left." Juliette nodded toward half a dark—almost black—loaf of bread with a few vegetables beside it. Food they presumably intended to save for dinner, but felt obliged to offer to their guest.

"We don't have much to offer in these times of rationing."

"I'm fine, thanks," Sven said, even though his stomach was rumbling. "I might take a walk into the village and buy myself something to eat. I have a return ticket booked for the day after tomorrow. It seems credible for me to stay for two nights, if I'm your relative."

"Isn't that a bit short?" Juliette wondered.

"Not at all. If anyone asks, I'll say I have business in Paris."

Juliette nodded, then pulled out a chair for him. She fetched a piece of the bread, two lovely red slices of tomato, and a glass of water and set everything out in front of him.

"Our guests don't need to buy their own food, not even in times of rationing," she said firmly. Sven was too tired and hungry to protest; his mother would have been furious with him. Now that his mission was complete, all the tension left his body, and the appetite that had disappeared during his journey came back with a vengeance.

He saw the couple exchange a dubious glance, as if they were trying to communicate something. They both seemed hesitant and anxious. He reminded himself that his arrival had taken them by surprise. Plus everyone was affected by the war, always on their guard, and no one was their true self. You couldn't ever allow yourself to trust someone completely.

Sven sat down at the table and tried the tomato. It was soft and juicy and warm, as if it had just been hanging on the plant in the sun. He looked at Juliette.

"It tastes wonderful."

In fact, it was one of the most delicious things he'd ever eaten. He'd never had access to such fresh vegetables before, and during the war it was even more difficult to get ahold of that kind of produce.

Juliette topped off his glass of water. The bread was hard and dry, but that was because of rationing; these days, flour was stretched out by adding other things. Juliette and Hugo joined him at the table, where they drank some sort of herbal tea.

"Thank you so much for lunch," Sven said after a while, once he'd assuaged the worst of his hunger. "But I'm going to go down to the village later anyway—I don't want to take advantage of your hospitality."

"No—stay here," Juliette insisted. "You've had a long journey. We have enough for dinner."

"And I could do with a hand with a broken thresher out there—it's too heavy for me to manage on my own." Hugo nodded toward the back of the house.

Juliette stood up. "I'll go and get the guest room ready."

"I don't want to be any trouble."

"You're not," Juliette and Hugo both said, practically in unison.

Sven realized that he *wanted* to stay for a few days. A sense of peace had come over him when he stepped into this house, the sense of being in a *home*. He hadn't been in a home, a place where people actually lived, for such a long time. Over the past five years he had lived in barracks, quartered with other soldiers.

Of course the vineyard was very different from his own home in many ways. He remembered the wooden kitchen sofa where he would sit eating an early breakfast before starting work on the farm, the creaking floorboards in his family's living room, his mother's rocking chair and her little sewing corner. Most things here were made of stone—the floor, the kitchen bench. It was considerably warmer than a spring day in Sweden, and different smells surrounded him here. But the feeling was still the same—this was a home.

When he had finished eating, he accompanied Hugo to a wooden building that resembled a barn, and that housed the machinery needed for wine production. Hugo showed him the thresher, and together they moved it into a toolshed—although the shelves in the shed were empty.

Hugo saw Sven's questioning look. "The Germans have requisitioned most of our tools, but I've managed to replace the essentials."

Several other machines needed repairing, too, and Sven knew exactly what to do. This was his area of expertise. They worked in silence. Hugo and Sven's father were alike in that way—neither of them said more than was necessary. Sven used to love it when he and his father worked side by side in silence, fixing the farm machinery.

"Is there anything else I can do?" he asked when they'd finished. He was tired after the journey, but he hoped that Hugo would say yes. Doing physical work on something tangible was familiar and relaxing.

"I'm busy plowing at the moment," Hugo said, and Sven nodded as if he understood, though he had no idea how a vineyard operated. "We plow up the ground so that the root systems are protected against heat and drought," Hugo told him. "It also makes the rainwater run down into the earth more easily."

Sven followed Hugo out into the field. He studied the older man's movements as he worked the wooden plow, then took over and tried to do the same thing while also pulling out the weeds, as he had seen Hugo do. The feeling of working the soft earth was completely different from holding a gun. That was more or less the only thought Sven gave to the Legion and his real mission here in France in that moment.

Then he allowed the physical effort and the expanse of the vineyard to take over.

13

Frederic's Paris office was in the Opera quarter. He had left his years as a sommelier behind and now worked with the family's vineyard in Bordeaux. From his office in Paris, he represented his family's business, plus the businesses of several other winemakers, selling their wines to restaurants, bars, and stores.

He and Bente had last seen each other three years ago, following the scandals over the unpaid bill and Bente's alleged cheating on Henrik, and after all the stories were written about her. She had needed the temporary distraction that Frederic offered. They had met for dinner, then followed their usual route visiting various wine bars before going back to his apartment, where she spent the night. On that point he was totally reliable—one night together was all he expected, nothing more. This had suited Bente very well, though there was no denying that the burning attraction they experienced never seemed to fade.

Frederic met them in reception. His once-wavy, medium-blond hair was now cut short in a typical man-over-forty-five style. He was one of the vainest men she knew, and she was surprised that he had gone for something so practical. He looked at her with that familiar glint in his eye. They exchanged air-kisses, and when the smell of him enveloped her, her stomach flipped.

He greeted Elnaz in the same way, then shook Didrik's hand.

"This is fantastic," Bente said as they walked along the corridor with its dove-gray rugs. Dark woods had been used to stylish effect, with occasional details in Bordeaux red: a nod to the business's representation of winemakers.

Frederic nodded. "Thank you. I share the office with some other smallish winemakers from all over France."

He showed them in. Wine bottles were lined up on shelves around the walls. The room was Spartan in its decor, with neat rows of folders and only a few essentials on the desk—a notepad, an ink pen, and the computer.

As they sat down, Bente could see that Frederic was looking Didrik up and down. He was the one who had broken her heart all those years ago, not the other way around, yet here he was, behaving as if Didrik were some kind of threat.

Why did that bother her? Once upon a time she would have taken it as a compliment. Instead of going for a practical haircut, maybe her way of changing and growing up was simply acquiring the ability to see right through Frederic.

A young woman with a wide mouth and a cute upturned nose arrived with coffee.

"This is Emma, my assistant." He gave her an appreciative look. A little too appreciative. Emma glanced over her shoulder on the way out as if to make sure that Frederic was watching her, which of course he was.

He was sleeping with her. It was obvious.

Bente found this irritating, and it bothered her that she cared. What had she been hoping for? Possibly a little fling for old times' sake, no more. So what did it matter if he was fucking his assistant? She made an effort to pull herself together, tried to focus on the real reason they were here.

"So you arrived in Paris yesterday evening?" she asked, meeting Frederic's gaze.

"Yes, I booked a ticket as soon as you said you were coming over." He was now looking at her as if she was the most important person in the whole world.

Nonsense. He hadn't answered her email for several days. And yet, though the inattentiveness was his, *she* felt inferior, just like she had back when she had been his pupil during her sommelier training. How she had looked up to him back then!

"You know Bordeaux well, and we have a bottle we'd like to know more about."

"I followed up on the information you sent." Frederic began tapping on the computer.

"Is it okay if I film this?" Elnaz picked up the camera.

"Of course." Frederic nodded happily and ran his fingers through his short hair. "I wanted to see if I could find any vineyards that used brass plaques back then. Brass was very difficult to get ahold of during the Second World War, but a handful of vineyards worked with it before the war began." He turned the laptop so they could see the list.

"Thanks—can you send that to me?" Bente asked.

"No problem. There are a couple of details I need to double-check, but then I'll email it to you. Do you have the bottle with you, by the way?"

Bente took the box out of her bag and passed it to Frederic. He held it as if it were his firstborn child, gazing at it with that level of reverence. This was the Frederic she knew—passionate about wine, dedicated to both his work and his family.

He guessed at various villages, based only on the seal and the glass the bottle was made of.

"Do you know of any vineyards in Bordeaux that were involved with the resistance movement?" Didrik asked.

"Several worked with the movement—there's plenty of information available in books and articles," Frederic said with insincere politeness. He was always civil, but clearly disliked the competition Didrik gave him simply by being present.

"I understand."

"When was the bottle shipped?" Frederic asked Bente.

"In 1945, just after the liberation of France but before the end of the war."

Frederic nodded. "And as we can see from the plaque, the wine was made in 1944. That was a pretty good year, favorable weather conditions, although with quite a lot of rain during the harvest." He was like a human reference book when it came to wines from that part of the country. "I have an acquaintance who works at the city archive in Bordeaux; I'll ask him if he can find anything. There's lots of old material that no one's gone through yet. He might know more about the cargo or the ship."

"Thanks, that's very kind. And if you need more details about the ship, just let me know. Camille has all the information—she was part of the expedition that found the wine bottle."

"Ah yes, Camille. Give her my best." Frederic plastered on a smile. He and Camille had always butted heads. Camille had thought from the start that he treated Bente badly—failing to communicate with her and frequently keeping her waiting—and she hadn't been afraid to let him know exactly what she thought.

Frederic wrote something on his notepad, turned to his laptop, then apparently changed his mind. "I'll get back to you with a contact."

They stood up, and Frederic held Bente's gaze as Elnaz and Didrik headed for the door.

"So what are you doing this evening?" He moved toward her, drawing very close, and tucked a strand of hair behind her ear.

Bente felt uncomfortable. Her colleagues were in the same room—what would they think? Her cheeks were burning, and she wanted the floor to swallow her up. She took a step back.

"We're having dinner and discussing the show." She added the latter so that he wouldn't invite himself along.

"I understand. Another time."

Bente only cleared her throat in response.

"So how do you know Frederic?" Elnaz asked as they left the building. Didrik looked searchingly at her.

"We met when I was studying to be a sommelier. And we . . ." She hesitated, but decided she might as well be honest. "We dated for a while."

"He seems to know his wine," Didrik said diplomatically.

"He does, especially when it comes to Bordeaux."

◆ ◆ ◆

The hotel was a twenty-minute walk from Frederic's office. Bente left the others and went off on her own for a little while. When she reached a market, she bought fresh flowers to put in the vase on the desk in her hotel room. She continued on to one of her favorite perfumeries, where she treated herself to a luxury shower gel to complement the perfume she had brought with her.

Then she walked back toward the hotel, stopping in at a small wine shop on the way where she chose a half bottle of Meursault. She put it in the minibar's refrigerator as soon as she got back to her room, then put on some soft French jazz, which always put her in a good mood. When she was living in Paris, she had owned a record player, which she took back to Sweden with her, and she used to seek out vinyl albums in old stores. Today she had to make do with Spotify on the hotel's Bluetooth speaker.

She stepped into the shower and used her new gel, which lathered up beautifully and felt wonderfully soft against her skin. The bathroom floor was warm as she reached for a lovely thick towel. She put on the silk robe she had brought with her and opened the balcony doors, letting the heavy smells of the city swirl into the room.

After she opened the wine and poured herself a generous glass, she pushed the desk chair out onto the balcony's narrow stone ledge so that it was balanced on the threshold, then sat down and closed her eyes. There was a cold wind even though it was April, and Bente reached back for the soft, fleecy cover from the bed and wrapped it around her body. She wanted to absorb the smells of Paris, hear all its sounds.

The wine was smooth, buttery, and voluptuous in her mouth. It was one of her favorites, the very best wine to drink by itself before dinner while she was getting ready—even better than Champagne.

After a while she put on a thin rust-red dress; it was loose, but clung in all the right places. Was she taking such care for Frederic's sake, in case he called? No, she decided, she was doing this for herself, and for the city. She was choosing the perfect dress to go out and meet one of the great loves of her life—Paris. She gathered up her hair in a loose bun on top of her head, then quickly put on her makeup, making her lips red to match her dress.

She was about to grab her purse and leather jacket when her phone buzzed. She smiled when she saw that it was a message from Frederic.

Maybe we could meet after your dinner? We didn't have enough time today—after all, we haven't seen each other in years.

Ha! She knew it. The fact that she hadn't fallen at his feet had triggered him, of course. The tone of his message didn't impress her—he really did take her for granted.

We have lots of meetings tomorrow, so I'll be heading back to the hotel after dinner.

Frederic answered immediately.

Just an hour with me, and I promise you'll sleep better than ever.

A ridiculous response, and yet she found herself considering his suggestion. They had enjoyed many passionate nights together, and maybe there was still something there. She didn't reply yet, leaving her options open.

Maybe a night with Frederic was exactly what she needed.

14

They went to Bente's favorite bistro, located on a narrow street five minutes from the hotel. A place that wasn't in the least trendy, but was all the more authentic for that. Classic bistro food like boeuf bourguignon and the best *moules frites* she had ever eaten, plus a perfect steak tartare. Bente would be happy to eat in restaurants for the rest of her life, and she found it difficult to choose, but eventually she opted for the mussels.

While they shared a bottle of wine and enjoyed their meal, they went through the schedule for the following day. The atmosphere was relaxed, but Bente had a feeling that Didrik was having to make an effort to join in. Sometimes he seemed to lose himself in silent, brooding thoughts, as if he were somewhere else. He was nothing like the carefree, popular Didrik she had seen on TV—but as long as he did his job properly, she supposed that was okay.

When they left the restaurant, the cold struck Bente's hot cheeks. It had been warm inside, and in the clear air her powdery, spicy perfume was much more noticeable—then it vanished completely as the wind carried with it the smells of the city and the river. The taste of the fresh Sancerre she had drunk with the mussels lingered in her mouth, a mixture of gooseberries and a mineral-based flint.

They wandered toward the wine bar where she'd first met Camille, and where she had worked sporadically during her time in Paris. They walked through the lively Quartier Latin, past cafés where students were drinking cheap coffee, and bookstores whose illuminated windows cast a warm glow over the streets. Down toward Montparnasse, then onto the street where the wine bar lay—it was on the ground floor of one of the old low-rise buildings. The facade was white plaster, with green-painted wooden panels at the bottom.

As soon as they walked in, Bente heard a shriek of delight as Marion, the owner, came hurrying over.

"Bente, how lovely! I saw Camille the other day and she said you might drop by." Marion kissed her on both cheeks and gave her a hug. "I'm so happy to see you!"

"Marion, these are my colleagues—Elnaz and Didrik."

They greeted one another, and Marion beamed. "Bente was one of the best sommeliers I've ever had."

Bente smiled, well aware that Marion always heaped praise on all her employees.

"It's true," Marion insisted. "You're fantastic when it comes to wine knowledge, but what makes you special is that you love the wines and guests equally. You always wanted to give them the very best wine experience." Marion hugged Bente again and showed them to a table.

Being here sent Bente spinning straight back to her time in Paris.

◆ ◆ ◆

She had been twenty-one years old when she came to Paris to study French and wine. Marion had employed her as a waitress and table clearer. Bente worked in the bar in the evenings, absorbing every scrap of knowledge she could glean from the bar's qualified sommeliers and from Marion herself, and studied French during the day. Gradually she began to assist the sommeliers more and more, learning how to match the wines with the simple dishes the bar served. Before long Marion offered to lend her the money to train as a sommelier herself—saying Bente could pay her back via a slight reduction in her wages.

The course was run by a well-established institution in the eleventh arrondissement. In the big dark rooms with rustic old wooden tables and hard wooden benches, the walls lined with shelves and cabinets displaying new and old bottles of wine and countless books, Bente could almost smell the corks from all the wines that had been studied and tasted. Her tutor was Frederic Revy, a top-notch young sommelier who was considered to be something of a pop star in wine circles. Bente fell in love at first sight. His charisma and passion when he talked about and described the wines took her breath away. He taught his students to link everything to their personal experiences, which made it easier to memorize the characteristics of each wine.

Bente found that she associated a Bordeaux with a dusty old library, its windows open to the garden where rotting autumn leaves swirled around and the smell of the wood-burning stove tickled her nostrils. A young Pinot Noir from Burgundy made her think of a cool evening in early summer, when the first, slightly tart strawberries were sold at Marché Bastille—the local food market in the eleventh arrondissement—the sweet, fresh smell of the river in the air. A Beaujolais would always remind her of a particular Thursday when the students in her training course went to a wine bar a couple of streets away, and she tasted the young, fruity wine for the first time. When they were all seated around a narrow table at the back of the bar, Frederic said: *This wine is like your first, hopeless love when you were young.* While he talked, he looked straight at Bente, and even though she wasn't naive enough to imagine she was his first love, she realized that the attraction was mutual.

They visited many bars together. After she took her sommelier exam, they spent the summer in Paris in each other's company. He took her to small wine bars in Montmartre and Pigalle; they swirled and sniffed and drank the wines. She built up her entire stock of aromas and tastes during that period. Cocoa beans, croissants, old leather jackets, recently fallen rain on sun-warmed cobbles, freshly picked raspberries, bales of hay, a leather girth, compost heaps.

Looking back on them now, the five years she spent here felt like a dream. In that same period, Bente had gotten to know Camille, who was already a qualified sommelier. During the day they studied wine together; in the evenings they worked until closing time, then hit the nightclubs and bars with their colleagues. Frederic would come to meet them, and Bente always went back to his apartment. They went to the wine cellars of the best restaurants in Paris, which kept their wine lists in leather-bound books as thick as the French novels she studied in her small apartment when she wasn't hanging out with either Frederic or Camille.

She had been madly in love, both with the city and with Frederic.

She had never experienced anything like it before, nor had she done so since.

◆ ◆ ◆

They each ordered a glass of *crémant* and sat down. Toastiness, crispness layered with a wonderful creamy freshness, finishing with a sharpness that gave away the wine's origins in the cool climate of Alsace. Delicious.

The hip-hop coming through the speakers was almost drowned out by the buzz of conversation as more and more people came in. The three of them moved their chairs closer together so that they could chat.

"Great place," Elnaz said, looking around. "Here's to our show, and here's to Paris." They clinked their glasses together.

"Have you been here before?" Bente asked, and both nodded.

"A couple of times," Didrik said, "but not with someone who really *knows* the city. It's going to be so cool, hanging out here with you."

"Your French is excellent," she replied. *Sexy*, in fact, was the word that came to mind. "Have you studied in France?"

"Yes, in Lyon."

That explained it. Just like Didrik himself, his French was accurate, with a rich vocabulary. His foreign accent, though, was obvious, the way it always was when someone could speak a language but hadn't heard it enough to get the nuances right.

"When were you there?"

"God, it must be more than twenty years ago now. I'd just graduated from high school and went traveling around Europe on an Interrail Pass, as a kind of rebellion against my mother."

Bente grinned. "That was brave."

"You haven't met my mother."

He gave her a meaningful smile and leaned closer to pick up the water carafe. She noticed a few laughter lines at the corners of his eyes.

"I had a place at university and was all set up to start my studies, but I dropped out. Mom went crazy—I'd embarrassed her in front of her university colleagues."

"So your mom is in the academic world too?"

"Professor of history." He topped off his water glass, and as he set the carafe back down, his upper arm brushed her shoulder. It was the gentlest touch, but the feeling seemed to linger on her skin. Bente noted this with a sense of surprise.

"Interrailing," Elnaz said. "That's something I wish I'd done."

"It's never too late." Didrik smiled. "I could easily imagine doing it again, but in a different way. Not just hanging out at the Prado in Madrid for hours and visiting the Colosseum and other sights. Although I would like to go back to my maternal grandparents' hometown in Estonia."

"Did your history-professor mom make your itinerary?" Bente's eyes twinkled at him over the rim of her glass.

Didrik laughed. "Sounds that way, doesn't it?" The laugh turned into a smile, and he gazed at her for a few seconds, which made her heart skip a beat. Why was she reacting like this?

Elnaz checked her phone and sighed loudly.

"What is it?"

"Palento's got a press shoot for a drama series tomorrow, and the photographer we booked has to stay home with a sick child again."

"Is it one of your productions?" Bente asked.

"No, it's actually Ted's, but I've helped him out with a few things. I'll figure something out."

Bente thought about how hard Elnaz always worked. She had no experience with Ted, but she had encountered other male colleagues who were in the habit of letting younger female employees do the grunt work.

"Why do you always have to cover up for Ted?" Didrik asked, as Bente was about to say the same thing.

"I know you think that's what I do."

"You're doing it now," Bente pointed out.

"I heard you did everything for the *Let's Get Baking* Christmas special. You were the one who made it a success," Didrik added.

"I don't know about that. I mean, I did work hard, but . . ."

"Elnaz, take the credit. Your situation is common knowledge in the industry. You *don't* need to carry on doing Ted's job—you're a producer, and everyone knows you're better than him."

"I agree with Didrik," Bente said. It was depressing to see Elnaz still working so hard, covering up for male colleagues and doing their jobs, even now that she'd been promoted. Bente loved the fact that Didrik had noticed what was going on, and she gave him a look of mutual understanding.

"Thank you—that means a lot," Elnaz said quietly.

Didrik's phone buzzed. He read the message and immediately lost himself in whatever was on the screen. He sat back, gazed blankly into space. Something had upset him.

"Since we're saying exactly what we think . . ." Elnaz placed a hand on Didrik's shoulder. "How are things with you, Didrik?" She looked genuinely concerned, but he responded only with a deep sigh.

"It was a message from Lovisa." He cleared his throat, looked away. Then turned back to face them, took a sip of wine, and blinked several times. *"Erm . . ."* He gave an embarrassed smile, as if he wasn't sure his voice would hold. Once again he glanced away from them, blinking fiercely.

Bente knew exactly what he needed. She rose to her feet. "I'll go and order more drinks."

She came back hoping that whatever was going on, the moment had passed. But Didrik and Elnaz were sitting very close together, speaking in low voices. Elnaz had her arm around his shoulders. Had he actually been on the verge of tears?

They both looked up at Bente as she placed three glasses of wine on the table and sat down.

"Do you want to tell me about it?" she ventured hesitantly. It seemed stupid not to ask, although maybe she didn't really want to know.

Didrik shook his head. "I'm sorry I've been so out of it during our meetings today. And for being hard to get ahold of, and for almost missing the train. Things are a little difficult at home." He rubbed his chin; Bente thought she could almost hear the rasping sound of his fingers against the stubble. "My wife and I are getting a divorce."

Bente searched for the right words. "I'm so sorry."

This explained a great deal. His strange behavior suddenly seemed entirely logical.

"She's the one who wants the divorce. So that's why I wasn't sure about the show, and why I haven't really been myself." He shrugged. "You might say everything's been upside down. And before I left home for the station the day before yesterday, she contacted me and said she wanted to meet. Out of the blue. She needed to . . . talk about something. That's why I was so late."

Elnaz's phone buzzed. She glanced at the screen and apologized. "I'm sorry, I really have to take this."

Didrik nodded as Elnaz put the phone to her ear and hurried outside.

Please don't leave me alone with Didrik.

What the hell was she supposed to say now?

"So have you spoken to each other? Do you know what she wanted to say?" she managed eventually.

Didrik shook his head. "I wanted to catch the train. I thought whatever it was, it could wait." He sighed. "I've kept hoping she'd change her mind, that's what I was waiting for, but now . . ." He ran his fingers through his hair. "I don't know what I want. I don't know if I want to hear what she has to say. If she wants to try again, maybe I don't, and if it's something else . . . well . . ." He didn't finish the sentence.

"I really am sorry."

He leaned back in his chair. "What can you say?" He rolled up his shirtsleeves, and the movement drew Bente's attention to his forearms. He was wearing a blue dress shirt that went beautifully with his olive skin, which had acquired a slight tan after a day's walking around Paris. She tried to imagine what would make someone decide to dump Didrik. He seemed like such a great catch. The unreliability that had bothered her had now been explained away. Now all she could think about was the fact that he was at least as nice as he appeared to be on TV.

Only a hundred times sexier.

He finished off his *crémant*, and Bente pushed the glass of red toward him as she sipped hers. A light, soft, and fruity Pinot Noir. Perfect to drink when there wasn't anything to eat. A good snack wine.

"Thanks. Good choice—delicious."

His phone buzzed again. He glanced at it, then turned it over.

"Is it your wife?"

"Yes. I told her I'm in Paris and it's not a convenient time, but she's insisting that I call her. She needs to talk about whatever it is over the phone."

"What do you think it might be?"

"I have no idea."

"Has she said anything about the breakup, why she wants a divorce?"

"She's met someone else."

"Oh dear."

"Indeed. Oh dear." He took two big gulps of his wine.

"But are you thinking of forgiving her and taking her back? If that's what she wants?"

"I thought that was what I wanted, but like I said, now I'm not so sure." He looked at her. "Don't judge me—a person never knows what they'd do in a situation until they find themselves in it. I assume you weren't cool and unmoved when that guy Frederic was messing with your heart?"

Bente gave a little start—she hadn't expected that question. "Why are you so sure he was messing with my heart?"

"It's what he does—that's his vibe."

Bente nodded, then smiled. "You're right."

Elnaz reappeared. She picked up her black coat from the back of the chair and put it on. "I'm so sorry, but I haven't managed to sort out tomorrow. I need to get back to the hotel and see if I can fix things."

Didrik shook his head. "Don't do Ted's job."

Elnaz shrugged. "I don't have any choice. I'm not doing it for Ted, I'm doing it for the company. You two stay and have more drinks, and give me the receipt. We'll cover it." Bente looked warily at Didrik—did he want to stay, now that Elnaz was leaving? They didn't know each other very well—maybe he'd rather go back to the hotel and rest?

But he smiled at Elnaz.

"See you tomorrow, don't stay out too late." Elnaz winked at them both.

"We promise." Didrik looked at Bente and held her gaze for a fraction too long. She felt a tingle run right through her body. Was it her imagination, or was he telling her something with that look? *Pull yourself together, Bente. This is Didrik Holgersson—who has just opened up and told you he's heartbroken. Plus he must have plenty of other women standing in line waiting to date him. Don't get carried away!*

The electricity between them disappeared when Didrik's phone buzzed once more.

"Your wife again?" Should she have said ex-wife?

"Yep." He put the phone aside and turned his attention to Bente. "How about you? You're not in a relationship?"

She shook her head. "I've stayed single since I split with my ex."

"Of course . . . Henrik Eklund? From *Let's Get Baking*?"

"Exactly. Henrik." She took another sip of her wine and gazed out across the room. "Relationships are . . . tricky."

The place had gotten even noisier, and Didrik edged his chair nearer so that he could hear her. He leaned across the small section of the table that separated them; he was right next to her now. She could smell him. An incredibly manly scent—bergamot, like a newly opened box of loose-leaf tea, leather, and citrus. She found it comparable to the most beautiful, most sensual aromas of a vintage wine.

She cleared her throat. "Especially when a person has lived alone for some time." It was as if the words took on a fresh charge of electricity now that he was so close. "How long were you married?"

"Eight years. And we've been a couple for . . ." He thought for a moment. "Thirteen years."

"That's quite a while. So how do you feel now? Are you done with women?" She rolled her eyes and gave an artificial little laugh. God, what was wrong with her? Why had she said that?

"I don't know. I thought my wife . . ." He broke off. "My ex-wife. Her name is Lovisa, by the way. I thought Lovisa was the love of my life, but that wasn't the case. I haven't had time to think it all through yet, but I assume I have yet to find that person."

"So you still believe in true love?"

"I'm way too much of a hopeless romantic to believe anything else. I refuse to accept that this was my one chance, and now it's gone. My actual true love *must* be out there somewhere."

Bente smiled. Of course that was what he thought. After all, he was Didrik Holgersson, everybody's darling. At the same time, there was something incredibly charming about that way of thinking.

"And you?"

She waited for a while before answering. The adult relationships that had shaped her life, and that had to a great extent been her role models for adult love, had all been deficient in one way or another. Aunt Lydia's husband had left her when Uno was little more than a newborn, and Bente's parents, who'd seemed to have everything—they'd *loved* each other—had also separated from one another in the most brutal fashion. If Bente had learned anything about love, it was that however fantastic and true it might be, it was never enough.

"Maybe I don't think it's that simple, that there's one forever person for every one of us." Saying she didn't believe in true love seemed much too dramatic.

Didrik inhaled sharply, adopting a theatrical expression of horror. "Ouch." He placed one hand on his heart. "You've just destroyed everything I've ever believed in."

She laughed. "Sorry. Of course I'm sure that *your* one true love is out there somewhere." She meant it. Didrik had charm and charisma. It wouldn't be long before he was in a wonderful, loving relationship again.

"But you don't think there's someone special for you?"

"I've grown up surrounded by adult relationships that didn't really work."

"Your parents?"

"Among others. My mother and father were always very loving, but . . . it didn't end particularly well." She swallowed hard. She did *not* want her voice to start trembling, and she couldn't go into the details. One detail always led to another, and telling Didrik her entire story was out of the question. This wasn't a therapy session.

"But you're happy living alone?" he asked.

"I don't feel as if I'm living alone." She smiled. "At the moment I'm actually living in my sister's apartment, with her and my mom. A slightly unconventional intergenerational arrangement."

"Do you enjoy living with them?"

"Would you want to move back in with your mom?"

"Not a chance."

"Being with them during a fairly tumultuous time has been good, but now I'm looking forward to moving back into my own place. I've given my tenant notice, so it won't be too much longer now." The payment she'd already received from the production company plus the money she had saved during her time at Rendezvous meant that she had enough to live alone at last. "Do you have brothers or sisters?"

"A brother. Who is about to become a father. I'm going to be an uncle."

"Fantastic—congratulations!"

He smiled proudly. "It feels huge!"

"Becoming an aunt would be a dream. Unfortunately, my sister has already found the love of her life—her business. It's hard to imagine that she'd be able to sustain a relationship for any longer than Elnaz's colleagues can run a production without her."

"By that you mean she's never had a relationship that's lasted past afternoon tea?"

"Kind of." Hanna had been with one guy for almost a year, but he had ended it because she worked too much. Then she had dated a woman quite seriously for a while, but Hanna had decided she couldn't cope with having to send messages and keep in touch.

"All the anxiety, all the misunderstandings that have to be sorted out before everything is okay again." He shook his head slowly. "Is that what I can expect if I start dating again?" He looked at Bente and sighed. "Maybe it's better to try to stay in the present? Right now I'm sitting in a bar in Paris, talking to an interesting woman."

Had his knee just brushed against hers? She felt as if an electric shock had surged through her body, her heart was racing. She felt her face burning—from the wine, from the heat in the room, from Didrik's proximity.

She took a deep breath. "Shall we drink to that?"

He raised his glass, met her gaze. Then smiled. "You're . . . unexpected, somehow."

"Unexpected?"

"Yes . . . I don't know . . . but I'm enjoying talking to you."

"Perhaps that's because you've lived a regimented life as a married man for the past few years, spending your evenings drinking tea and looking forward to the excitement of a new British crime series on TV . . ."

He laughed. "Marriage can be more exciting than that. And you're forgetting that I work in TV; it's very fast-paced and you meet all kinds of people. Who find themselves interesting, at least, even if no one else does." He paused, seemed to be gathering himself. "But I mean what I said. I think you're interesting. I recognize myself in you, your passion for wine."

"Same. You're . . . interesting too." *And absolutely gorgeous.* She hardly dared move, he was so close. At that moment her phone buzzed and she picked it up. Frederic. She quickly rejected the call.

"Let me guess—Frederic?"

Bente raised her eyebrows. "Frederic, yes."

"So what's the story with you two?"

She told him about meeting Frederic in Paris, about him being her tutor when she was training to be a sommelier. "We started dating. He showed me the city." She was turning her glass around and around as she talked. "I fell in love and he broke my heart." She finished her wine. "When we saw each other today, I realized I'm too old for men like him."

Didrik nodded and gave a faint smile. There was clearly some satisfaction in that smile, the same one Camille wore when she tasted a really fruity Shiraz from the New World—her "guilty pleasure" wine.

That smile made Bente's heart beat even faster.

There were plenty of people out and about on this Parisian spring evening. The streetlamps along their route back to the hotel looked like a necklace of glowing beads. They were surrounded by the typical hum of a big city, the typical hum of Paris.

They stopped outside the hotel.

Didrik glanced around and began to laugh, then he looked deep into her eyes.

"What?" Bente was confused. "Is something wrong?"

Didrik didn't answer. He leaned toward her . . . and wiped something off her cheek.

There was silence all around them, as if the world was holding its breath.

The *crémant* they had drunk, the red wine, the good food, all those spices, the shimmering lights all around them, the smells of the city—she almost felt dizzy. Or was it his closeness that was to blame?

What if he kissed her? What would she do? Kiss him back? They were colleagues. And he was in the middle of a divorce.

As if he could read her mind, he looked away and turned toward the door. They walked inside.

"Tomorrow will be exciting," he said, as if nothing had happened.

"I'm looking forward to it."

"By the way, I booked a meeting with a military historian for tomorrow. Apparently she knows a lot about the French Foreign Legion."

Bente stopped in her tracks. What had he just said? *He'd* booked a meeting? Wasn't *she* the one who was supposed to be running the production side of things—or had she misunderstood? He'd taken the meeting with the man who ran the blog on the Foreign Legion, and now this.

"Okay . . . When did you do that?"

"Sometime last week."

"And can we fit it in tomorrow?"

"Yes, around lunchtime. Elnaz thought it sounded great when I mentioned it to her."

"Did she. And when did the two of you discuss it?" God, she sounded difficult—she could hear it in her voice. Was she overreacting? Was it arrogant to think that everything should go through her? After all, Didrik was the star of the show.

"I don't remember—I think we did it via email." He looked warily at her. "I just wanted to help out."

They had reached the elevator. She turned to him.

"Thanks, but I can handle the show myself." She forced a smile. "See you tomorrow." She left him standing by the elevator and headed for the stairs.

When she reached her room, she slammed the door behind her. What had just happened? Had she reacted too strongly? They'd had a fantastic evening. Didrik was nicer than she'd thought, and somewhere deep down she knew that his taking the initiative with aspects of the show was a sign of his commitment. Of course she wanted him to be fully involved. But he was already the natural star. He would obviously take the lead role when the show was launched. But now? No. The whole thing was her idea. Couldn't she at least be the one to pull the strings when it came to the production?

With a sigh, she went over to the balcony, opened the doors, and stepped outside. She thought about the bar, the wine, the heat. And about Didrik's knee touching hers. The look that had been in his eyes. She hadn't been imagining things.

She went back inside and slammed the balcony doors.

Had she made a fool of herself?

15

I know you had to leave the other day, but I really need to talk to you. Have you got time for a phone call?

The message woke Didrik the following morning. Lovisa had sent something similar the night before, making it three messages in total. She was obviously keen to talk to him. God, was she dying?

He put down the phone, pulled the soft, thick coverlet up to his shoulders, and closed his eyes. He didn't want to think about Lovisa and whatever she had to say.

Instead he thought about the evening. It had been fantastic—up to a point.

He and Bente had had an interesting and rewarding conversation. He had been curious about her, and she had listened to him. He realized that he had felt listened to for the first time in . . . months.

After a while, he got up and went for a run beside the Seine to clear the wine from his body, and while he ran he thought more about the evening's conversation. About Bente. About those green eyes that almost always sparkled, and about how she had shown *her* Paris to him and Elnaz with such enthusiasm.

He had meant it when he said that she was unexpected and interesting. His first impression had been that she was a determined person, perhaps a little cold. But in fact they had discussed things that *meant* something. Bente had shared her thoughts and feelings. Most of all, she had allowed him to talk about his failed marriage.

There had been something there, hadn't there? Until he sabotaged it all by marching into her territory. *Shit.* He stopped to catch his breath, then stretched and gazed out across the river. An early tourist boat glided slowly by as the water sparkled in the morning sun.

What must Bente think of him after he had behaved with such a lack of concern? That he was an arrogant TV star who was used to getting his own way? Didrik set off again.

He vowed that he would think before he acted in the future. He didn't want Bente to feel as if he had walked all over her. He knew how much she cared about this show.

◆ ◆ ◆

Bente sat in the hotel's inner courtyard wearing a dark-blue dress and low-heeled black shoes, her auburn hair loose. *Le Monde* lay open in front of her, next to a cup of coffee and a croissant.

Didrik went over to her table and said a cheery "Good morning!"

She smiled—not coldly, but with a certain reserve. "Morning."

Elnaz emerged from the restaurant carrying a tray laden with bread, orange juice, and a large café au lait.

When Bente didn't say anything else, Didrik turned and went in to the generous breakfast buffet. He loaded up his tray with a fresh-baked baguette with salad and thick slices of rustic French cheese, a large café au lait, and freshly squeezed orange juice. He could eat breakfasts like this for the rest of his life.

Back in the courtyard, he sat down on the white cast-iron bench by the wall, where lush green ivy scrambled up the white-rendered facade.

Bente was laughing at something Elnaz had said.

"There's been a slight change to today's schedule," Bente informed him.

At last, Didrik thought. She seemed ready to get back to work, and ready to talk to him again; now maybe they could leave the awkwardness behind them and move on.

"Frederic contacted me," she continued. "Apparently he has some information that might be useful, and he wondered if I had time to see him so he can tell me more." Those green eyes sparkled. "I thought I'd meet him for lunch, so could we maybe postpone the visit to the museum?"

Didrik nodded. "No problem." *I* thought I'd meet him for lunch, she'd said. Clearly she intended to go alone. "Or I could go to the museum by myself."

"Why would you do that?"

"Just to stick to the schedule." He took a bite of his baguette, which was perfectly crusty. "If I find anything helpful at the museum, we could go back tomorrow?"

It annoyed him that she wanted to change their plans for the sake of that unreliable guy.

Elnaz nodded. "Sounds good. We really need a breakthrough—we have no time to lose."

Bente shrugged and turned her attention back to the newspaper.

◆ ◆ ◆

After breakfast they headed off to the morning's first meeting, with a historian specializing in the history of French wine. The woman explained how the winemakers had lived during the occupation, about the challenges they'd faced, and the pride they'd felt as they continued to do their utmost to produce their beloved wine: both because they needed to bring in money and because making wine was a part of the cultural heritage of France, and such a large part of their personal lives.

They showed her the bottle and the box, and Didrik asked specifically about the little space in the latter. The historian told them that many winemakers had worked with the resistance movement. She added that some of those were collaborators who also worked with the Nazis and the French police.

Afterward they went for coffee at a small café just off Place de la Madeleine.

Elnaz, who seemed unaware of the tension between Didrik and Bente, was on the lookout for filming locations they could use with the production team later.

"I think we've found some good places," she told them now, "like that sweet little museum. And it would be great if the two of you talked to the historian, if she wants to be on the show. And your friend Frederic—you could chat to him in a wine cellar, for example."

Elnaz beamed at them, clearly hoping for an enthusiastic response. "And I love the idea of us filming with our own camera sometimes—it feels really authentic. Like a nicer version of *The Blair Witch Project*. With wine." She laughed, then sighed. "But we need more material than we've got if we're going to have enough for a series."

Bente nodded as she jotted things down in her red notebook. "I agree—we don't know much at all." She sounded resigned. "It's going to be difficult to build a show on the fact that a bottle at the bottom of the sea had a Swedish inscription and was apparently on the way to an address in Vetlanda."

"Where a man was born who later joined the Foreign Legion," Didrik added.

"Yes, but we don't know for sure that it was this Sven who sent the bottle. We need more. *Something* at least. Where was the bottle from? Which vineyard? From what we've heard from the people we've met so far, that all seems almost impossible to track down. Of course we may find out more about this Sven, but even if we do, it still feels a bit . . . sparse."

Didrik sensed a certain desperation in Bente's voice and did his best to sound encouraging. "Maybe Frederic will have information that will take us another step forward. Plus I'm meeting that military historian. She might be able to point us in the direction of some good reading material if she doesn't have any concrete details."

Bente gave a brief nod.

◆ ◆ ◆

When they parted company, Didrik walked to the military museum. He was met there by an elegant woman in her early fifties, wearing pants and a shirt, her hair in a neat chignon. She greeted him with a firm handshake. As they walked around, she told him about all the exhibits—books, uniforms, old weapons—and talked about the development of the Foreign Legion throughout history, and its role during the Second World War.

She hadn't heard of a Swedish legionnaire who ended up in Bordeaux during the occupation, but she gave Didrik an important tip: A legionnaire in occupied France probably would have traveled under a different identity, and might even have claimed to be of a different nationality. She recommended a diary written by a priest who had been active within the resistance movement in Bordeaux—he might have mentioned Sven. She pointed Didrik in the direction of one or two antiquarian booksellers in the city who might have a copy—apparently it was difficult to obtain.

When Didrik left the museum, he took a stroll in order to get some exercise and see a little more of Paris.

He hadn't replied to Lovisa yet. He ought to just get it done.

Back in the hotel room, he called her right away, before he had time to change his mind. He sat down on the bed, and she answered after three rings.

"Thanks for calling."

Didrik didn't say anything.

"How are you? How's Paris?" Her tone was hesitant.

"It's great, but I'm mostly working. What did you want to talk about?"

"I wanted to tell you before you found out from someone else." Her voice was trembling now. "Niklas and I, we . . ."

Niklas. It hadn't even occurred to Didrik that her new partner had a name.

"We're expecting a baby."

"Expecting a baby? What, so you're . . . pregnant?"

"Yes."

Didrik took a deep breath. "Why are you telling me this now?"

"Like I said, I didn't want you to hear it from someone else."

"Someone else? I'm in Paris, I don't know a soul here. Why couldn't it wait until I got home?"

She was silent for a few seconds. "Because I'm showing . . ."

What had she said? She was already showing? She couldn't be that far gone, they'd only just split up. What the hell? That must mean . . .

With a sigh of despair, he ended the call and flopped back on the bed.

16

1944

When Sven woke up the following morning, he heard subdued voices from the kitchen. He got dressed and went downstairs. A short man was standing opposite Juliette and Hugo.

Juliette turned to Sven. "This is our neighbor, Monsieur Marcel Fossey. He also works for the resistance." Sven shook hands with Marcel Fossey, who was holding his beret. His shirt was creased, and he had the air of someone who was feeling stress. Sven got the sense he had gotten ready in haste before rushing over.

"The Allies' successes are making the Germans nervous. There are rumors that they're tightening up their checks on travelers," Marcel said. "They're stopping anyone traveling to or from Bordeaux, and they're letting hardly anyone through."

Juliette looked at Sven. "You can't leave now."

"The Germans already know I'm here—I can't stay with you indefinitely."

"Best to lie low," Hugo said. "If they call here and ask, it won't seem strange that you're staying on with relatives, but if you try to leave, they'll check your ID papers and ask lots of questions."

"Thank you, Marcel." Juliette squeezed the man's hands. "Thank you for warning us."

He nodded and turned to leave, then stopped. "So you'll be putting out the bottles this evening?"

"We will, as usual. This evening. On the steps."

"Good. Good." Marcel nodded, then left.

Juliette and Hugo exchanged anxious looks.

"You don't need to think about me, of course I must go. I won't stay here unnecessarily. I'll keep a low profile."

"We can't risk you getting caught," Juliette said firmly. "It's dangerous for all of us, and you're more than welcome to stay here."

Sven nodded slowly. If he was caught and exposed, then Hugo and Juliette would be in danger. And yet he was another mouth to feed, and who knew how long he would be forced to stay? Then again, he had some money with him—not a great deal of it, but enough to make a contribution.

"I could do with a hand in the vineyard," Hugo said encouragingly.

"Yes, because Mathieu isn't here," Juliette added.

They had told him over dinner the previous evening that their son was in Paris, helping relatives with their shop. Mathieu was obviously missed—it was hard for the two of them to do all the work in the vineyard on their own.

That settled the matter. Sven could be of use, and of course it was safest for everyone if he stayed on for a while.

◆ ◆ ◆

The flickering flame of the candle chased away some of the darkness in the cellar. Mathieu had spent a whole twenty-four hours down here. Considerably longer than usual—he normally hid for short periods when unexpected visitors showed up, either the Germans or strangers.

His parents had explained that their guest, a man who worked for the resistance movement, would be staying on for a while, and until they had worked out what to do, Mathieu must remain in the cellar.

He moved along the vaulted brick corridor to his desk. Lit another sconce, then another; took down one of the candles and sat down at the wooden table, placing the burning candle in a candlestick made of tin. He smoothed out the map he had drawn and tried to remember where he had stopped the previous evening, what point he should continue from. He looked up at the ceiling, listened for footsteps. He really wanted to get out of here.

Suddenly it felt to him as if all the oxygen was sucked out of the room. The dampness and the darkness seemed to seep into his body, into his veins. He needed air and daylight. Maybe he could creep upstairs while Mom, Dad, and their guest were asleep.

A second later he heard murmuring—his parents were awake.

He continued working on the map while listening hard, hoping to make out what they were saying. Perhaps the guest would be leaving soon.

Mathieu allowed one hand to slide into his pocket, where it caressed the silver chain and the flat medallion. The cool metal against his fingers always calmed him.

Gerard

Then he stood up and sighed deeply, paced up and down the vaulted corridor. It had been dug out and built after the First World War; his parents and paternal grandparents had learned from the Germans' progress back then. The plan was to create an easy passage to the next vineyard that they could use to smuggle and hide bottles of wine, or as an escape route if they needed to flee.

Mathieu's family had chosen to stay put when the Germans came to the village this time. It had been too late to run by the time they found out that France had capitulated and that the Germans had begun to occupy large parts of the country. The family had stayed even after the Germans reached Bordeaux; they had nowhere else to go, and they wanted to protect the vineyard as much as possible.

The cellar and these corridors had become Mathieu's refuge.

He moved toward the hatch and took a couple of steps up the wooden ladder, taking care not to let it creak.

He was so tired of being a prisoner in his own home, but even before the war there had been rumors about him and Gerard. He had never mentioned their relationship to his parents, and they hadn't asked. Maybe they didn't want to know. He and Gerard had kept it a secret, as far as they were able, but once the rumors started, his parents had warned him to be careful.

Gerard's parents, on the other hand, had been furious when they heard.

Then both Mathieu and Gerard had been called up to join the army. When Mathieu later returned to the village, Bordeaux was occupied. He and his parents tried to live as normal, even though everything had changed. That's when they became a part of the resistance movement.

Then the deportations began. Jews and communists. Mathieu's family helped out as best they could. They received reports from other parts of France: Men were being taken prisoner and removed from the villages, herded onto trains and buses and transported far away—no one knew where they had gone. Men who had sexual relations with other men were taken away along with the Jews and the communists. Mathieu didn't know what the Nazis might have heard about him, but he knew that they were going around with lists asking about this and that—trying to get people to inform on their neighbors.

One cold gray day in the fall, after Mathieu had been out in the forest foraging for mushrooms, his mother came to meet him on his way back to the vineyard. She was running, her cheeks were red.

"Mathieu, Mathieu. My son, my darling son." She drew him close.

"Mom—what's happened?" Her gray eyes were filled with tears. She was smiling with relief even as horror was etched on her face.

She held his face between her hands. "They came looking for you. The Nazis. They came and asked about you." She took a breath. "Come back to the house, you can't be outside."

Since then Mathieu had hidden whenever anyone came by. Not because he and his parents didn't trust their friends—everyone in the village stuck together. The solidarity since war broke out had been unshakable. Still, the fewer people who knew where he was, the better. Only their closest neighbors, Monsieur and Madame Fossey, knew that Mathieu was still at home. It wasn't clear why the Nazis had asked about him—perhaps they suspected he was involved in the resistance, or maybe they had heard the rumors about him and Gerard.

So Mathieu had stayed hidden. And although he was tired of it, he knew it was the safest option.

He had cooperated mainly for his mother's sake, but now he felt he couldn't stand it for a second longer. If the guest was a part of the resistance, then surely he wouldn't say anything about Mathieu to the Nazis? If he was taken prisoner and forced to talk, then they would be lost anyway. All of them.

He would speak to his mother later in the day. But first he was going to sneak upstairs and get some fresh air before their guest came down.

It was worth the risk.

◆ ◆ ◆

When Sven woke up on his second day at the vineyard, after a deep, sound sleep, he sat on the bed for a little while. It was still early, the sun had just risen. He opened the window and let the pleasant morning breeze sweep into the room as he listened to the birdsong. Sometimes it was hard to grasp that half of Europe was at war, in flames.

He got dressed and went down to the kitchen. Hugo and Juliette were still asleep, and he thought he would make them breakfast.

He was peeling the hard-boiled eggs when he heard a thud from the bedroom, then another, followed by the sound of whispering voices. Hugo and Juliette seemed to be talking to someone. Had they had a visitor during the night? Someone from the resistance?

Then the noise level rose, and there were more loud thuds. It almost sounded as if a fight was going on in there—was it an intruder? Sven rushed toward the bedroom door. The soldier within him was on full alert, his senses sharpened, and he glanced into the hallway to check if there was anyone else there. The voices in the bedroom were clearly agitated now.

"Please," Juliette begged.

Was it the Nazis?

Sven flung open the door.

Juliette, wearing a nightdress and with her hair in a loose braid, was holding a young man's shoulders in a firm grip. A hatch in the floor next to the bed was open, and it looked as if she was trying to force the young man down into the hole, while he did his best to resist. Hugo was standing to one side, watching the spectacle.

"Let him come up, *chérie*," Hugo said with a sigh.

"I refuse to be a prisoner in my own home!" the man said.

Only then did they notice Sven.

The man was around Sven's age, slim, of medium height. He had the same big gray-blue eyes as Juliette, and Hugo's chiseled jawline. Tousled light-brown hair that made Sven think of poets and artists.

"Is everything okay in here?" he asked as he backed away. It was clear that the man was no stranger. Sven realized this had nothing to do with him, and he needed to apologize. "I'm so sorry, but I heard voices and there seemed to be some sort of argument going on, so I . . ."

"There's always some sort of argument going on." Hugo shook his head slowly.

"Hi—I'm Mathieu." The young man twisted free of Juliette's grip and ran his fingers casually through his hair, a gesture that took Sven's breath away. He came toward Sven holding out his hand.

"Our son." Juliette gave a resigned shrug.

"Sven Steen." Sven shook Mathieu's hand. "I believe you live in Paris—did you arrive home last night?"

Mathieu looked at his mother, then his father, as if he was working out what to say.

"He doesn't live in Paris," Juliette said. "He's not officially at home, so sometimes he has to hide in the cellar."

Sven nodded. Realized he shouldn't ask any more questions.

17

Frederic was already waiting for Bente at an outside table at the wine bar. As soon as he saw her, he stood up and kissed her on the cheek.

"I wanted you to see this place," he said, waving to a man inside who was arranging wine bottles behind the bar. "I work with them a lot. They have an amazing wine list, and have bought our new lines, the ones I told you about."

Bente knew that Frederic worked hard to modernize the family vineyard. He wanted to maintain the traditions, but he also liked to experiment with styles and blends.

He waved again to the man behind the bar, who came over to introduce himself as the owner and say hello. He then hurried away and came back with a bottle. Bente recognized the label from Frederic's family business.

"Our latest blend. You have to try it."

He spoke intensely about the wine, a classic Bordeaux blend but in a modern style—Cabernet Franc, Merlot, and Cabernet Sauvignon. He looked expectantly at her. She had always appreciated the fact that he valued her opinions on wines, especially the ones he produced. Because she was *gifted* in the field of wine, as he put it.

They clinked their large glasses together, then she inhaled the aroma of juicy, mature, dark cherries. Next came black currants, plums, and a delicate touch of herbs.

She took a sip. The taste reflected the aromas, but unlike a classic Bordeaux, the wine wasn't harsh, and it had a wonderful, spicy aftertaste.

"Fantastic—it will definitely appeal to the public." She smiled at him.

He returned her smile. "You think so?"

"It's complex, but incredibly easy to drink." She took a larger sip. "This would be perfect for cozy Friday evenings in Sweden. Depending on the price tag, of course."

Frederic looked pleased. "Good to hear." Getting a wine into the state-owned Swedish liquor stores would be an achievement, and give Frederic's business a considerable advantage. The government-run chain placed large orders and was the best buyer imaginable. Frederic liked to discuss the Swedish market and national preferences with Bente.

"So let's hear it," she said, putting down her glass.

He looked at her inquiringly.

"The wine bottle," she clarified.

Frederic sipped his wine, then gazed into her eyes and smiled mischievously, the way he always did when he wanted to do more than just talk. Which irritated her enormously.

"What did you find out about the bottle?"

He took a deep breath and leaned back on his chair. "I might have a good contact you can speak to, but I'm not sure yet."

"You *might* have a contact?" She laughed. "So why did you ask me to come here?"

"I wanted to see you." He tried a winning smile.

His phone rang, and she saw the name on the screen. Emma.

She sympathized with his poor assistant; she knew exactly how it felt to be the one who was kept waiting. After those whirlwind summer months when she was newly in love and had his full attention, when it felt as if she were floating on the pink fluffy clouds drifting over the Seine on summer evenings, Frederic had become increasingly distant. He needed to go back to Bordeaux, while she carried on working at the restaurant.

She hung out with Camille and her other colleagues at the wine bar, but couldn't help waiting and waiting . . . and waiting, for Frederic. Weeks would go by without him returning to Paris, for one reason or another. Then he would show up again for a week or so, behaving as if nothing had happened. He even surprised her with the occasional weekend trip to Bordeaux, only to disappear again. This went on for months.

When he was in Paris, he gave her his full attention at first, but after a while he became very busy with meetings. Meetings that went on all night. And once again she waited.

In the meantime she tried to enjoy this wonderful city, but Frederic was always there in the back of her mind. She wanted to be *with* him, yet she wasn't in a position to make demands since they had never promised each other anything. Eventually she realized that he was seeing other women, but thought she had no right to be angry—once again because she felt she had no right to make demands. After all, they weren't a couple, were they?

Their unpredictable relationship had gone on for almost a year when she decided to give up hope. And yet they continued to see each other, albeit more sporadically. Because they had never been exclusive, she'd found it hard to let him go. And maybe she hadn't been prepared to admit to herself that she had real feelings for him.

After a while, she'd gotten a job as a sommelier with a prestigious restaurant in the historic district of Marais, but continued to work the odd shift at Marion's wine bar because she loved the place. One evening as she was serving a Swedish woman, Bente was talking, as usual, in some detail about the wines on offer. The customer was asking lots of questions, and it turned out that she was an editor on TV24's morning show. She loved Bente's descriptions, the way Bente *took down the wine from the crystal chandeliers*, as she put it, and before long Bente was offered a slot on TV.

She didn't tell Frederic she was leaving Paris until a week or so before she was due to go. He was in town for meetings, and as was their habit, they had gone to some club before going back to his apartment.

Toward dawn, as the city was waking up, she had told him. She had imagined the scene beforehand, the way he would suddenly realize what he was losing, but that simply didn't happen. It was obvious that Frederic had never felt the same way about her as she had about him.

She left Paris with a broken heart. Back in Stockholm, once TV filming began, she created a new life and a new world for herself as a celebrity sommelier. It wasn't something she had dreamed of, but when she became famous, it was as if a desire had been awakened within her. A desire for the recognition, the attention. The *validation*.

The fame had satisfied a need she didn't know she'd had. But it struck her now that the feeling it once gave her—that of being drunk on life—reminded her of the way she'd felt with Frederic for a while.

She looked at him sitting across from her. He wasn't all that exciting, if she was honest about it. In fact, she found it hard to understand what she'd seen in him. Okay, so he was a typically charming Frenchman, and he was knowledgeable and passionate about wine. But at the end of the day, he was probably even more lost in life than she was. The flirting that had once been so appealing now seemed unattractive. And then there was his hair—why had he had those beautiful curls cut off?

He leaned across the table and tucked a strand of hair behind her ear.

Suddenly she knew exactly how he had expected the day to play out. He had arranged this meeting in order to have some time alone with her, after she had behaved so dismissively. Back in the day, she might have been flattered that he had made the effort, but right now she had a show to make. She didn't have time for this.

Frederic gazed at her searchingly, a small smile playing on his lips. "Why are you hesitating? What am I missing?"

She leaned back in her chair. "I . . ." What could she say? He was used to the game between them. Which always ended in the same way. In bed. "I'm thinking that maybe we're . . . done with each other? We have history, but it doesn't really appeal to me anymore."

He laughed. "Done with each other?" He reached over, placed a hand on her cheek. "You and I will never be *done with each other*."

If she hadn't been so disappointed that he had no information about the bottle, by the fact that she could literally see the show disappearing before her eyes, she might have stayed and finished the delicious wine, maybe tried another exciting bottle that the bar had to offer, indulged Frederic with some friendly flirting. But as it was, she just wanted to get out of there.

"Thanks for the wine, but I . . . To be honest, I don't have time for this. I'm only here for a few days, and I've got so much to do on the TV show."

"Please stay, Bente." Frederic got to his feet, realizing that she was serious. "I apologize, I . . . I just wanted to spend some time with you."

Bente looked at him. "And I wanted to see you, but I know now that I'm done with this. Give me a call. If you find out something about the bottle, that is." She stood up and left the wine bar.

A cold wind was blowing up the street. Bente pulled her leather jacket closely around her body and headed for the hotel, feeling like an idiot. She had wasted two meetings with Frederic in the hope of learning something useful, and the worst part was that she had arranged the first meeting partly because she had wanted to see him. For so long she had nurtured the idea that Frederic and the way he lived were what she wanted, that they were right for her. How much had she allowed that perception to steer her actions? Would she have seen Henrik and her relationship with him in a different light if Frederic hadn't been on her mind?

She would probably never know the answer.

◆ ◆ ◆

She thought about visiting a museum, but she really needed to prepare for the day's meetings.

When she reached the hotel, she went straight to the bar to order a large café au lait to take up to her room. Didrik was sitting at the bar, shoulders slumped, with an untouched glass of whiskey in front of him. He was staring at it as if he was wondering what to do with it.

"Are you going to drink that?" she asked as she slid onto the stool next to him.

He glanced at her, shrugged. "That's what they always do in movies—knock back a large whiskey."

The bartender came over to take Bente's order.

"I'll have the same as him."

They both sat in silence, watching as the bartender poured whiskey into a crystal glass and placed it in front of her. The glow of the lamps was reflected in the amber liquid, causing tiny flickers of light to spin around the glass on the brass counter.

Didrik picked up his own glass, then changed his mind and put it down again.

"I thought you liked whiskey?"

Another shrug. "The odd sip is okay."

"I thought you were the type who drank quite a bit."

He gave her a questioning look.

"When I came to your office that day, I got the impression you'd put away half a bottle."

"Right. Yes. I tried the same thing then as now. Isn't that what brooding, distinguished men do when they're trying to numb their feelings?"

"It's very Don Draper." Bente picked up her glass and knocked it back in two gulps. "I think I needed that. So how are you? Why do you need to numb your feelings?"

"My wife—sorry, ex-wife—is pregnant by her new boyfriend."

"Fuck."

He nodded. Sipped his drink and pulled a face. He didn't seem to like the taste. "So what did Fredrik have to say?"

She gave a half smile. "*Frederic* didn't really have any more information. The meeting was probably just . . ."

"An excuse to see you?"

She nodded.

"I thought so."

She raised an eyebrow.

"I know his type."

"So how did your meeting with the military historian go?"

"It was helpful. She pointed me in the direction of some useful reference material, and made me realize that we might be taking the wrong approach in our search for Sven."

"How so?"

"If he sent the bottle, and he was in Bordeaux during the occupation, he was probably using a different identity, and possibly a different nationality."

"Why?"

"My best guess is he was working for the resistance."

Bente sighed. "That makes it even more hopeless—we don't even know *who* we're looking for."

Didrik stared blankly into space. "Exactly."

Bente buried her head in her hands. "I just don't see how we're going to make any progress."

Didrik said nothing. She had hoped for words of encouragement, but he seemed incapable of stepping up, and she could understand why. He was now watching as the bartender inserted a corkscrew into a bottle and opened it with a loud plop. Didrik's hair was tousled, his glasses lay on the bar, and his shirt was partly unbuttoned. He had a very attractive three-day stubble that made the manly contours of his face appear even more pronounced. He took a sip of whiskey and grimaced again, but looked like maybe it didn't taste quite so bad this time. Being off his game really suited him. This was something very different from the neat tweed jackets and the perfect bow ties, a look that was reinforced by his round glasses.

He dragged his attention away from the bartender. "Listen, that business yesterday evening. I'm sorry I took liberties with the show. I should have checked with you first."

Bente nodded. "It's fine." She knew she had overreacted, but she didn't want him to see that his involvement in the show bothered her; she didn't want to come across as anxious. "So far the show has existed only in my head, so it's kind of hard to relinquish control. But I guess I have to, sooner or later."

"You do. And you've come up with a fantastic idea. I'll do my very best to make the show as good as possible." He was smiling now.

"I don't doubt that for a second."

He adjusted his wristwatch with a slightly clumsy movement, then ran his fingers through his already messy hair. The gesture gave him the look of a cute high school guy with a guitar. Bente had loved guys with guitars when she was in high school. She felt warm inside. What was it she actually found attractive? The way everyone's darling Didrik was off-kilter—was she seeing something more genuine there?

"Okay," he said after a while, putting on his glasses. "Shall we tackle the rest of the day? We have a few more meetings."

"Why not? I think Elnaz is checking out possible filming locations—she said she'd meet us at the sommelier school later. How about we start at that antiquarian bookstore by the Jardin du Luxembourg?"

"Visiting a dusty antiquarian bookstore with historical literature by the Jardin du Luxembourg after knocking back a glass of smoky whiskey. I can't think of a better way to spend the afternoon."

Bente couldn't help noticing the movement of Didrik's shoulder muscles as he stood up and put on his tweed jacket.

Or the fact that he was sexy even when he was talking about a dusty old bookstore.

18

The sunshine outside the hotel's main entrance was almost painful to Didrik's eyes after the subdued lighting of the bar. The whiskey had gone straight to his head. There was something weird about feeling slightly drunk in the middle of the day as they walked along the street among strolling tourists and Parisians hurrying back to work after lunch.

They reached the Jardin du Luxembourg, where the treetops bursting into life swayed above the gardens. On a street corner, Bente stopped at one of those stands where artists with varying degrees of talent sold pictures featuring motifs of Paris.

"It might be stupid, but . . ." She picked up a painting of the Arc de Triomphe. "My father always bought one of these on vacation when I was a kid. A little picture to remind him of where we'd been. So I always buy one too." She looked at Didrik. "I've got quite a collection now." She laughed and put it back, then took down a watercolor of the Moulin Rouge in pastel shades. "No, I mustn't, I've already got way too many little pictures from Paris, I've been here so often." She shook her head. "Shall we move on?"

"You should buy a picture, if it means something to you."

She shook her head again. "It's too hard to choose."

They set off again and soon arrived at the antiquarian bookstore. The walls were covered with overfilled shelves, as if someone had just kept on cramming in more and more books, then added even more shelves until the little store had become something of a labyrinth. Bente helped Didrik find the right section; there were lots and lots of old books that featured accounts of the war.

While Bente slipped across the road to look for books on Bordeaux in another store, Didrik went to the counter and asked for assistance from the clerk, who began searching for a title on her laptop. Its metallic angularity seemed totally out of place in this setting, which otherwise consisted entirely of organic material—wood, leather, and paper.

Leaving her to it, Didrik wandered around the shelves. He found the biography of a woman in the resistance movement in Bordeaux, which contained extracts from her diary. That might be useful. He added a couple of other interesting volumes about the resistance and the Foreign Legion and took his haul to the clerk. She told him that unfortunately she didn't have the book he wanted, but could order it. Didrik explained why he was in Paris, and she offered to mail the book to Sweden when it came in. Didrik picked up one or two other titles on French history, and the assistant wrapped everything in rustling brown paper, then tied it up with a piece of string. Didrik paid and left the store just as Bente reappeared.

They went to a café farther down the street where they ordered sandwiches and coffee. They chose a table by the window and sat down.

"Look what I found." He undid the string and took out one of the books. "It's the biography of a woman who was active in the resistance movement in Bordeaux. I thought she might have written about a Scandinavian man, or there might be some information about messages sent via wine bottles. I don't know, but hopefully the book will be useful." He tried to sound positive, wanting to give her hope. "And I've ordered the priest's diary, the one the military historian mentioned. Apparently he had lots of contacts, so we might spot something, find the odd detail that will help us."

Bente sipped her coffee as she listened to him. She looked quite cheerful.

"What did you find?" Didrik nodded in the direction of a shopping bag on the floor.

"Some books about winemakers in Bordeaux, and the history of the region." She took out a book with a red fabric cover, then leaned back and took another sip of her coffee. Her lipstick left red marks on the white rim of the cup. She was wearing a white cotton shirt and black pants, with a black-and-white-striped silk scarf knotted around her neck. Her large sunglasses were pushed up onto the top of her head. She blended well with the Parisians.

"One thing I don't get," she said. "If Sven was in France, what was he doing there? And specifically, why was he in Bordeaux? There was no fighting at that time—France had already capitulated."

"There was no armed conflict between military forces, but the resistance never gave up the struggle." Didrik took out the notes he had taken while conducting his own research, and during his discussion with the military historian. "Sven belonged to a Foreign Legion battalion that fought for France in Narvik, when France and Britain helped Norway to defend itself against Germany."

Bente nodded. "So what happened to the Legion when France capitulated?"

"Things got kind of messy." He flicked through his notes. "Parts of the French army chose to join the Free French forces, led by de Gaulle. Some parts of the Legion did the same, while other sections of both the army and the Legion were loyal to the Vichy regime, which agreed to a ceasefire with Germany. Sven's brigade remained in Britain, so I assume they chose the Free French."

"The liberation army?"

"Exactly."

"So if the Foreign Legion were working for the liberation army, it's not impossible that they might have sent people to help from inside France?"

"Not impossible at all."

Bente went to the bar and ordered a glass of wine for each of them to drink as they continued to look through their purchases.

"That's delicious," Didrik said when he had tasted the cold wine. "Chablis?"

"Correct. Well done." Bente looked impressed.

"I've drunk quite a lot of Chablis—you could say it's my house wine. In fact, I think you might have recommended it on one of your shows."

"When Chablis is good, it's excellent. And this one is fantastic—dry, with a mineral flavor." Bente tasted again, let the wine roll around in her mouth before she swallowed, then sniffed the bouquet as she swirled the glass. "Some people insist they would never touch Chardonnay, only Chablis. My mother, for example. Although Chablis is made from only Chardonnay grapes," she explained.

Didrik laughed. "Lovisa says exactly the same. 'Only Chablis!'" He imitated her voice.

Bente smiled. "It's a common misconception, and it's not really surprising. Chablis is the actual place where the wine is produced, and it has that typical minerality, fresh and with elements of citrus, while American Chardonnay is stored in oak barrels, which gives flavors like butter and nuts. Some link the name Chardonnay with those wines."

He tasted again, noting the freshness and the hint of citrus. "So you didn't inherit your interest in wine from your mother?"

Bente shook her head. "Mom's drink of choice is my sister's Manhattan cocktails, which are revolting. But they love them, for some reason. I have no idea how my sister manages to mix perfectly reasonable ingredients and end up with something that resembles a witch's brew."

Didrik grinned. "So where does your interest come from?"

Bente's expression grew serious, as if she was thinking about something.

"From my father," she said after a moment.

"Is he a sommelier?"

"No. He was an accountant. He and my mother ran an accounting firm together."

"Ran?" He felt as if he was having to drag the words out of her. Bente could be so chatty and sociable, asking him questions with interest, but right now it was as if she had completely shut down.

"Yes. He died when I was thirteen."

"Oh . . . I'm so sorry."

She managed a small smile. "Thanks. It was tough." She sipped her wine, turned away, and gazed out across the street.

She couldn't have given him a clearer signal that the conversation was over.

19

1944

Mathieu now had breakfast with the others. Sometimes he went outside to get a little fresh air before going back in to continue working on the maps. Sven usually went out with him, and they would sit and chat for a while on the stone bench by the house.

Sven told Mathieu what it had been like when he joined the Legion, and when he was sent into battle for the first time. Sven had fought the Germans at Narvik. It had been a weird feeling, he said, to be in the country that bordered his own and to be fighting. He confided that he had helped injured civilians, but then he fell silent. Mathieu understood; he had met so many men who couldn't talk about the war.

In turn Mathieu told Sven about the vineyard and tried to teach him the basics of wine production. Sven listened with interest.

Mathieu had quickly realized that Sven came from an agricultural family. There was something about those broad shoulders. He saw how efficiently Sven worked when he was helping Hugo. As a soldier he was strong, of course, but the kind of raw strength he displayed when it came to physical work, the strength it took to run a vineyard, could come only from years of hard physical toil. He also had a sure hand in repairing and maintaining the tools and machinery. As for the vines, he worked with incredible care and meticulousness. Mathieu would often sit and watch him, before raised eyebrows from his mother would send him back indoors.

They had also gotten into the habit of having lunch together, with Sven joining them at the table. A simple snack, then dinner in the evenings. Sometimes Mathieu would sneak out in the afternoons to watch Sven work. He hadn't seen anything so wonderful for a long time.

Even more wonderful, perhaps, was watching Sven when he talked. When they chatted over dinner, Mathieu would catch himself being utterly captivated by Sven. Those full red lips. The way he spoke broken French, that fantastic accent that made the words strangely sensual.

◆ ◆ ◆

A week or so after Sven's arrival, two German soldiers came to the vineyard.

The Nazis showed up at regular intervals to "buy" wine at such insultingly low prices that the whole thing was nothing more than pure theft.

Apart from the wine, the family had little of value left. They had hidden the silver in the cellar, but the linen cloths from Hugo's parents, the lace cloths that Juliette's mother had ordered from Paris—the Nazis had taken them all. There was nothing here to interest the Germans except the wine, and they had scheduled the pickup times so they didn't have to wait around while Hugo searched the wine cellar for the best bottles, so what were they doing here now? They weren't due for another week.

As soon as they heard the car, Mathieu ran down into the cellar, while Juliette went outside to call Hugo.

When the Nazis came by, Mathieu could always hear every word from his hiding place, because the soldiers spoke loudly. His parents did the same so that he would know if he needed to flee along the secret corridors.

He heard his father speaking German to their visitors. They liked it when he spoke their language. He had learned it when he fought in the

First World War—the war he had hated, the war that had changed him. That was what he always said, that the war had changed him, which was why he had wanted Mathieu to avoid it for as long as possible. But of course Mathieu had been called up. He hadn't had time to do much of anything, let alone fight, before the French government capitulated. He had never witnessed those terrible battles, which in hindsight he was very grateful for. He already had too many dreadful thoughts about the fate that must have befallen Gerard.

He loved Gerard.

At the thought of him, Mathieu's hand slipped into his pocket, as it always did, and he touched the silver chain, then the cold medallion. His fingers traced the engraved letters and numbers.

Mathieu didn't understand German, but his father translated for his mother as he spoke. The soldiers asked if they could take a look around the wine cellar. Access to the wine cellar was from the other side of the house; there was a passageway leading from it to the cellar where Mathieu hid, but its opening was well concealed.

"Of course," Hugo replied in German. Then he said something else. Naturally it was good to be able to speak the language, it made the Nazis slightly more well disposed toward them. At the same time it was important not to go too far, otherwise people might start saying you were a traitor. Doing business with the Nazis wasn't exactly accepted, but on the other hand, everyone in the village realized that they had no choice. There were no longer any other options when it came to exporting the wine; plus it was impossible to refuse—no one wanted to give the Nazis an excuse to arrest anybody.

One of the soldiers asked a question, and Hugo translated for Juliette.

"Yes, that's my nephew," she replied in French. "He's here to help us with the work in the vineyard while our son is helping relatives elsewhere."

"Oh? Which relatives is he helping, if your nephew is here?" The other soldier spoke French; most in the higher ranks were familiar with the language, while others had begun to learn. "Seems a bit complicated, all this moving about."

"He's with my elderly aunt," Hugo said quickly.

"I see. So could we say hello to your relative? The Swede?"

"Of course. This way." Mathieu heard the sound of boots crossing the floor, then fading away.

His heart was pounding. What did they want with Sven? It was hardly surprising that they wanted to meet him, but what if they saw through his story? Meanwhile, Mathieu was hiding down here like a coward. He sighed in frustration. After half an hour, which felt like an eternity, he heard footsteps again, followed by a thud—presumably a wooden box—and the clink of bottles. They must have spoken to Sven and visited the wine cellar.

"Thank you—always a pleasure to do business with you, Monsieur Latorre."

"Thank you," Hugo replied. Mathieu could hear how difficult it was for him to force the words out. No one really wanted to do business with the Germans.

After a while, his mother opened the hatch.

"Everything okay?" Mathieu asked as he clambered out. Juliette nodded.

Mathieu hurried through the house. He wanted to see Sven with his own eyes, wanted to know for sure that he was all right.

Hugo was in the hallway, about to return to the vines. Mathieu went with him. Sven was outside, standing by a row of vines. Mathieu rushed over, then stopped in front of him. What had he intended to do? Throw his arms around him?

"Did they suspect anything?" Mathieu asked, his heart in his mouth.

Sven shook his head. "No."

"Good."

"You can't trust them."

"I want you here," Mathieu said.

Sven looked surprised, then gave a brief nod before getting back to work.

◆ ◆ ◆

Sven liked the monotony of the days. Routine was something he had appreciated during his training in the Legion.

Being able to help the family meant a great deal to him, and he reluctantly began to accept that he liked it here. He saw his life as a soldier and a member of the Legion as a vocation, and his decision to join the Legion had meant leaving his old life behind him. However, now that he had the opportunity to live something that resembled his former life—a normal everyday life—he experienced for the first time in years a sense of calmness, of harmony.

The thought of home and family, and the fact that he couldn't speak to his mother or sister, lay over him like a suffocating, wet woolen blanket.

He would never forget the expression that had come over his father's face when he realized what a mess Sven had gotten into. Father, who never lost his temper, who rarely showed his emotions at all, had gone crazy and said that Sven was *sick*. He had spat out the word.

Sven's father was a good person, with high moral standards. He cared about those who were worse off, and he had taught Sven that a decent man shows kindness toward everyone. Sven looked up to his father, respected him, loved him. He was everything a son could wish for. He had taught Sven all he knew. Sven would always remember how his father had defended him when Sven was teased and bullied by older boys in school, how he had stood up to not only the teacher, but also the father of one of the boys, who ran a factory in their small town. He had found the courage to face him because it had been *the right thing to do*. He had made it clear to Sven that the two of them had a special connection. The best times in the day were the ones they spent working together. Probably both of them assumed that this would continue for as long as they both lived. When Father became too old, Sven would take over the farm.

But then Sven had let his father down, disappointed him. Had kissed another man. Looking back, Sven wondered if it had been worth it. He hadn't had any strong feelings for the man in question—a former classmate who had left Vetlanda to work elsewhere, but had now returned to get married.

They met at a crayfish party hosted by mutual friends. Sven had noticed the man watching him; he hadn't dared to encourage the attention, didn't really know how he felt about this chap, even if the feeling was not unfamiliar. He had been attracted to other men before, and had tried to suppress his desire, but when this man kissed him, he had responded, curious to explore the possibilities.

They were caught. Sven's parents found out.

Shortly after that Sven joined the Foreign Legion in order to cleanse himself and get rid of those sick tendencies.

Perhaps Father would be proud of him now. Sven had fought at Narvik. His battalion had then ended up in Britain, and shortly afterward Charles de Gaulle had established the Free French forces. Sven and several of his fellow legionnaires decided that they would continue to fight for France's liberty, even if Pétain and his government collaborated with the Germans and allowed them to occupy half the country in order to maintain the ceasefire. Sven's brigadier had given him the task of delivering documents to the resistance movement, an incredibly dangerous job in occupied France.

So yes, he thought Father would be proud.

He had told himself that eventually, when he was done with the Legion and they were done with him, he would return home as a new man, a man worthy of Father's respect. They could go back to working together. Sven would take over the farm, maybe even meet a woman and start a family of his own.

Carry on living his life.

And now that fantasy about home, the red house with the white gables behind the huge oak tree in Vetlanda, everything he longed for, had become tangible—only it was happening here.

With the Latorre family.

◆ ◆ ◆

One morning when he was in the kitchen, he noted the morning light coming in through the narrow window, casting long, soft stripes over a single onion. Sven was struck by how beautiful the simple motif was. He noticed a pen and a piece of paper on the table, and couldn't help starting to sketch the contours of the onion.

When he heard footsteps, he stopped and turned around.

It was Juliette.

"Don't let me disturb you." She looked at what he had drawn.

"I'm so sorry, I didn't mean to waste paper, but . . ."

"Don't apologize, I understand. We all need an outlet for our creativity. And we need to breathe, in the middle of all this. It can't just be work, worry, and misery." She smiled. "We have to devote time to things we enjoy in order to survive. Did you do any drawing when you were in the Foreign Legion?"

Sven nodded. "I had drawing and painting equipment."

"But you didn't bring any of it with you?"

He shook his head. "If the Germans searched my things . . . well, it's important not to reveal too much. I didn't bring any personal possessions apart from my watch." Even the clothes he wore were not his own, but had been supplied by the resistance specifically for the journey.

"Wait a moment." Juliette disappeared into the hallway, and he heard her rummaging around in a closet in the bedroom. She returned with several sheets of paper and a pencil. "Use these for the time being, and I'll see if I can get ahold of some proper supplies for you."

"But this is perfect—are you sure you don't need it?"

"It's fine. We can get more."

"Thank you, Madame Latorre. Thank you so much." Sven thanked her over and over again. No one could understand how much this meant to him. Drawing and painting was his way of resting, of escaping those thoughts of his mother, his father, his sister. His sister's children, whom he adored and had had to leave. It also meant he could keep certain images at bay, things he had seen during the war. It gave his brain a respite from seeing beautiful Europe in flames, all the innocent civilians who had died, all the young men sent to the front as cannon fodder.

Like the physical work in the vineyard, this creative work would enable his brain to switch off for a while.

◆ ◆ ◆

One afternoon when Sven was taking a break from his labors, he sat down on a stone bench in the shade of the house so that he could see the huge oak he had admired on the day he arrived. He drew its magnificent network of branches, gnarled like an old woman's hands, the small leaves.

"That's beautiful."

The voice from behind Sven made him jump. His pencil slipped and drew a line straight across the sketch.

"Oh, I'm so sorry!" It was Mathieu.

Sven turned around. Mathieu was leaning over his shoulder, and they came face-to-face. They were only inches apart. For a second Sven held his breath. He saw something in Mathieu's eyes. Desire. Or was he mistaken?

Mathieu ran his fingers through his hair in the nonchalant way that made Sven go weak at the knees—in fact, it made every bone in his body soften like butter that has been left out too long.

"Should you be on this side of the vineyard?" Sven said after a moment. "What if someone sees you?"

"I've only come out for a little while." Mathieu shrugged and slipped one hand in his pocket. Sven caught a glimpse of the silver chain that Mathieu often took out and held. He wondered, not for the first time, what it might represent.

"You should be the one drawing our maps. You're far more talented than me."

"Maps?" Sven didn't know how he got the word out; he was still holding his breath because of Mathieu's proximity.

"Yes—they're part of our work for the resistance."

Until now, Sven hadn't been involved in this aspect of the family's life. He hadn't been allocated any tasks by either the resistance or the Legion since he arrived here. No doubt his superiors had only just found out that he'd been forced to stay on. If he was going to operate from here, he needed instructions, and he was still waiting for those.

In the kitchen that evening, by the light of a single candle, Hugo, Juliette, and Mathieu introduced him to their work.

"You're a member of the Legion, which means you're helping the resistance, so we know we can trust you," Hugo said with a certain formality. "We need all the help we can get."

They explained that they were currently helping a Jewish family in the neighboring village to flee. The family was heading to Switzerland. Mathieu showed him the map he was currently working on.

"We draw maps on the back of the wine labels, showing escape routes. Then we stick those labels on the bottles that are going to be delivered to other members of the resistance. You can't see the map until you've emptied the bottle, and the label falls to pieces, making the maps completely unreadable, if you try to remove it."

"How do you make sure the Germans don't get these particular bottles?"

"We provide them with plenty of wine—this one is the cheapest we produce, and they think it's not good enough for them," Hugo said with a snort. "They leave the table wine to the French. Yes, of course there's a risk—but it's a risk we're willing to take."

They sat up until late that night.

"Do you miss home?" Mathieu asked when Hugo and Juliette had gone to bed.

"Sometimes, yes. I miss my mom most of all. She . . ." Sven cleared his throat in order to hide the tremor in his voice, which always came when he spoke about his beloved mother. "She doesn't know where I am right now, and it's hard, not being able to speak to her or send a letter. She doesn't even know if I'm alive or dead."

"And your father?"

"My father . . ." He broke off. "He'd be proud of what I'm doing here. Proud of the fact that I'm helping you." Sven didn't look at Mathieu. He focused on correcting the line that showed the escape route along the road on the map. "It's so kind of your parents to let me stay." He wanted to shift the focus from his father—it was too hard to talk about what had happened.

Mathieu nodded. "They're good people. Thoughtful. And sending you away might mean sending you to your death."

"So the whole village thinks you're in Paris?" Sven asked eventually. He had been wondering why Mathieu's parents were so determined to hide him.

"Yes, Mom and Dad felt it was for the best." He took a deep breath as if he were about to say more, but at that moment the kitchen door opened.

"Are you two still up? Don't you think you should go to bed?" Juliette was standing there in her nightdress.

"Absolutely, Madame Latorre." Sven put down the pen and got to his feet.

Mathieu simply rolled his eyes. "Okay, Mom."

Sven went up to the guest room and lay down. What had Mathieu been going to say? And had Juliette been eavesdropping? Whatever was going on, it was clear that Juliette didn't want Mathieu to reveal the real reason why they were keeping him hidden. Had he committed some crime?

Even more difficult to stop thinking about was the sense that there was something *between* them. A kind of chemistry. He couldn't describe it in any other way. Was it just his imagination, or did Mathieu feel the same?

He suddenly sat up as a thought struck him. Had he infected Mathieu with his . . . with his *sickness*? Shame and guilt flooded his body.

Hugo and Juliette, the wonderful couple who had done nothing but help him, had taken him in—and in return he'd infected their son with that dreadful, disgusting sickness.

Those unnatural urges.

He had to get out of here, he couldn't stay.

But he had nowhere to go.

That didn't matter, he reasoned as he paced up and down. He couldn't stay here and drag Mathieu into depravity.

It was too late to go right now, so instead he went back to bed.

He barely slept a wink all night.

20

In order to get to their next meeting, Bente and Didrik hired bicycles and launched themselves into the Paris traffic.

They rode through her old district. The streets were so familiar to her, with patches of grass where early spring flowers bloomed. Somewhere beneath the earth, the summer flowers were beginning to grow, too, and Bente knew they would provide the neighborhood with glorious color in only a couple of months.

"I used to live along there," she said, nodding down one quiet road. The sand-colored stone block hadn't changed at all. "There's my apartment." She pointed up at a small French balcony made of black wrought iron.

The bakery across the street, the best in Paris to her mind, was still there.

"Would you like to try the most delicious croissant in the world?"

"Absolutely."

They parked their bikes and went inside. Everything was exactly the same as she remembered it. It was like stepping into an earlier part of her life.

They bought a whole bag of croissants and shared one on the way out. The buttery, flaky consistency was like something from a dream. She closed her eyes. Opened them and realized that Didrik was watching her.

She smiled. "Good, aren't they?"

He smiled back. "They certainly are." He reached out a hand. "You've got something just . . ." He wiped a crumb from her chin. The touch was gentle, but it burned her skin and set all her pleasure receptors on full alert.

Her phone rang. It was Elnaz.

"Oh God, our meeting!" Bente inhaled sharply.

"Are we late?"

She nodded. They jumped on their bikes and pedaled as fast as they could until they reached the sommelier school where Bente had once studied. They had arranged an appointment with the principal, who was the most knowledgeable person Bente knew when it came to wine. Elnaz was waiting for them outside.

"Where have you been?"

"We went to the antiquarian bookstore we mentioned," Bente explained.

"And I got to see where Bente used to live."

"And we bought croissants." Bente happily held up the bag.

Walking into the sommelier school was also like revisiting a part of her former life, but she had no time to reflect on her memories of how she had met Frederic and what life had been like back then—she had to focus on the reason why they were there. Didrik's presence, however, made that difficult. It was as if she could feel the nearness of his body even though he was sitting three feet away. That touch, that brief moment, had changed something between them.

The head of the school, unlike the school itself, was virtually unchanged—just an older version of the man she'd known. They told him they wanted some guidance on how to track down more information, and he had plenty of suggestions.

"Would it be possible to analyze the wine from a small sample?" Bente wondered.

"Unfortunately, that wouldn't help. You can't establish the origin based on chemistry alone. Have you checked the ship's log?"

"We have, but it's not very specific—it just states that the wine was sent from Bordeaux."

"So that leaves the packaging—the box and the bottle itself." He looked at the bottle, held it up to the light. Took off his glasses and went over to the window to examine it in daylight.

"I can't see anything unusual. Certain vineyards had a slightly different-shaped bottle or special glass, but this one is standard for both the region and the time. Apart from the brass plaque, that is. But I believe Frederic was looking into that for you?"

Bente nodded.

The man moved on to the box. "It might be worth taking a closer look at this—the kind of wood, the craftsmanship. I have one or two contacts who might be able to help us there."

"That would be fantastic," Bente said, feeling more optimistic now. "This has been very useful."

"Absolutely." Elnaz nodded.

◆ ◆ ◆

It was late afternoon by the time they emerged from the gloomy interior. Elnaz was in a hurry to get back to the hotel and jumped in a cab, while Bente and Didrik decided they felt like a walk. They returned their bikes to the nearest docking station and set off. They stopped at a small market on the way and bought peaches to eat as they strolled along.

They cut through the Jardin du Luxembourg, passing the boules courts. Didrik watched the men playing. "I've always dreamed of becoming one of those old men. Wearing a beret and playing boules in the evenings."

"I've never played boules in Paris. Or *pétanque*, as it's called here."

"Never?"

Bente shook her head. "I've only played at home, at the odd staff party. And with friends a couple of times in Rålis skate park."

"Then we need to try it." Didrik headed for the court.

Bente shrugged. "Sure, why not?" They were in no rush to get back.

"It's more fun if you play for something," he said, picking up a boule.

She laughed. "Okay—what shall we play for?"

"The loser has to reveal a secret."

"That's not fair—I'm not exactly an expert when it comes to boules."

"And I am?" He grinned.

"Well, I don't know, do I? You might already be halfway to becoming one of those old men. You might have picked it up secretly, perhaps meeting up with your little gang of old men in the suburbs every evening?"

"Maybe—you'll never know."

"So are you thinking along the lines of . . . truth or dare? Like we all played in high school?" She winked.

"Exactly." There was a flicker of uncertainty in his eyes behind those round glasses.

Had she gone too far? Was he embarrassed?

"Cool, let's do this," she said quickly before he could change his mind. Actually, she didn't know if this was going to be cool at all; revealing secrets wasn't her strong suit, but there was something about Didrik's playful spontaneity that drew her in.

Didrik threw the smallest ball, the jack, then the first large one, which landed in the sand with a thud.

"Your turn," he said, looking up at her.

The court was framed by trees in blossom, white flowers like little tufts of clouds against the sky. The shimmering pink glow of the setting sun made his brown eyes sparkle.

Her ball landed only inches from the jack. "Yes!" she shouted.

It was an even and enjoyable game, but no matter how hard Didrik tried, Bente was always the closest, and won in the end.

She was taken by surprise when he gave her a big hug. "Congratulations!"

He held her in his arms for a fraction too long, and she rested her head on his shoulder. His coat was rough against her cheek and smelled of him.

"Sorry!" He let go and took a step away from her. Smiled. That smile. The one that had possibly been written about even more than the Mona Lisa's smile, at least in Swedish magazines. She thought about a song whose lyrics said the singer wanted to drink a particular woman's smile. Slightly macabre, in Bente's opinion—but now she understood the sentiment. She wanted to *drink* that smile. She immediately began to wonder what it would taste like. As sweet as honey, a little salty. Maybe with a hint of peach.

"So," she said, clearing her throat and attempting to pull herself together. "Tell me a big secret."

"No problem." He thought for a moment. "I steal plastic folders from TV24's photocopying room."

She laughed. "I don't think that's much of a secret."

"Okay. In that case I've got something else." His eyes twinkled, as if he had something really juicy up his sleeve. Something naughty? She hoped he wasn't going to reveal something about Lovisa, about how the two of them had had a wild sex life. That would be embarrassing, and she would prefer not to know. She was pretty sure Didrik wasn't the kind of guy who would kiss and tell, though. Or was he?

"The reason why I said yes to this TV show was you."

Suddenly, it was as if the world was holding its breath again. Her heart was racing, and the expression in his eyes made her head spin as if she had knocked back a whole glass of *crémant*. She looked at him warily. Was he flirting with her?

"I've said too much." He shook his head. "This . . . My mom hates this side of me. Too talkative."

"I think it's fantastic." She meant it.

"Oh?"

She nodded. "It makes me feel special. The fact that you share things with me, it's wonderful. It's a great quality, being vulnerable and opening up to someone else."

"It's naive."

"I think it's a sign of trust. And it shows you're genuine." She wanted him to understand how valuable that side of him was.

He nodded slowly, never taking his eyes off her.

She didn't really want to break the mood, but she cleared her throat anyway and bent down. "Ready for another game?" She gathered up the boules, the dust whirling around her as she moved across the court.

They positioned themselves at the short end of the court. He touched her on several occasions: placed a hand on her arm when he laughed, squeezed her shoulder when she achieved a good throw. It was intoxicating. At the same time, a clear voice inside her head said, *This is not ideal.* Although this guy clearly appealed to her, the last thing she needed in her life was a man in crisis. He hadn't gotten over his wife; this flirtation was just a way of making him feel better. A rebound. Which Bente could usually tolerate, and might have this time if it wasn't for the fact that this attraction felt so different from her usual ones.

Plus a relationship between them could scuttle the show.

She couldn't help returning his touch, though. She wanted to be near him.

They played a second game, and once again she won.

She gave him a triumphant smile. "Another secret, please."

"So *who's* been playing boules in their spare time?" He laughed. She loved that laugh. Deep and clear. Just like his voice—he could sing tenor in a choir.

"Come on, what's your next secret?"

He smiled and thought for a moment, then the smile disappeared. He cleared his throat and ran his fingers through his thick, wavy hair.

"This might be too personal, I . . ." He broke off. "No, I can't."

"Surely that's the definition of a secret? Secrets are personal. Isn't that the whole point of a secret?"

"Maybe." He bit his lower lip. Oh God. She couldn't get enough of gazing at that mouth.

"Okay." He swallowed hard, looked at her. "I don't know if I can have kids."

The atmosphere changed in a heartbeat. She didn't know what to say, so she nodded and left him the space to say more, if he wanted to.

"We tried to have a baby for a long time. Several years. And when Lovisa met someone else, she got pregnant right away, so . . . What other conclusion can I draw?"

◆ ◆ ◆

Had he really just said that? It was the first time he'd put it into words, even in his own mind. Bente's green eyes were fixed on his.

At first he'd thought she wouldn't go along with this silly competition. She was so incredibly private, it had been a ruse to try to make her reveal something, get a little closer to her. Instead he had ended up babbling about himself. And now this—the words had just slipped out somehow. He hadn't intended to tell her, but in hindsight it felt good, as if he had *wanted* her to know.

Presumably this was a way of processing the whole thing. Lovisa was pregnant, by someone else. So the fault for it not happening for them must lie with Didrik.

He clapped his hands. "So shall we continue our Parisian adventure?"

Everything had gotten so serious, and now he wanted to leave it behind for a while. To try to have some fun—he didn't want Bente to feel she had to act the role of therapist.

She smiled. "Good idea. One thing I think you have to do in Paris is buy a bottle of Meursault and drink it on a hill with a fantastic view of the city."

"Meursault?" He smiled. The name was familiar—maybe he'd drunk it in the past, but he couldn't be sure.

"One of my absolute favorites. It's also a Chardonnay, but it's completely different from Chablis. It's from a different region of Burgundy and is stored in oak barrels, which gives it that buttery, rounded taste. American Chardonnay wines often try to imitate that style, and certain producers are pretty successful—I love American oak-stored Chardonnay." She grinned. "But you're going to sample the French version."

They wandered along to a small wine store she said she knew well. It didn't look like much from the outside, but Didrik assumed that they offered a wider selection than most of the state-owned liquor stores in Sweden.

As soon as he walked in, he saw that the shelves were crammed with bottles. No flashy signage, though—this place wasn't aimed at tourists; it was a store for those who were genuinely interested in wine. Bente browsed happily and eventually placed three reds in her basket.

"I'm going to take a couple of bottles home to Sweden—that's the best thing about traveling by train." Then she chose a Meursault from one of the refrigerators at the back of the store. She also bought two large, cheap wineglasses, which the assistant wrapped in tissue paper and placed in a shopping bag with the wine.

They took the Metro a distance, and then made their way up the hills in the Parc des Buttes-Chaumont. As they walked, Didrik noticed that Bente's bags appeared quite heavy. He offered to carry them.

"I was the one who was stupid enough to buy so many bottles," she said, allowing him to take them.

"As a thank-you, maybe you could let me share one of the bottles when we get back to Stockholm," he said, glancing at her.

Bente smiled, then nodded.

They had reached the top of the hill. From here they could see Sacré-Coeur and Montmartre, bathed in the soft glow of the setting sun.

"Are the skies always more pink in Paris?" Didrik asked as they sat down and contemplated the streaks of white clouds against the rosy background. The view really was magnificent.

"I don't know, maybe it's because of the pollution." Bente grinned. "But it sounds lovely—the idea that the skies are more pink in Paris."

She opened the bottle while he unwrapped the glasses. She poured and they toasted each other.

He felt relieved that his revelation about children hadn't completely ruined the mood. Sitting here with a view over the rooftops of Paris at sunset was something he would never forget.

He took a sip of his wine. "Delicious. So this is from the place called Meursault?"

She nodded. "It's quite exciting to drink this—several years ago they ripped out the white wine vines in Burgundy because it was believed their grapes made bad wine; the whites became considered out of fashion. Scandalous, when the green grapes in Burgundy are so fantastic. Today Burgundy wines are considered the best in the world! You can taste it—burnt butter, nuttiness, but also a hint of floral notes. And as smooth as silk. Completely different from Chablis."

Didrik had to agree. Very different. "Absolutely delicious."

"There's something seductive about it. I once heard someone say it makes a person think of white silk sheets, and they could well be right."

He nodded slowly and caught her gaze. There was a spark when their eyes met, and the soft sunlight was reflected in those green eyes.

"What made you fall for Frederic?" Didrik asked after a while.

Bente laughed. "I don't know—maybe the fact that I could be myself with him. And I learned a lot about myself. I discovered new things with him. Apart from that . . . I guess I was young. And you? What did you fall for?"

"His masculinity, that incredible French . . ." He grinned at Bente, who burst out laughing. "All joking aside . . ." He took a deep breath. "Lovisa made me feel secure, she was . . . everything I was looking for. But I also valued her passion for her subject—maybe I told you she's a lecturer in philosophy? I've always found it attractive when people are passionate about something. It could be work, music, some form of art, anything." He looked at her. "Even wine."

That hit home—she was clearly embarrassed.

"How did you two meet?"

"At a mutual friend's thesis disputation dinner. I was sitting next to Lovisa, and . . ."

He began to tell her the story, but after a while he realized he had been too long-winded again. Why would she be interested in hearing about his ex?

"Anyway," he said. *"Skål."*

His phone buzzed. *Shit.* He sighed.

"Lovisa?"

"Just Mom."

"Just Mom?" She raised her eyebrows inquiringly. "Take it if you want."

"She doesn't know we've split up, so I'm avoiding her calls right now."

A second later a message flashed on the screen.

I've just spoken to Lovisa. Are you getting a DIVORCE?

He sighed. Answered quickly:

Haven't got time to talk at the moment, but yes, we're getting a divorce.

For a few seconds nothing happened. He looked at Bente.

"Okay?" she said, just as his phone buzzed again.

You need to fix this, Didrik.

He shook his head and groaned. Of course in his mother's eyes it was *his* fault that Lovisa had met someone else.

"Are you all right?" Bente placed a hand on his arm, which made him jump. She immediately drew back. He cursed his reaction, but he had been unprepared.

"She's found out that Lovisa and I are divorcing, and she wants *me* to fix it. We're so far apart, Mom and I. We've never understood each other."

"How do you mean?"

"For one thing, she can't understand why I want to work in television when I could go all in and become a professor. Maybe it's my way of rebelling against her. My way of resisting."

"Why is she so set against TV?"

He shrugged. "I suppose it's her academic leanings. She doesn't believe it's good enough. But I also think . . ." He paused, sipped his wine. "I think she doesn't like it because her sister is Kristina Storm. Part of this is rooted in sibling rivalry."

"Seriously? Is Krissie your aunt?"

He nodded. "*Mm* . . . and Mom has never liked the fact that she's famous, though she would never admit it. So when I started appearing on TV, too, it felt to her like a slap in the face."

Bente smiled, but quickly grew serious again.

"So what does she say to you?"

"I suppose she imagines she's being subtle, but what she thinks is as clear as day to me. She makes little digs all the time, hidden criticisms." He knew that his mother's attitude was unhealthy, even though he didn't spend a lot of time thinking about it. But now, talking about it to someone on the outside, he realized just how true that realization was. Before this, he had always accepted that the fault lay with *him*, believing that his choice of career was controversial and unsatisfactory in some way.

Bente remained silent for a little while, as if she were letting what he had told her sink in. Then she took a big gulp of wine and looked at him. The sun had gone down now; all that remained was one last shimmering strip of light that made Bente's hair glow.

"I don't know your mother, and I'm not familiar with your relationship. But the fact that she criticizes you feels . . ." She broke off. Once again she placed her hand on his arm. This time he didn't jump, even though her touch seemed to be burning a hole in his sleeve.

"You explain history to viewers. A colleague in the wine bar told me that her nephew developed an interest in history thanks to you. He never liked school, but then they started watching *The Experts* together in the evenings, and he became really curious about the stories you brought to life. What you do is important—you teach anybody and everybody about the past, you reach out to them, and you do it brilliantly. You're popular, you're nice, everybody loves you. She's your mom, for God's sake, how can she criticize someone she loves like that . . ."

Her tone made it clear what she thought about his mother, which was something entirely new for Didrik. Lovisa and his mom had always been united in their dislike of his TV career, as if it were some kind of crazy whim. But somewhere deep down he had always considered it a cool thing to do.

"You're absolutely fucking fantastic, Didrik." Bente took her hand off his arm, looked him straight in the eye, and raised her glass in a toast.

Didrik knew he was appreciated, but to hear Bente talking about what he did as if it were something important, actually hearing someone praise him like that, made a wonderful warm glow spread through his body. He nodded slowly and took her hand.

"Thank you."

21

They stopped off at the hotel for a quick change of clothes before meeting Elnaz and setting off for the bistro where they had eaten the previous evening. On the way they passed people on the way home from work on Vespas or on foot—men and women in suits, carrying briefcases, and students heading for cheap bars.

All three of them ordered boeuf bourguignon accompanied by a robust red wine. Then they moved on to a wine bar where they drank a fruity red Beaujolais that Didrik loved.

When Bente went to the bar to order, Didrik accompanied her. His hand rested on her hip, which sent tingles all the way down her leg. She looked over at their table, where Elnaz sat watching them. She gave Elnaz a quick smile.

After that, they went to yet another wine bar. Bente would remember the next two hours only as a series of snapshots. They stayed in the bar's outdoor area, where people were drinking wine in the chilly spring evening. It was necessary to move closer to one another to be heard through the hum of conversation. The warmth of Didrik's body was tangible to Bente. And his smell. That fragrance.

They ended up in a club with low ceilings, where the *crémant* was served in tumblers. The sensation of bubbles on her tongue. Didrik moving even closer. A cover band playing nineties music. Bryan Adams's "Summer of '69," Oasis's "Wonderwall."

When they lost Elnaz in the crowd, his hands clasped both her hips. Standing with her back to him, feeling his warmth enveloping her whole body, she felt as if she were on fire. He drew her to him as they listened to the band. Sang along to "Lemon Tree" by Fools Garden.

Elnaz returned long enough to say she was going home with a tall blonde. When the band finished playing, Bente and Didrik left the club.

"They were surprisingly good," Didrik said.

"Really good. But then everything about the nineties was good."

Didrik considered this assertion. "You could be right. Movies and music—the best was created in the nineties."

Bente nodded in agreement.

"The movies are clever, well made, and brilliant, and . . . most important of all, good storytelling," he went on. "And maybe that's the magic of it all. It was a special time, I still remember when my brother and I first saw *The Usual Suspects*." He smiled and took her hand.

"We used to go to the movies once a month, always on a Friday." Bente smiled as the memories came rushing into her mind like a spring flood. Memories of Dad. Maybe it was the wine, the reminiscences about the nineties, or simply the effect Paris had on her. She felt melancholy and happy at the same time.

"Fantastic—the whole family?"

"Yes. I loved our movie Fridays. But most of all I loved Saturday afternoons with my dad in the kitchen. While he cooked dinner, he danced and sang along to Springsteen, always with a glass of red wine in his hand." The memory made her smile. "I danced, too, and helped out. Mom would join us later. Sometimes we had people over, sometimes it was just us."

She fell silent. Realized what she was doing. She didn't usually babble about her father like this.

When Didrik had asked about him before, she had answered with practiced ease, said what she always said so that the first question wouldn't lead to more. Now the words were bubbling out of her. At least she had stopped herself in time. It wasn't that she couldn't talk about her father. It was simply that she didn't want to go into everything with just anyone. Did Didrik even want to hear her story? He was on a work trip, he was trying to get over his wife. Yes, there was chemistry between the two of them, but that didn't mean he wanted to listen to Bente's life story.

"So what's your favorite nineties movie? Is it *The Usual Suspects*?" she said in an attempt to change the subject.

"It's a strong candidate, obviously. But nothing can match a really good American teen movie. *American Pie*, *Dazed and Confused*. Those were fantastic."

"American teen movies . . ."

He squeezed her hand and she stopped.

"There's just something about those adolescent emotions, those carefree American teenagers," Didrik said, turning to face her.

Maybe it was the reference to tumultuous teenage feelings, or nostalgia for the nineties, but something had made the air between them vibrate. When he took a step closer, she drew him to her and kissed him. His lips were soft, his tongue cautious as it sought hers. A shiver ran through her entire body when the tips of their tongues met. Although she had dreamed of and wondered about his kisses, she hadn't been prepared for what it would actually be like. He really did taste of peaches—but also of cherries, from the wine. And honey and a hint of saltiness.

He kissed her hungrily, much more intensely than she had imagined, and it was impossible not to respond to that hunger.

They were standing by a doorway, and even though she knew she shouldn't—she had to stop now, they were colleagues, he had to get over his wife—she pulled him into the opening. Pushed him up against the wall and kissed him even harder.

He was soft, smooth, warm. Totally, totally glorious, and it made her wonder why she had wasted her kisses on other men all her life, when Didrik Holgersson had existed all along.

The door opened, a young girl came out, and they quickly stepped apart.

"God, I feel like a character in one of those teen movies—caught in the act," Bente said, allowing the girl to pass. The girl looked horrified, which made them both burst out laughing, and Bente kissed him again, kissed him while he was laughing.

She drank his smile. And she wanted more.

He pulled her along with him in the direction of the hotel, and soon they were in the foyer. He was still holding her hand. They half ran up the stairs, with him leading the way, and Bente had barely enough time to tell herself again that this was a bad idea. He was just about to divorce, he was going through a breakup. And she . . . She was supposed to be professional, making a serious TV show. She couldn't jump into bed with her cohost.

And yet: It wasn't forbidden. Definitely not. They were two adults, free to do exactly what they wanted.

At the top of the stairs he turned to her. The niceness, the humor, had gone from that much-loved, cheerful expression. Instead his eyes were burning. With desire. And she threw herself into his arms. They carried on making out as they stumbled toward the room. At that moment she wasn't sure whose room it was, but one of them found a pass key, and Didrik threw open the door.

"I've wanted to kiss you ever since you showed up at my office," he murmured in her ear.

"I've wanted to kiss you ever since I saw you at Rendezvous with Elnaz."

"Have you now?" he whispered in her ear. Then he looked at her again, and she knew that he wanted her, knew that she wanted him in return, their shared desire heightened by what they saw reflected in each other's eyes. Bente knew what he felt, because she felt exactly the same.

She let her leather jacket slide down her arms and onto the floor. Then she slipped her hands inside the collar of his coat, let her fingers play with those thick curls. *Oh God.* Continued inside the coat. The tweed fabric was rough, but his cotton shirt was smooth to the touch.

His shoulders were so warm. She caressed his cheek, felt the stubble rasp beneath her fingers.

His hand was on the base of her spine. The other hand crept into her hair and took a firm grip, which sent a shiver right through her body. She stroked his shoulders, broad and solid beneath the layers of neatly ironed, respectable clothes.

She so wanted to rip off those clothes. She just wanted Didrik, exactly as he was, nothing more. She could be the woman he used to get over his wife—right now she didn't care what that might lead to: wild emotions, unrequited love. None of it mattered.

She just wanted him.

She took off his coat, then his jacket, kissing him all the while, deeply and intensely, playing with his tongue. She couldn't get enough of his kisses, and yet she wanted so much more.

Quickly she unbuttoned his shirt and slipped it off.

A shirtless Didrik Holgersson was better than she could ever have imagined. She wanted to touch his body, and she did exactly that, stroked and felt him. She was out of control. His skin was burning.

He pulled down her dress, kissed her shoulder, up along her throat, and she shuddered.

He edged her over to the bed with an unexpected briskness. Quickly removed her dress and gazed at her with a look in his eyes that made her inhale sharply with pleasure.

She propped herself up on her elbows so that she could take off his pants and underpants while he eased her out of her panties.

He caressed the inside of her thigh, gently with one finger, making her whimper impatiently. He continued with his hand, higher and higher, and she whimpered again. Grabbed his shoulders, pulled him down, wanted to feel his weight on her. Meanwhile, that hand was still working, stroking her labia, one finger finding its way to her clitoris, moving in circles, gentle but determined.

She stroked him in turn, loving how hard he was. She paused, dug a condom out of her purse.

He carried on caressing her, and just as she was about to come, he pushed into her. She tried to hold back, suppressed the first wave that tried to take over her body and focused on him, touching him, the back of his neck, his back, his weight on her.

When she could tell that he was close, she let go. Allowed that wonderful wave of pleasure to surge through her body as he thrust harder and harder.

And there it was again, that fantastic pleasure, as she looked up at him through half-closed eyes.

22

When Bente woke up the following morning, her head was pounding and she had a weird feeling in her body. Warm yet slightly nauseous, as if yesterday's alcohol was overheating her blood. She rarely drank so much that she finished up with a hangover; she loved wine too much to sabotage the experience like that. But yesterday she had . . .

At that moment she remembered, and suddenly became aware of something else. Someone was lying next to her, and she had a memory of something wonderful: that warm, relaxed feeling that came only from having sex. She turned her head to see Didrik moving slowly. Seeing his tousled hair, his lips swollen from all the kissing, the stubble that had grown even darker during the night, caused a sense of tenderness within her to wrestle with much more earthy, swirling emotions.

A second later he opened his eyes.

Her heart was racing. She wanted to kiss him, snuggle up close beside him, cancel the train home, stay in this hotel room with him for the rest of the week.

This was not good.

She reminded herself that he'd only needed someone in order to get over his ex. She had to get out of here, save them both from this uncomfortable situation.

But Didrik acted first, pulling her close with complete confidence, as if doing so were the most obvious move.

She had no intention of letting herself be fooled. He was only doing this because he regarded himself as a gentleman. She had to be professional. She sat up. Pulled the sheet over her body.

"Are you okay? Does this feel . . . wrong?" Didrik asked hesitantly.

"Not wrong, but . . ." She pulled the sheet right up to her chin, wanting to conceal herself. "I don't think this was wrong, or bad or anything, it's just that we work together and you're . . . in the middle of a divorce."

"Yes."

"It's not ideal." She gathered her thoughts. She wanted to be honest, these few days had been . . . fabulous. No, that was too weak a word. These few days had been pure magic. "I really like you, and these few days have been . . . fantastic. But . . ." She sighed. "We're going to be working together, I don't know if this is such a good idea, and besides . . ." She shuffled over to the edge of the bed. The window was open, the curtains were fluttering in the breeze, and the scent of lavender from the pots in the courtyard was drifting into the room. "Besides, you're still married . . ." Didrik tried to protest. She raised a hand to stop him, went on: " . . . and I assume you'll agree when I say it's best if we don't continue with this. We're at different . . . stages in our lives."

Bente stood up and felt Didrik reach for her. She wrapped the sheet around her, leaving him completely naked. She quickly turned around, muttered an apology as she threw the sheet back at him, and put on her panties and her dress as fast as possible.

"So we just forget this, okay?" She shook out her hair, slipped on her shoes.

He watched her thoughtfully as she gathered up her things and scurried out into the corridor, letting the door close behind her.

Back in her own room, she threw herself on the bed.

What had just happened? What was that all about? What the hell had she done? Didrik was a celebrity, for fuck's sake, a much-loved TV star. Why on earth would he want to be with her? To get over his wife, yes, that was definitely it. During the night it had felt perfectly okay; she had wanted to go to bed with him, and it had been fantastic. Better than she could ever have dreamed of. But . . .

Didrik Holgersson. A man like him didn't fall in love with someone like her. He was unattainable. Everyone loved him, and he had everything. She, on the other hand, had a slightly messy life, lived with her mother and sister, and harbored pathetic aspirations about returning to TV.

Why had she gone to his room? Why had she slept with him when she knew it could ruin so much?

Because he had aroused something within her, it was that simple, and she had been unable to resist. They could talk to each other. He was interesting, and interested in her. She felt seen when she was with him. And he was such a decent person. More than that, she felt the tingle. And when you felt the tingle, a one-night stand was no good, because sex led to deeper feelings.

She rolled over, buried her face in the pillow, and screamed. Screamed out her anguish over the night, and over the fact that she had walked out, leaving him there. Screamed out her frustration.

Because Didrik was the only man she really wanted.

◆ ◆ ◆

After a while she managed to summon up enough energy to take a shower and get changed. They had been given permission to take the wine bottle back to Sweden so they could use it for filming and for further research, so she wrapped the wooden box that held it in newspaper and placed it in her suitcase, protected by her clothes.

Afterward, she sat on the balcony for a few minutes, inhaling her last breaths of Paris before meeting up with Elnaz and Didrik outside the hotel. Didrik arrived at the last second, hurrying across from the other side of the street.

Bente felt as if an electric shock passed through her body when she saw him.

"I just had to do something," he said, before dashing into reception to retrieve his suitcase. When he came back, he had taken the plastic folder with all the travel arrangements out of his briefcase and was double-checking the train's departure platform. Always in control.

Maybe it was that air of safety and security that she found so frightening? Even now, when he was in the middle of a crisis, he appeared totally secure. If anything, this trip had recruited Bente into Didrik's huge fan club.

She now got why everybody loved him. People enjoyed his company, that unshakable calmness, but also the fact that he listened with such interest. He was curious about her. She reflected on her answer to his question about Frederic and why she had fallen for him. She had been able to be herself with Didrik; she didn't need to pretend when she was with him.

But that also meant that he had just let her be.

It occurred to her that he hadn't really asked questions about her background, or seemed to wonder about who she was and how she operated. Henrik Eklund, her ex, had wanted to get to know her, had wanted to know everything about her, and she had told him about her father and what had really happened; it would have been odd not to share that with her boyfriend. But she had given Henrik the simple version and thereafter avoided the subject. She didn't really know why she acted that way.

Didrik had shown interest in her, but no good could come of imagining she was unique in that respect; no doubt he was the kind of guy who was generally interested in people. Thank goodness she hadn't opened up too much, or she would have scared him off. That was why it was probably best that they didn't continue, best that whatever this might have been was finished now.

Before things got too complicated.

◆ ◆ ◆

They woke up in Hamburg the following morning and ate breakfast in the restaurant car as the outskirts of the city swished by.

Bente had just sat down with a cup of coffee when she received a message from the head of her former sommelier school.

> Based on the kind of wood and the craftsmanship, the box was probably made in Deux-Sèvres in western France, near Bordeaux. Unfortunately we can't find any more information.

She looked up at her companions with a resigned expression, and passed on the message.

"So nothing to link the bottle to a specific vineyard," she concluded, "or even a specific village in Bordeaux."

"That's a shame," Elnaz said. "We really do need some kind of breakthrough." She spread butter on her toast. "I've kept the production company and Don, the exec producer with TV24, updated during our trip, and . . . well, they're not too impressed with what we've found out."

Bente held her breath.

"I mean, *I* believe in this," Elnaz said, "and I *know* it would make an interesting program, even if we can't get to the whole truth about the bottle. And the company and TV24 still want to make the show."

Bente exhaled.

"But with a slightly different angle. A little more personal."

"Personal? In what way?"

Elnaz gazed steadily at Bente as she answered, with some hesitation in her voice. "More focus on the two of you. Didrik is incredibly popular, everyone wants to know more about him, and everyone is . . . curious about you." She spoke slowly, as if she were choosing her words with care.

What did that mean?

"I don't really understand," Didrik said.

"Well, think more *Stars at the Castle* and *So Much Better*," Elnaz said, citing two famous Swedish reality programs: one featuring celebrities who live together for five days, discussing their lives and careers; the other starring musicians who stay together at a hotel, reinterpreting each other's songs. "You chat to each other during your journey, get to know each other . . ."

Bente couldn't suppress a small smile. If Elnaz only knew. She didn't dare look at Didrik.

". . . through the wine, the history, the food. Maybe you invite some guests," Elnaz continued. "Other well-known personalities who have some kind of food or wine profile. I haven't quite thought it through, but it was an option I suggested to TV24 when they initially were hesitating, and they asked us to keep it in mind. A different angle. We've been discussing that option, and I've found some fabulous locations in Paris. It could be terrific—the two of you have amazing chemistry."

Didrik laughed. Bente turned to him and saw that he was looking out of the window. She turned to Elnaz again.

"So *you* suggested this?"

"Not exactly, I was just giving them an alternative option." She sighed and took a big gulp of her coffee. Put on her sunglasses to protect her eyes from the rays of the low sun. "Or would you prefer they cancel the whole show?" Her tone was neither harsh nor unpleasant, simply matter-of-fact. "I've put together everything we've got, and they still think it's too thin."

Bente gave a cautious nod but didn't say anything.

"I assume we can think it over," Didrik said, giving Bente a meaningful look.

She gazed out of the window. Forest. The forest had taken over from the built-up suburbs.

Yes, she could probably go along with Elnaz's suggestion, but she still wanted to tell the story of the bottle; it had gotten hold of her. It *meant* something. But if there was nothing to tell, what would she do then? Was it worth making a TV show she didn't believe in at all, and wouldn't feel comfortable with? Could that show lead to other possibilities, the chance of making one in the future with a concept she really did care about?

This was her opportunity to get back into the world of TV.

So maybe she should just grab it with both hands.

23

1944

A month went by, it was now the middle of summer, and Sven was still at the vineyard. Ever since the Allies had landed at Normandy, the Germans had been on high alert.

It was too dangerous to leave now.

One morning he was out pruning the vines just as Hugo had shown him. The sun was rising slowly, appearing as a burning hemisphere on the horizon as Sven moved along the rows, working with a knife that was getting pretty blunt. The Germans had only visited a couple of times since they first asked why he was staying with the family. These days they didn't bother with him at all, but because they were more nervous than before, and unfortunately also more aggressive, there was a risk that he would be caught if he left. Questions would be asked, papers checked, and he might be arrested if they had even the slightest suspicion about him. The more time went by, the more he felt torn between his desire to return to the Legion and his preference to stay here.

He had recently extended his contract by another five years. A legionnaire was not allowed to break his contract early, and in times of war, desertion was particularly serious. Maybe the Legion already regarded him as a deserter. The thought was terrifying. He had heard tales of penal servitude on Devil's Island, even rumors of execution. Whatever the truth of those stories, desertion was unthinkable.

Once the war was over—he believed that France would be liberated—he would have to go back. He couldn't live with Hugo and Juliette forever, and he felt like a traitor when he realized how grateful he was that he had been allowed to stay at the vineyard for so long.

Mathieu came out, crossed the lawn, and helped Sven for a while before taking a break and sitting down among the vines. "'When a vine is standing firm with its feet in gravel and can see the Gironde estuary, it gives its best wine.'" Mathieu gazed out across the field.

Sven looked at him inquiringly.

"It's a saying that describes where the Cabernet Sauvignon grape grows at its best. We can *almost* see the estuary from here, it's just beyond the forest. That's why our wine is so good." Mathieu smiled.

Sven had tasted the wine that the Germans allowed the producers to keep. He had enjoyed it, but he doubted he would be able to tell the difference between that and a more sophisticated wine. That was why he loved the division of labor. He completed the practical tasks, tending the vines and the earth under Hugo's supervision, and this gave Hugo more time to focus on the production itself, along with Juliette and Mathieu. Together they worked on the blends—deciding when the grapes were ready to harvest, how long they should be stored in oak barrels, how long the bottles should be stored—and made sure the vines were nurtured so the grapes were at their happiest.

"Thousands of years ago, sandy gravel was washed down here from the Pyrenees by the rivers Garonne and Dordogne, and it formed these fields." Mathieu nodded toward the vines, then picked up a handful of the gravelly soil and let it trickle through his fingers. "The drainage is fantastic. The water drains away quickly, leaving the earth warm and dry." When he talked like this, it was like beautiful music to Sven's ears. He loved it when Mathieu told him about his precious Médoc region and about his wine.

They continued on along the rows, working methodically. At times like this, Sven existed entirely in the present, focusing only on the vines that needed his care.

No, that wasn't entirely true. There was one other thing—he couldn't stop thinking about Mathieu, couldn't stop watching the young man's slender figure as he moved ahead of Sven. Spending time with Mathieu made life at the vineyard better, even if Sven's feelings about him were conflicted.

Mathieu had an effect on him. His carefree attitude made Sven's heart lighter. Sven was learning to develop a more positive view of life, and also to take pleasure in the moments he was able to enjoy—like these conversations about grapes and the history of Bordeaux. They also discussed culture and literature. Sven wasn't used to talking about books, or reading for enjoyment. Mathieu had taught him to do that, to live in the moment. To find pleasure in a book, but also in simple things like the feel of the morning sun's first rays caressing his face, or the afternoon breeze cool on his skin after a hard and sweaty task.

As a result, now when Sven was working, he focused on what he was doing, just as before, but he was also able to contemplate nature's simple beauty. Things like the dewdrops on the green leaves of the vines, sparkling in the morning sun. He mustn't think about the attraction he felt for the man beside him. Quite the reverse. Suppress, suppress, suppress. Push aside. That was the only thing that helped.

Never give in.

◆ ◆ ◆

That afternoon Sven sat down to do some more drawing. As soon as he had the opportunity, he took out his pad and the pencils Juliette had managed to acquire for him. He realized this was the only time of day when he didn't think about Mathieu; drawing absorbed all his senses. He had continued to draw the oak; this particular sketch was taking longer than the rest, and he was sitting by the wall concentrating hard when Mathieu appeared in front of him. Sven stopped and looked up.

He wanted to draw Mathieu.

He was the most beautiful man Sven had ever seen. There were imperfections, certainly—his eyes were slightly too large, his nose wasn't completely straight—but this gave him character. It was his aura, though, that really captivated Sven. There was something dreamy about him—that tousled hair, the gangly body. The melancholy in his eyes. And yet he could be so carefree, laughing and telling his stories. Sven wanted to capture all of that.

He blinked a few times, didn't want to stare. "Should you really be out here?"

Mathieu didn't answer, but looked at the pad instead. "So you're still drawing the oak?"

Sven nodded.

"You miss home."

Sven had told him about the oak tree back home, and the fact that it resembled the one at the vineyard.

"I don't know, but I do think about my family a lot. Especially my mother. We've written letters to each other the whole time I've been in the Legion. I'm afraid she'll be worried about me." He knew she was worried about him. Sven and his father had always had a special bond, but it was Mom who had given him and his sister all her love. Several people in the village said that she spoiled the two of them with her hugs and kisses, but Mom said that was nonsense, and always hugged them a little too tightly for a little too long. Even after they were grown up, she had still been there with those hugs. He missed her and her unconditional love so much. Somehow it had become even stronger after Sven and the other man had been exposed.

Did she think he was dead? His heart broke at the thought of it, of her anxiety.

"You could send her a message." Mathieu's eyes were sparkling.

"It's impossible, the Germans check everything."

"I don't mean a letter, I mean a bottle of wine. With a message only she will understand." Mathieu paced up and down, thinking. "Does she know you draw?"

Sven nodded. "I've drawn and painted lots of things for her over the years."

"Okay. Well, we have brass plaques, round plaques that are embedded in the glass bottles for our finest wines. You can etch the oak onto the plaque, and when she sees it, she'll know it's from you. Maybe you can send a letter, too, if we make a box with a secret compartment? And if she opens the box, she'll find the letter." He walked around in circles and raised his arms in the air as he spoke, as if they were making epic plans, which made Sven smile.

"I don't know if I dare write too much in a letter in case the box is confiscated and the Germans go through it. That could put us all in danger. If they find out I'm a legionnaire and I'm here . . ."

"You're right. But how about a note with a short message telling her to open the bottle? We can put something inside the cork, maybe an address?" Mathieu's face had lit up with excitement. He sank down on the bench next to Sven and took his hands. "She'll realize you're alive."

Sven's eyes filled with tears. His beloved mother. Quickly he blinked away the moisture. What would Mathieu think of him? A man crying!

"I'll set aside a brass plaque." Mathieu got to his feet, ready to hurry away and make a start on the project right now. Sven stood up, too, and stopped him, placed a hand on his arm.

"Thank you. For helping me."

"It's not a problem—I can see that you miss your family. I can see how much it means to you. I've lost a great deal, but at least I still have my family." Mathieu looked at him for a long time. Placed his own hand on Sven's. This time his touch burned.

After Mathieu had gone, Sven sat down again, thinking over what had happened. He had expected Mathieu to say that he was returning the favor because Sven was working in the vineyard, but in fact he wanted to help Sven contact his family because he *cared about him*. Then there was the touch, the look.

The whole thing took Sven's breath away.

No. He couldn't read anything into this. Just because Sven suffered from this . . . affliction, it didn't mean that Mathieu suffered the same urges. Sven was seeing something that wasn't there.

After a while he went back to the vines, driving himself hard in order to numb his feelings. He mustn't act on his impulses. The emotions that had blossomed recently simply proved that he had to get back to the Legion soon to cleanse himself once more.

He couldn't stay here for much longer.

◆ ◆ ◆

It was in the evenings when they were drawing the maps that Mathieu got to know Sven better. Sven would tell stories about his nieces that made Mathieu laugh so loudly that on at least one occasion, his mother ran into the kitchen, thinking that someone was hurt.

In the afternoons Sven always took his break on the stone bench in the shade, sketching away while Mathieu read aloud. Sven listened, and would pause his drawing to discuss the passages. Mathieu loved having someone to talk to like this, because neither of his parents had any interest in literature.

Mathieu always tried to be around when Sven was drawing. He liked to watch him, to see the way the muscles in his wrist moved as he swept his hand across the paper.

In the evenings, as they worked in the candlelight, Mathieu tried to sit close to him. He wanted to feel Sven's proximity, to inhale the smell of him, yet at the same time he was careful not to make his approach too quickly. He found it difficult to interpret Sven's intentions, and didn't want to scare him off.

He didn't want to destroy their friendship.

And yet he had seen the way Sven looked at him, gazed at him. But then it was as if he always caught himself, turning away or pretending to be busy with something else.

One evening after they had finished a map, Sven continued working on the brass plaque. He completed the trunk of the oak tree and held the plaque up for Mathieu to see.

"What do you think?"

Mathieu took a step nearer. He was only a couple of inches away from Sven. He took his hand and pulled it closer even though he could see perfectly well. Ran his thumb over the plaque to remove the tiny brass shavings, caressed Sven's finger, saw Sven's entire body tense at his touch. He seemed to be holding his breath.

Mathieu continued, gently moving his thumb along Sven's hand, then his forearm, over the tiny blond sun-bleached hairs. Over the fabric of his shirt on his upper arm, along his throat. He could feel Sven's pulse beating fast beneath the warm skin. *Oh God.* Mathieu had to fight hard not to throw himself at Sven.

But Sven still stood there, holding out the plaque, as if he had been turned to stone.

Mathieu kept going, stroking Sven's cheek. Then he placed his other fingers on Sven's cheek and drew Sven toward him, closing the distance between them. Kissed him cautiously, hesitantly.

Sven didn't recoil, but neither did he press his body against Mathieu's. He simply stood there, parted his lips, and allowed Mathieu to insert the tip of his tongue. After a while he responded, meeting Mathieu's tongue with his own.

It was a slow, tentative kiss.

A second later Sven dropped the plaque on the floor. The thin metal made a loud clang, as if a glass had fallen onto the hard stone. He made an initial attempt to tidy up everything on the table, then left it and hurried toward the door.

"Sven, you don't have to go!"

But Sven ran up to his room without a word.

Mathieu understood that Sven needed to process what had happened.

He let him go.

24

Over the next two weeks, Bente and Didrik communicated only by email. She always felt a little rush of excitement when she saw his name in her inbox. *This is about work, Bente,* she had to remind herself, which became more than obvious when the messages contained nothing but dry references to something Didrik had recently read that might help them in their research. Still, she always managed to find an excuse to reach out and ask questions. Like the time she got the list of vineyards from Frederic—the vineyards that had used brass plaques during the first half of the twentieth century. She didn't recognize any of the names, but forwarded the list to Didrik.

> We could visit these vineyards in Bordeaux and do some more research.

Did that sound like an invitation? Yes. But they were working together, so it was a work-related invitation.

> Interesting!

That was the response she got, nothing more.

Next she asked about the diary Didrik had ordered from the antiquarian bookstore, and when he told her that it had arrived but he hadn't had time to read it yet, she suddenly became convinced that they must read it as soon as possible, because it might contain interesting information.

> Can I come and pick it up tomorrow?
> Absolutely. I'm not in the office tomorrow, but I'll leave it outside the door.

He added the address of the office in Gärdet. So he wasn't going to be there. Okay. She couldn't say she wasn't coming now, even if it no longer seemed quite so important to go through the diary immediately. She could easily have waited a few days.

> Great. I'll come by around ten.

Why had she written that? Did it seem too pushy?

Oh well, at least he knew the book wouldn't be sitting outside his office all day.

And still she found herself standing at the door of the office with her heart pounding the following day. She picked up the shiny green paper bag on the ground. Maybe he would appear?

She waited a few minutes until the whole thing felt seriously pathetic. *He isn't here.* Slowly she wandered down the stairs and out into the spring sunshine without having seen any sign of Didrik.

She set off for home, telling herself yet again that what had happened was just a one-time event, prompted by the seductive atmosphere of Paris, too much wine . . . and their mutual attraction, of course. She had to admit that Didrik Holgersson going through a crisis was one of the sexiest things she had ever experienced.

She'd had sex with a hot guy; it was a one-night stand. It was no more complicated than that. She just had to forget that he was also kind, understanding, interested in her as a person, and had a passion for history that made her love talking to him.

When she got home, an email from Elnaz was waiting for her. Bente had written asking for more details about the change of angle Elnaz was suggesting, as well as updating her on the research they had done so far.

> Had a meeting with TV24 and just wanted to keep you both in the loop. Because we still don't have any information about the bottle, they don't think the story is strong enough.

Bente felt a surge of panic. She had to come up with something.

Her mother and sister were going to visit Lydia and Uno the following week; Uno ran the infrastructure for Hanna's company remotely, and they needed to update the platform; plus changes of environment apparently did wonders for Hanna's technical creativity. Mom was taking the opportunity to go with her so she could gossip and hang out with Lydia.

An excellent chance for Bente to invite everyone over. Show some initiative.

If she was going to realize her vision, she had to take control of the discussion surrounding the show. She had to *own* it. The whole thing was slipping out of her grasp, and she had to grab it back. If she plied Don with delicious food and fine wines, maybe she would be able to convince both him and Elnaz that her format was the right way to go, assure them that they would be able to track down more information.

That very evening she sent out an invitation—short notice, but everyone said yes.

Including Didrik, albeit with a brief *Cool! I'll be there.*

◆ ◆ ◆

On the day of the dinner, she went shopping, brought up some wines she selected from the storage unit in the cellar, and got back to the apartment with plenty of time to spare. She put down the large shopping bags and the rucksack containing the wine and unlocked the door. As she opened it, she heard voices. Her heart sank. Hadn't they left yet? Had she misunderstood?

Hanna wandered into the hallway carrying her laptop, on her way to her enormous home office located next to the living room.

"What are you doing here?" Bente asked, dropping all her bags on the floor.

"Excuse me, I live here," Hanna said without looking up.

"But I thought you were going away?"

"Do I have to explain why I'm in my own home at a particular time?" Hanna glanced at her from beneath her dark bangs.

"Of course not, it's just that I . . ."

At that moment her mother appeared in the hallway and started rummaging through the bags. She found the packet of chips and tore it open.

Goodbye to snacks with the predinner drinks.

Bente sighed. "I've invited people over for dinner."

"How lovely! We can come too." Mom grabbed a handful of chips and stuffed them into her mouth. "Uno has a broken heart. Mirja has left him, so we all thought it would be better if he came to the city."

"Bente, is that you?" Aunt Lydia's voice came from the bathroom, and the door flew open. "Darling Bente!" Lydia emerged in a cloud of her signature perfume, Shalimar by Guerlain. She flung her arms wide and embraced Bente.

Bente returned the hug. The scent would cling to her clothes, it always did when she encountered Lydia. She liked it; it felt as if something of her aunt lingered after they had said goodbye. Bente was usually pleased to see Lydia—but not today.

Uno joined them, also carrying a laptop. "Hi, Bente," he said listlessly. He gave her a quick hug and then went into the kitchen. Bente took off her trench coat, and Lydia helped her with the bags. Uno was making himself a coffee.

"Can't you eat out?" Bente looked pleadingly at her mother, then Lydia. "Didrik and the producers are coming here." Instantly she knew she'd made a big mistake.

Lydia inhaled sharply. "Didrik? As in Didrik Holgersson?"

When Bente first started working in TV, Lydia would call her on a daily basis wanting to know which celebrities she had met or seen. Now that Bente thought of it, that had continued throughout her TV career. No one had been more upset and disappointed over her breakup with the TV baker Henrik Eklund than Lydia; she had loved having him at family dinners. Her pleasure was genuine, she had really liked him, and she had also loved having a real star in the family.

"What fun—in that case I think we'll eat here. But we'll stay in the background," Bente's mother said with a wink. She held up her empty cocktail glass and looked meaningfully at Hanna, who immediately put down her laptop and turned her attention to the various bottles of spirits on the counter.

If there was one thing Bente's family was incapable of, it was staying in the background.

She sighed. "I don't know if I've got enough food for all of you," she said, hoping they would take the hint.

"I can run down and do some shopping," Lydia offered. "What do you need?"

Bente realized she had no choice.

While Lydia hurried off to the grocery store, Bente unpacked the bags. Hanna headed into her office, where Uno was now busy tapping away on his computer. It was six o'clock, but they were perfectly capable of working night and day. Mom sank down on the sofa with the chips, Candy Crush on her phone, and the cocktail Hanna had mixed for her.

Bente opened a bottle of Merlot, put on some soft jazz, unpacked the rest of the wine, and lit the candles in the holders around the kitchen.

Lydia soon returned.

"So tell me more about your new show. Agneta mentioned a few things, but . . ." Lydia glanced over her shoulder and leaned closer to

Bente. "She doesn't seem to think this TV business is a good idea, but I like it. As long as it makes *you* happy, sweetheart." Lydia's expression was serious as she looked at her niece. Her calm voice struck a chord with Bente, and she had to clear her throat before she answered.

"I'm happy." She smiled and poured Lydia a glass of wine.

She was planning to serve hash browns with fish roe as a starter, followed by oven-roasted portobello mushrooms with a potato bake and a red wine sauce. She had heard from Elnaz that ever since Don had started playing padel, he had become a little more careful about what he ate, and was avoiding meat these days. So she was going vegetarian, with the exception of the roe. Elnaz would eat anything, and thanks to their trip to Paris, Bente knew that Didrik liked most foods. She had loved having dinner with him; he always studied the menu with interest and curiosity, and was keen to try something different whenever he had the opportunity. Maybe it was his curiosity that had attracted him to history in the first place? The chance to make discoveries, learn something new.

She pushed aside thoughts of him and focused on dinner.

Hanna and Uno soon came over to help. Uno made a salad while Hanna opened the windows to air the room. A chilly spring breeze carried in the smells of the city—frying food from the stall down on the corner, budding trees, earth and grass that had just started to grow.

After a while her mother laboriously got to her feet and came to lend a hand too. She set the table while balancing her Manhattan between her thumb and forefinger. The air was filled with anticipation and excitement. Lydia was thrilled at the prospect of meeting a celebrity, Hanna was pumped over the major technical update they had just completed and were due to launch the following week, and Mom always looked forward to a lovely dinner. Bente herself was nervous, but also eager to discuss the format of the show with her guests. Only Uno was somewhat subdued, because Mirja wasn't answering his calls.

Fifteen minutes before her guests were due to arrive, Bente slipped away to freshen up. She changed into a long dress but remained barefoot.

She shook her hair loose but didn't run the comb through—it was tidy enough for a dinner at home. She put on some red lipstick. Was she taking a little extra care? No, she was just making an effort—this dinner was important. She was doing this not for Didrik's sake, but because the people who would make important decisions about her career were coming. That was the reason.

Next she took the old wine bottle out of its box and placed both items on the kitchen island to show Don. With a bit of luck, he would realize how fascinating the story was—and what an amazing show it could be—if he actually saw and held the bottle.

At least that was what she was hoping.

25

Elnaz arrived first, clutching a bunch of tulips. As Bente welcomed her in the hallway, the sound of cheerful voices came from the living room—so much for "staying in the background"—and Elnaz seemed to give a little start.

"I'm so sorry, I couldn't get rid of my . . . family." Bente gave a half smile and showed her guest into the apartment. The whole gang was standing there, at the ready. They stepped forward to say hello, one by one.

Elnaz shook Hanna's hand for rather too long, while Bente's sister gazed deep into her eyes.

Oh no, Bente thought, well aware of what that might mean. Hanna was *not* allowed to develop an interest in Elnaz, that would be a seriously bad idea. Bente knew her sister well, and she needed to keep her relationship with Elnaz and the production company on a professional footing.

The doorbell rang again and Bente went to answer it.

Didrik. It felt like forever since they had seen each other. Now he was standing here, right in front of her, in his usual coat and with his hair slightly tousled, as if the spring breeze had ruffled it. His gaze held hers, and for a little while they looked at each other in silence. He smiled tentatively and her heart began to pound. She didn't know what to say.

Didrik got there first. "Hi."

She cleared her throat. "Hi! Come on in!" She made a vague sweeping movement with one hand, and he took a step toward her. He surprised her by trying to give her a hug, but it turned into nothing more than an awkward pat on the back. The brief touch was enough to make her body react. And his smell. *Oh God.* His smell.

Beneath his coat he was impeccably dressed as always—chinos, tweed jacket, a checked shirt in the same dark-blue shade as his chinos, matching tie.

He hung up his coat and handed over a flat package wrapped in shiny pale-gray paper.

"Thank you. Is this from . . . ?"

"From me. Just something small I thought you might like."

She clumsily unwrapped the gift as if it were made of glass. Inside was a small watercolor. Tall trunks topped by fluffy treetops against a perfect sky, painted in matte pastel shades. Below the trees were the long boules courts where several men and women were playing—the Jardin du Luxembourg.

"I know you were thinking of buying a painting, and I found this one just before we were due to leave."

"Thank you. It's . . . it's perfect." She held it in front of her with both hands.

"I thought about you when I saw it, and—" He broke off.

Bente sensed that someone was watching them, and turned to see her mother standing by the kitchen island with sadness in her eyes. *Dad.* He'd brought home pictures from every trip. She found a vase and arranged the tulips Elnaz had brought.

Don arrived a couple of minutes later, and Bente took out the chilled bottles of wine and the large Chardonnay glasses—particularly well suited for oaked Chardonnay.

"To go with the appetizer, a Chardonnay from Burgundy." She served them the buttery wine, perhaps not a common choice to accompany an appetizer, but she loved it. It was a little more robust, a little softer, and ideal for stimulating the appetite.

"I don't drink Chardonnay, haven't you got any Chablis?" Agneta asked, as she always did.

Bente rolled her eyes. "For the millionth time, Chablis *is* Chardonnay, it's made entirely from Chardonnay grapes."

Didrik gave her a meaningful look and Bente smiled.

"Well, I don't drink that pretentious Chardonnay then." Agneta sighed. "That's because when I was in jail, one of the guards smuggled in wine for New Year's Eve so we could have some fun. And it was sickly Chardonnay—I haven't been able to touch it since."

"You can't compare this wine with something you were offered decades years ago. It's excellent." If they'd been alone, Bente would have pointed out how much it cost.

"You were in jail?" Don's curiosity had been aroused.

"Yep. Serious tax evasion. Three years."

"Wow."

Bente looked wearily at her mother. "There's Champagne if you prefer. It's to go with the starter, but I can open it now."

Uno had been silent so far, but suddenly his face crumpled and he let out a sob. "Mirja loved Champagne."

Lydia patted his shoulder.

Bente looked apologetically at Don as she passed him a glass of wine. "His partner has just left him."

"I understand—we've all been there," he replied sympathetically.

"*Skål* and welcome," Bente said, raising her glass in a toast.

◆ ◆ ◆

Don immediately launched into a discussion with Agneta about what could be smuggled into jail. Elnaz went and stood next to Hanna, praising the apartment. Uno sat down by himself on the sofa, and Lydia had laid claim to Didrik. Bente was standing with her mother and Don, but couldn't find a natural way of bringing up the topic of the production. It would just have to wait—she had all evening, so she went to heat up the hash browns she had already fried. She slid them onto plates, then topped them with roe, chopped red onions, sour cream, dill, and lemon wedges. She carried the plates to the table, took two bottles of Champagne out of the refrigerator, and asked everyone to sit down.

"Once again, *skål*. I'm so pleased you could come." She looked at Elnaz and Don, then at Didrik. Her heart rate shot up, and she quickly turned away and looked at the members of her family. "And you too. So pleased." She couldn't quite hide the sarcasm.

They all sipped their Champagne and began to chat about the show.

"I thought we could talk over the format one more time and see where we might take it. I know you guys have discussed a slightly more personal angle," Bente began, hoping Don and Elnaz would join in. "But there's one thing we haven't had time to dig into yet, which might lead us to the right vineyard. We now know which vineyards used brass plaques back then, and it would be well worth traveling to Bordeaux to see if we can find more information once we're there on the ground." She looked from Elnaz to Don, but Elnaz's attention seemed to be elsewhere. On Hanna, to be precise.

"Elnaz?"

"Sorry, what did you say?"

"I said that—"

She was interrupted by Don, who took a large slurp of his Champagne. "That's delicious." He smacked his lips.

"I was actually locked up with the daughter of Italy's largest wine producer." Agneta twirled her empty glass around.

"Seriously, Mom?" Bente sighed.

"Well, maybe not the largest producer, but her family was some kind of big deal down in southern Italy, the biggest producer of some table wine or other." Agneta pointed to her empty glass, and Bente obligingly refilled it.

Don gazed with interest at Agneta as she kept talking.

"She told us so many crazy stories! They really did live the Mafia life down there. Oh my God. Everyone was terrified of her. One time she and my cellmate had an argument about the last bit of marmalade at breakfast. The rest of us thought, Jesus, she has no idea who she's messing with." Agneta laughed. "And do you know what the Italian did?"

Don shook his head and leaned forward expectantly.

"Wrote a message on the mirrors when she was in the shower. None of the rest of us ever found out what it said, but it must have been something horrific, because my cellmate, who was also in for financial crimes, by the way—she was a bit of a snob, really—was too scared to go to sleep. And when she did finally fall asleep, she woke up the following morning to find the bed full of blood. I mean, it was actually lingonberry jelly, but she woke up and thought she'd been stabbed." Agneta slammed her hand down on the table and guffawed. Don joined in the laughter.

Bente stole a glance at Didrik. If she could draw him into the conversation, get him to present the information they had so far, then maybe Don would listen? But Didrik was fully occupied with Lydia.

"History has society and people at its heart . . ." she heard him say. Lydia was captivated by his deep voice, and Bente couldn't help staring at that beautiful mouth for a second. ". . . the memory disappears but the history remains. However, it varies depending on who is writing it. That's why it's so important, everything depends on how we—you and I—choose our angle . . ."

Didrik paused there, as if he sensed that he was being watched. Looked in Bente's direction. She smiled apologetically, trying to convey that she hadn't been staring at *him*, but at her aunt. He returned the smile and she felt her cheeks flush red.

Maybe it was the wine.

Meanwhile, Agneta was shaking her head at her Italian story. "Pure *Godfather*."

Uno's face crumpled yet again. "*The Godfather.* Mirja and I used to watch *The Godfather* once a year," he burst out.

Bente turned to her mother. "I thought you guys were going to stay in the background," she murmured.

Needless to say, Agneta took no notice whatsoever. "I love reality TV, it's like psychoanalysis in prime time, of such interesting people. During my time in jail, I . . ."

Bente got to her feet. There clearly wasn't going to be a discussion about the show.

There was a natural pause as everyone started eating, and Bente seized her chance. "Like I said before, Don, we have a list of vineyards that might lead us to Sven Steen. I really think we could find out quite a lot if we had the opportunity to . . ."

"Your mom should be on TV." Don was beaming, not listening to a word Bente said.

"Absolutely. But I'm thinking that if we go to Bordeaux, I take my handheld camera, and we visit the city archive and maybe a few vineyards, we should be able to gather some really good material. What do you say?" She looked at Elnaz, who was laughing at something Hanna had said. Then Elnaz whispered something in Hanna's ear that made her giggle. Giggle? Since when did her sister giggle? And Don wasn't listening either; he was laughing at yet another of Agneta's jail stories.

Bente sighed. She might as well just give up.

26

The balcony door was ajar, and Bente thought she could hear Didrik's voice from outside. She peeped out and saw him sitting at the wrought iron table with Don.

As Bente went out to join them, Don got to his feet and held up his coffee cup. "Just going inside for a refill."

Didrik looked up at her and pushed out the chair beside him so that she could flop down.

"Okay?" he asked.

"Not really. I'm afraid that this show is going to be reduced to some kind of nonsense where we talk about feelings with other celebrities, me wearing stripy Breton tops and you, creased linen shirts."

"Don't be too disappointed—I look really good in a creased linen shirt." Didrik winked, and once again her stomach flipped. Creased linen shirts and Didrik Holgersson seemed like a lethal combination. His expression grew serious. "Don't worry, we'll bring them around."

She nodded. "Thank you. It means a lot that you think the show is important too." It was a great comfort to know that he was on her side, after all.

She allowed herself to gaze at him for a moment in the soft twilight, which would soon be swallowed up by darkness. His hair was more tousled than ever, and the stubble made him even more attractive.

"By the way, I found something that I think Don was interested in," he said.

"Oh?"

"Yesterday I got the diary of that woman who was in the resistance movement. I wanted to tell you in person—she mentions a Scandinavian guy at a vineyard. His name was Per, but he seems kind of anonymous, and had very pale skin and hair. That fits with the photos we've seen of Sven. As we discussed before, Sven was almost certainly using a different identity. It might be a long shot, but it's worth looking into."

She nodded. "Absolutely. And you've told Don?"

"Yes, just now, when I managed to get him to myself for a while."

"And he listened to you?"

"He did. He thought it sounded exciting."

Bente managed a smile. "Great." She ought to be pleased that they'd captured Don's interest, but it bothered her that he had ignored her all evening.

"Time for more Manhattans!" a voice announced from the kitchen. Hanna appeared in the doorway with another tray of cocktails, with Lydia, Don, and Agneta right behind her. Clearly the premium wines had been abandoned in favor of Hanna's hastily mixed Manhattans.

The others took a glass, then Hanna shoved the tray under Bente's and Didrik's noses.

"Thanks, I'm fine." Bente held up her wineglass.

"Er . . ." Didrik's eyes flickered toward Bente; he obviously remembered her comments about the dubious quality of her sister's cocktails, but he picked up a glass like the polite guest he was. "Thank you." He nodded to Hanna, then took a sip.

"Good, isn't it?" Hanna said.

"Fantastic." He pursed his lips. Bente could see that he was trying not to grimace, and she only just managed to stop herself from laughing.

"It's okay, you can pour it in that plant pot," she said when Hanna had gone back inside.

"Are you sure the pansies won't die—along with anyone else who drank one of these?" Didrik asked before tipping out the contents of his glass.

Don, Agneta, and Lydia sipped happily as Agneta fiddled with her phone. Soon music was pouring out of the speakers in the living room, and the small speaker on the balcony. The trio started dancing, Agneta in Dad's old oilskin coat and her Wellington boots. Bente and Didrik stayed where they were, watching the three of them.

Bruce Springsteen's "Dancing in the Dark" came on, and as always when Bruce began to sing, Bente felt the pain in her heart, in her bones.

The dancers bellowed along with the lyrics, singing about a spark being needed to make a fire.

"So what do you say?" Didrik held out his hand, and Bente got to her feet. The balcony floor was cold beneath her warm soles. They joined the others, dancing in the dark, with the sparkling lights of the city all around them.

Next came the opening chords of Springsteen's "The River." Bente sank down on the sun lounger in one corner with Didrik beside her as the others shimmied in the living room, singing away and clutching their cocktails.

She rested her head against the wall. Listening to Bruce always made her feel ambivalent. To her, his music meant weekends. Childhood. Security. Normality. It reminded her of Dad, who always wore a suit to the office but jeans and a T-shirt at home, sang and danced to Bruce while cooking dinner, drove her to and from sports practice and other childhood activities, and played badminton with a group of local dads on Tuesday evenings. In so many ways he had been a perfectly ordinary father. But the darkness had always been there. At the time, Bente had noticed only that there were periods when he was low.

"Thinking about your dad?" Didrik asked.

"Yes . . . or rather the way life used to be."

There was such a clear division in her mind between before and after. A before with a dancing dad at the weekends who cooked meals for his family and their friends; when their family went on skip trips with other families and were invited over for dinner in return. When everything was carefree. And then there was an after—a time when

Bente, Hanna, and their mother had no friends left. When they were excluded from the community, brutally and completely.

And when they no longer had Dad either.

"And how was life back then?"

"It was . . ." She looked at him, smiled. "I like that."

"What?"

"The fact that you're curious about me." She couldn't resist placing a hand on his arm. Feeling the tweed fabric of his jacket, rough and almost prickly beneath her fingers. She completely forgot that she was trying to remain objective when it came to Didrik.

"Of course I'm curious about you. I loved experiencing Paris with you."

"I feel the same."

For a few seconds she allowed herself to get lost in his eyes.

"I don't think much of this wine . . ." Hanna's voice drifted to them from inside, then she stepped out onto the balcony. She was holding an almost full wineglass in one hand, and a bottle in the other. Bente didn't register what was going on at first; her vision was too clouded by the whole situation—by the wine, by being so close to Didrik again. She blinked, focused on the bottle, and her eyes widened. *No!* It couldn't be . . .

Shit.

"Fuck" was all Bente managed to say before she leaped to her feet. "You opened *that bottle*?" She snatched it out of Hanna's hand.

"Yes—it looked a bit sad, it didn't even have a label. It reminds me of the stuff our neighbor mixed up in the bathtub when we lived on Lövvägen. You remember the guy who—"

"Hanna, you can't drink that wine—it's almost eighty years old." Bente felt her desperation rising.

"Don't worry, I'll reimburse you," her sister said cheerily. She took another sip and grimaced.

"It's irreplaceable!" Bente snapped. "Stop drinking right now. That's the bottle we're working on." She took the glass away from Hanna.

"But how was I supposed to know . . ." Hanna rolled her eyes. "You always complain about my cocktails, so I thought I'd pour you a glass of wine." She sighed loudly. "Like I said, I'll reimburse you."

"It's not about that." Bente groaned. Gazed at the bottle. "How am I going to explain this to Camille?"

The others had heard the argument, and now they came out onto the balcony.

"Well, since it's open, maybe we should all have a taste?" Agneta suggested with a shrug. "I mean, it's the reason for this evening's dinner party, isn't it? It would be a shame to let it go to waste."

Bente was about to protest, then realized that her mother had a point. They could try it. And it might make good content for the show—if Didrik had managed to talk Don around.

She ran and fetched her camera while everyone gathered around the dinner table.

She provided each of them with a clean glass, and gave brief instructions on how to treat the wine. She contemplated the pale-red liquid in her glass. The sediment swirled around when she moved it. There was nothing wrong with the color, she thought as she tilted the glass and studied the contents against the white surface of the table. However, she had no great expectations about the taste, which must have deteriorated over the years. It was only the very best wines that opened up and improved during such a long storage time, and she wasn't sure this one fell into that category.

They all sniffed their glasses simultaneously.

Elnaz reached for Bente's camera and began filming. Bente stuck her nose in the glass and inhaled, then glanced up at Elnaz and the others, feeling both pleased and surprised. "I'm getting dried berries." She sniffed again. "Tobacco and cedarwood." She took a deep breath. "There it is, leather and mushrooms." She usually allowed everyone else to say what they thought when she conducted a tasting, but right now she was completely caught up in the moment. She realized what she was doing, and looked to the others. "What are you getting?"

"The same, I think." Don swirled his glass just as Bente had done. "Maybe a little earthiness?"

"Good," Bente said.

"And . . . stables?" Didrik looked inquiringly at her. Bente nodded eagerly—she could smell that too. "Shall we taste?"

"I already know what it tastes like," Hanna said.

"Yes, but try again—take your time. Think about what you're really getting. Close your eyes." Hanna did as Bente instructed, and the others followed suit. "Although I guess your cocktails have probably already destroyed your taste buds for the evening."

Bente swirled her glass again and took a small sip. The taste reflected the nose, but she was also picking up pine needles. The wine wasn't particularly mellow; back then the alcohol content was relatively low, unlike today's Bordeaux wines. But it was clearly from a good vineyard, and had been made using high-quality grapes. There was very little roughness on her tongue—the tannins had faded over time.

"Just imagine, this was bottled eighty years ago," Didrik said. "And it's been lying at the bottom of the sea until very recently."

Bente nodded. "Unbelievable. That's what's so exciting about wines, the way they change and develop. The acidity would have been much greater when the wine was bottled, but it's since rounded off; the flavors of mushrooms, an earth cellar, and a stable come from age. But the taste can deteriorate if it's aged for too long. It could even be that those flavors were more noticeable twenty years ago, when it was probably meant to be drunk. It's hard to know for sure."

She held up the bottle to the light; the sediment had dropped to the bottom.

"How do you think the conditions have affected the wine? The darkness, the pressure at the bottom of the sea?" Don seemed genuinely interested.

"The darkness and the cold temperature are why the wine has kept so well. The relatively constant temperature and the water pressure made it keep for longer. It might not have survived that length of time in an ordinary wine cellar."

They all looked at one another in silence. Even Agneta and Hanna seemed to appreciate the magnitude of the occasion, because this was clearly something special—the wine had a history. The story of this bottle was the most complex Bente had ever come across. She turned it around as she gazed at it. The cork must have kept well—there were no fragments whatsoever in the wine.

"Where's the cork?" She wanted to sniff it.

"I think I threw it away," Hanna said.

Bente went into the kitchen and saw the corkscrew on the counter, with the cork still attached. She gently unscrewed it and headed back to the table. She sat down, holding the cork between her thumb and forefinger. It had darkened over the years, but had retained its shape, and expanded slightly when it was removed from the bottle.

Then she saw it.

"Look. There's something here." She peered more closely. What she saw was very small—tiny, in fact. That's why they hadn't seen anything when they looked through the neck of the bottle before. "It's . . . numbers and symbols."

"What could it be?" Didrik leaned across the table, and Bente gave him the cork while she fetched a pen and paper.

Outside it had started raining. Hanna had lit the candles on the table, and Bente switched on more lamps so they'd be able to see better. Once she was seated again, she wrote down the numbers and symbols; the numbers were separated by a circle and two apostrophes.

"I think those are coordinates," Agneta said, looking over her shoulder.

Didrik nodded. "I think you're right."

Bente glanced at Don, who seemed fascinated. She picked up her phone, opened Google Maps, and entered the details.

Then she froze as an image appeared. Could this be the breakthrough they'd been waiting for?

She stared at the screen. It was showing Bordeaux, more specifically a small village in Médoc. When she zoomed in, she couldn't see a vineyard, but there was a building and an address—16 Rue des Templiers.

They had an address!

She beamed at Don, then Elnaz, and finally Didrik. She held up her phone to show them the map.

"I've found it!"

27

They were definitely on the trail of something. Didrik understood that Bente wanted to find out more, so he stayed behind when the others went home. Don and Elnaz had been fired up by the unexpected turn of events, and seeing the relief on Bente's face, Didrik had realized how uneasy she had been over the idea of making a show with a different angle than the one she'd planned.

They drank mineral water and black coffee all night as they continued their research. They looked at the coordinates again and used Google Maps to "walk" around the roads in the Médoc in the vicinity of the vineyard.

"Look at this!" Bente was pointing eagerly at the screen.

Didrik leaned closer, picking up her powdery, slightly spicy scent: the way the sheets in the hotel room had smelled after she had left his room a couple of weeks ago. It had been so ridiculous, but he had stayed put for a long time that day, not wanting to leave the bed and the scent of her.

He had also needed time to think—of course she had been right to say it wouldn't be a brilliant idea to embark on a relationship when they were working together. And yet those days with her had done something to him. He had come alive, had done what he loved best without constantly questioning his decision to work on a TV show. Working on a show together with Bente had been fun; their collaboration had made the job even more enjoyable. And it had been interesting to get to know her.

That was why he had been somewhat taken aback by her sudden departure.

Once again he was surrounded by her scent, causing his stomach to flip. He glanced at her profile, those beautiful red lips that he had been allowed to kiss to his heart's content for one night. She had swept her hair to one side; the nape of her neck was exposed, and he followed its contours with his eyes. He so wanted to caress that soft curve near the top of her shoulders. Her hair shone in the glow of the candle on the table.

She prodded him gently in the ribs. "Hey, check this out!"

He focused on the screen.

"This could be the main building of a vineyard."

"A vineyard?" Didrik gazed at the simple stone building on Google Maps Street View.

"Vineyards aren't always as grand as you might think," Bente explained. "Even a château doesn't necessarily have to be a castle, despite the name. But if you look here . . ." She moved the cursor to a nearby building.

"Château du Boda," Didrik read aloud.

"That's the neighboring property, and it seems to be in use. Maybe we could reach out to the owners, see if they know anything about the address we have."

Didrik nodded. "So it seems likely that the bottle was sent from there."

He stared at the map—was it Sven who had sent the bottle? Had he been there—in that stone building?

"I recognize the name Château du Boda—it's not one of the bigger producers, but I think it's old," Bente said. "We should definitely contact the owners."

They flicked through all the books Bente had on Bordeaux and gathered as much information as they could about Médoc, and more specifically about the area around the address they'd found.

Many hours later, after the sun had begun to rise, casting a faint light through the closed curtains, they booked train tickets to Bordeaux.

"This little hotel looks super-cozy, and they've got rooms available!"

She reserved two single rooms. Didrik couldn't help feeling disappointed, but realized it would have seemed odd if they'd booked a double. They weren't a couple, and the receipt would be going to the production company.

The relaxed atmosphere between them was such a relief. Didrik had been nervous about this evening—how would Bente behave toward him? Would she be cold, like after their . . . night, their wonderful night together? She had made it very clear how she wanted things to be—and now she had suggested another trip. She had clearly softened her posture toward him, and he'd even had the opportunity to look into those sparkling eyes again.

They were going to travel the week after next, getting back just in time for TV24's annual summer party, which was on a Thursday evening. He guessed that she hadn't been invited, as she'd only just started working for the company again.

"Listen, would you like to come to the summer party with me? My ticket is for two people."

Her face lit up. "Oh yes—I'd love to!"

He immediately started wondering how they would go to the party—as colleagues?

She looked at hm in the gentle morning light. "Thanks for a great night's work."

He smiled. "No, thank you." He met her gaze and saw her pupils dilate just before he leaned forward and kissed her.

She responded. At first it was a simple kiss, perfect and all they needed, as if they'd never done anything more. He felt as if the kiss had been in the air all night, and here was the proof. Her soft, smooth lips tasted of coffee, her tongue tasted sweet, and he thought he could also pick up the flavor of wine they had drunk—dried berries and cedarwood.

Then the kiss grew more urgent. He pulled her close, onto his lap so that she straddled him as he buried his hands in her hair, then slowly caressed the nape of her neck. He continued along her arms, her skin hot beneath his fingers. Down to the curve of her waist, then her hip, pushing up her skirt so that he could touch her bare thigh. She let out a quiet moan as he stroked the sensitive skin. He bit her lower lip, kissed her even harder, and pressed her close to his body.

She quickly unbuttoned his shirt and took it off. Kissed her way down his throat, her warm, light touch making him whimper.

For a second he stopped. Met her gaze. It was growing light outside, the first rays of the sun giving the room a bronze-colored glow. Her green eyes were almost luminous.

To think that sex could be like this. That he could feel this way about a woman. He couldn't compare the attraction and desire he felt right now with anything he had experienced before. In one rapid movement, he picked her up and carried her over to her bed. Put her down, took off her dress, and looked at her lying there for a little while. When he saw her pale-pink underwear, it was all he could do not to rip it off her body right away.

Instead he slowly unhooked her bra, then stroked her breasts as he slipped off the shoulder straps and dropped it on the floor. Caressed the outside of her lacy panties before taking them off. Then he buried himself in her. He wanted to taste her, smell her. Wanted her wetness, her warmth to swallow him up.

He had longed for this moment.

◆ ◆ ◆

He woke late in the morning—it was almost lunchtime. Unlike the previous occasion, Bente looked at him with affection when she woke up. She stretched her arms above her head like a contented cat and rolled over to face him. Ran her fingers over his chest and kissed him.

He grew hard straightaway. It didn't matter that they'd had sex only a few hours earlier, he wanted Bente again, and again.

Afterward she pulled on a robe and went into the kitchen, but came back a minute or so later.

"The coffee is on, but I wanted to curl up with you while I'm waiting."

He smiled, held her close, played with a long strand of her auburn hair.

"Just think, in two weeks we'll be in Bordeaux," he said, tucking the strand behind her ear.

"I know, it's unreal." She smiled up at him. "I'm so looking forward to going there with you."

"Have you been before?"

She nodded. "A few times."

Of course. That was where Frederic was from.

"But it'll be cool to discover new areas." She gave him a kiss. "Coffee." She moved to get up, but he stopped her.

"Let me serve you." Didrik got out of bed. "This whole project makes me feel like an investigative journalist—I love it!" He pulled on his boxers.

She laughed. "I can see you as a journalist!"

"It's actually my dream job."

"I thought being a historian was your dream?"

"It is. But if I hadn't been a historian, I would have liked to be a journalist. I've written about history for a few periodicals, but I've always wished I could write investigative pieces."

"You think traveling around Paris and Bordeaux, meeting winemakers, and going to museums counts as investigative journalism?"

He responded by throwing a pillow at her. "Shut up and let me pretend." He sank down on the bed, laughing, and threw another pillow at her.

"I will absolutely let you pretend, and I'll keep that dream in mind. We'll be doing some filming, and you can deliver some serious, explanatory monologues to camera, with subdued lighting so we get that real *Mission: Investigate* atmosphere."

"Can we disguise the voice of someone we're interviewing?"

"That would be perfect." She nodded in agreement.

"So what's your dream job?" He looked at her with curiosity.

"Working with wines. On TV." She said it as if it were the most obvious thing in the world.

"But if you weren't doing that, what would you do?"

She thought for a moment. "I honestly don't know, this is what I want to do."

"What did you want to do when you were little?"

She laughed, shook her head. "No idea."

"No cute dream job? Breeding cats, being a ballerina?"

"I don't think so." Her tone became slightly distant, as it always did when she didn't want to get into something, so he didn't pursue it. A second later she grinned at him. "How about you? What did you want to be?"

"Easy. A firefighter."

"Oh, I can definitely picture you as a firefighter." She drew him close, kissed him. "With a sooty face after rescuing a kitten from a burning building, with your helmet askew. And one of those big jackets with nothing underneath, just this fantastic naked chest." She whispered in his ear, sending shivers of pleasure down his spine. "Although these days I find historian the sexiest profession, without a doubt." He could feel her smile against his ear. He loved being described as sexy by her.

"It's great that you're working with your passion."

She nodded slowly, kissed him on the lips.

"Did your dad want to do similar work? He loved food and wine, didn't he?"

Her smiled died away. "Yes. He mentioned it now and again."

This was clearly a topic she didn't want to discuss. Should he drop it? Or did she want him to ask? After all, she had said she liked the fact that he was curious about her.

"You don't really seem to want to talk about your dad."

She let go of him, moved away.

I got that wrong, then.

"I've talked about him so much with the rest of the family."

"I understand. What . . ." He broke off, suddenly feeling unsure. Perhaps she just needed a little help to get going, to let him in. "What happened when he died? Was he sick?"

She shrugged. "It's hard to explain."

They had said so much to each other, but . . . No, Didrik realized: *He* had said so much. He had opened up, exposed his innermost thoughts and feelings. About his breakup, the divorce, his and Lovisa's relationship. His longing for children, his fucking infertility, for God's sake. He'd told her that he probably couldn't have children, while she . . . What had she actually revealed about herself?

Once again he got the sense that this relationship wasn't real as far as she was concerned.

"Sorry," she said. "I don't mean to . . ." But she didn't complete the sentence.

He was at a loss. He'd been about to do something when they started this conversation—what was it? Oh yes, he remembered now.

Didrik went into the kitchen, which was filled with sunshine and the aroma of freshly brewed coffee. He opened a cupboard hoping to find two mugs, but a box of baking powder fell out instead. He put it back, closed the door, and moved on to the next cupboard, where he found what he was looking for.

What was it that she had said about their night in Paris? That it was a mistake. That they were colleagues, so it wasn't a good idea. Admittedly it had all happened so fast, he hadn't been sure, either, that he wanted to embark on something new. But had she just been making excuses for a lack of interest on her part?

He poured the coffee.

"Come back," she called from the bedroom.

He looked at the clock. Suddenly he wanted to get out of here. He left one mug on the counter and took the other in to Bente.

"I should be heading home."

"Please stay," she begged. "We can talk."

"Talk?" He gave a harsh, toneless laugh that he barely recognized. "About what? You don't seem to want to talk at all."

She sat up, fixed him with her gaze. "I do, just not about certain things."

Really? What exactly had she shared about herself? Anything at all? No. And it wasn't because he hadn't asked. He was interested in Bente, curious about her, but he was the one who had babbled away. He'd *thought* that she had opened up to him, just because she had shown him her Paris. But now he realized the revelations had all been superficial—the apartment where she had lived, the bakery where she had shopped, her favorite wine store.

"The problem is that I know *nothing* about you. You don't tell me anything."

She didn't speak, she just sat there as if she were trying to find the right words.

He went on: "I want to get to know you, I want to know more about you, but you only let me scrape the surface. It's so obvious now. You don't talk about your dad, or your childhood. You can't even fucking tell me what your dream job was when you were little. For some reason you don't think I'm the right person to share your innermost thoughts with."

"It's not like that . . ." Bente began.

"Maybe not, but that's how it feels." He turned away, picked up his pants.

"He killed himself."

He stopped in mid-movement. Turned to face her. Met her eyes, which were not sparkling now.

"Oh God, I . . ." He took a step closer to the bed. "I didn't know . . ."

"No, you didn't know. Because my father's suicide is not something I like to talk about. It's painful, it brings up a lot of hurt, and I don't tell just anybody."

"Bente, I . . ." He reached out his hand, then realized what she had said. Ah. There it was. Those two words summed it all up. "So that's how you see this? That I'm *just anybody*?"

She didn't say anything.

"I'd better go." He sighed. "I'll be in touch about the trip to Bordeaux."

Bente didn't protest as he finished getting dressed.

He felt torn. Should he think about her in this moment, or about himself? Part of him wanted to throw his arms around her, take away all the pain she was feeling, destroy it.

Another part just wanted to get out of here.

He turned and walked out of the apartment.

Bente made no attempt to stop him.

28

1944

"His name was Gerard," Mathieu said one evening a few days later when they were working on the maps in the kitchen. It hadn't escaped him that Sven had been avoiding him since they kissed; he hadn't sat outside drawing during his breaks, like usual, but had gone up to his room. They had continued on with the maps in the evening, but Sven hadn't engaged in conversation with Mathieu. Instead he had remained silent, focused on the task at hand.

It made sense that Sven would be confused after what had happened, and Mathieu wanted to tell him about his own transformation and his journey to becoming his true self.

Without Gerard it would never have been possible.

"Who?" Sven glanced up from the map.

"The young man who made me realize who I am, and helped me to accept it."

Mathieu stood up, feeling that he needed to move while he was talking.

"We met at a dance in the village. He'd just arrived here; his family had bought Lassac, the vineyard three properties away." He took a deep breath, gathered his thoughts. "He was the kind of person who was always surrounded by others—both men and women. The women wanted to be with him, and so did the men.

He saw everyone, paid attention to everyone. He was warm, friendly, and somehow world-wise, even though he'd never set foot outside Bordeaux."

Mathieu smiled as he spoke. "I saw him as soon as we walked in. The friend I was with knew him and introduced us. I felt something the second our eyes met. Love at first sight, if you like. His family were also winemakers, and we had lots to talk about—the latest harvest, the work at the vineyard. But he also told me about his dream of going to Paris and training to be a doctor. He loved to study and learn new things, and he really wanted to go to university. Hearing someone speak of their dreams like that was very unusual. Here in Bordeaux everyone stays and helps out in the vineyard, then takes over their parents' business—that's how it works. We talked for hours that evening and became good friends. That was how it began."

Mathieu smiled again at the memory.

"He came by a day or so later, and I showed him around. Then we cycled down to the river, laid a blanket on the sand dunes, and read books. Spring had arrived early that year. Every evening after our work was done, we met by the river. We brought cheese, bread, and fruit, and we read books and ate our food as the sun went down. Swam in the river when it was warm enough. It felt like that summer went on forever, in a good way. And we . . . we fell in love. At night we crept along to see each other through the underground passageways between our vineyards. No one has ever made me laugh like he did, and he taught me to love. Passionately. We kept our relationship secret, of course, but rumors started to circulate. Gerard's parents were furious." Mathieu paused. "Around that time the war broke out, and we were both called up."

Another pause as he prepared to tell Sven the rest—the painful conclusion.

"Just like me, he went away to war. We kept in touch at first, but then the letters stopped coming. A couple of weeks after France surrendered and I came home, my parents received this."

He dug into his pocket and fished out the long silver chain with Gerard's dog tag. His full name and date of birth. Mathieu stroked the cold metal.

"His parents had sent it to me." He let the chain run through his fingers. When the tag arrived it had still carried bloodstains, and he hadn't wanted to touch it, hadn't wanted to risk erasing the final traces of Gerard. At the same time he'd wanted to keep it close, because it was the last thing that had touched Gerard's warm chest. By now the blood had been worn away by his pocket and his fingers.

It seemed to Mathieu that telling Sven about Gerard, their relationship and the death of his beloved, signified a new beginning—maybe because he'd spoken of it he could start afresh now? But it was also a way of doing for Sven the same thing that Gerard had once done for Mathieu. He could see how Sven was struggling, trying to fight against his urges. Which made Mathieu sad. What kind of life was it if you didn't allow yourself to love? Even if the person you loved was the wrong person in society's eyes.

"I'm so sorry," Sven said quietly. "So your parents . . . know about Gerard? Is that why you're in hiding?"

"They've never said anything directly, but . . . The Nazis showed up one day and asked about me, so that's why they're hiding me here. Everyone knows that the Nazis want to track down people like us."

◆ ◆ ◆

People like us.

Sven thought that he perhaps ought to place a consoling hand on Mathieu's shoulder after what he had just shared, but he was finding it hard to take it all in, so instead he carried on with the map. He couldn't look at Mathieu. He needed time to process everything he'd heard.

The kiss had terrified Sven. He had been convinced that he had infected Mathieu with his sick urges. He'd heard that this was possible, so he had lived under the delusion that he had somehow driven Mathieu to kiss him.

But now he realized that if Mathieu had once loved another man, then his *unnatural tendencies* had nothing to do with Sven. Mathieu had already been like that before they met, before Sven came into his life.

Sven had not led Mathieu into depravity. Mathieu was who he was, and his parents had accepted it.

When Mathieu said that he had loved Gerard *passionately*, Sven had been struck by an immediate and instinctive pang of jealousy. Gerard sounded so full of life, so carefree, everything Sven associated with Mathieu. Nothing like Sven, who brooded over every little thing, who suppressed all that he felt through work—either as a soldier or at the vineyard. Even when he was supposed to be resting, he needed to draw, in order to avoid thinking too much.

A second later he realized how stupid it was to be jealous of a dead man. He could see how Gerard had helped Mathieu become the person he was—the person Sven was in love with.

He ought to be grateful to Gerard.

◆ ◆ ◆

In the days that followed, Sven processed this new information and tried to understand who Mathieu was, who *he himself* was, while continuing to work peacefully in the vineyard. No soldiers came calling, and the only people they saw were the Fosseys, the owners of Château du Boda, the vineyard next door, and their little boy, Jérôme. They visited regularly with news and food, and the families exchanged produce from each other's kitchen gardens.

They also tried to keep up to date with the Allies' successes. The Germans were still fighting, but there were frequent reports of increased aggression. They were taking more prisoners, arresting anyone and everyone. It was a dangerous time.

The days were unbearably hot, and during the hours when the temperature was at its highest, Sven and Mathieu rested in the shade behind the house, while Hugo and Juliette sought refuge indoors.

On one of those days, Mathieu asked Sven to draw a portrait of him for his mother's birthday. They disappeared down to the cellar where it was cooler, and by the light of the flickering candles, Sven worked on Mathieu's portrait. He drew those beautiful, characteristic features, spending a long time on the slightly crooked nose, that thick hair. The chiseled jawline was easy to capture, but the gray eyes with a hint of melancholy were more challenging. Sven loved those eyes—they held the joy of life, but that joy was edged with sorrow. This was something Sven had come to recognize in occupied France—the people were living under oppression, but no one could take away their hope and lust for life. Sven tried to encapsulate all this in Mathieu's portrait.

They worked like this for three days. On the third day, when Sven had finished, he put down his pencil and asked Mathieu to take a look. Mathieu gave the drawing a brief nod.

He then asked, "Do you want to start a new sketch?" Mathieu's voice was hoarse as he slowly took off his shirt.

Sven was dumbstruck at first. Did Mathieu want Sven to draw him without his shirt on? Should he do that? But then he stood up and carefully placed the portrait for Juliette on the wooden shelf. Fetched a clean white sheet of paper, laid it on the table, and picked up the pencil. He drew the first stroke, the line of Mathieu's shoulder, then continued to work with focus.

Mathieu removed another piece of clothing, then another, until he was naked. Sven studied every shadow, every curve, every single hair. He drew frenetically, as if this were his first and last chance to see Mathieu's naked body, even though he knew that this image would be etched on his consciousness for the rest of his life.

"I need a break," Mathieu said after a while. He stood up and stretched. Took a step toward Sven. He wiped the perspiration from

Sven's brow with his thumb. Sven hadn't even noticed that he was sweating, but now he realized that his shirt was almost soaked through.

Then Mathieu leaned forward. Kissed him. He tasted of salt, and something smooth. He played with Sven's tongue, sucked on his lips, and Sven let himself be kissed. Waves of pleasure surged through his body.

This was what it was like to kiss someone you desired.

◆ ◆ ◆

The unbearable heat continued. Early one morning a few days later, Mathieu was helping with the work in the field. Both men were sweating profusely.

"I need to cool down," Mathieu said, glancing at Sven.

"In the house?"

"In the river." He gazed at Sven for a long time, and Sven's body immediately came to life. After the kiss in the cellar, he hadn't been able to think of anything else, but they hadn't had an opportunity to be together. He wanted to go with Mathieu now; he *had* to go with him. As if he were under a spell, he put down his tools and followed Mathieu in the direction of the forest.

Mathieu confidently led the way along the forest tracks. They were hidden by the dense trees, Sven told himself. No one could see them. No one could see Mathieu. What would happen if someone did see him? If he gave himself away? People would start asking questions, wondering why the Latorres' son was home. The Germans would hear about it, and Mathieu was already on their list.

This adventure was dangerous. A lethal game.

They kept going, and when they reached the edge of the forest, they continued down the riverbank. The water was shimmering, almost azure blue.

Mathieu pulled off his shirt, his pants. Then his underwear. With only a few strides, he was in the water. Sven remained standing on the bank. Mathieu beckoned him, and eventually Sven took a few hesitant steps, then removed his shirt and pants. The sun was burning his shoulders. He hesitated for a few seconds, then took off his underwear. He made his way resolutely down the bank and waded out into the river, the reeds scratching his calves, then kept on going in the crystal-clear water that was so wonderfully refreshing around his ankles, cooling the blood pumping through his overheated body. He felt free. He could almost forget about the German soldiers who were just a mile or so away.

He heard Mathieu laughing out loud. It was a fantastic sound.

"What if someone sees us?" Sven said as reality suddenly caught up with him.

"It's only for a little while," Mathieu said. "I can't stand being a prisoner in the house and the vineyard any longer." He splashed the water all around him. "I want to breathe." He turned his face up to the sky, spread his arms wide, and fell backward, allowing the water to embrace him.

Sven did the same, then dove and swam underwater with his eyes open. The fractured sunlight filtering down through the surface of the river danced in front of him until his eyes hurt.

When he came up again, Mathieu was spinning around and around, causing the water to ripple in wide circles around him. When he was done, he swam along the shore until he reached a tree trunk growing out across the river, then clambered up it.

"Come here!" he shouted, and Sven followed him. Mathieu jumped down and made a big splash, not graceful in the least. They kept on swimming back and forth, competing to see who could swim to the trunk the fastest. Sven won every time, until the last time. He was almost there when Mathieu seized his foot, pulled him back, and quickly overtook him.

"That's cheating!" Sven laughed, grabbing hold of Mathieu's bare shoulders, slippery from the water. He pushed him under the surface as Mathieu fought back and bounced back up, laughing too.

"How can you be so happy? You're amazing," Sven said as they breathlessly treaded water in the shade of the tree's long branches. He thought about how much he had laughed since he had gotten to know Mathieu. He hadn't laughed like that for several years.

"You have to live, find happiness where you can." Mathieu moved closer to Sven, tucked his hair behind his ears, gazed at him for a long time. They were close to the bank now, their feet touching the bottom. Sven felt the muddy, soft, sandy riverbed beneath his toes.

"Painting, drawing, swimming, sneaking away from home. In spite of everything that's going on. That's the happiness we need," Mathieu said. "Kissing. Is something we need." He gently kissed Sven's lips. "We have to dance in the darkness," he whispered, letting his wet lips caress Sven's.

Sven nodded in agreement as the words, the kiss, and Mathieu's touch sank in. Mathieu was probably right.

Then he pressed his body against Mathieu's and kissed him harder. He tasted sweet, from the river water. Sven put his arms around Mathieu's neck, felt Mathieu's thick, wet hair against his arms. His naked body, so close. His hardness against Sven's thigh, Mathieu inhaled sharply, deepened the kiss.

A sound interrupted them. The snapping of a branch echoed across the river, and they drew apart. Sven turned around.

A shadow was moving among the trees.

29

When Didrik had gone, Bente remained sitting up in bed for a while. She was surprised that he had gotten so upset. Certainly it wasn't strange for her not to share personal stuff with someone she'd met only recently? Okay, so they'd spent a couple of nights together, had sex, had a good time—but surely he saw this as something temporary, like she did? She'd never for a moment thought it could be anything else. Why would Didrik, who could easily have anyone he wanted, be seriously interested in her? Was this about his bruised ego? Maybe he was used to people turning to him for all kinds of reasons, just because he was famous?

Yes, their night had been amazing, and she loved being with him. Still, she couldn't understand why he would want her. He had come so far in life with his stellar TV career; he'd been married and had been planning a family. Meanwhile, she lived as if she were ten years younger than she actually was. Until a few months ago, Didrik had had everything he'd dreamed of. She couldn't contribute to any of those dreams, so why would he want to be with her? No matter how she looked at things, she always came back to the same conclusion—he needed to get over his ex-wife, move on with his life, and Bente was a perfect way to achieve that aim. In that context, she couldn't open up to him. Which meant that she had to let him go.

Even though everything within her wanted to run after him.

Her coffee had gone cold. She carried it into the kitchen and poured it down the sink. The machine was empty, so she refilled the pot with water and scooped coffee into the filter.

Hanna came in and put down her empty cup. "Has Didrik gone?"

"He has."

"He's nice. He seems to like you." Hanna smiled.

"I'm not sure about that. When he left we'd . . . had a bit of a falling-out."

"About what? Something to do with work? You both seem really passionate about this show, so I can imagine there might be the odd disagreement."

"No, nothing like that. He thinks I don't open up to him, that I don't tell him things. About Dad, for example."

"And that made him angry?"

"Not angry exactly, but . . . he's the kind of person who talks, shares everything. The mood between us got a bit strange."

"Why don't you want to talk to him about Dad?"

"We don't know each other very well yet."

Hanna looked thoughtful. "I think Didrik has a point. In order to get to know someone, to become really close, you have to share, find out more about the other person. You can't get to know each other well without doing that."

"But I'm not sure what this thing between us actually is. And I do let certain people in. You and I talk about everything."

Hanna tilted her head to one side. "We do—but we're sisters. This is about letting a man get close. Have you ever done that? Give Didrik a chance. He obviously wants to get to know you. Not all men are like Frederic—he wasn't interested in that level of commitment, which I suspect suited you perfectly, because that meant he couldn't see the real you. Henrik tried, but he didn't succeed. It's all because you find it so difficult to open up, to let people get to know you. Which may be because you still haven't properly worked through what happened with Dad."

Bente didn't know what to say to that. However, Hanna was right when she said that Bente had always kept a certain emotional distance when it came to relationships with men, a bit like an invisible barricade. Henrik had done his best, and she had talked about her dad a little bit. But after that she had avoided the subject, and Henrik had respected her wishes.

But when she thought about it, she always came back to the knowledge that one of the people she loved the most, the only man she had ever loved unconditionally, had taken his own life. Bente's love hadn't been enough. All these emotions formed what felt like an enormous dark hole, at the bottom of which might be fear. She didn't really know what she was afraid of. She just felt a kind of primal instinct to keep any man she could fall for at a safe distance.

When she went back to her room, her phone was flashing with a new message.

It was from an editor on the TV show *Krissie*.

Hi, I heard about your new show from Elnaz, it sounds super-exciting. Would you like to come on Krissie to talk about wine one evening?

Krissie was the show that aired five evenings a week, hosted by Didrik's aunt Kristina Storm. Bente had been on the show a few times in the past, and in the time since she'd left the limelight, it had gotten even bigger.

She quickly replied, saying she'd love to do it.

After that, she got ready to go meet Ellie at Rendezvous. Her friend was picking her up there in her car, and they were going to drive to the storage unit that held Bente's possessions.

It was wet and windy outside, and by the time she reached the restaurant, Bente was glad she'd pulled on her raincoat at the last minute. She was about to slip into the covered doorway next to the wine bar when she saw a notice taped to the door of Rendezvous. She went over and read:

RENDEZVOUS HAS CLOSED BUT WILL RETURN SOON WITH A NEW LOOK. LOOK FORWARD TO SEEING YOU AGAIN!

So Tomas had finally managed to sell the place.

At that moment, Ellie pulled up. Bente jumped in.

"So the bar has closed?"

"Yes. We found out yesterday." Ellie set off along the street. "We don't know who's bought it yet. We all got two weeks' paid vacation before the new owner takes over. Generous," she said with a wink.

"That was very quick."

"It was—crazy."

"But you all get to keep your jobs?"

"It looks that way. All Tomas knew was that the new owner still intends to run the restaurant; I don't think he bothered to try to learn more than that."

"So how do you feel?"

"Good. It looks as if it will still be a wine bar, and it will be good for all of us to carry on working together—minus Tomas. A fresh start."

Bente's mind was whirling. She had always loved the place. It could be so much better than Tomas had made it—it had huge potential. An owner could conduct classes and hold wine tastings in addition to serving fantastic wines and delicious food.

And that wonderful wine cellar. Tomas had mostly filled it with crap, apart from one section of wines, but Bente imagined the walls lined with shelves and racks full of wine, with new lighting so that diners could sit in there. Clear the place out, clean it, bring in a table and chairs, and hold small tasting sessions for guests, but also for the staff. The wine bar could really take off with a different owner.

All it needed was a new, more ambitious concept.

30

That evening they made pizza with Dad's tomato sauce recipe.

"Isn't it great that the cork took your story to the next step?" Agneta put down her phone (open to Candy Crush, of course) as Bente placed the steaming-hot pizza on the chopping board she'd set atop the table. "It was such fun to see it all happen."

"Yes, it was definitely a turning point," Bente replied.

Hanna sat down at the table. Agneta gave her an encouraging look, but Hanna simply smiled and shook her head. What was going on? Now that Bente thought about it, the two of them had been whispering together while the pizza was being made.

Agneta poured them all chilled cola from the big bottle on the table—nobody felt like cocktails or wine today. "Was there a risk that the show might not happen?"

"Well, there would have been a show, but with a more personal approach. A bit more in the line of reality TV, with Didrik and me talking about ourselves and inviting along celebrity guests who would also . . . talk about themselves."

"Oh dear," Hanna said.

"Yes—it doesn't really feel like my thing."

"You don't say."

"Didrik seems lovely," Agneta said after a moment.

"Yes, he is." Bente sliced up the pizza and served them. There was no point in denying anything or pretending that nothing had happened;

Agneta always knew what was going on, and was well aware that he had stayed the night. "He's *too* good," Bente added.

"Don't say that—nobody is too good for my daughter."

"She's right," Hanna agreed. "Or for my sister."

Bente sighed. "It's just that we're so different. He lives in a house. He dreams of a family and wants children, probably enough for a seven-person soccer team. And me . . . I don't want that life. I don't even know if I want kids. That guy has everything, and he can have anybody he wants." It was a relief to put her troublesome feelings of inadequacy into words.

"But he wants you," Hanna said firmly. She took a bite of her pizza.

"It's not that simple."

"He does. I saw the way he looked at you," Agneta said with a smile.

"I understand what you're saying," Hanna went on, after swallowing her pizza. "Feeling insecure about the other person's feelings and your own means it's easier to keep everyone at arm's length. I'm the same way. But is it worth it—keeping everyone at a distance? Shouldn't we both take more risks? When we're lying on our deathbeds someday, will we regret the fact that we took a chance?"

Bente smiled. "Probably not."

They carried on eating while Hanna talked enthusiastically about her company's platform launch. Bente's phone buzzed with an email from the editor on *Krissie*.

She excused herself in the middle of Hanna's monologue on the synergy effects of the new operating system, and opened the message. Could she possibly come on the show tomorrow? Friday—the show with the highest viewer ratings. Watching *Krissie* that day had become a regular ritual for many people: partly a way to mark the end of the workweek, partly a way to wind down on a Friday night.

Bente was smart enough to realize that another guest had probably canceled, since they were asking her to appear at such short notice. She didn't actually care that she wasn't their first choice—she wanted to do it. She could be their millionth choice and she would still say yes on any evening they cared to invite her.

"I'm going to be on *Krissie* tomorrow," she informed her mother and sister.

"How exciting," Agneta said.

Then it struck Bente. Didrik would be there too. He had told her last night that he was the guest for Krissie's Friday profile this week. The Friday profile guest was always different, but he or she stayed for the whole show—being interviewed, helping the Friday episode's cook prepare food, chatting about book recommendations, tasting wines.

She would see Didrik tomorrow. They would be on-screen together. They might see each other behind the scenes during the ad breaks.

Shit, she wasn't ready for this. Still, they had to talk to each other sooner or later. They were going to Bordeaux soon, and then would come the next stage of the show's filming. Their quarrel couldn't be left unresolved.

"So when are you sleeping in your apartment for the first time?" Agneta asked.

Bente smiled. "I need to unpack my stuff and organize things first, so maybe at the beginning of next week."

Agneta nodded as her eyes filled with tears. "I can't believe you're leaving us."

"Mom, we'll still see each other." Bente went and sat beside her and gave her a hug, feeling tears rise to her own eyes.

"I know, but it's been so lovely living with both my girls again. It's as if we got back those three years we lost."

A sob escaped before Bente could stop it. Hanna, who was sitting on the other side of their mother, joined in the hug.

"We'll miss you," she said, squeezing Bente's shoulder.

"And I'll miss both of you."

"We know, sweetheart." Agneta stroked Bente's cheek.

"I've really needed this time with you. But now I think I have to move forward."

"Speaking of moving forward . . ." Agneta swallowed hard as if to pull herself together. She looked at Hanna. "Don't you think you should tell her now?"

"Okay." Hanna smiled, rubbed her hands together, and looked at her sister.

"What's going on? What are you two up to?"

"I've made an investment."

"Great." Bente took a sip of her cola, put down the glass, and waited for her sister to go on.

"I've bought the wine bar. Rendezvous."

Bente was completely taken aback. "What? You're the one who's bought the bar?"

"I am."

"'An investment.'" Bente laughed. "I thought you were going to say you'd bought another company offering a cloud-based platform that could revolutionize a client's current business. But . . . you don't know anything about the restaurant industry. Oh, I know! You can make Ellie the manager. You've met her, she's amazing, she . . ."

"Tell her the best bit," Agneta interrupted.

"The bar is yours." Hanna's eyes were twinkling.

"Mine? I don't understand."

Hanna placed her hand on Bente's. "I've bought the wine bar for you, so you can make Ellie the manager if you want. As you say, I know nothing about the restaurant industry. I know nothing about wine bars. I'm completely ignorant when it comes to wine, though I do mix an irresistible Manhattan."

Bente pulled a face at this claim.

"You see—you're already dismissing the only thing I think I'm good at within the culinary sphere," Hanna protested. "I can't run the wine bar. It's yours."

"It's out of the question. I can't accept it."

"I told you she'd say that," Agneta said.

"We knew you'd say that," Hanna went on. "If you won't let me give it to you, then I'd like you to run it for me. Then you can buy it from me over time, when you can afford it. But you have to run it for me."

"I've got the TV show to . . ."

"Yes, well, you know what I think about that, but . . ." Hanna sighed. "I can see how passionate you are about this story, and I'm happy for you. I really hope the show turns out well. You can do both, can't you?" She squeezed Bente's hand. "Running your own business is your dream, isn't it?"

Bente didn't know what to say. She wanted to say yes, but the TV show seemed to be making progress. She could step back into the limelight now, maybe work on more shows. Would she even have time to run a wine bar?

"If you're not interested, I can convert it into a tech hub," Hanna continued. "A kind of tech nursery. Bring in keen young people who can spend all day every day coding, creating, and programming." She gazed dreamily into space. "I'm thinking loads of green plants along the walls, table tennis, pinball machines. Maybe a room with couches and pillows where anyone can go for a little rest." It sounded more like a day-care facility than a tech hub to Bente. The very idea gave her palpitations. "The wine cellar would be perfect for the servers; it's cool down there. Plenty of space. All the bottles of wine were part of the deal, so we can use them to mix drinks for our after-work gatherings—sangria, Aperol spritz . . ."

"No, you can't do that." Bente took a deep breath. "And you can't use those wines to mix drinks—I selected some of them personally."

Hanna gave a little smile. Shrugged.

"In that case, you'd better run it for me."

31

Didrik smiled at his aunt. The interview had gone well.

She had asked him some probing questions. The Friday show always included a longer, more in-depth conversation with the special guest, and of course Krissie was a journalist—he wouldn't have expected anything less. For example, she had asked what his parents thought of his career choice, which had made him laugh before admitting that while his father was his greatest admirer, his mother wished he had stuck to the world of academia. Honesty in prime time—Mom could handle that. Krissie had smiled in mutual understanding; over the years she had suffered her own share of digs and jibes from her sister.

She hadn't mentioned his separation, though. When he got back from Paris, Krissie had contacted him to offer sympathy on the split. Sometime later, she had come by his office with lunch, and he had told her most of the story. It had been easier to talk to Krissie than to his own mother.

Appearing on *Krissie* made for a nice break from brooding over his conversation with Bente. They hadn't been in touch since she'd insinuated that he didn't mean that much to her.

Just anybody.

He couldn't let it go.

They were due to travel to Bordeaux in a couple of weeks. Didrik believed in the show. He wanted to be involved, and he had managed to book several exciting interviews during their trip that he believed could take the content they already had to another level.

But were they going to be able to work together?

The cooking segment came next, and he helped Krissie and the guest chef prepare a chicken dish. After that, the book panel offered tips on what to read over the weekend. Didrik had also brought a book to recommend, a biography of Queen Elizabeth. He loved the whole concept of Krissie's show, and realized he was really enjoying the live broadcast. His aunt was so good at making everyone feel comfortable.

Krissie looked into the camera. "And now it's time for our wine slot. This evening we are joined by the sommelier Bente Hammar."

Didrik gave a start. Bente?

"Bente is going to tell us about the best wines available this spring."

And there she was, wearing a pale-green, silky, knee-length dress with long sleeves.

She went over to the table where four bottles of wine were waiting, with three glasses in front of each one. Didrik didn't move for a second or two. He was completely unprepared. Then he felt Krissie's inquiring gaze.

"I believe you two are working together on a new show?" Didrik put on his most professional expression, got up from the sofa, and went over to join the two women. He was almost dazzled by the reflection of the spotlights in the highly polished glasses.

"That's right," Bente said. "It's going to combine wine and history, and we're actually heading off to Bordeaux in a couple of weeks, where we'll attempt to track down the origins of a mysterious old bottle of wine."

"Sounds great," Krissie said. "Definitely a show to look forward to!"

Didrik nodded in agreement. He looked into Bente's eyes. Their deep-green color reminded him of green wine bottles under those studio lights. She smiled politely. Coolly. How could she be so frosty? So distant?

Didrik had never been able to love half-heartedly. He couldn't feel an attraction and a passion for someone and then simply move on. He found it so hard to understand how someone couldn't open up completely when they really liked the other person.

The wine had already been poured into large glasses.

"Are we tasting Bordeaux wines today?" Krissie asked, picking up the first glass before swirling it around and sniffing.

"No, I've selected Pinot Noir, which is mainly associated with Burgundy and the New World. It's a fantastic grape at this time of year, springtime, especially to accompany lighter dishes. It's used to produce reds, but also sparkling wines and rosés. I have a wonderful Austrian rosé to begin with."

They sniffed and sipped while Bente talked about the wine, then she moved on to an American Pinot Noir.

"*Mmm . . .*" Krissie said. "A wine for the hammock!"

Bente smiled. "If you take another sip, I think you'll find this wine has slightly fiery, smoky notes. You can almost taste a charcoal grill! And caramelized tones—it opens up gradually."

Unlike certain people, Didrik thought, hoping she couldn't see how hurt he was.

Bente closed her eyes. "This is one of my favorites—I love it."

She spoke with such intensity about wine. Would she ever be able to feel even *half* of that passion for him?

Didrik nodded. Made an odd comment about licorice even though he couldn't taste any licorice at all. She lobbed a quick response back at him, said there might be a hint of aniseed, a touch of something herbal.

He couldn't help himself. "Don't you think there's an element of thatched roof in this wine?" His tone was awkward. He hadn't meant to sound exactly the way he felt; he'd planned to hide it a little better. He swirled the glass around. "Dish soap?"

Krissie gave him an uncertain look. Laughed disarmingly. "You're being very creative, Didrik."

Bente smiled. "Maybe—there's certainly a freshness, perhaps a little fruitiness."

When it came to the next wine, Didrik managed to comment first. "I'm getting . . ." He paused, and his poor aunt forced a smile. "Sweaty horse." He was sure he'd heard that stupid description somewhere.

"Sweaty horse." Bente's expression grew serious, and she remained silent for a few seconds. "Funny you should say that." She sniffed the red wine, turned to face him, and fixed him with her gaze. "The person who first got me interested in wine sometimes used that description for red wines." She stared meaningfully at Didrik, and something happened deep inside him. It was as if she wanted to show him that there was a little leeway, after all, that she could open up. But there was also a tentative little smile on her face, as if she were saying sorry.

"He'd picked the term up from a TV show in the eighties," she added.

"And who was it who got you interested in wine?" Krissie asked.

"My father." Her voice trembled, and he saw that her eyes were shining with tears.

"He must be so proud of you," Krissie said.

"I'm sure he would have been."

It was all Didrik could do not to close the distance between them, take her in his arms, and hold her. Instead he reached out his hand under the table so that no one could see. Squeezed her hand.

As he watched, she closed her eyes, holding back the tears that threatened to spill over.

◆ ◆ ◆

Bente had hoped that Didrik would understand—this had been a huge step for her to take.

She made her way to the greenroom while he remained on set, talking about the new season of *The Experts* that was to be filmed after the summer.

She could see him on the big screen in the greenroom. The show was live, and he was laughing and joking, being completely himself. He was always like that. His authentic self. But the fact that he had shared his innermost thoughts with her meant that he had been more than just genuine with Bente; he had made himself vulnerable too.

She thought about Henrik; she had always kept him at arm's length. And before him she'd done the same with Frederic, who in turn had always kept his own innermost feelings a very long way from Bente. This had suited her very well because it meant their relationship made no demands on her.

Didrik, on the other hand, had expected her to open up, exactly as he had done. Maybe doing so was worth it. Maybe she needed to do that in order to give him—to give *them*—an honest chance?

When he emerged from the studio, she was waiting. She looked him in the eye.

"Running a restaurant," she said, because she didn't know how else to start.

"Sorry?"

"Running a restaurant. Or a wine bar."

He raised his eyebrows. Apparently she needed to explain why she was standing here spitting out alternative careers.

"That's what I dreamed of when I was a child—running a restaurant."

"Okay?"

"And that's what I'd choose to do today, if I were to do something else. A wine bar rather than a restaurant, though. But I have to explain why. Everything kind of hangs together."

He nodded.

"Do you want to talk?"

He gazed into her eyes.

"I'd love to."

◆ ◆ ◆

They wandered through Gärdet. Today Stockholm was offering its entire repertoire of spring weather. A storm had just passed, and now the steel-gray bank of clouds was resting on the horizon, appearing to swallow the setting sun, which was staining the sky the color of a blood orange. The air was heavy with rain and dampness.

"First of all, I want to say that I really do want to share more," she began. "I want us to get to know each other, it's just that I'm not sure . . . what this is, what we have. I mean, you're Didrik Holgersson. One of Sweden's most likable personalities. You can have anyone you want." She laughed. "I guess this is my way of telling you I'm insecure." She stopped, smiled.

He smiled back. "Anyone I want? I want you." Those dark eyes twinkled.

His words made her heart pound.

I want you.

He gave a little laugh, sounding almost embarrassed. "I like you very much." He kept his gaze fixed on her and she had to look away, but she was still smiling. They set off again and she continued to talk.

"My parents were accountants, but Dad's passions were cooking and wine. He often talked about running a restaurant, something of his own. Nothing major, just a modest local eatery in the suburb where we lived. He had big dreams, and in the end his dreams became my dreams too. And somehow they have lived on."

She realized how stupid it must seem to him: her not being able to tell him about a simple childhood dream. It was just that if she started to talk about that kind of thing, about herself, her goals and her dreams, it seemed like she wouldn't be able to avoid digging up everything else. One question would lead to an answer that would lead to another question, and suddenly, she would find herself back at her father's death.

But she had to let Didrik in. If she wanted to hold on to him.

"That's very interesting," he said.

"It's hard to tell the story because it's all connected to my dad. I find it so difficult . . ." She fell silent.

"But you still dream of running your own restaurant?"

"Sometimes, yes." She thought about Rendezvous and Hanna's offer. She wanted to accept. "When the opportunity to work in TV came into my life, I loved it. But the dream of a restaurant has always been there."

"I like the sound of your dad, with his passion and his dreams, and the fact that you got those things from him. How were things before he died? What kind of person was he?"

"He was fantastic. Well, I thought so, but of course you don't see everything as a child. My sister and I were quite protected, I think. I guess both Mom and Dad wanted to shield us from the worst, and Hanna and I didn't realize how bad he actually felt. We lived in our little suburb in a lovely community. Everyone helped everyone else. If one person was painting their house, we all stepped in. Three parents painted while a fourth watched the kids and a fifth took a group of teenagers down to the store, and afterward we all had a barbecue. We were all welcome in one another's houses. It was like an Astrid Lindgren children's book." She couldn't help smiling at the memory.

Their house had been at the end of the street, closest to the lake in a residential neighborhood south of the city. All the properties had been built in the early 1990s and purchased by families with children. Bente's family lived in a fairly modest wood-paneled house that was painted yellow and had a garden that was easy to look after, a fantastic lilac arbor, and a showy drive. Dad had put up two columns on either side of the front door, like a frame. He had done it just as the neighbor across from them did the same thing—part of a kind of suburban-dad competition. A competition that her father eventually lost, in every possible way.

"But then a series of things happened. Their accounting firm . . . I don't know all the details, but they were suspected of accounting violations."

Everything had changed one windy Saturday afternoon at the beginning of November. Winter was well on its way. When Bente headed home from handball training, darkness was already falling, and she expected to be greeted by appetizing aromas in the kitchen, homemade tomato sauce to go with the pizza she would help make, the sports roundup on TV, more sports live on the radio—the announcers' tinny voices drowning out the TV commentary, because Dad thought the radio commentators were much better. Plus music on the little CD player in the kitchen.

Bente hurried home, but when she got there, there were no appetizing aromas, no radio or TV, only murmuring voices upstairs. Something was wrong. Mom and Dad came down and told her to go and take a shower. They were going to buy burgers instead. That was the day everything changed.

"Soon everyone knew that they were suspected of a crime, and nothing was the same again. Everyone avoided us. We were no longer invited to friends' houses for dinner; my sister and I weren't asked to come over to movie nights or to hang out after our handball matches. Then friends began to avoid me in school. Nobody would talk to me anymore. It all happened so fast, within a few weeks. In the end Mom and Dad were arrested. It was . . . horrible. When they were taken out of the house . . . all the neighbors came out onto the sidewalk and just stood there watching. No one spoke to me and Hanna. No one tried to console us. No one. They just stared as the police took our parents away, leaving us screaming and crying."

"Were there no adults to help you?"

"Social services came over until Lydia could get there. But no one on the street came to see how we were. None of the grown-ups we'd shared dinners with, the moms and dads who'd put a dressing on our knees when we fell off our bikes, or a bag of frozen peas on a swelling or a sprain. People whose children Mom and Dad had helped with their homework. I'd thought of them as family, but when the scandal broke, when we became tainted with shame, when that fluffy-pink Astrid-Lindgren life gave way to something bad, they withdrew completely."

"And then you moved away?"

She nodded. "They were convicted, and while they were waiting to be sentenced, Dad took his own life. The shame and everything else was too much for him. Once Mom was serving her sentence and Dad was gone, both Hanna and I felt we might as well move away. So we lived with Lydia on Gotland for a few years until Mom was released. She sold the house and bought a small apartment in the Söder district."

She fell silent for a while. "It was hard for me to make close friends after that."

"I'm not surprised—it's difficult to trust after you've been treated so badly." Didrik put his arm around her shoulders and gave her a hug.

They continued along Djurgårdskanalen and Strandvägen, before eventually reaching Skeppsbron. They then strolled along the southern shore of Lake Mälaren, with the City Hall on the far side. The red sky had faded to a peachy hue, sending swirling reflections across the waters of Riddarfjärden.

"Did he have a history of mental health issues?" Didrik asked tentatively, as if he were feeling his way in their conversation. She appreciated his tact but couldn't help feeling sad that he seemed so uncomfortable. But maybe that was only natural? It was a difficult subject, after all.

She shook her head. "In hindsight I can see that he had his ups and downs, but there was nothing at the time to suggest he was capable of taking his own life."

They stopped and he took her in his arms, held her tight. It was just what she needed, she realized. A hug. No more questions.

Didrik seemed to understand this, and afterward, they walked on in silence.

◆ ◆ ◆

"Do you want to come back to my place?" Bente asked as they passed the rocky viewpoint known as Skinnarviksberget.

"Yes, please."

"I mean *my* apartment."

"Sounds great. So you got it back?"

She nodded. "It's all happened really fast, and I've brought my stuff out of storage. I haven't had time to sort it all out yet, though, so it's a bit of a mess."

Didrik was thrilled that she had asked. The conversation had been heavy, and he now understood perfectly why it was so hard for her to talk about her past. He shouldn't have judged her so harshly. She was the kind of person who brooded on things, and he liked the fact that he had discovered that side of her. It made sense that it was a side she didn't show to *just anyone*.

They bought Thai takeaway and took it up to her apartment. There were boxes piled up everywhere, but behind them he could see pale-pink walls. A dark-green velvet sofa stood in the middle of the living room on a cream-colored rug. A large square mirror in a brass frame hung above the mantelpiece over the open fireplace, and a built-in bookcase covered one wall. It was already partly filled with books from an open moving carton. A small shelving unit with sections for storing LPs already housed a record player, and there was a speaker in the corner of one windowsill. The rest of the sill was occupied by potted plants, and a couple of smaller plants hung in crocheted holders attached to hooks in the ceiling.

Bente grabbed a couple of brass candlesticks and put them on the highly polished walnut dining table. Then she found candles and lit them.

"This is lovely." He looked around.

"Thanks. I'm guessing your place is a little . . . tidier?"

He smiled. "Right now I don't really have a place, but I've found a rental apartment in Gärdet. This feels as if . . . as if we're back in Paris."

He loved her apartment. Could he live like this? He'd always dreamed of a house and garden, and had moved out of the city as soon as he could. He'd enjoyed city life, but moving to the suburbs had been the next step in wanting to move on with his life.

It had started to rain again, a light drizzle this time. They sat down at the table by the window and ate their food straight out of the plastic containers, using the chopsticks they had brought from the restaurant.

"Thank you," he said after a while, reaching across the table to take her hand. "Thank you for sharing everything with me. Your story. And this."

"Talking about his death and what caused it brings up so many emotions." She picked up a piece of chicken. "It always makes me think so much, I feel as if I'm processing it all over again. All the whys . . . He had two children and a wife, he said he loved us, and I always *felt* loved when I was growing up. And we loved him. But our love wasn't enough."

Didrik had listened in silence. Now he wanted to say something consoling. "You do know it's not because your love wasn't enough. That it was all about how he was feeling," he said cautiously.

She nodded. "Deep down I get that, but every time it comes up, my mind starts whirling again and I have to remind myself and it's . . ." She sighed. "Fucking hard work." She put down her chopsticks, put her hands together on the table, and gazed out the window. "After he died, I felt so terrible. There were days when I didn't want to live, either, because he'd gone. When the grief tore me to pieces, the pain and the sense of loss, I sometimes thought the only possible solution was to do the same thing. Just take my life. But what stopped me was Mom and Hanna—I could never do that to them. Because I love them. Which makes what my dad did even more inexplicable. You don't *do* that to the people you love the most. But that's exactly what he did to us."

Didrik stood up, moved to the chair beside her, and pulled her close. She rested her cheek on his shoulder and let herself be held.

"I'm really sorry I behaved so badly the last time we were together," he said after a while.

"Don't apologize."

"I have to. I realize now how emotionally draining it must be for you to process this over and over again. I'm so sorry I went on and on at you."

"You couldn't have known. And they say it gets easier every time you go through it all like this, putting your feelings into words." She raised her head, looked at him. "And I've never put it into words like this before, so thank you for making me feel safe enough to . . ." Her voice trembled, she swallowed hard. "To take the risk."

They gazed at each other for a long time, and then he kissed her gently. She kissed him back.

"A cup of tea would be good," Bente said to him then. "The previous tenant left some behind, and I think I know where the cups are . . ."

She made the tea and dug out two cups, then she carried on taking things out of boxes. She hung several small pictures on a wall where there were already nails—motifs from France, Italy, Copenhagen, a small Alpine village. Memories of her travels.

"And . . ." She went over to a large leather bag next to the sofa, took out the picture he had given her, and hung it in pride of place.

She moved on to another box and began unpacking books with an air of concentration. "There's an old one about Bordeaux in here somewhere, I think it's from the fifties. It might contain old maps or something, pictures of what the area around the address in Médoc looked like back then."

Didrik nodded and helped her unpack a number of cookbooks and books on wine, which she arranged on the shelves. Many were in French, they were all well thumbed, and in some cases the covers were falling apart.

"Here it is!" Her face lit up and she brandished a volume with a red woven cover.

Didrik's phone buzzed with a news alert. He was taken aback to see Bente's name in the headline. What the . . . ? He clicked on the article. TV sommelier on her grief after losing her father.

He grinned. Typical headline on a slow news day.

"That was quick. You're topical again." He showed her the article. She looked shocked, then anxious. Then she read the piece and managed a smile.

"I guess they had nothing more worthwhile to write about."

He shrugged. "That's usually what happens."

They sat down and wrote up a schedule of the places they were going to visit in Bordeaux and the meetings they'd arranged, but he noticed she was a little quiet.

"Are you okay?"

"Yes, it's just . . . I'm not used to showing up in the media."

She shook her head and went to sit on the sofa with the book open on her lap. He joined her and they leafed through the pages together, reading selected passages that looked interesting. After a while Didrik could feel his eyelids growing heavier. It had been a long day. Beside him Bente was yawning too.

"Look at this!" she said suddenly, not a trace of tiredness in her voice now.

He followed her finger across an old map.

"This must be 16 Rue des Templiers, mustn't it?"

He nodded.

"And this must be the stone building we saw on Google Maps the other night. I suspected it was a vineyard, and I was right!" She was beaming now. "Look at the name!"

Didrik did.

CHÂTEAU DE CHÊNES

32

1944

Sven got out of the water as fast as he could and pulled on his clothes. It was difficult to do when his body was soaking wet.

Mathieu stayed where he was. "Wait!" he shouted.

"Someone saw us. We have to get away from here. You need to go back to the vineyard," Sven said quietly.

Mathieu shook his head. "No. I won't do it. I'm out of there for the first time in years." Slowly he waded to the edge and climbed the bank, like a naked, somewhat sinewy Greek god. He stopped next to Sven.

"Are you crazy? Get dressed and go home. We don't know who saw us. The Gestapo or the police could show up and arrest us at any moment."

"You don't know what it's like, having to hide away. For the first time in years I felt *happy*." Mathieu spread his arms wide, emphasizing his words.

"Mathieu, you can't search for happiness now. There's a war going on. France is occupied by the Nazis, who are looking for people like . . . like . . ." He just couldn't say it.

"Go on—people like us." Mathieu's expression was challenging. "Are you ashamed of us?"

"Ashamed? It's not about that. I'm terrified that we'll be caught. Your parents have kept you hidden for a reason. Doing what we did here, letting ourselves be seen, was just stupid. Totally idiotic. I shouldn't have stayed at the vineyard. I've exposed your family to . . ."

Mathieu snorted. "Fine. Just go. You think I don't know that you're planning to return to the Legion?"

Sven shook his head slowly. "Not planning exactly. But they're expecting me back, and soon they might start searching for me."

"So you want to go back?" The look on Mathieu's face was wary.

"I have to, eventually. I signed a contract."

In fact, Sven wanted nothing more than to stay here with Mathieu. Of course he did, but the Legion would never allow it. As a deserter, he risked being sent to jail. If you joined the Foreign Legion, you had to remain loyal.

"A contract." Another snort of derision. "As if soldiers haven't already done enough?"

"We can't talk about this now—someone has seen us." Sven began to walk away, but Mathieu didn't follow him. "Are you mad?"

Mathieu simply stood there, watching him go.

Sven hurried back to the vineyard and continued working on the vines from where he had left off, as if nothing had happened. He waited for Mathieu. Why, why had he gone with him? Why had he taken such a huge risk? What danger had he exposed Mathieu to?

He gazed over toward the edge of the forest on the other side of the vines. The minutes passed. Mathieu didn't come.

What if something had happened to him? What if he'd already been arrested?

Eventually Mathieu emerged from the trees. Sven let out a long breath. He felt like throwing up with relief. His stomach turned over and he let out a sob. Hugo was working nearby and looked up, but Sven simply held up his hand.

Mathieu wandered along a row of vines. Hugo stared at him in surprise. It was almost nine o'clock; at this time Mathieu was usually indoors, working. Mathieu didn't even glance in Sven's direction, but continued into the house.

Sven sighed. Right now Mathieu was safe. He had no idea who had seen them, but right now Mathieu was safe. *Mathieu is safe,* he repeated over and over again in his mind, like a mantra.

The day passed, and Sven jumped at every sound from the road, but they were spared a visit from German soldiers, the Gestapo, or the French police.

Mathieu stayed out of the way and didn't show up until dinner. Sven couldn't bring himself to think about their quarrel. He was still too shaken and frightened because they'd been seen.

After dinner, Hugo went outside to carry on working. Sven was about to join him when Juliette asked him to stay for a while.

She began to clear away the dishes. "I saw the two of you in the river earlier."

Sven's heart was pounding. A wave of relief flooded his body. It wasn't an outsider who had spotted them. No one was going to report them to the police. Then the shame hit him. Then the guilt. Then the fear. Juliette would never report her son, but what if she reported him? Maybe she thought that Sven had led Mathieu astray?

"I'm so sorry, I . . . I can turn myself in to the police or the Nazis. I don't want anything to happen to Mathieu." He tried to pull himself together. "It was my fault. It was my fault."

Juliette stopped what she was doing. "Calm down—nobody is going to report anybody, and I know it wasn't *your* fault. I know my son, the hopeless romantic. I also know that he was the one who put you in danger."

"I should have had more sense."

Juliette nodded. "Yes, you should have." She pulled out a chair, indicated that Sven should take a seat, then sat down opposite him. "But love makes us indiscreet. Love makes us crazy." She smiled. "After we heard about Gerard's death, a part of Mathieu died too. But he's come back to life since you arrived. He's himself again. It's so good to see, and I'm so grateful to you, Sven."

He didn't say anything.

"But what you did today was dangerous, and I'm well aware that Mathieu doesn't always consider the consequences of his actions."

"I won't do it again, and I won't allow Mathieu to take off like that."

"That's not your responsibility. But Mathieu listens to you. You make him feel safe." Saying that, she smiled again, wider this time. "The two of you took a huge risk today. Even if love is what enables us all to survive right now."

"What we were doing, Mathieu and I, it wasn't . . ." Sven searched for the right words. "I mean, we're not . . ."

Juliette shook her head. "We don't need to talk about that. With all the terrible things that are going on, how can tenderness between two people be wrong? Love is life-affirming. It's what makes the world go round. How can it be bad for two people to love each other?"

Sven took in what she said; it sounded so straightforward, so self-evident a truth. A million miles from her describing him as having a disgusting, revolting sickness, which is what Sven had imagined everyone else thought.

"Was that why you joined the Foreign Legion?" Juliette asked.

He nodded. "I thought it would cleanse me, that I'd change. And it gave me a new place to be. I was able to get away from home, where I was no longer welcome."

◆ ◆ ◆

Mathieu considered the large map in front of him. It would be used to help another family escape from Bordeaux, from occupied France. Mathieu and his parents never knew the names of the people they helped, so there was no risk of them revealing anyone's identities if they were arrested and tortured as a way to make them talk. Whoever they were helping now could easily be someone he knew. He'd had classmates who came from Jewish backgrounds, and it was strange to think that none of them were still around. Some had been sent to labor camps where they might well have died. Others had gone underground or managed to flee. Mathieu and his parents could have been involved in making that happen—he really hoped they were.

He sighed. He knew that Sven thought he'd been careless and rash, but Mathieu lived in these conditions all the time, just like Sven did. He just tried to handle it in a different way, in order to keep from going under completely. If he worried as much as Sven about everything that had happened, he wouldn't be able to cope.

Gerard.

Friends and acquaintances they hadn't heard from for months.

Had they been deported?

Killed?

And then there was the loss of his own personal freedom.

The constant fear.

Mathieu's way of dealing with it all was to find those glimmers of light in the endless darkness, like searching for a twinkling star on a cloudy night. Recently Sven had been Mathieu's star, the source of his happiness.

The candle flickered in a draft. The hatch opened and Sven clambered down, moved toward Mathieu.

"I'm sorry about our argument earlier."

"Is that an apology?" Mathieu asked. "Because if so, it's a terrible one."

"No, it's not an apology. I meant everything I said, even though I was angry. We have to be careful."

"I understand," Mathieu admitted. "And I know I should have been terrified because we risked being caught—but I can't live like this." He looked Sven in the eye. "You asked how I can be so happy. But it's a question of survival. Right now you make me want to live. And being with you is what makes me able to keep going."

Sven gave a faint nod. "But think about your parents. The Nazis have already come looking for you; you're on some kind of list. If you're caught, that will put your parents in danger, because they've hidden you. I won't be safe either."

Mathieu let the words sink in. He realized that his behavior had been selfish. If it came out that Mathieu had been kept hidden, then of course the Nazis would take a closer look at his parents and they'd be in harm's way. Plus their work with the resistance movement would be at risk of being revealed.

"We can live here," Sven went on. "We can be together. Here. But we have to be careful."

Mathieu didn't say anything.

"Here at the vineyard, we can dance in the darkness," Sven said.

Mathieu thought about Gerard again. About how he had once said almost those exact words in order to teach Mathieu how to carry on. When the war broke out and they both were called up, Mathieu had been inconsolable. But Gerard had wanted to spend their last few days together behaving as if nothing had happened. He didn't want to talk about the war anymore, he had said. He wanted them to have fun together, to live life to the fullest. *Dance in the dark.*

Mathieu later said the same thing to Sven. The fact that Sven had repeated those words, had tried to *understand* Mathieu, made his heart break.

"And the Legion?" he asked.

Sven looked at him for a long time. "I don't know. I wish I had an answer, but what can I do? I haven't been able to get back, and there's nothing they can do about that, but sooner or later I'll have to return."

"Do you *have to*?"

"What else can I do?"

"I've been living like this for four years now."

"And I've signed a contract, taken an oath. A soldier doesn't break his word." Sven was whispering now, as if someone from the Legion might be lurking around the corner in one of the passageways.

Mathieu gave a brief nod. So he was going to lose Sven too.

He couldn't bear it. He turned away.

Sven gripped his shoulder, but Mathieu shook him off and left the cellar.

◆ ◆ ◆

The following morning Mathieu woke early. He couldn't stop thinking about the quarrel. Sven had tried to make amends, but Mathieu hadn't been able to let go of the question of the Legion. Once again he thought about what Gerard had said, what Sven had said. Who knew how much time he and Sven had left together? Something terrible could happen tomorrow.

Mathieu knew exactly how to surprise Sven. A little gift to make up for yesterday. Previously, Sven had talked to Mathieu about the wild raspberries and strawberries he used to pick back home in Sweden in the summer. Mathieu knew a place where delicious raspberries grew in abundance. So before breakfast, before the sun had even risen above the treetops, he grabbed two mugs and crept out. No one would see him at this early hour.

He arrived back just after Sven had woken up, and met him in the doorway. Mathieu had found wild strawberries, too, and both mugs were filled to the brim. This would make a fantastic breakfast. Triumphantly he held up his treasure, showing Sven the dark-pink berries.

"Where did you get those?" Sven looked neither pleased nor surprised, just suspicious.

"I picked them in the forest. I know the perfect place from when I was a kid."

"So you snuck out into the forest?"

"I wanted to surprise you. I wanted to talk about yesterday and apologize for . . ."

Sven's expression hardened. "So even after what happened yesterday, you snuck out into the forest?"

"Yesterday was fine, it was only Mom. No one saw me this morning. I was careful and I was only out for a little while, less than a hundred yards away. I wanted to apologize for pressuring you about the Legion last night."

"To apologize for . . ." Sven raised both hands in a gesture of resignation. "What is it you don't get? This was how everything started yesterday." He spoke calmly even though he was clearly furious; the vein protruding in his forehead gave him away. "So you put yourself in danger, and now you're trying to say sorry by doing the same thing again." He shook his head.

"But I did it for you." Mathieu placed a hand on Sven's cheek, but he pushed it away.

"Someone might see us."

The dismissive action broke Mathieu's heart. "Like who? My parents? I'm prepared to stand up for this, for our relationship. I'm prepared to stand up for my love for you, but you've made it perfectly clear that you're not ready to reciprocate."

He put the mugs down on the bench and one fell over, the little berries tumbling out onto the ground. Then he ran away.

Down into the cellar, where everyone thought he belonged.

◆ ◆ ◆

After dinner that evening, Sven sat in his room with the small brass plaque on the desk in front of him, etching away fervently. It would soon be finished, but he had no idea when he would be able to send the bottle. Right now it was too risky; he might have to wait a month or more, depending on how the war progressed. The thought of how worried his mother must be made him feel sick. She hadn't heard from him for what seemed like an eternity.

He liked working with the metal, which was cold and hard to the touch. The work was slightly painful, and the pain took away all the thoughts in his head.

Hearing the sound of fast-moving footsteps outside, he stopped his work and slid the little plaque under his bed with his tools. The Germans confiscated—or requisitioned, as they put it—everything they could. Maybe they'd want the piece of metal too.

Sven hurried to the door, heard stressed voices, people speaking French. One sounded like Marcel, the owner of Château du Boda, the neighboring vineyard. Sven ran downstairs to see what was going on.

"They've started asking around again," Marcel said. "They're looking for Jews, communists, homosexuals." He looked very anxious. "And . . . I don't want to worry you, but Jérôme saw Mathieu in the forest the other day. He asked me if Mathieu was allowed to be outside."

Juliette inhaled sharply. Hugo and Sven remained silent.

Marcel continued: "I told him nothing has changed, and that he absolutely mustn't tell anybody."

◆ ◆ ◆

Sven went back upstairs and returned to working on the plaque. He couldn't stop thinking about the last couple of days, how Mathieu constantly pushed the boundaries and risked attracting attention. He was putting so many people in danger—Mathieu's parents and friends.

Sven made up his mind. He had to leave, for everyone's sake.

Maybe his absence would give Mathieu the chance to start behaving sensibly and go back to the life he had lived before: listening to his parents, staying hidden, focusing on simply surviving. Until the hell of occupation was over.

He packed his few possessions. Put on the clothes he had been wearing when he arrived. He hadn't worn the shirt and suit during his whole time at the vineyard, or the change of outfit, which he now pushed into his bag.

He looked at the brass plaque, which he'd left lying on the bed. He slipped it into his pocket; maybe he would be able to get back to the Legion now. The plaque would be a special memory of the vineyard.

He gathered up the last of his things, then left the house.

◆ ◆ ◆

Mathieu clambered slowly up the ladder to join his parents for supper, which on these warm evenings and in these difficult times usually consisted of a little boiled water and, if they were lucky, some stale bread.

He had considered missing supper in order to avoid Sven, but his mother would have come looking for him, and he would have had to come up with some excuse. He was really bad at lying to her.

Only Juliette and Hugo were in the kitchen. Mathieu helped himself to some water and cut a small piece of the bread Juliette had set out. He sat down. "Where's Sven?"

"He hasn't come down yet," his mother said.

Mathieu took a bite of the bread.

Always a polite guest, Sven never missed a meal, or showed up late for supper. Maybe he was sick?

After a few minutes, Mathieu said, "I'll go and take a look." He went up to Sven's room, but it echoed with emptiness. The window overlooking the yard was wide open. An envelope on the bed fluttered in the breeze. Mathieu's name was on it, in Sven's neat handwriting.

He picked it up, opened it, and read the letter inside.

Taking in the words, he was overcome with the same pain he had felt on the day he and Gerard had been separated. But this was even worse, because Sven had chosen to leave him.

For Mathieu's *own sake*. For his safety, Sven wrote.

Mathieu tried to hurl the piece of paper at the wall, but it only drifted as it left his hands, and fell slowly until it reached the floor.

33

A week later, Bente and Didrik traveled to Bordeaux. Elnaz was busy with another production and had decided to stay home, and they were looking forward to spending some time together, just the two of them.

They arrived early in the morning, and after dropping their luggage in their respective rooms, went downstairs for a late breakfast. The small boutique hotel had a beautiful inner courtyard where the staff served a generous breakfast every morning, and cocktails every afternoon. The air was filled with the scent of honeysuckle and the aroma of café au lait and freshly baked croissants. Bente got there first and sat down at a table, and Didrik soon appeared. He gently touched her shoulder and sat down beside her.

He went through the notes he'd written down on the train journey while Bente glanced through her own research. Château de Chênes seemed not to exist anymore—they had searched everywhere, gathering up every scrap of information they could find in Sweden. Bente's book on Bordeaux had been published in 1955, and at some point after that the vineyard had ceased production.

She had even asked Frederic about it. He discovered some notes about bottles from the vineyard in an old wine cellar whose list was available on some network he belonged to, but the owner knew nothing more—he had acquired the cellar as part of the house purchase. Frederic had never personally heard of the vineyard either.

The Bordeaux city archive was quite a distance from the hotel, but after so much time on the train, they were both looking forward to walking on this beautiful early-summer morning. On the way, they passed Porte Cailhau, which with its medieval turrets and towers resembled a miniature Disney palace. Bente allowed herself to be enveloped by the atmosphere of Bordeaux, which was always warm and welcoming. Maybe she would record a piece for her YouTube channel at a sidewalk café later?

Following her appearance on *Krissie*, her channel had gained considerably more viewers and subscribers. Despite her reaction when Didrik showed her the news item—one bordering on terrified panic—she had plucked up her courage and gone through the comments on Krissie's Facebook page. Though she'd felt nervous, there had been nothing but positivity in the comment box beneath the clip of her slot on the show. The director had been in touch to book her again, and they had discussed Bente making more appearances during the summer and fall.

Things were looking up for her.

She looked at Didrik, walking beside her across the bridge over the Garonne River toward the eastern bank where the archive lay.

Yes, things were definitely looking up.

◆ ◆ ◆

The modern building that housed the archive was cool, thanks in part to its stone floors. Bente and Didrik registered at reception, then continued into the high-ceilinged reading room, where a man with graying hair, glasses, and a blue checked shirt welcomed them. He was Frederic's contact; they had corresponded with him by email before leaving Sweden, and he had the material they'd requested waiting for them.

There were several large boxes containing documents on Médoc and the small area of the peninsula where they believed Château de Chênes was once located. Bente took the first file out of the top box, and Didrik took the next.

Bente paused and thought for a moment before opening it. What if they didn't find anything? She had so much faith in these files, these bundles of old documents. She hoped they would provide the key to the rest of the story. But what if there was no trace of Sven, or any Scandinavian?

As she looked through the plastic pockets, her mind continued to whirl. What would happen to the show if they never discovered the truth about the bottle?

She turned page after page, read and read. Finally she saw something and beckoned Didrik over. "Look—in 1991 Château de Chênes was bought by the neighboring vineyard."

"That explains why we haven't been able to track down any information about it."

"We need to ask the owner of Château du Boda what she knows."

Didrik nodded. They had already booked a meeting with the vineyard owner, and were due to see her that afternoon.

As they carried on with their task, Bente was taken aback to see an old newspaper article that mentioned Château de Chênes. She asked Didrik to film her while she talked.

"So this was written postwar, and it's about the winemakers who owned the vineyard known as Château de Chênes." She looked down the page and read the piece more closely. "It says the couple helped the resistance movement." She beamed. Things were beginning to fall into place.

"They were honored after the war for their efforts," she continued. "Apparently they sent secret documents in hidden compartments in wine boxes. They drew maps on the back of the wine labels to help people escape the Nazis—Jews, communists, homosexuals, and dissenters, among others."

Didrik put the camera down and examined the article.

"If Sven really did end up there, maybe they worked together in some way?"

◆ ◆ ◆

Two hours later they were in a rental car, a lemon-yellow Citroën—the color made it appear more sporty than it actually was—on the way to Château du Boda, which lay nearly an hour to the north of Bordeaux.

As they drove along the sun-drenched route, it struck them that they were probably making the same exact journey that Sven had once made.

Didrik was behind the wheel, dressed in cool shorts and a thin cotton shirt. Bente glanced at him, then turned and looked out the window. Vineyards, row upon row of vines, but also fields of crops whizzed by on both sides of the road, and she reveled in simply being here, in this moment.

They soon turned onto a narrow dirt track that led them to a large circular graveled area in front of the main building, with hand-painted "P" signs directing them to the parking lot.

They parked and made their way to the main building—a modest entrance hall with a round table and two armchairs. There was no one in sight.

Bente took out her phone and glanced at the comments on her video clip again—she had done this frequently since publishing it a few days ago. For some reason, this time she suddenly realized what she was looking for—negative comments. Every time she scrolled down the screen checking for updates, her heart started racing. Was this really healthy?

After a minute or two, the owner appeared and introduced herself as Sylvie. She led them out to the back where there was a large pergola. The view of the vineyard was stunning, with closely packed rows of lush vines stretching down toward a small grove of trees, and a black church tower in the distance.

"Would you like something to drink? Wine? Water?"

"Please," Didrik said, and Bente nodded in agreement. While they were waiting, they watched the workers, who were toiling away in the warm sunshine. At this time of the season, side shoots were pruned from vines in order to expose the grapes to as much sunlight as possible.

Bente had come to Bordeaux with Frederic on several occasions and helped out in his family vineyard, which had given her a completely different understanding of the work and the thought that went into every single grape that was harvested.

Sylvie returned with a carafe of red wine, a jug of water, and glasses.

They sat down on sun-bleached cane chairs at a worn but sturdy wooden table. Sylvie poured wine and water, and Bente sniffed her glass. Cabernet Sauvignon was the most dominant grape on the Médoc peninsula, and she immediately recognized its characteristic notes—black currant, plum, but also a hint of cedarwood and grassiness. When she tasted, she detected the typical harshness associated with Bordeaux, followed by an herbal quality. In Médoc, slightly harsh wines with very good aging potential were made mainly from Cabernet Sauvignon grapes grown on deep free-draining gravel.

She loved the wine. "Delicious." She smiled at Sylvie. She would really like to serve this at Rendezvous—imagine the stories she could tell, both about classic Médoc and about this particular vineyard! Maybe she could source wines made from grapes grown at Château de Chênes—what a dream that would be! "By the way, is it okay if we film our conversation? Obviously we'd get your permission before showing anything on TV."

"No problem. How long are you staying in Bordeaux?" Sylvie asked once the camera was switched on.

"Only a few days," Bente replied, taking another sip of her wine.

"You must try one of the beaches here in Médoc, on the Atlantic coast. The water isn't warm, but the beaches are so beautiful."

"We'll definitely do that. How long have you had the vineyard?"

"Only a few months. I bought it from an elderly man whose children weren't interested in taking over."

"I read that on your home page—Jérôme Fossey, wasn't it? And he acquired the neighboring vineyard, Château de Chênes, in the nineties?"

"That sounds right—I think it was sometime in the nineties. That's the part of the vineyard you can see from here." Sylvie pointed to the right. "Over there. Those vines used to belong to Château de Chênes. We can look at an old map if you like?"

Sylvie went inside and came back with a yellowed map, which she unfolded. It clearly showed the boundaries of the property. The main building of Château de Chênes was no more than five hundred yards from the main building of Château du Boda. The two vineyards with their rows upon rows of vines were located right next to each other.

"We found out from the city archive that the owners of Château de Chênes worked for the resistance movement," Bente said.

"Really? That could well be true. Now that you mention it, I seem to recall Jérôme's children saying something about that."

"Do you happen to know if there was a Swedish man living here toward the end of the war?"

Sylvie shook her head. "I'm afraid I don't know much about the vineyard's history."

"And you don't know why Jérôme took over Château de Chênes? The Latorres had a son, Mathieu—was he not interested in running the business?"

Once again Sylvie shook her head. "I'm sorry, I have to admit that I don't know. I ought to read up on the history of both vineyards." She laughed. "It's really Jérôme you should be talking to."

Bente was thinking exactly the same thing. He might be able to answer all their questions.

"Unfortunately, he's not entirely . . . He suffers from dementia, and it can be tricky to have a conversation with him."

Bente wasn't too keen on disturbing an elderly man with dementia with her questions. "Let's start with what we can find out here," she said, smiling at Sylvie.

"I can call the care home, see if they think Jérôme might be able up for a visit tomorrow?"

"That's very kind of you," Didrik said warmly.

"And there's lots of old stuff over at Château de Chênes," Sylvie added. "No one's taken the time to go through it all. Jérôme's kids made a start, but there are a whole lot of boxes and papers, and they gave up. I know the cellar has more or less been left untouched since the old owners handed the place over—I'm sure there will be things of interest to you. You're welcome to walk through the passageways down below where we are now—now that would be worth filming! You can get to the main building of Château de Chênes via our wine cellar. The underground passageways were constructed after the First World War—several of the vineyards here in the village are connected."

"That does sound exciting," Didrik said. "We'd love to take a look."

"There's electricity and lighting for a short distance, but you can easily find your way with flashlights."

They all exchanged smiles at the prospect of an adventure.

Sylvie led them down into the wine cellar. If they'd had more time, Bente would have happily studied the hundreds of bottles stored beneath the vaulted ceiling. Instead they continued along the damp, winding passage. Sylvie handed them each a flashlight.

"Keep going as far as you can. When you see a small staircase, that means you're right under Château de Chênes."

"Thank you so much for your help—we'll be fine from here," Didrik said.

"You're welcome. I'll leave the door open so you'll be able to see your way out when you come back."

They set off along the narrow passage. After a while they saw a plain door, and went through it.

They found themselves in a small, pleasant cellar. There was a desk in the middle of the room, piled high with boxes. A couple of benches and a bookcase lined the walls, and at the far end they saw a staircase leading up to a wooden hatch.

"Here we are!" Didrik announced.

There were boxes of various sizes piled up all around the desk, as if someone had begun to sort everything out but had given up the attempt.

They began to look through the boxes, but found only old newspapers and books filled with notes on the harvesting of grapes and the storage of wines. Didrik shone the beam of his flashlight around the room while Bente kept on searching. He walked over to the bookshelves where there were several old wooden boxes.

He opened one, then called, "Look at this!"

Bente joined him. He shone the flashlight into the box while she filmed. It contained yellowing sheets of paper covered in pencil sketches.

They took one out to look more closely and saw it was an image of two hands, one resting on the other. The hands were strong, male hands. It was a very simple drawing, but intimate. Bente couldn't explain how, but the artist had managed to convey something incredibly tender and loving in those hands. Perhaps it was because the thumb of the upper hand appeared to be stroking the other person's wrist—she couldn't quite put the impression into words.

They unrolled another sheet of paper. This one was a drawing of a naked man. Judging by the style, it had been done by the same artist, who was clearly extremely talented. Once again, the artist had managed to convey so much. The eyes of the man in the picture were filled with desire, so much so that Bente almost felt embarrassed, as if she had walked in on an intimate moment, the beginning of a sexual act. She wondered if Didrik had had the same reaction. In the bottom corner was the letter *M*—as if it were the name of the subject rather than a signature.

"The *M* is drawn the same style as the oak tree on the plaque," she said.

"You're right." Didrik nodded and looked straight at the camera, which Bente was still holding. They turned the paper over, and there it was.

Sven Steen, 23 June 1944.

Their eyes met. *At last.*

"He was here," Bente said, smiling at Didrik before zooming in on the signature.

"We've finally found Sven." Didrik reached for her hand in the darkness, and they clasped their fingers together.

Bente turned the camera on herself. "So we've discovered drawings done by Sven Steen here in Bordeaux, in the cellar of the former vineyard where the coordinates on the cork led us. We still don't know who arranged for the bottle to be put on the ship—we're guessing it was Sven, but what were his intentions for it? And how does that fit with the fact that he was sent away to a prison camp and died before the bottle could have been posted?"

She continued looking through Sven's intimate drawings of the winemakers' son. "They were in a relationship," she said quietly. "Sven and Mathieu."

Didrik nodded. Gazed at the images. "Undeniably."

They switched off the camera and carried on looking through the boxes. Once they were done, they gathered up the drawings and put them back in the wooden box. They took some items that seemed relevant—notebooks, letters, and so on—and then retraced their steps.

At least they had something to work on now.

After they'd reemerged, Sylvie showed them into a room where they could study what they had found by daylight.

Bente started with a box that contained items that she thought had probably belonged to Sven. Small half-finished drawings.

And a bundle of half-written notes.

34

Didrik filmed Bente as she read aloud:

"Open the wine bottle. Your Dejje."

She opened several notes, each one a variation on a single message, as if the writer had been trying out different phrases.

Open the wine bottle. Then you'll find me. Your Dejje.
Drink the wine. Find me. Your Dejje.

Your Dejje. The same words as on the brass plaque on the wine bottle.

"Since the note is in Swedish, Sven must be the one who wrote it," Didrik said, and Bente agreed.

"Maybe he'd intended to send the note with the bottle."

Didrik thought for a while, trying to piece the story together. "Perhaps it was Mathieu's parents who shipped the bottle, after he'd died. They might have added a note of their own, but it perished in the water?"

Bente nodded. "Could be."

They gathered up all the papers and put them back in the box, just as Sylvie appeared with yet another box.

"Good news! Jérôme is having a good day today, and he'd be happy to see you tomorrow, if you like?"

Didrik glanced at Bente, who looked as eager as he felt.

"Absolutely!" he said as Bente nodded.

"Great—I'll give you the address." Sylvie placed the box on the bench where they were working. "This might be of interest too. Jérôme's mother corresponded frequently with her sister in Paris, so I wondered if there could be something helpful in the sister's letters. You're welcome to take them back to your hotel."

"Yes, please," Bente said. "That's very kind of you."

"To be honest, I'm glad that someone is doing the job for me. I'd love to know the history of these vineyards, but the thing about the war is that you have to dig for information people wanted to hide back then. Which makes the search more exciting, of course." She glanced at the other boxes on the bench. "You can take those too."

As they walked through the hallway, Bente stopped in front of a pencil sketch hanging on the wall. A naked man.

Sylvie followed her gaze. "Beautiful, isn't it?"

Bente nodded. "We found several similar drawings down in the cellar—the artist is the Swedish guy we asked about. Sven Steen."

"Oh, really? I didn't know he was Swedish. Now that you mention it, I remember Jérôme saying that someone at Château de Chênes did quite a lot of drawing, and that he was very good. Apparently several of his pieces have been sold and can be found all over the area. If you contact an art dealer, you might be able to track down more. I know Jérôme tried to find as many as possible. I guess he didn't know he had such treasures in the cellar."

Bente smiled. "Once again, thank you so much for all your help. We'll be very careful with the drawings and the documents."

At that, Didrik couldn't help smiling too.

Sylvie didn't know that the last time they had borrowed something old, French, and valuable, they had literally drunk every last drop.

◆ ◆ ◆

That evening, they went out to eat, choosing an empty table outside a restaurant on a square. A street musician was playing melancholy pieces on a violin in the warm evening. Twilight was already falling.

All the tension between them had melted away, thanks to the progress they had made in their search. They were able to relax a little more tonight. It was as if the two men's love story had impacted their own. They talked about what it must have been like to live as lovers—and homosexuals—during that period, and in occupied France. How the war must have affected the men, even if neither Bente nor Didrik could really imagine it, of course. All at once Bente's own problems seemed so insignificant—and maybe they were?

After they'd eaten, they ordered a café crème each and sat in silence for a while, letting everything sink in.

In this fresh environment, Bente wondered: What kind of life was it that she was choosing, one that involved constantly worrying about what others thought of her? Why chase fame and recognition from people she didn't care about? Her reaction to the newspaper headline, her obsession with updating and searching for negative comments . . . Suddenly she found herself viewing it all as if from a distance, and could see the matter from outside herself. Was what she was doing even worth it?

"Are you okay?" Didrik's voice brought her back to reality, and she put down her cup.

"I just have some stuff to think about. That news piece on what I said about Dad on *Krissie* . . . I had such a weird reaction when you showed it to me."

"Tell me." His eyes were full of concern.

"My heart started racing. Everything went black and I thought I was going to faint. It was so . . ." She shook her head. "My reaction was totally out of proportion to what the article said. It was as if I was reliving everything that was written before, during that terrible time. As if the feelings are still there, lying dormant in my body."

"If I'd known, I would never have shown it to you."

"You couldn't have known. But after reacting so strongly, I've been doing some thinking. Why do I want to get back into it all? Why do I need the attention?"

"Redress," Didrik said quietly, almost as if he was talking to himself.

"Sorry?"

He cleared his throat, sat up a little straighter, and gazed out across the square. The violinist fell silent, and the gentle hum of conversations around them took over. "You've been through so much—is it that you want some kind of redress? Restitution?"

Bente nodded. She'd considered that explanation herself, but at the same time she didn't really care what their friends and acquaintances from her childhood thought of her.

At least that's what she'd told herself.

"And validation." As she said the word, everything became obvious to her. Her thoughts fell neatly into place inside her head, as if she had just solved a crossword she'd been working on her entire life. "The kick of being popular. When I was most in demand, when all the invitations for appearances came flooding in, I got totally high on the whole thing." She looked at him. "It made me feel accepted."

"You and I are driven by different things. For me I guess being on TV is maybe some kind of revolt. For you it's validation. And now that you know that, you can handle it in the right way."

She nodded pensively. Didrik was also driven by passion. She was passionate, too, at least about *this* project, but she still didn't know if that passion was worth everything that went with it. The reasons why she wanted to go on TV were complex. And possibly not entirely healthy.

On their way back to the hotel, Bente stopped walking and looked at Didrik.

"Hanna has invested in a wine bar, and she wants me to help her run it. Rendezvous."

"Seriously? Wow!"

"Seriously! I think it could be really good." She felt so happy, and at that moment she knew she wanted to run the bar. Somehow she would make it work with the TV show. "Something occurred to me," she went on. A nagging anxiety, a thought that she would have preferred to dismiss, but one that had taken root in her mind. "Sven finished up in a prison camp, and no one seems to know anything about Mathieu. If Sven and Mathieu were in a relationship . . . what if they got caught? Is that why we haven't found any more information?"

They looked at each other in silence. A homosexual couple who'd gotten caught during the time when the Nazis occupied Bordeaux.

Didrik didn't say anything. Bente's heart ached—she hoped she was wrong.

◆ ◆ ◆

That night they made love slowly and tenderly, driven by a sense that they needed to make the most of what they had because nothing, not even love, could be taken for granted.

35

Jérôme's care home lay between the city and Médoc, and consisted of a small building covered in pink plaster. Bente and Didrik strolled through a fantastic garden with a small white marble fountain bubbling away. Shortly after they entered the reception area, a nurse arrived and showed them to Jérôme's room.

"I'm afraid Monsieur Fossey isn't having a very good day today, but when we asked him yesterday, he said he'd be happy to see you."

"I suppose it's still worth a try," Didrik said as they continued along the corridor. What else could they do, now that they were here?

"Your visitors, Monsieur Fossey," the nurse said. A man with a cloud of gray hair was standing by the window watering some potted plants. He turned, and they saw dark-brown eyes behind his glasses, bushy eyebrows.

"My visitors?"

The nurse looked apologetically at Bente and Didrik. "I hope it goes well. Try asking your questions and see what he says." She turned to Jérôme. "You wanted to see Bente and Didrik. Two young people from Sweden." Bente couldn't help smiling at the description. "They want to ask you some questions about your vineyard."

Jérôme's face broke into a smile. "My vineyard, how nice. It's not for sale," he chortled. Bente wasn't sure if he was joking.

"We're making a TV show," Didrik explained, sitting down opposite the old man. "We have one or two questions."

"We're trying to find out who sent a bottle of wine—this one." Bente took the empty bottle out of her bag and showed it to him. Jérôme screwed up his eyes and took a step back, as if he needed to look at it from a distance.

"I don't recognize it."

"No, we didn't expect you to, but we think it was sent by a Swedish man, Sven Steen, toward the end of the war. He was at Château de Chênes—he arrived there in connection with the resistance movement in 1944."

Jérôme looked at them. First Bente, then Didrik, with an expression that suggested he was wondering whether it was worth talking to them or not.

"I don't know anything about that," he said.

Didrik cleared his throat. "What about Mathieu Latorre, the son of Juliette and Hugo, the couple you bought Château de Chênes from? Do you know if he stayed on at the vineyard after the war?"

Jérôme shook his head. "No, he was sent to Paris after he came home from the front, and I think he stayed there."

Bente and Didrik exchanged a glance.

"Do you know of anyone from Scandinavia who was living in Bordeaux during the war?" Bente ventured.

Jérôme appeared to be thinking. He gazed out of the window for a moment, then looked back at her.

"No. I don't know anything about that."

◆ ◆ ◆

They took a detour and drove out to the coast. Didrik challenged Bente to take a dip in the sea; he didn't think she would do it, but she made it clear that he had underestimated her, and she even managed to persuade him to do the same. He bought two blue-and-white-striped beach towels from a tourist store, then they returned to the deserted shore and ran laughing into the water in their underwear. It was absolutely freezing cold. Afterward they wrapped themselves in the towels and held each other until they were warm again.

Back at the hotel, they lay down on the bed in Didrik's room and gazed up at the ceiling fan as it spun around and around. They'd hung the towels up to dry, and they flapped in the breeze from the open balcony door.

Didrik listened to the sounds of the city. The unmistakable sound of a French traffic jam, a cacophony of car horns. Laughing children on the way home from school. The scrape of chair legs on the concrete slabs outside the café down below.

He reached out and took her fingers in his.

"What cold hands you have," he said.

"What warm hands *you* have." He could tell that she was smiling, and he turned his head and looked at her.

"This is a very different work trip." He stroked her cheek and laughed. "My best work trip ever."

"All work trips should be like this."

He thought about all the times he had traveled for work, conferences at other universities, guest-lecturing overseas, filming in Sweden as a guest on various TV shows. At first he hadn't minded the traveling; it had been an exciting aspect of his career. Then he had found it boring being away from Lovisa. What would life be like in the future? What would a life with Bente look like?

"What are you thinking about?" she asked.

He smiled. "What my life is going to be like. What do you expect your life to look like in ten years' time?"

"I'll be doing a job I'm passionate about, possibly running Rendezvous, which by then will have become a fantastic wine bar. I *might* also be making the odd appearance on TV, but I'm absolutely not interested in fame."

"And family?" He couldn't help noticing that she hadn't included him in her dreams.

"I don't know . . ." She gazed at him. "I'm not sure if it's right for me. Having children."

When he saw her uncertain expression, his mind began to spin. Could he go through this again? With someone who wasn't sure? Investing all his emotions in a person and a relationship that didn't lead to where he wanted to go.

"So family life isn't for you?"

Bente shrugged. "I just don't think it's my thing."

He nodded slowly.

"Is that a problem for you?"

"No. Or rather, I don't know. I don't even know if I can have kids, but there are other ways to build a family."

Bente didn't say anything.

He wasn't sure why he felt so awkward about the whole thing. Maybe it was because he had always imagined the future so differently. Was he ready to let go of the dream of a family?

"Why haven't you told me this before? That you don't want kids."

"What do you mean? It never came up until now, when you started pushing me for information, as usual."

"'As usual'? I think I took a clear step back, and I've given you every chance to tell me."

He took a deep breath. Tried to slow his racing heartbeat. This was stirring up his emotions. Once again he felt shut out by Bente, excluded from her thoughts and innermost feelings. It was as if she had suddenly become a different person. He couldn't help wondering what she really wanted. Did she even want to be with him?

"It's just that I devoted several years to a marriage with a person who didn't know what she wanted, or at least wasn't honest with me," he said eventually.

"But I *have* been honest." Bente propped herself up on her elbows, looked at him. "I've been honest all along."

"I don't know if I have the energy to fight for it again." He was thinking out loud.

"Fight?"

"Yes—I don't know if I can do it." He suddenly felt incredibly tired. Should he really have to fight like this for love? Shouldn't it be simpler? If two people were meant for each other, surely that relationship developed spontaneously? Everything went smoothly, and you just knew. Wasn't that what happened with true love?

"Are you trying to break up with me?" Bente's expression was serious.

"I don't know, but . . ." He took a deep breath. "I'm not sure if this is what I want."

There it was again: a sense of constantly being changed by someone else. It seemed to him that he had found a new side of himself, something that Bente had helped him discover. Yet at the same time, he didn't want to give up on other dreams. The dream of marriage and a family.

All his life he had tried to fit into a template that someone else had created for him—starting with his mother. He had always made an effort to fit into her image of what her son should be like. It had been the same in his marriage—Lovisa had been opposed to the person he was, to the person he became. Of course Didrik realized that everyone has to compromise within a relationship. But ever since the breakup with Lovisa, he had realized that their compromises had been about his entire personality. About the way he wanted to live. This business of children and a family—could he really walk away from all that? He didn't want to change yet again within a relationship. He wanted to be himself, 100 percent.

"I don't get it. What do you mean? Are you trying to find a way out of this?" Bente looked searchingly at him, her eyes burning into his.

"No, it's not like that. I'm just questioning what we both want, wondering if our goals are too different."

She nodded. "It's fine. I understand if this was just a way for you to move on. To get over your fantastic ex-wife." She got up off the bed.

"It's absolutely not about that, and you know it." He reached for her, but she pulled away.

"Oh, I know it, do I? Then why are you determined to invent some kind of conflict? This issue shouldn't be a problem—you're *making* it into a problem."

"So my dreams of a family are invented?"

She rolled her eyes. "Don't twist my words." She sank down onto the bed, put her head in her hands, then looked up at him, her eyes shining with tears. "Maybe you're right. Maybe we're too different. Maybe we need time."

His stomach contracted. Was she right? Did they need more time? Did *he* need more time? Was Bente right? He had no idea. He was completely confused. Why did love—life!—have to be so demanding all the time?

"I think we do," he heard himself say. "I need to give this some thought."

"And what about the summer party?" Bente said. "Are we . . . are we still going together?"

"The party?" She was asking him about a fucking party? They were in the middle of breaking up! "Why bring that up?"

"It's not important, I was just thinking about the show. It will be good PR if we go, and—"

"How can you think about TV24's summer party right now? What upsets you the most—the fact that we won't be seeing each other anymore, or that you'll be missing the party?"

Unbelievable. He'd thought that he had finally found his way to the person Bente really was, had gotten her to open up, to let him in. And now this.

He gazed at her in silence for a few seconds. "Like I said, I need to think. And maybe you should think about why you want to be with me—if you even do."

Bente looked shocked, as if she couldn't believe he was capable of raising his voice. But he was, and he had—and he had no intention of giving in. He wasn't going to let anyone walk all over him again.

She simply nodded slowly.

"I'll go back to my room," she said quietly as she got to her feet.

36

1944

The evening air was oppressive, suggesting that a thunderstorm was on the way. Sven headed for the village, hoping to catch a late train. He didn't meet a single car as he walked along the main road, which was something of a relief.

The soldiers were sitting in the restaurant as usual. They were eating and talking loudly, but there was no sign of any of the villagers—surely the curfew hadn't yet gone into effect? It was too early. There was a strange atmosphere; he thought he saw the odd movement at a window, as if people were on the lookout. Something was happening.

Then he saw. Several buses were parked on the square, and there was feverish activity outside the town hall. German soldiers were going around with lists, talking with each other about something, leafing through documents. One of them was directing a group, although Sven couldn't quite see what they were doing. He didn't want to stare—this was not the time to draw attention to himself.

A young woman hurried past, keeping her head down. Sven stopped her with a gentle touch on her arm. "What's going on?" he asked quietly.

She looked at him with terror in her eyes. "The Germans have been given orders to remove people," she whispered. "People they believe have gone underground. Jews. Deviants. Communists." She spat out the last three words. "They've been given new lists of names. But if you're not in one of those categories, you've got nothing to worry about." There was a clear value judgment in the final sentence, and Sven was relieved when she scurried away.

He quickly crossed the square, making for the station. Should he really be traveling now? Then he saw a familiar face—the soldier who had given him a ride on that first day. He had a list in his hand and wore a troubled expression. He spotted Sven at the same moment.

"Good evening." The German soldier glanced over his shoulder before coming over to Sven. The troubled expression gave way to something more like resignation. Sven couldn't work out what was going on in his mind, or what was on the list. For a second he was afraid that the soldier knew everything about him.

"Good evening," Sven replied.

"It's been a while. My name is Max, if you remember me?"

Sven took off his hat. "Of course I do. Thanks again for the ride." Sven didn't smile but he spoke politely, trying to keep his voice steady.

"You were at Château de Chênes, weren't you?"

"That's right."

"Have you been there all along?"

"I have."

"I understand." Max cleared his throat. "Have you seen anything of the son?"

"No, he hasn't been around at all. He's in Paris."

"I see." Max glanced over his shoulder again, as if to make sure that no one was listening. Then he took a step closer to Sven, looked him in the eye, and lowered his voice. "Listen to me, and listen carefully. Some members of the Gestapo will soon be going to the vineyard to check out the rumors we've heard about him. His name has been on our lists for a long time, and now they're determined to go and conduct a thorough search."

Sven nodded but didn't say anything.

"They'll be leaving in about twenty minutes." The German nodded toward a group of armed soldiers. "I might be able to delay them for another ten minutes."

Sven looked at him with gratitude to show that he had understood the warning, that he realized what a risk Max had taken.

Then he walked quickly across the square, turned the corner, and slipped into the shadow of the buildings. He continued out onto the road, back the way he had come. His shirt was sticking to his body. His suitcase felt heavy, but he kept going. Only when he was out of sight of the square and the village did he dare to speed up, and after a couple of minutes, he broke into a run. He hurled his case into the ditch so he could run faster, lengthening his stride. He ran so fast that he was gasping for breath. He had to get there before the Germans.

The distant sound of an engine made him slow down. Could he jump into the ditch, hide among the trees? But then he was dazzled by a car's headlights, his own figure casting long shadows on the road behind him. They'd seen him. Definitely. It was too late now. He should have picked up the sound earlier, but it was as if his panic and all his turbulent emotions had canceled out his senses.

He slowed down, ambled along as if he were out for an ordinary evening stroll.

Please let them drive past. Please let them drive past.

When the car continued at the same speed, Sven exhaled. It drove past him, then stopped after a few yards. Reversed. Sven stopped too.

"In a hurry?" Two German soldiers looked out of the window.

"Your papers. ID," said the soldier in the passenger seat.

Sven swallowed hard, took the documents out of his inside pocket. They were damp with sweat. He handed them over, and the German took them between his thumb and forefinger. Unfolded the papers, checked everything. Showed the driver.

"Jump in, we'll take you to the village. We need to ask you a few questions."

Sven thought about the buses he'd seen in the square. Thought about Mathieu. He wasn't going to make it in time. *He wasn't going to make it in time.* Were the Germans already there?

He didn't know.

Would he ever find out?

As he got into the car and it set off toward the village, he felt as if he was headed straight for the notorious labor camps.

◆ ◆ ◆

Mathieu was still in Sven's room. His parents had come up, seen him, and immediately realized what had happened. He had twisted free of their consoling hands, brushed aside their soothing words, then run down the stairs to look for Sven. What if something happened to him? But Mom and Dad had persuaded him to stay. Mathieu's presence out on the roads and in the village would cause all kinds of problems.

He was lying on the bed, breathing in the smell of Sven from the sheets, when he suddenly heard a noise and sat bolt upright. Footsteps on the gravel, then his parents crossing the wooden floor.

Had something happened to Sven? But it could be anyone out there. Mathieu had to hide. He flew down the stairs, and as he ran into his parents' bedroom, someone hammered on the front door. He yanked open the hatch, and as he reached the bottom of the cellar steps, he heard Jérôme's voice—the boy from the neighboring vineyard—and slowly exhaled. Then he heard what Jérôme was actually saying.

"The Germans are on the way."

"What's happening?" Mom's agitated voice.

"I think they know about Mathieu. The priest ran over to our place; he'd heard something about Château de Chênes being on a list. Apparently there's a lot of activity among the Germans in the village. He asked me to warn you; he was going to speak to the others."

"Thank you, Jérôme. Are you all right?"

Mathieu didn't hear Jérôme's reply, but the door soon closed. He assumed that the neighbors weren't in any danger.

The hatch opened and Mom came down. She handed him his old rucksack and a water bottle. "You have to get away, Mathieu. As far as you can. All the way to Lassac."

To Lassac, to Gerard's parents. Mathieu hadn't heard from them since Gerard died, since they sent him their son's dog tag.

He looked at his parents. "What about you?"

"We'll be fine. Don't think about us, it's you they're after."

What if the Germans forced his mom and dad to talk? Maybe he should stay. Then the Nazis would get the person they were looking for.

"Please, Mathieu. Run. We'll be fine." Hugo put a protective arm around his wife's shoulders, then looked sternly at his son. "Go."

Mom held out a lit candle.

Mathieu quickly kissed each of them on the cheek, shrugged on the rucksack, and took the candle. He then set off along the winding passageways leading to Château du Boda, the vineyard next door. The darkness and dampness surrounding him were dense. He could hear the storm rumbling overhead, or was it the Germans' running footsteps? He didn't know, he just kept on walking through the darkness for several minutes.

Eventually he reached his destination. He recognized Château du Boda's cellar with its long wooden shelves, which were usually full of bottles of wine, but now stood empty because the Nazis had requisitioned every harvest.

Then on through the passageways to the next vineyard. From time to time he had to claw at the cobwebs that stuck to his face and clothes. All the cellars were empty and dark. He felt as if he were heading into eternity. The fact that he was now using these passageways, that he was finally on the run as he and his parents had constantly feared he would be one day, gave him a feeling of having arrived at his fate.

Eventually he reached the heavy door at Lassac. From here he could leave the passageways and continue out into the fields and forests.

Hide as best he could until he found help somewhere. At least he would be alive.

The door opened and there stood Gerard's mother, Madame Bresson. Her expression was grim as she looked at him.

"Madame . . ." Mathieu began, but he fell silent when he heard footsteps up above. Voices. German. Someone shouting orders, more running footsteps. What were the Germans doing here? Had she *reported him*?

Gerard's mother didn't like Mathieu's type. Maybe the solidarity between the vineyards meant nothing to her. *He* meant nothing to her.

The next moment he heard boots clattering down the cellar steps.

37

That damned summer party meant absolutely nothing. For some reason, possibly as an emotional defense mechanism, Bente had simply started going through the practical details in her head during their discussion. The journey home from Bordeaux, contact with the production company, the rest of the research, the summer party. And that was where she had gotten stuck—what were they going to do about the party? It was just something she had blurted out in the moment, a meaningless thought that for some reason had come out of her mouth.

But yes, they did need time to think. She needed to give Didrik the chance to do that. And she needed time herself.

Was she going to lose him? If he had time to think, would he realize there was someone better out there? Some famous, successful woman who, unlike Bente, wanted children. But who, unlike Lovisa, also understood Didrik's career and way of life. Someone who was *perfect* for Didrik.

Someone who wasn't Bente.

The thought was like a thorn in her flesh. She wasn't good enough for him, of course she wasn't. How could she have believed anything else?

She stayed in her hotel room until dinner. They still had material to go through; she might as well distract herself by making a start.

She took the box of Jérôme's mother's letters down to the outdoor dining area in the inner courtyard—she wanted a change of scenery. She ordered a salade Niçoise and turned her attention to the letters. They were all written by Jérôme's aunt, his mother's sister.

She read each letter carefully, first while drinking a glass of white Bordeaux, and then, a coffee. The letters were well written, and were mostly about life in Paris during the occupation. However, a lot of information was omitted, so the content was often sparse. The love between the two sisters shone through; no doubt they'd written to one another as a way of trying to maintain some kind of normalcy.

Then she saw it.

This particular letter opened with the usual details about the availability of food and other essentials. Jérôme's aunt wrote that it was hard to obtain eggs, then she added a few details about how her husband had been spending his time. Next came the fateful words. Everything inside Bente froze, and the last spark of hope she'd felt was extinguished.

She paid the bill, gathered the letters together, and went up to Didrik's room. She stood outside his door for a few seconds. Closed her eyes. Should she disturb him? Yes, they were here to do a job. She knocked.

Didrik opened the door and gave her a questioning look. Silently she handed him the letter. He took it and read, first to himself and then the shattering words out loud.

"My beloved sister, the news you shared with me is heartbreaking. So many people who have disappeared. Darling Mathieu. It feels like only yesterday that he was running barefoot among the vines when I came to visit. Please, God, let him survive. All this time I thought he was in Paris. Poor Mathieu. Again, please let him survive."

Didrik glanced at the top of the letter. "This was the summer of 1944."

Bente nodded. "And no one seems to have heard from Mathieu after that. He must have been arrested."

Didrik looked pensive.

"So I presume we've solved the mystery," Bente continued. "He and Sven were taken prisoner, and neither of them was ever seen again." She couldn't stop her voice from trembling, and quickly cleared her throat.

"Mm," Didrik said, gazing at her.

Was he going to hug her? She didn't think she could bear that right now. "I'll go and fetch the camera—we ought to film this." She hurried to her room and returned with it. She placed the letter on Didrik's desk, then read it aloud.

"But we still don't know how, when, or why the bottle was sent to Sven's parents," Didrik said, looking into the camera.

"Like we said before, maybe Hugo and Juliette sent it after Sven disappeared?" Bente speculated. "Because Sven wanted his parents to have it."

"That's one possible explanation."

They switched off the camera. Didrik came over to her, put his arms around her, and she allowed herself to be hugged. They had searched for the origins of the bottle, found the sender, been astonished by the love story of the two young men at the vineyard, and now they had reached the end of the narrative. A heartbreaking end, one that made her feel a sense of resignation. What had made her think she could hope for more? This was the Second World War. Millions of people's stories had ended in tragedy—why should Sven and Mathieu have been any different?

She looked at Didrik. They had shared their own story, but now it was over too. She took a deep breath. "I'm going back to my room to pack. I can return the boxes to Sylvie first thing tomorrow."

"No, don't bother—I'll take them. You have an early train to catch."

"Won't you be on the train?"

"My brother is coming down—I just found out. So I'm going to stay for another day and meet up with him—he's working on a project here."

"Okay," was all she could manage.

She made her way slowly to her room. He really had been serious. They had definitely broken up.

38

The following morning Didrik went through Sylvie's boxes, which Bente had left with him. He had found nothing new, and was placing the last bundle of documents in a box when a receipt dated 1982 fell out. It was the amount of money that caught his attention: 19,500 francs, a huge sum of money at that time.

The receipt was from an art dealer who had paid the money out. Didrik saw that it had been signed by the dealer, and then he saw a familiar name. *Ida Steen.* He'd seen that first name somewhere before—was she a relative of Sven's, maybe his sister? Did this mean that Sven's family knew that he had been in Bordeaux? He opened up his laptop and scrolled through their notes until he found the address list from the National Archive, which Bente had sent him earlier. Ida Steen. Sven's mother! He took a closer look at the receipt. Ida had brought in some artwork to sell to the dealer, and the artist's name was . . . Dejje Steen.

Didrik leaned back against the wall, his thoughts whirling. What was going on here? Had Ida traveled to Bordeaux after her son's death and found his work? In that case, she must have somehow learned that Sven had been in the Médoc region. So had she come here in the autumn of her life—she must have been pretty old in 1982?

The receipt had been issued by Galerie Doré. He googled the name and discovered to his delight that the gallery still existed. A shudder of excitement ran through his body. How he loved this kind of thing! He made a note of the address, checked the hours of business, looked at his watch. They opened in half an hour. He went down to the breakfast room and ordered a baguette and a cup of coffee. Then he drank the coffee quickly, took the baguette with him, and set off into the morning rush hour.

◆ ◆ ◆

The art gallery was on a street of old buildings, its entrance tucked into an arched portal, the name painted in a handwritten style directly on the facade. Tall windows overlooked the street, and the glass doors were also modern in style.

Didrik walked in and took a deep breath. Paintings were displayed on every wall, from floor to ceiling. Behind the desk stood an older lady who was inspecting a small watercolor. She rubbed at the frame with her thumb, then set it aside as he approached.

"Good morning, my name is Didrik Holgersson." He held out his hand. "I'm a historian, and I'm looking for pieces by a Swedish man who lived here in Bordeaux just before the end of the Second World War. He might have been known as Sven Steen or Dejje Steen." He took the receipt out of his pocket. "I found this in the cellar of the vineyard where he was living. Do you know this artist?"

The woman examined the receipt, then said, "Goodness me. Dejje Steen."

Didrik realized that he ought to be filming this. He clicked on the camera on his phone, then paused and asked: "Is it okay if I do some filming?"

The woman nodded. "It's fine." She took off her glasses and looked at him. "I know Dejje Steen. He's a local artist who has been popular for a long time. A bit of a hidden gem, but hugely appreciated by those who have discovered him, particularly in this area. We might even have something of his at the moment." She smiled. "Come with me."

Didrik followed her through the room.

"Here we are." She looked up at the wall. The only pictures hanging there were watercolors. None of them matched what he knew of Sven's style. The woman picked up a low stool and clambered onto it with some difficulty.

"I can do . . ." Didrik began, but the woman simply reached up and took down a painting before he could finish the sentence.

It was a watercolor in a gilded frame, slightly larger than A4. The subject was a vineyard, painted in muted shades of green—from the pale-green bunches of grapes to the emerald-green grove of trees at the edge of the picture. The rows of vines were executed with sweeping strokes, yet gave off an air of precision. A slender man was walking between the rows with his back to the observer, as if he were heading toward the horizon. As a guess, Didrik thought the subject was middle-aged, based on his posture and the graying hair just visible below his hat.

"But this can't be by Sven," Didrik said hesitantly, looking more closely now. "Or rather, Dejje Steen. It looks so . . . new." Had Sven perhaps had access to watercolor paints during the war?

"It definitely is." The woman smiled and turned the canvas over.

And there it was, *Dejje Steen* on the back. But . . . it was dated 1979. And farther down, the word *Mathieu.*

"So you deal in paintings by Dejje Steen?"

"Sometimes. There are a few around."

"And this is dated 1979."

"It is."

"But he died in 1944."

The woman laughed. "I don't think so. He's probably dead now, but we were taking new paintings from him until the eighties. Unfortunately, I never met him, even though I've worked here for many years. He never came in himself; others brought the pieces in for him. On one occasion it was a neighbor, as far as I recall, and on another his elderly mother, who didn't speak a word of French." She laughed again at the memory.

"Can I buy this?"

"Of course—let me see how much it costs." She went behind the desk, tapped away on her computer, then gave him an eye-watering price. Didrik didn't need to think for too long; he took out his card, then watched with satisfaction as she carefully packed up the painting.

◆ ◆ ◆

On the way back to the hotel, he let the information sink in. How could Sven have painted this picture? The only possible explanation was that he hadn't died in the prison camp, as they had believed all along. Which made his sending of the wine bottle entirely logical.

So what had actually happened to Sven? Had he managed to escape from the camp?

Didrik supposed that, unlike in Hollywood movies, the Foreign Legion probably didn't hunt down its deserters over land and sea. But if Sven had left the Legion and remained here in Bordeaux, and his identity had become known, he would certainly have faced a jail sentence for deserting. If he had stayed in France, then it was likely that he would have used his nickname, Dejje Steen, for his paintings.

According to everything Didrik and Bente had read, Sven had been an outstanding legionnaire and a dedicated soldier. Giving all that up and deserting must have been a big thing—so big that he had decided it was better to let the world believe he had died.

This was too much to take in. He had to tell Bente! He didn't want to do this on his own. He took out his phone and called her without the slightest hesitation.

But there was no answer.

◆ ◆ ◆

Didrik returned the boxes to Sylvie later than day, and told her what he'd found out. She urged him to contact Jérôme again.

"Sometimes he has better days."

That was probably true, but it was already late, and his brother was due to arrive soon. Plus he wanted to talk things over with Bente; conducting research without her just wasn't the same. If he was going to see Jérôme again, then Bente had to be there. They would do it together.

His brother drove up to the hotel in a rental car. Didrik was waiting and gave him a hug right away.

They had dinner at a small bistro. Didrik ordered wine confidently, and Victor was impressed by his newfound knowledge.

"So Bente has already gone home?" Victor said when their main courses were served.

"Yes—we were intending to travel together, but I changed my ticket so I could meet up with you."

"Cool. How's it going, working with her?"

"Pretty well . . . but to be honest, there were other reasons why I didn't want to catch the same train. She . . . we . . ." He didn't know quite how to put it, but Victor picked up on his discomfort. For some reason Didrik wanted to talk about what had happened.

"Have you fallen out?" Victor helped him out.

Didrik sighed. "Kind of. There was definitely something between us, but somehow it's slipped through my fingers. I feel like I need time to think."

Victor nodded. "Maybe it's too soon after the divorce?"

Didrik shrugged. "It's not that exactly, it's just that we both have things to consider. We're very different." He leaned across the table and looked at his brother. "I've spent my whole life trying to fit in, being a version of myself that doesn't actually reflect the person I really am. Starting with Mom's dream that we follow her into an academic career . . ."

"Which you did." Victor grinned.

"Absolutely, and I enjoy what I do, but then Lovisa had her say and constantly told me that all this TV stuff was a bad idea."

"So what does Bente want? Does she find your public profile difficult to deal with?"

"I don't think so. It's just . . . She's unsure about children. She says she doesn't want kids, it's not her thing. And I've always wanted a family, it's always been my dream. That's what life's about." He spread his hands wide.

"Hang on, isn't that also something that Mom has always drilled into us?" Victor took a sip of his wine. "I mean, I do want to be a dad, but for as long as I can remember, she's made her opinion crystal clear. It's always '*When* you have children, *when* you become a dad, *when* you have a family,' as if there's no alternative."

"You're right. She always been pretty pushy on the subject."

"Is it possible you're fooling yourself, Didrik? Are kids really *your* dream? Is having a family the main goal for *your* life? Or is this about Mom's expectations of you? Surely you have plenty of other qualities? And imagine what this is like for Bente. You're in the process of getting divorced, you've just started seeing each other, and you start asking about children. Then suddenly you need time to *think*. If I were Bente, I would absolutely feel like I was just your rebound."

Maybe Victor was right? If so, the thing that had driven him all his life, the dream of what he thought would make his existence perfect, had once again caused destruction. Old sorrows and conflicts were destroying the wonderful joy that Bente had brought with her. Didrik had looked at life quite differently ever since he'd gotten to know her, and yet all his old baggage had continued to affect their relationship.

Dreams and goals were important, and he had always lived by the belief that a person should allow their dreams to guide them.

At the same time, Bente had shown him something new. She didn't limit him. She opened up fresh possibilities. Maybe children weren't the most important thing, after all—and certainly not at this moment. Plus with Bente he felt more alive than he ever had in the past. Wasn't that worth pursuing? Suddenly he knew, he felt it in every fiber of his body: He had made a big mistake. It was Bente he wanted, more than anything else.

And he had to tell her. Right now.

39

The lights inside Rendezvous came on just as Bente opened the door. The staff were already busy. Ellie was behind the bar arranging glasses. Tonight they were open only for friends and employees.

Bente hadn't yet worked out what she was going to do with the place, and still hadn't given Hanna a definitive answer one way or another. In Bordeaux she'd thought she'd decided, but over the past few days she'd received multiple inquiries about appearing on various TV shows, and she felt incredibly flattered. She was reluctant to say no now that a new TV career was knocking at the door. If she was going to run the bar for Hanna, she wanted to do it wholeheartedly.

She had, however, helped organize everything in the lead-up to the reopening: planning the wine list, buying the wines, working out the staff roster for the coming week with Ellie. Losing herself in the preparations had been calming—it had stopped her constantly thinking about Didrik. She had spent full days in the bar, working into the evenings over the past week, and during the last twelve hours she had gone home only to shower and change. For the evening, she had chosen a pale-green dress in a thin fabric, shot through with metallic threads. It was possibly too dressy for a bar opening, but she had bought it for TV24's party, which she would no longer be attending, and she'd figured she might as well get some use out of it.

As she walked over to the bar, her mother popped up from behind the counter. She had found a bottle of vermouth, which she set down with an air of triumph. Hanna emerged from the kitchen carrying a bundle of paper straws, and a moment later dropped one into a ready-mixed cocktail.

"Hi." She smiled at Bente. "I'm trying to persuade Ellie to let me mix cocktails here once a week. A kind of guest appearance. She's just tasted my Manhattan."

"I have," Ellie said with a somewhat strained smile.

Hanna passed her mother the tall glass with the straw. Agneta closed her eyes and took a sip. "So. Delicious."

Ellie gazed at the two of them, then looked at Bente. "I'm amazed that you managed to become a sommelier with those genes."

Bente grinned at her friend, who slipped behind the bar and took a bottle of sparkling wine out of the refrigerator. Bente picked out two ordinary wineglasses—they both loved to drink their bubbles that way. Ellie opened the bottle—a *crémant* from Alsace that was going to be their house fizz. She filled the glasses and they toasted each other.

One of the kitchen staff put on the opening-night music playlist, and then the first guests arrived—Lydia, as well as Uno and Mirja, who were happily reunited. A few minutes later, the place began to fill up with families and friends of the staff. There were light bites on offer, along with bubbly, wine, and beer, plus Hanna's cocktails.

When Elnaz walked in wearing a black sparkly long-sleeved dress, Hanna whistled appreciatively before greeting Elnaz with a kiss on the lips. Bente knew they were dating, but she had no idea how serious it might be at this stage.

Elnaz came over with flowers for Bente, and gave her a hug.

"You look fabulous," Bente said.

"Thanks—I'm going on to TV24's summer party. You're not coming?"

"No, I wasn't invited."

"Would you like to come with me? I have a plus-one—my sister was supposed to come, but she dropped out."

"I don't know . . . Maybe I ought to be here." Bente gestured with her arms wide. She didn't really want to leave the celebration now, and of course she knew that Didrik would be at the party.

He had called, had left a voicemail message saying he wanted to see her and talk. He had something *important* to say. She hadn't called back. Hadn't wanted to talk. He was the one who had asked for time to think, so time to think was exactly what he was going to get.

Then she had received a text message yesterday.

I'm back in Stockholm, have been trying to call you.

She assumed that he thought she wanted to go to the party, and had found that quite hurtful. So she had ignored his text. And she had no intention of going to the party. If she saw him there, she wouldn't be able to keep her distance, which she was determined to do.

Hanna drifted over and served Elnaz a Manhattan, which she accepted with apparent reluctance.

"I'm trying to drag your sister along to the TV24 party." Elnaz took a cautious sip.

"Good idea—Didrik will be there, won't he?" Hanna grinned.

"I assume so." Elnaz looked inquiringly at Hanna.

"It's just that Bente has been very down since she got back from Bordeaux."

"Why? I thought the research went really well. All the material you sent was fantastic. I've already got a team cutting together your video clips to make a little teaser."

"That's not why she's down—it's because of Didrik." Hanna sounded serious, but there was a mischievous glint in her eye.

"There's something going on between the two of you, isn't there?" Elnaz asked.

"There *was*. I don't know . . . We broke up in Bordeaux."

"But why? You're perfect for each other."

"I don't think so. He's popular, loved by the public, he's got a fabulous TV career. And he really wants children."

"Okay, so he's popular with the audience, but he's a perfectly ordinary guy, which is what I like about him," Elnaz said.

"I'm not . . ."

Was Elnaz right? She knew Didrik, possibly better than Bente did, and Bente was well aware that she could be a little stubborn sometimes. After all, Didrik had only said that he needed time to think.

"Look, why don't you come to the party? It might be good to do a little networking with people in the industry."

And Didrik, Bente thought. She would have the chance to see Didrik. She'd been avoiding him. But what if he wanted to tell her something good, something she wanted to hear? She didn't have to start dating him again . . . But if he was there, she could at least listen to what he had to say.

She smiled at Elnaz. "Okay—why not?"

◆ ◆ ◆

Two hours later they arrived at the venue Cirkus in the Djurgården district, where they were met by velvet drapes, happy party guests, and twinkling lights. Everything seemed to shimmer—sequined dresses, spotlights, jewelry, shiny hair, and smiles fired off toward the clatter of flashing cameras. Bente searched among the faces but couldn't see any sign of a historian in tweeds and round glasses.

She stayed close to Elnaz as they made their way to their seats for the evening's entertainment and awards ceremony. They had a good view of the stage, and when a young guy who Bente vaguely recognized from a children's show went up to receive the award for TV24 profile of the year, the audience's enthusiasm seemed boundless. Drawn in by it, Bente applauded energetically. It was clear that the winner was very popular, but she had very little idea of what he'd actually done. At that moment she realized how far she had drifted from this volatile, ever-changing world. New stars had come along, others had disappeared. This was not the place for her anymore, not really.

During the intermission, Elnaz was swallowed up by a gang from the production company. She introduced Bente to them, but once Bente had finished talking about her show, she couldn't think of anything else to say, and started to wonder how the evening was going at Rendezvous. Had a lot of people shown up? And what if Hanna and Mom were engaged in some kind of cocktail-making competition. That was a terrifying thought—they would scare all the clients away. No one would come back.

She kept on looking around, hoping to spot Didrik. Had he changed his mind about coming? What the hell was she doing here anyway?

Was it too late? What if he'd given up? She should have dropped her guard long ago, let him get close to her instead of keeping her distance. Standing in the middle of this crowded room, she suddenly knew just how much she missed him.

All at once the hum of conversation grew louder. There was movement farther down the room, and Bente tried to see what was going on.

Then she saw the suited figure making his way through the crowd. Her heart began to pound. Not a hint of tweed, but instead a dark-blue, well-fitting suit. The thick hair had been combed, but was still doing its own thing. This was definitely Didrik, confidently entering the venue like the popular star he was.

He met her gaze, and a shudder of pleasure ran through her entire body. She stood there frozen to the spot. She couldn't stop staring. He was looking straight at her, no one else.

He was beaming as he hurried over. "Bente! I hoped you'd be here. I've called you, messaged, I—" He broke off, took both her hands in his, and looked her up and down, from top to toe. "You're so beautiful. Unbelievably beautiful."

Her cheeks were on fire, she looked away. "Thank you."

He put his hand under her chin, tilted her face up to his. "I want to apologize for . . . everything. Above all I want to say that I don't know what I'm doing." He drew her closer. She could feel the warmth of his breath on her forehead.

Seeing him like this, hearing him like this, made every last scrap of anger melt away. Her whole body felt soft. She just wanted to be hugged, to inhale the intoxicating smell of him.

"I don't know what I'm doing either," she said. "What *we're* doing." She laughed, then became serious. "I don't want to change you. You're perfect just the way you are."

"I know you don't want to do that. I know, I *know*." He took a deep breath. "And that's why I'm so in love with you. Because you want me exactly as I am. And it's not just that—you've made a real effort for me. Opened up, shared your thoughts and feelings with me."

He placed his hand over hers. "What's so fantastic about you is that I don't have to pretend. I can just be myself. I thought I needed to change and look to the future so that we could be together. But the thing about you is that you give me space, all the space I need to be myself. You bring out the best in me, Bente." He glanced around, seemed not to notice all the curious looks. "I apologize for all the dumb things I said. About the party." He closed his eyes. Shook his head as if he were trying to erase the memory of his stupid question. "I was searching for some way to validate the insecurity I felt. I don't even know why I asked the question. Maybe because I needed to focus on some practical detail, because I couldn't bear the thought of us splitting up. I can be kind of pragmatic and solution oriented sometimes—I need to work on that."

He smiled his wonderful smile and tucked a strand of her hair behind her ear, causing her to shudder with pleasure at his touch. "Bente, will you please continue dating me? My life is richer than it's ever been when I'm with you. I have never been more sure of myself and what I want. Every day I spend with you is a fun day. Until now, I've been blinded by all kinds of expectations, by how it seems things *ought* to be. With you I feel so secure, even though I never know how the day is going to turn out. Children aren't important—being with you is important. We can take every day as it comes. The main thing is that I get to be with you." He spoke quickly, desperate to get the words out, then fell silent.

Bente smiled. "You've said everything I need to hear."

"Everything?"

She nodded. "I've also been carrying my own insecurity; it's blinded me, held me back. That's why I've been on my guard, but when I opened up to you, I felt . . . safe." She paused. "I felt safe because I knew you could help me, and you have. Taking that first step was tough, but once it was done, I felt a sense of calmness, because I knew you'd handle things in the right way. Because I thought you'd stay around."

"And then I said I needed time to think . . ." Didrik said.

"And then you said you needed time to think." She smiled. "But that's okay. You're here now."

He rested his forehead against hers as she continued talking.

"During the last few days I've done a lot of thinking, too, about how I want to live my life," Bente told him. "It's been so hard to find my place. But now, with you . . . I think I know my place and where I ought to be."

He looked into her eyes. "So what is your place?"

She gazed around the room. "Not here, anyway. It's been there all along, I just thought I needed something more, when in fact I'm perfectly satisfied with what I have right now. Especially with you."

Didrik kissed her, deeply and for a long time. Then he said: "Let's get out of here."

40

Rendezvous was virtually empty when they arrived. Didrik had insisted on dropping by the office to pick something up, and had returned to the cab with a bag containing something wrapped in brown paper.

Ellie was just locking up, but opened the door when Bente waved to her from the cab.

Outside the car the air was fresh; it smelled of an early-summer night, with the fresh dampness of new growth and the dry warmth of asphalt gradually cooling in the chill of the evening.

Didrik came around to her side, and they walked into the bar hand in hand.

Agneta was sitting at a table distractedly stirring a cocktail, her attention focused on her phone. Candy Crush, no doubt. Hanna was behind the bar cleaning up.

She looked up at them. "Back already? Hi, Didrik!" She broke into a smile and hurried over to give him a hug.

"How did it all go?" Bente asked, joining Ellie and Hanna at the bar.

"Above expectations—we're definitely ready for the real opening," Ellie assured her.

"That's great to hear," Bente told her. "And I have news too. I've decided this is what I want to do—full-time."

"Seriously?" Ellie's hands flew to her mouth and she let out a cheer. "So you and I are going to run a wine bar together?"

Bente laughed. "I guess so." She looked at Hanna. "But I don't want you to give it to me. I'll run it for you until I can afford to buy it from you."

"Whatever you want." Hanna smiled at Bente and Ellie. "What a dream team." She grabbed a bottle of Champagne, moving around the bar as if she'd been a bartender all her life. Maybe it came naturally now that she owned the place. "I think this calls for bubbles!" She opened the bottle with a loud pop and foam went everywhere, much to everyone's very vocal delight.

"By the way, I have something new for our wine list," Bente said, looking at Didrik. "I got a fantastic email from Sylvie today, and she can let us have several cases."

"From Château de Chênes?" he asked.

"From Château de Chênes."

"This all sounds wonderful," Hanna said. "But for as long as I'm the owner, I insist on coming down at least one evening a week to mix cocktails."

"You mean after closing time?" Bente said, laughing as Hanna punched her on the arm. Bente accidentally kicked over the paper bag on the floor, and Didrik quickly picked it up. "What have you actually got in there?"

"I thought you'd never ask." Didrik fished out a package, unwrapped it, and placed an item—a painting—on the bar.

It didn't take Bente long to recognize the style. "That's by Sven Steen."

Didrik nodded. He turned the picture over, and there was Sven's name . . . or rather *Dejje Steen, 1979.*

"I don't understand."

Didrik told the story of the receipt he had found, signed by Ida Steen. And recounted his conversation with the woman in the gallery.

"And the art dealer was buying paintings by him through intermediaries right up until the eighties?" Bente's eyes filled with tears. "So he *survived*? *They* survived?"

"Sven must have survived, and I'm guessing the man in the painting is Mathieu," Didrik said.

"But are you sure it's Mathieu?"

Didrik shook his head.

"Maybe this is just how Sven imagined Mathieu would have looked." Bente's voice was trembling.

Didrik placed his hand on hers. "Or that's actually Mathieu in the picture."

She smiled, took his hand, and squeezed it. She really hoped he was right. "Maybe we should try talking to Jérôme again. If we bring some information, help prompt his memory, he might be able to recall something."

"Sounds like a good idea."

Bente looked back at the painting. So Sven had survived. How amazing was that?

But what had happened to Mathieu?

◆ ◆ ◆

They called Jérôme the following day, sitting at Bente's kitchen table. In an email exchange between Bente and Sylvie the previous evening, Sylvie had offered to go to the care home to be with Jérôme during the conversation. She thought it might be easier for him to remember if someone he knew was there, someone he associated with the vineyard.

"Hi." Sylvie appeared on the screen. "Jérôme is here, he's got a cup of tea and would love to speak to you." The image flickered as she adjusted her phone so that they could see the old man. He stared into the camera, brought his face closer. It took a minute for him to figure out how to look at the screen and at them. But once he did, Bente saw that his expression was different from when they'd gone to visit him—much clearer. He suddenly looked younger to her.

They introduced themselves and his face lit up.

"Oh yes—it was you who had some questions about Château de Chênes, wasn't it?"

"That's right," Bente said, edging a little nearer to the phone. "We've found a picture painted by a Swedish guy—Sven Steen, although he was known as Dejje Steen. We're wondering if you know why there was a Swede living at the vineyard toward the end of the Second World War, and in the years that followed?"

Jérôme thought for a moment. "I don't know anything about that," he said.

Bente's heart sank. She'd had such high hopes for this call. This would be the last time they spoke to Jérôme, they couldn't disturb him again. They had enough of a story for the TV show. Maybe they would never know what had really happened to the two men, and she and Didrik would have to accept that.

"So you're not aware that there was a Swedish guy at the neighboring vineyard?" she tried again.

Jérôme gave a cunning smile. "That's what I was told to say. 'I don't know anything about that,'" he repeated with a secretive glint in his eye. "That's what I had to say if anyone asked about them. Mathieu and Sven." He looked almost boyish now, and she could see a glimmer of eight-year-old Jérôme. "Or Dejje, as we called him. It was a name he used to call himself as a child."

Bente glanced at Didrik, who was also smiling. They both turned their attention to Jérôme, who took a sip of his tea. He clasped his hands on the table in front of him. "But now I think I can tell you everything I know. The only people who might be damaged by it are long dead. I hope you have plenty of time?"

41

1944

Sven sat on the seat behind the two soldiers.

The driver set off again, but after only twenty yards or so the car began to judder, the sign of a slow puncture. He stopped, the soldier in the passenger seat moved to get out, and in that brief moment of confusion, Sven seized his opportunity.

He hit the driver hard over the head, then jabbed his elbow into the other man's temple, and before either of them could work out which direction he'd taken, Sven had jumped out and fled into the darkness. He heard their voices, swearing and shouting to him, but they didn't use their guns. Presumably they didn't want to waste a bullet on him.

He ran back toward the vineyard, along the edge of the forest where he couldn't be seen. Within minutes he heard the sound of engines, and a convoy of five vehicles drove by, their headlamps lighting up the night.

They were heading in the direction of Château de Chênes.

He wasn't going to make it in time.

But he kept on running anyway. Maybe the soldiers had another mission?

He ran and ran, his lungs were burning, but he didn't stop for even half a second to catch his breath. His legs moved faster than ever. He knew he was several minutes behind the soldiers, and he couldn't bring himself to think about what they might have already done. He raced into the courtyard, which was deserted. Either they had driven past, or they had already achieved their goal and gone.

He flung open the double doors, and when he saw the devastation, he realized he was too late.

The hall table had been knocked over, and the vase that always stood on top of it was smashed to pieces. That was what the Nazis did: They destroyed everything in their path. No doubt their aim had been to frighten Hugo and Juliette into talking.

Hugo and Juliette.

The house was silent. Sven walked through the chaos, then he heard a sob from the kitchen and rushed in.

Juliette was on her knees on the floor next to the tipped-over kitchen table. Hugo was beside her, with a bleeding gash in his forehead.

They glanced up in terror as Sven came crashing in. At least Hugo was conscious, even though the wound looked nasty.

"They hit him," Juliette said.

"Are you all right? How's . . . Where's . . . Did they take him?"

Juliette scrambled to her feet. "He managed to get away. Shortly after he left, we heard that someone in the village had organized a truck for Mathieu and a few others—they'd had advance warning, and so had we. This man is going to get them out of Bordeaux, and to a vineyard farther south."

Sven slowed his breathing. The relief was overwhelming. His efforts caught up with him, and he sank down onto the floor next to Hugo.

The Germans had checked his papers—oh God, they had kept his papers. They knew he'd been at Château de Chênes, they knew *everything*. Would they come looking for him?

He dragged himself to his feet. "I'm going with them."

"Wouldn't it be safer for you to stay here?" Juliette asked, concern etched on her face. Sven's heart broke—they knew exactly how much danger Mathieu would be exposed to by fleeing.

Sven had to get to Mathieu, he had to go with him. "How is this man going to get us out of Bordeaux? Surely the Germans are patrolling all the roads?" Sven asked as he and Juliette headed for the neighboring property. He didn't want to criticize the plan, but he needed to know.

Juliette looked at him, a little smile playing at the corners of her mouth despite her serious expression.

"By delivering wine."

◆ ◆ ◆

"In," Madame Bresson hissed as she pushed Mathieu back through the opening and down into the cellar. She took hold of one of the big wine shelves and *pulled it out*. It was like a false wall, and behind it was another cellar. Not a very big one, but she shoved him inside it, and just before she pushed the shelf back in place, Mathieu saw that the walls were covered in wooden shelves filled with wine bottles.

Seconds later the Nazis came storming in to the cellar on the other side of the false wall. They were yelling in German, and Madame Bresson answered calmly in French.

"There's no one here. You're welcome to search."

They continued to shout at her in German.

Please don't let them hurt her.

"Who are you looking for?" she asked.

"Your son—is he here?"

Mathieu was able to understand the gist of the German words. Surely the soldiers should be better informed? Maybe they didn't know what to believe anymore.

"He died in the war." Madame Bresson sounded furious. "You took his life. You don't need to look for him here."

Soon Mathieu heard the sound of boots moving away, then clomping up the cellar steps.

He slowly exhaled. A minute or two later, Madame Bresson pulled out the shelf, then took his arm.

"Come with me."

They hurried through the house and out into the vineyard. The storm had broken, and rain was pouring down on the dry plains in huge, warm drops.

Madame Bresson ran between the rows of vines, with Mathieu close behind, then took shelter by the wall of one of the barns. As they made their way around the building, she looked around them constantly to make sure no one had spotted them. Mathieu had no idea if the Germans were still close by.

Soon they reached a minor road. She pulled Mathieu behind a tree, keeping her eyes firmly fixed on the road.

Before long a small truck appeared and slowly came to a halt.

They emerged from their hiding place as a man jumped out of the driver's seat. Mathieu recognized him—he was a winemaker from the other side of the village.

"The Germans are waiting for their wine," he called out through the rain.

"The safest way out of here is via the enemy," Madame Bresson said firmly, waving Mathieu toward the truck. He opened the door and started to climb in, then looked back at Gerard's mother.

"Thank you."

She nodded, gave a cautious smile. "I hope you make it."

The driver had come around to the back of the vehicle. "Go farther in, behind the curtain," he said. "There are some others there, we've picked up a few people."

Mathieu made his way between the boxes of wine, right to the back of the truck behind the curtain. He could make out five bodies pressed close together in the gloom. Soon he was able to distinguish faces. A married couple, both teachers, rumored to be communists. He nodded to them; the man patted him on the shoulder. Then Mathieu saw a woman who had worked in the bakery for years; she was of Jewish heritage. He didn't recognize the fourth person, a young woman sitting with her eyes downcast. And the fifth . . . Sven.

It was Sven, curled up between the boxes. He looked up at Mathieu.

"Sven," Mathieu said.

"Mathieu."

What he noticed first was how relieved Sven sounded. Then Mathieu saw the tears pouring down his cheeks.

"You're here." Sven gave Mathieu a hug.

"For God's sake, keep quiet when the truck is being unloaded. And don't make a sound if you're stopped," Madame Bresson said behind Mathieu before slamming the door.

The truck set off, bumping along the road. The small space was stuffy, but fresh air seeped in through the gaps between the doors. Rain hammered down on the roof, and the interior was damp from where it had found its way in.

"Do you think we'll make it?" Mathieu whispered to Sven.

"I don't know. But this is our best option—they'll come looking again. And again. We have to get away from here." He put his arm around Mathieu in the darkness.

Mathieu felt safe.

Whatever happened, he was with Sven.

Epilogue

One year later

Bente went down into the wine cellar, selected one of the bottles that had just arrived, and returned to the bar. So far she was the only one in. She'd wanted time to go over what stock they had, and to consider whether to update the wine list with some interesting new wines they would serve by the glass. Her highest hopes concerned one certain special wine from Bordeaux, although she was afraid it might be too young to drink now.

She pulled out the cork and contemplated the numbers on it with a smile. The wine was made from the vines that had belonged to Château de Chênes. Sylvie had liked the idea of putting the longitude and latitude on the cork and had done the same for all her wines—the exact geographic coordinates of each vineyard, to show precisely where the grapes had been grown.

The show was due to premiere tomorrow—*The Extraordinary Story of a Wine Bottle*. Once she and Didrik had gotten to the truth, recording had been straightforward. They had filmed during the fall. Many of the people they'd met during the course of their research were happy to give more interviews, so they had traveled back to film with Sylvie. They had also gone to Paris to see Camille, and while they were there, Bente had gone on a diving expedition with her, seeking out new shipwreck wines. Interviewing Camille in full diving gear out at sea between France and the UK had been something very special. Even Frederic had appeared in one segment, to talk about today's wine producers in Bordeaux. The material Bente and Didrik had filmed themselves over the course of their research added an exciting, slightly more authentic vibe to the show, and Bente had been very pleased when she saw the first episode. She was looking forward to the premiere, to giving more people the opportunity to share in the wine bottle's story.

Other than that, the wine bar was occupying virtually every waking hour. Regular clients had returned after the reopening, but they also had plenty of new customers. Sometimes she appeared on the morning show on TV24 to present different wines, and she also guested on *Krissie* occasionally. She had been offered several TV shows of her own but had turned them all down. She wanted to devote most of her time to the wine bar—this was where she was happy and where she belonged.

She poured the wine into a large glass and swirled it around before sniffing. She could tell immediately that the wine was too closed. It had been stored for only a year—not long enough.

She took a sip; it was harsh on her tongue, but she thought it would be good in a couple of years. Particularly good in five to ten years. Fantastic in fifteen. She would follow the progress of the wine as it developed in the cellar at Rendezvous.

The door opened and Didrik came in, his face beige from his TV makeup. He had just been filming his own new show—*The History Lesson*—in which he took viewers through major events in history in an educational but entertaining way. "Historical events you ought to know about" was the show's tagline.

"Did it go well?" she asked.

"Yes, but I couldn't wait to be here with you."

He came around the bar and gave her a long, tender kiss. She laughed and wiped off the makeup that had transferred itself to her cheek.

"*Mmm*—you taste of wine."

"I do—this one." She held up the bottle.

"So it's arrived!"

She handed him the glass. "It's perfectly okay, but it needs a few more years."

He tasted, smacked his lips. "I assume you're right." Then he kissed her again. "I've got something to show you. Elnaz sent me this." He fished a USB stick out of his briefcase. "The last episode of our show—you haven't seen the final edit, have you?"

Bente shook her head.

"Have you got time now?"

"Absolutely."

She poured Didrik a glass of wine as he opened up his laptop and inserted the stick.

The episode began with interviews with the historian in Bordeaux they had gone back to visit, then the material they had filmed themselves: the visit to Château du Boda, and the discovery in the cellar at Château de Chênes. This was followed by a longer interview with Sylvie, in which she talked about the history of Château du Boda, then Didrik's visit to the art gallery. Bente felt her pulse speed up when the woman took down the painting—it was as if she was hearing it all for the first time.

And finally: the interview with Jérôme.

His voice was clear and strong, his French wonderfully elegant and old-fashioned, as he explained how the man in the village, risking his own life, had rescued the two young men from Bordeaux and driven them to a vineyard farther south.

"After the Allies liberated France from the Nazis, Sven and Mathieu came back. However, the fact that Sven was there had to be kept secret. It proved quite easy to concoct a lie, a mystery around Sven's fate. My parents and I, but also Monsieur and Madame Bresson over at Lassac, were able to confirm that Sven had been taken away by the Germans that night toward the end of the occupation. We'd managed to rescue the couple who were teachers, the woman with Jewish heritage who worked in the bakery, and the young woman whom the Nazis suspected of some minor offense: That was what we told the police once order had been restored and all the collaborators within the police had been rooted out and punished. But we were unable to rescue Sven. We assured them that we never saw the Swede again.

"During the Germans' rapid and chaotic departure, local administration suffered somewhat, and at that time witness statements often became accepted fact. The Foreign Legion was informed that Sven had been taken away, so he was able to continue living in secret at Château de Chênes with the love of his life. Our word became the truth. No authorities ever came looking for Sven. The Foreign Legion never questioned the information they'd been given, but *if* anyone ever asked about him, we were all say that we didn't know anything about him."

"How did his mother eventually find him?" Bente asked. The entire conversation with Jérôme was included in the episode, and there was something beautiful about the old man's unedited story, and something intimate about seeing both Bente's and Didrik's reactions to it.

"You mean Sven's mother, Ida. She spent her final years at the vineyard, did you know that?" Jérôme chuckled. "I think she reached about the same age I am now. But for a couple of years, she thought Sven was dead."

Jérôme explained that the Foreign Legion had told Sven's parents they'd been informed that he had been arrested and taken to a labor camp. They hadn't succeeded in tracking him down, and had therefore concluded that he was dead. Sven's father passed away shortly afterward, and his mother, Ida, always said he'd died of a broken heart.

Until the end of the war, it was too risky to communicate openly, so Sven had decided to send the bottle with the brass plaque as a greeting to his mother—a way of communicating without arousing suspicion. He'd placed a note, telling her to open the bottle, in a secret compartment in the box: an innocent message in Swedish that wouldn't give anything away if the box ended up in the wrong hands. He figured that if his mother didn't find the note, the brass plaque was a message in itself; plus one day she would open the bottle and see the coordinates.

And then she would understand. At least, that was what Sven hoped would happen.

But the ship struck a mine, and Sven's greeting never arrived.

After the war ended, Sven made a fresh attempt, now that everyone believed he was dead. No one would be interested in confiscating letters or going through whatever he sent, so he was finally able to be completely transparent.

This time, Ida received her son's letter.

Jérôme laughed again. "We often wondered about the bottle and how it was doing at the bottom of the sea." He winked at the camera. "Have you tasted the wine?"

And there the interview ended.

Bente raised her glass and looked at Didrik as he closed his laptop.

"Here's to a successful collaboration," she said. "What a team we are! Let's keep . . ."

But she didn't manage to say another word, because Didrik leaned forward and gave her a kiss.

About the Author

Photo © 2023 Lina Eidenberg Adamo

Heléne Holmström is the author of *Time to Rise*, *After Hours*, *Office Affair*, and *Working Late*. Heléne still works part-time as an associate attorney. In addition to writing, Heléne's other interests include food and wine, and she has also studied to become a sommelier. For more information, visit www.heleneholmstrom.com.

About the Translator

Marlaine Delargy studied Swedish and German at the University of Wales, Aberystwyth, and taught German for almost twenty years. She has translated novels by many authors, including Kristina Ohlsson, Helene Tursten, John Ajvide Lindqvist, Therese Bohman, Theodor Kallifatides, Viveca Sten, Johan Theorin, with whom she won the Crime Writers' Association International Dagger in 2010, and Henning Mankell, with whom she won the Crime Writers' Association International Dagger in 2018. Marlaine lives in Shropshire in the United Kingdom.